D1172828

CODE BLACK

by Philip Donlay

ibooks
NEW YORK

For my son Patrick

"When once you have tasted flight, you will forever walk the earth with your eyes turned skyward, for there you have been, and there you will always long to return."
—Unknown

ibooks

1230 Park Avenue
New York, New York 10128
Tel: 212-427-7139 • Fax: 212-860-8852
bricktower@aol.com • www.BrickTowerPress.com

Library of Congress Cataloging-in-Publication Data

Donlay, Philip
Code Black
ISBN 978-1-59687-368-X
Library of Congress Control Number: 2007935780
Thriller/Adventure
Hardcover, Adult/General Fiction

Copyright © 2007 by Philip Donlay

First Edition

Cover Art & Design Les Munoz
Typeset by The Great American Art Company

10 9 8 7 6 5 4 3 2 1

ACKNOWLEDGMENTS

A heartfelt thanks goes to all of the aviation professionals around the world whose tireless work and dedication keep our skies safe. A further thanks goes to the men and women at Chicago's O'Hare Airport—day in day out, you're the best in the world.

For their patience, friendship and insight, I offer a special thanks to Sheren Frame, Bo Lewis, D. Scott Erickson, Rebecca Norgaard, Emily Burt and Tony Moss; you've played a bigger part in this than you'll ever know. Thanks to Kimberley Cameron, Roger Cooper, Nicole Barron and Adam Marsh for your steady hands and professional guidance. To Dr. D.P. Lyle, for spectacular help with all things medical. A final heartfelt thanks goes to my family. To my brother Chris, who is by far the smartest person I've ever met. To my Mom and Dad for their unwavering support in everything I've done. Finally, to my son Patrick, whom I love dearly, thanks for letting me see the world through your eyes.

PROLOGUE

"Don't touch him, he's still hot!" Roy Wickstrom shielded his eyes as fiery sparks arced up from the body slumped against the high-voltage feeds. Wickstrom was the foreman of the maintenance crew, and one of his crew had just made a terrible mistake—the worker was now only a charred corpse that danced and convulsed on the short-circuited conduit. Wickstrom turned and fought the bile rising in his throat as the dead man's clothes burst into flames. "Pull the breaker—we have to get him off of there!"

"We can't!" came the frantic reply. "The junction box has ignited! We've got to shut off the main power or this whole place is going to burn!"

"Shut it down then!" Wickstrom instinctively reached for his flashlight as one of his crew slammed down the heavy metal handle attached to the breaker box. The deep hum of the electrical current in the room came to an abrupt halt. Wickstrom waited in the darkness for the backup generator to pick up the load, but all he heard was his own breathing and the sharp peal of thunder as it echoed through the dark building, finally reaching the basement. Someone emptied a fire extinguisher on the burning body, and the rush of compressed gas was followed by groans as the acrid smell of burnt flesh filled the room.

"Get him off there and call 911," Wickstrom said as he clicked on the flashlight and played the beam over the smoldering body. "I want the main power back on as soon as possible!" He shifted the beam to a worker standing nearby. "You're with me! We have to get to the generator."

The twin beams from their flashlights lit the way as they both hurried to another part of the basement. Wickstrom put his shoulder against the thick steel door, and as it opened he was met with the sound of cascading water. He pointed his light toward the source and found a stream of rainwater pouring from the ceiling onto the standby generator.

"Find a tarp or some plastic!" he yelled as he peeled off his jacket and plunged under the icy shower to try to protect the components. As the water continued to soak the generator, a cold stab of fear swept over Wickstrom. He pictured the air traffic controllers upstairs, responsible for guiding airplanes over a six-state area, and who were now sitting in the dark.

*   *   *   *   *

The room around him went pitch black. Mark Dresser watched helplessly as his radar screen died, leaving only a small bright dot in the center. Above the distant exit an emergency floodlight flickered and then came to life, casting its harsh beam across the room. Mark keyed his microphone, the ghostly images of the dozen airplanes under his care clearly etched in his mind.

"Wayfarer 880, this is Indianapolis Center. Descend and maintain flight level 310." Mark paused as he mentally counted to three, and then broadcast the message again. "Wayfarer 880, do you read Center?"

His calls were met with silence. The noise in the room was starting to escalate with the buzz of other air traffic controllers growing equally desperate to talk to the pilots in their airspace. Mark had less than five minutes before his situation went critical. He snatched a phone from its cradle and waited for the familiar ringing of the direct line to Chicago Center. If he could talk to his counterparts in the neighboring facility, they could direct Wayfarer 880 to descend and head off what was rapidly becoming a problem, but the phone in his hand was as lifeless as the screen in front of him.

Mark banged his fist on the useless radar console. He was torn between staying at his station, hoping that everything would come back online shortly, or leaving the heavily insulated room to get outside where his cell phone would work. In the darkness he turned toward his supervisor's desk. "Tom! I'm going to have a big problem if I can't move some airplanes around."

Tom Keller was already up on his feet and covered the distance in three strides. "What have you got?"

"I was about to descend a Boeing 737, Wayfarer 880. I needed the separation from a Military KC-135. They're both going through the same hole in the weather."

"The backup generator should come on any second. How long until there's a problem?"

"Less than five minutes. I needed Wayfarer to turn or descend, then I lost the whole thing."

"Even if it's close, the 737 has TCAS," Keller replied. "They'll be able to avoid any serious problems."

Mark shook his head. "The transponder on the KC-135 isn't working right. It's been intermittent since he came into my sector." They both knew that without a working transponder on the military aircraft, the Wayfarer jet would have no way of knowing the KC-135 was even there. The TCAS equipment that alerted airplanes to a potential midair collision required both airplanes to have an operating transponder so they could "talk" to each other electronically.

"Oh God! How close is it going to be?" Keller pressed his fingers against his temples and pondered the unthinkable.

"Given that they're both going through the same opening in the thunderstorms at the same altitude—" Mark looked up in the near darkness at his boss. "These planes could hit."

"Go!" Tom reacted instantly. "Do whatever it takes to reach Chicago Center. Try the pay phone in the hallway or use your cell phone. I don't care how you do it, but find a way. I'll stay here and if this mess comes back up I'll make the call. What's his call sign?"

"Wayfarer 880." Mark yanked off his headset. "Just have him descend out of 36,000 feet."

Mark flew from his chair and ran for the door. He pushed through and raced down the dimly lit corridor. He rounded a corner and crashed into another person. The impact threw him into the brick wall. "Shit! Sorry." He propelled himself forward and ran as fast as he dared, leaving a stunned coworker sprawled behind him.

"Get out of my way!" Mark yelled as he rounded another corner. His left foot slipped on the waxed floor but he steadied himself. He could see the pay phone just ahead, and he prayed it was on a different circuit from the other phones. He slid the last four feet and yanked the receiver from its cradle.

He jabbed at the buttons furiously and tried to blot out the image of a collision between two airplanes. There wasn't a controller in the business who hadn't had nightmares about this very situation. A 737 could carry as many as 150 people, and the KC-135 had a crew of at least four. As hard as he tried, he couldn't escape the image of two airplanes colliding, the debris and passengers raining down from five miles above the earth. He pictured the tiny flags that the investigators would sink into the ground to mark each of the dead, and then the hundreds of body bags that would be lined up in somewhere in a makeshift morgue. The death toll was bound to be staggering.

"We're sorry, all circuits are busy. Please try your call later," the automated voice calmly requested.

Mark looked at the phone as if it had somehow betrayed him. He yanked his cell phone from his pocket, ignored his trembling hands and pushed the power button as he ran toward the front door. Moments later he burst through the double glass doors into the driving rain and huddled under the small awning. Breathing heavily, he turned his back to the deluge and checked that his phone had powered up. Vivid flashes of lightning danced in the clouds overhead followed by the rolling sound of thunder. Mark dialed the number for Chicago Center. As the hisses and clicks sounded in his ear, he waited and tried not to hyperventilate. Rain came in torrents; another explosion of thunder rattled the structure around him. He looked at his watch—it was going to be close, but there was still time.

Mark swore under his breath when he heard the busy signal. He disconnected the call and hit the redial button. He squeezed his eyes shut as waves of self-recrimination washed over him. Why hadn't he descended or turned one of the airplanes earlier? Why was any of this happening? His spirits soared as an encouraging click came over the phone, but he slumped as he heard the recording. "All circuits are busy."

Oblivious to the cold and being soaking wet, he tried over and over to reach Chicago—the mental picture of two airplanes hurtling toward the same point in space played out in his mind's eye—until he knew that he'd run out of time. He felt hollow as he tried to grasp the realities of a five-hundred-mile-per-hour impact, the screams that would follow and then be silenced forever. He pressed the send button again and when the recording sounded, his hand dropped to his side. Mark helplessly scanned the building for any sign that the power had been restored, that the aircraft had been reached in time, but the dark interior told him no such miracle had taken place. He stared numbly into the northern sky. Whatever was going to happen was now unavoidable.

CHAPTER ONE

Seated over the wing in 19F, Donovan Nash glanced at his Rolex and discovered it was only five minutes later than the last time he checked. If there had been any other option, he wouldn't have gotten on this flight. But with a blizzard brewing in the Midwest, he'd calculated that this was the last flight with a decent chance of making it into Chicago before the storm caused major problems. He guessed that they were probably still forty-five or so minutes out from O'Hare. He shifted uncomfortably in his seat and glanced uneasily toward the front of the plane. Behind the thin curtain up in first class sat a woman he desperately hoped would stay where she was.

Donovan himself held a first class ticket for seat 2B, but as he'd boarded the flight and had been about to take his seat he saw her—seated next to the window in 2A. Even though it had been nearly eighteen years since they'd spoken, he knew instantly that any exposure to her was dangerous. Audrey Parrish would be in her mid-forties by now, but with her refined elegance, slim figure and shoulder-length blonde hair, she appeared far younger. Though he knew he'd changed a great deal over the years, both from the surgeon's knife and the natural aging process, Donovan realized there was a very real chance that she could recognize him. If that happened, his carefully concealed world would immediately come undone.

Shocked at seeing her, Donovan had tried to remain calm as he walked casually past his assigned seat. As he'd passed, Audrey had looked up at him briefly. He'd wanted to turn away, but couldn't help himself as he searched her blue eyes for any hint of recognition. She'd gazed out her window, then back at Donovan again, as if she were about to say something, then changed her mind. Donovan had hurried through first class into the relative safety of coach. He'd quickly explained to a flight attendant that there was a business rival in first class, and that he'd prefer to sit back here. She'd shrugged and gestured rather indifferently toward several rows of empty seats.

Donovan often wondered what those who had known him before would think of him now, of all that he'd accomplished. When Audrey had known him he was quite literally a different man—very little about his former self bore any resemblance to who he was today. In all the years since he'd made his fateful decision, Audrey represented his first contact with someone from what had been the inner-circle of his previous life. He looked down at the paperwork he'd planned to finish on the flight, but the proximity to Audrey made it next to impossible to concentrate. He remembered her as being extremely intelligent and resourceful, somewhat feisty, and perhaps even a little over-ambitious. She'd been fresh out of law school, a junior attorney who had been assigned as part of an acquisition team he'd outsourced for the take over of a rival company. Donovan's thoughts tumbled back through the years as he dredged up the images of their last contact. It hadn't gone well.

Playing through his mind, he recalled how she'd caught him completely off guard by making what was clearly an overt sexual advance—and he winced at the memory of how poorly he'd handled the situation. How abruptly he'd dismissed her. It all seemed so long ago. He thought of how he looked now, as opposed to then. At forty-five years old, he was still in pretty good shape, though his six-foot-two frame wasn't as lean and muscular as it had once been. The normal changes of growing older hadn't escaped him either. The creases on his angular face were getting deeper and his short brown hair was peppered with gray. When he looked in the mirror he still found his deep blue eyes looking back at him, but his forties had seen the onset of full-fledged middle age. But unlike most men, Donovan welcomed the subtle changes—even relished them. Anything that distanced him from the man he used to be was a plus.

Had Audrey already dismissed him, or was she up there trying to decide where she knew him from? Would she connect him with a man she thought had died eighteen years ago?

He looked out his small window and studied the line of thunderstorms that marked the leading edge of the cold front. The cloud tops rose far into the stark blue sky. Donovan's usual place in an airplane was up in the cockpit, and he imagined himself there, threading the plane through a narrow gap in the weather. He'd been a pilot for half of his forty-five years—never an airline pilot, but he flew jets and had logged thousands of hours flying around the world. It was his one true passion, one he'd used to escape parts of his life that had proven far too difficult. His other passion was the company he'd formed. Eco-Watch was, in a word, everything Donovan had been searching for his entire life. In the eight years since its inception, Eco-Watch had grown from humble beginnings to become one of the leading private research organizations in existence. Eco-Watch's collection of specialty aircraft and ships were in constant demand and booked months, if not years, in advance. At any given moment, Eco-Watch teams and equipment were crisscrossing the globe helping governments, universities, and other recognized groups study the planet. The primary mission objective was to help facilitate an understanding of both natural and man-made events that presented any kind of threat to the world's population. Donovan liked to think that what he'd created was making a difference in the world.

Very few people knew that he'd founded Eco-Watch. Donovan operated under the title of Director of Aircraft Operations; it took him out of the spotlight and gave him far more freedom than he'd have otherwise. For the better part of the last two decades he'd carefully rebuilt his life, and at the same time, fiercely guarded his identity with every resource at his disposal, and his resources were vast.

A figure came through the curtain that separated first class from coach, and Donovan tensed, then relaxed, as he recognized one of the young flight attendants. So far, Audrey was up front, and the longer she stayed there the better. Donovan knew that once they landed, he would simply stay onboard until Audrey was well off the plane. After that, it would be easy to vanish into the terminal and disappear once again.

Donovan's thoughts turned to his fiancée. They had only been apart for two days but he missed Lauren terribly. Once he made it to Chicago, he and Lauren would meet up with Michael Ross, Donovan's best friend and colleague, and they would then fly the brand new Eco-Watch Gulfstream jet back home to Dulles.

From the beginning, she'd captivated him with her startling beauty and his pure physical longing for her had never ebbed. He imagined the subtle expressions she'd radiate, a flash of her emerald-green eyes, a smoldering glance over her shoulder as she absently brushed her auburn hair away from an inviting neck. He'd been instantly attracted to her, but it was her warmth and intellect that had won him over. They'd met several years earlier on a mission to study an Atlantic hurricane; Donovan had been the Eco-Watch pilot flying the sorties out of Florida. Lauren served as the lead scientist and he quickly learned she held a number of degrees, including a doctorate in Earth Science from MIT. She was one of the smartest, most complex, and most exciting women he'd ever known. He imagined her smooth skin, the faint scent of juniper when he kissed her, and found himself even more impatient to get to Chicago. It had taken him years to finally reach a kind of negotiated peace with himself, and now he'd finally met the woman he was going to spend the rest of his life with. Lauren was the reason that, against his better judgment, he'd stayed on this airplane instead of quietly turning around upon seeing Audrey. Lauren was one of four people in the world who knew the truth about who he'd once been. His secret had nearly cost him his relationship with her, and though their relationship had been at times tumultuous, it now represented the most important part of his life. Lauren, and their daughter Abigail, meant everything to him. Donovan removed his wallet from his pocket and extracted a credit card, then pulled the phone from the seatback and swiped the card through the slot. Moments later he had a dial tone and punched in the numbers to Lauren's cell phone.

"Hello." Lauren's firm voice was amazingly clear despite the airborne connection.

"Hey you, it's me." Donovan smiled. He knew she'd checked the caller I.D. on her phone and hadn't known who was calling. She was in "Dr." mode.

"Where are you? Please tell me you're about to land. It's snowing so hard right now."

"I should be there in less than an hour. Where are you?"

"I'm in the restaurant at the O'Hare Hilton having a cup of coffee. Do you want to just meet me here when you get in? From what I've seen of the terminal it's probably a mess. I was tempted to reserve us a room."

"Oh really. What have you got in mind?" Donovan said.

"Not that," Lauren said, laughing easily "I'm worried we won't be able to get down to Midway airport. I've talked to Michael, and he says the airplane is ready and we'll be able to leave when we get there. It's the roads I'm concerned about."

"I'm sure it'll be fine. Chicago knows how to deal with a little snow. How was the conference? Were you brilliant as always?"

"It went fine. I'll tell you all about it when you get here." Lauren paused. "So, did you get everything finished?"

Donovan knew she was probing. He'd been rather vague as to why he'd needed to dash back to Washington. Donovan thought of the small triumph he'd pulled off just before he'd raced to Dulles airport to catch this flight. Earlier today, he'd signed the papers to buy a house that they'd looked at last weekend. It had been a warmer-than-usual winter Sunday, and the three of them had been out for a relaxing drive. As they'd wandered the tree-lined roads of northern Virginia, they found themselves in a tranquil sub-division with stately homes situated well back from the road. There was an open house in progress and on a whim they'd stopped and taken the tour. Lauren had fallen instantly in love with both the house and neighborhood. They'd talked about it and finally decided it was perfect, but when they'd called the realtor, they discovered that the house had already been sold. Lauren was heartbroken. It had taken Donovan nearly three days of negotiations to finally convince all parties to drop the deal so he could purchase the house. Thankfully, he hadn't had to use any assets from the huge fortune he controlled; one of the keys to his secret existence was to hide what amounted to one of the largest personal fortunes in the world. While expensive, the house would just fit in with his and Lauren's known combined income, and no eyebrows would be raised. It would be his wedding present to Lauren. He couldn't wait to see the look on her face when he told her what he'd accomplished. "I'll tell you about it later."

"You haven't got anything else better to do at the moment. Later we might be too busy to talk."

"Nice try."

"That's right. Leave me hanging, mister—and maybe all you'll be doing later is talking."

Donovan glanced up as someone emerged from first class. He stiffened as Audrey Parrish swept aside the curtain. She slowly worked her way down the aisle, glancing at the seated passengers. It would only be a matter of seconds before she reached him.

"Donovan, are you there?" Lauren asked. "Can you hear me?"

"I'm here," Donovan whispered. "There's someone on this flight I used to know—from before."

"Oh no. Who is it? Is there any chance they might recognize you?"

"I can't say much right now." Donovan kept his voice low. "She just came out of first class and she's coming this way."

"You're in coach?" Lauren's said, her voice filled with disbelief.

"Yeah," Donovan admitted. "It was the only way to avoid her."

"Don't you think the chance of her recognizing you after all these years is pretty remote—especially after all the changes that have taken place?"

"We're about to find out." Donovan shifted the phone to his other ear to help block his face. Audrey seemed to be taking in each passenger as she walked by. Donovan turned and looked out the window. The thunderstorms were far closer now.

"Donovan. What's happening?" Lauren said.

"Nothing. I'm fine and I miss you," Donovan replied.

"Is she gone yet?"

Donovan was about to reply, but he was distracted as several passengers on the right side of the plane began pointing frantically out the window. Others moved across the aisle to see what was happening outside. Murmurs suddenly turned to cries of alarm.

Donovan felt nothing wrong with the plane. He leaned forward to look outside at the wing and right engine. Everything seemed fine. Then, impossibly close, he caught sight of a dark shape bearing down on them. Another plane was in and out of the clouds, appearing only briefly, but he recognized it as a military KC-135 tanker.

Donovan's practiced eye told him instantly they were on a deadly collision course. "Oh my God," he whispered, bracing himself for the evasive maneuver he was sure the pilots were about to make. His muscles tensed, but neither plane made any attempt to avoid the other.

"Donovan! What's going on?"

"Everyone sit down!" one of the flight attendants yelled from behind him.

Donovan looked up at Audrey. She was standing next to him, her attention locked on the growing chaos in the cabin.

"There's another airplane—I think we're going to hit." Terror swept through him as he realized there was no way the two planes were going to miss. The unthinkable was about to happen. Every pilot feared a mid-air collision. It was one of the few things you were powerless to stop no matter how good you were. Driven by a surge of adrenaline, and in a desperate attempt to do something, anything, he reached out and grabbed Audrey by the wrist and yanked her down into the empty seat next to him. Her small scream of protest was drowned out by the cries of the other passengers.

"Donovan, talk to me!"

Lauren's voice seemed to fade away—he didn't know what to say, there were no words to tell the woman he wanted to marry that he was going to die. All of his carefully thought-out plans for their future were now pointless. After all the times he'd risked death in the cockpit, he was going to die in the back of a plane—as a passenger.

Donovan dropped the phone, gripped Audrey's arm and held her in place. He stared helplessly as the KC-135 bore down on them. He found small bitter comfort in the realization that at least he wouldn't die alone.

CHAPTER TWO

Lauren McKenna's hands began to shake as she stared at her phone. The signal had been lost. Tears formed in her eyes and a giant void built in her chest and begin to spread. She fought the impulse to jump up and cry out that there'd been a plane crash—that the love of her life had died as she'd listened. Her breaths came in sharp jagged gulps.

"You're a scientist," she whispered, trying to get control of herself. "Deep steady breaths." Lauren blinked through her tears and managed to gather herself enough to sift through the numbers programmed into her cell phone. She needed to find Michael.

Michael was across town at Midway Airport. He'd stayed to oversee some repairs to the *Galileo II*. The plan was for her to call Michael as soon as Donovan's plane landed so Michael could start getting the Gulfstream ready for departure. Michael was the number two man at Eco-Watch, as well as Donovan's closest friend. Lauren loved Michael like a brother. As the phone began to ring Lauren closed her eyes and willed Michael to answer.

"Hello," came Michael's usual upbeat voice.

"Michael, it's Lauren." Her throat threatened to close off as she battled her emotions.

"You guys about here? We need to leave this winter-wonderland behind before we're stuck here until spring."

"Michael—there's been a—" Lauren swallowed hard and gazed up at the ceiling. "Donovan's plane…I think maybe something happened to Donovan's plane."

"What!" Michael's tone changed immediately. "What happened? What do you mean?"

"He called me from the airplane." Lauren spoke in a rush of words. "We were talking when all of the sudden I could hear screams in the background. When I asked him what was wrong all he told me was that there was another airplane—that he thought they were going to hit. Then I lost the connection."

"Where are you now?"

"I'm in the restaurant at the O'Hare Hilton."

"Okay, we're not going to find out anything with you there. I think you should go to the Wayfarer ticket counter and find someone in charge, anyone who will listen to you. Do whatever it takes to get their attention—make them talk to you."

"I will." A sense of purpose began to flow through Lauren's body. At least she had a plan. Anything was preferable to just sitting and quietly falling apart.

"I'll call you the second I find out anything firm and you do the same. And Lauren, I want you to understand that it's virtually impossible for two airplanes to collide. There are multiple systems in place to keep that from happening. Too many things would have to fail for that to be a reality. So don't dwell on the worst quite yet, okay?"

"I'll try not to. I'm headed for the terminal now. I'll talk to you in a little bit."

"I'm on my way," Michael said. "I'll be there as soon as I can. When I'm close, I'll call so I know where to find you."

"Please hurry." Lauren ended the call and quickly gathered her things. She put some bills on the table and left the hotel. Snow swirled and billowed against the large plate glass windows. If anything, it was beginning to come down even harder than when she was talking to Donovan.

As she made her way through the underground tunnel that connected the hotel to the terminal, Lauren's thoughts whirled in her head as she thought of their upcoming wedding. It was scheduled for the following Saturday in Florida. Lauren thought of their daughter Abigail, and suddenly she felt like she might be sick. She was finally forced to stop in the underground walkway. She leaned against the cold brick wall. Her world was shattering and she didn't know how to make it stop. Lauren couldn't help but question the reasons that Donovan was even on the airliner in the first place. Their usual mode of transportation was aboard one of Eco-Watch's Gulfstream jets. She, Donovan and Michael Ross had just finished the acceptance flights on the new Gulfstream in Dallas. The *Galileo II* had been delivered less than a week ago. It was a hurried replacement for the first *Galileo* that was now lying at the bottom of the Atlantic Ocean. The plan had been to drop her off in Chicago, and then Donovan and Michael were to fly on to Dulles. She was supposed to travel home on a commercial flight after the conference. But upon landing at Midway Airport, the new airplane had lost a hydraulic pump. With the jet grounded, Donovan had flown back to Washington to take care of some Eco-Watch business. Lauren choked back her tears. If the *Galileo II* hadn't been grounded, it would be her on a commercial flight from Chicago to Washington. Donovan would be waiting for her there—none of this would be happening.

"Excuse me, miss. Are you okay?"

Lauren turned and discovered an elderly gentleman with kind eyes standing next to her.

"Yes," Lauren lied. "Thank you. I just needed to stop for a moment."

"These airports are so confusing, plus they make us walk awfully far sometimes. Which way are you headed?"

"I'm fine. Really, I'm just going up to the Wayfarer ticket counter. I know the way. It's not much further."

"Okay, I hope your flight isn't affected by the weather. Have a good day."

Lauren watched as the man shuffled away. She forced herself to start walking until she located the escalators that would take her up into terminal three. As she neared the top of the rise, the noise level began to increase steadily. Five steps before the end and she could finally see across the large, high-ceilinged room. To her horror, hundreds of people stood, queued in lines that snaked back and forth across the tiled floor. It would take her forever to reach the Wayfarer ticket agents. Frantically, Lauren scanned the crowd for someone who might help her.

Through the crowd Lauren spotted a Wayfarer agent. The woman stood, unsmiling next to the entry point to one of the impossibly long lines. She seemed to be answering questions while directing passengers to different lines. Lauren could hear the woman's voice carry above the fray. Lauren zigzagged through the crowd until she reached the woman.

"I need to talk to a supervisor," Lauren said.

"What seems to be the problem?" the woman replied calmly, as she gave Lauren the once-over.

"Something may have happened to one of your airplanes," Lauren whispered, not wanting to be overheard and start a panic. "I was talking to my fiancé, he's aboard—."

"Not here," The agent hissed, then put her hand on Lauren's arm and escorted her to an empty area near the large windows. The agent turned and stood toe-to-toe with Lauren. "Now, slowly, tell me what it is you think you know?"

"Like I said, I was talking with my fiancé, he's a passenger aboard one of your flights. Before we were cut off, he told me there was another airplane and that they were going to hit. I need to find out if that airplane is still flying."

"Security!" The woman called out. She waved her arm to get a uniformed guard's attention. She spun back and clamped her hand around Lauren's wrist to keep her from walking away.

Lauren yanked her arm from the woman's grasp. "I need you to listen to me!"

"Stay right where you are!" the agent said.

Lauren wrestled with her emotions, a part of her wanted to run—find someone who would help her. Another part knew she'd said the wrong thing and wouldn't get very far. From the alarmed expression on the face of the agent, Lauren understood she was being perceived as a threat. Over the agent's shoulder, Lauren spotted a Chicago policeman as he weaved through the crowd, his eyes locked on Lauren and a hand on the butt of his sidearm.

A cold rush of air enveloped her and she turned and saw an airline pilot, luggage in tow, hurrying through the door to escape the harsh elements outside. His leather jacket was covered with snow. He still had his head down against the wind as he strode purposefully into the terminal. Lauren searched for the emblem affixed to his cap. She saw the gold braid on the bill that identified him as a captain. It took her a moment, but she finally recognized the distinctive logo of Wayfarer Airlines.

"Captain," Lauren said. "I need to speak with you."

"I beg your pardon." The pilot stopped, glanced at her and the agent and then stepped aside as he prepared to move around her.

"I need you to listen to me!" Lauren said with as much force as she dared. She realized she must sound like a madwoman.

"Miss, I'm going to have to ask you to keep your voice down." The female agent was growing even more agitated. She motioned for Security to hurry.

The policeman's fast approach would give her only a few more seconds. She read the pilot's name from the security badge hanging from his neck. His name was David Tucker.

"Captain Tucker. One of your airplanes might have crashed," Lauren said quietly. "I need your help."

"Who are you?" Tucker eyed her warily. "What do you know about a crash?"

"I was talking to my fiancé, who is on a flight from Washington D.C." Lauren leveled a dead-serious glare at Tucker; she had to convince him that what she was telling him was true. "He said there was another airplane, and that they were going to hit. He's a professional pilot and I trust what he was telling me."

"Officer," the agent gushed the moment the policeman was within earshot. "This woman came up to me and told me that we might have a problem with one of our airplanes."

"Let me explain," Lauren said. "I was talking to a passenger on flight—."

"Did you tell her there's a problem with a plane?" the cop interrupted.

"Yes," Lauren said. The policeman stood there, looking her up and down, as if trying to gauge how much of a threat she might be. She exhaled heavily. This situation was going nowhere fast. "I have reason to believe one of Wayfarer's planes is in trouble. I'm just trying to find out what's happened."

"I want everyone to calm down," the cop said. "I need to see your I.D."

"I'd be happy to," Lauren said. She opened her purse under the watchful eye of the cop and produced her Defense Intelligence Agency badge. She flipped it open. Though now technically only a consultant, she was still one of the DIA's top meteorological analysts.

The cop examined her credentials and carefully compared the pictures. He stepped away and spoke softly into the microphone strapped to the shoulder of his vest.

"What's the passenger's name?" Tucker asked.

"Donovan Nash," Lauren replied, relieved that perhaps she was going to be taken seriously. "He boarded a flight in Dulles to come here."

Tucker nodded at the agent to go check it out. She hurried across the terminal to the main Wayfarer ticket counter and began typing at a vacant station.

"Here you are Dr. McKenna." The cop held out her I.D. badge. "Now, will you please explain to me exactly what's going on here?"

As calmly as she could, Lauren recounted the conversation she'd had with Donovan. Just as she was finishing, the agent came running back toward them and handed a computer printout to Captain Tucker.

"I'm telling you the truth," Lauren said as she waited for Tucker to find Donovan's name on the manifest.

"He's listed," Tucker said as he looked up from the sheet.

"Dr. McKenna." The cop held up a finger for everyone to wait while he listened to a transmission through his earpiece. He acknowledged, and then continued. "We just ran a check. It confirmed you're DIA. As far as I'm concerned you don't pose a threat to security. You're free to go. But if you create another disturbance on airport property—I will arrest you and put you in jail. Do you understand me?"

"Yes."

"I want to check this out at our end," Tucker said. "Can you help me get her through Security? I think she needs to tell her story to someone besides myself. Just to be on the safe side."

"Makes sense. Follow me," the cop said.

Lauren followed Tucker and the cop as they made a beeline toward a security checkpoint. They went directly to the front of the line where a short conversation between Tucker, the cop and the TSA took place. Once cleared, she and Tucker breezed through the metal detector.

"I just want to say—" Lauren said to Tucker, as they walked away from Security.

Tucker cut her off mid-sentence. "If you turn out to be some crazy woman, I'll see to it you're right back in the hands of the cops—I doubt they'll be so accommodating the second time around. I don't want to hear another word from you until we get to Operations."

CHAPTER THREE

Like a giant 500 mph scythe, the wing of the military plane cut through the thin skin of the 737 just above the cockpit. Aluminum ribs and stringers snapped as the wing dug further aft. Debris was ripped out into the frigid atmosphere, rupturing the Boeing's fuselage. Instantly, the aircraft depressurized. A cloud of water vapor filled the cabin as the air condensed in the explosive decompression. In a fraction of a second, luggage, purses, blankets and magazines were sucked out of the forward section of the airplane. Large metal pieces from both aircraft gave way, tumbling back and tearing violently into the 737's tail.

The airliner reeled under the impact from the tanker. Donovan kept his grip on Audrey as they were both thrown into the seats in front of them. Donovan twisted sideways as the airplane lurched beneath him.

Razor-sharp pieces of aluminum shot through 880's passenger cabin. Plastic overhead compartments exploded, then splintered into a maelstrom of deadly airborne daggers. Glass from the shattered fluorescent lights flew into terrified eyes.

The carnage was far worse in the front of the plane. Those passengers seated in the forward section bore the brunt of the flying debris—their momentary screams absorbed by the roar of the slipstream pouring into the cabin.

Donovan tried to protect both himself and Audrey from the shower of fragments. The sting of objects peppered the exposed skin on his hands, while the pull of a powerful suction lifted Audrey off the seat. Donovan was sucked forward, his full weight pressed against his seatbelt. He braced himself with his feet as wrapped his arms around Audrey, keeping her in place. The roar penetrated to his bones, the freezing cold air shocked Donovan's lungs as he fought to breathe. He winced at the pain in his ears, he had to swallow hard, twice, to eliminate the pressure and relieve the agony.

Donovan raised his head and risked opening his eyes. He watched helplessly as rows of people in the forward cabin, still strapped in their seats, were sucked out of the gaping hole that had been ripped in the roof. With slow-motion clarity, he could see flailing bodies pummeled and slashed by the jagged metal before disappearing from sight.

As quickly as it appeared, the suction from the decompression vanished. Donovan knew the pressure differential had equalized and the threat of being sucked out of the plane had passed. He pulled himself up. Fighting the horror he had witnessed and his own rising fear, he looked into Audrey's frightened and confused face. At least she was still alive.

"The masks!" he yelled above the rush of air. They were dangling from the overhead compartment just above them. He hoped she understood they needed oxygen. It was now freezing cold, and his mind became cloudy and uncertain. A vague notion crossed his mind—their efforts were probably ridiculous and short-lived. They would be dead in seconds. There was no way they could remain flying after being in a midair collision.

Donovan pulled one of the oxygen masks to his face, tugged the lanyard to start the flow, then held out a second mask for Audrey. He breathed deeply into the yellow plastic cup, drawing the oxygen into his lungs.

Audrey squeezed his hand fiercely and Donovan looked into her widening eyes, then turned to the ghostly scene in the cabin. It took him a moment to comprehend that many of the oxygen masks had failed to drop. Those that had were being fought over by panicked, hysterical passengers. Some were up out of their seats, trying violently to yank the masks off the people who had them, but their struggles only reduced their time of useful consciousness. People dropped in the aisle and some thrashed in their seats before their oxygen-starved brains caused them to black out.

In the middle of the chaos, Donovan saw someone with a portable oxygen bottle. It was one of the young flight attendants, her long blonde hair whipped by the wind. She moved into the fray, trying to help. As she neared some of the panicked passengers, she was knocked off her feet, her shoulder slamming sharply into the seat frame. Her mask was ripped from her face. Two men then proceeded to battle for her oxygen bottle. She screamed in pain and collapsed helplessly into the aisle.

"Stay here!" Donovan yelled to Audrey. He felt light-headed, but steadied himself on the seat in front of him. The cabin was a whirlwind of blowing insulation and debris from the ruptured fuselage. He waited a moment, trying to calculate his movements.

Donovan forced himself forward, his walk unsteady. He made his way to an overhead bin marked "OXYGEN" and opened it. He could tell he was already suffering from the effects of hypoxia as a detached sense of euphoria fell over him. He strained to discern the simple commands on the oxygen tank. He had experienced this once before while training in an altitude chamber. If he was going to save himself and the young flight attendant still lying in the aisle, he needed to hurry. He pulled the green cylinder down and fumbled with the valve, his fingers numb from the cold. His vision began to fade, the blackness beginning at his periphery and moving inward. He tried to work faster, but the apparatus perplexed him. Somewhere in his befuddled mind he knew he had only seconds before he, too, would black out. His actions bordered on frantic, yet he was strangely calm. With a final twist he opened the valve and pressed the mask to his face.

Donovan felt the cobwebs evaporating as he drew deeply on the 100% oxygen. His strength and clarity returning, Donovan knelt and picked up the mask the two men had been fighting over. Neither had won the battle. He slid the mask over the flight attendant's face, her lips already a faint blue. He removed another portable bottle from the overhead bin and headed back to where Audrey sat. He repeated the process of opening the valve to start the flow of oxygen, then secured the mask around her face.

Surveying the destroyed cabin, Donovan tried to make sense out of what had happened. A torrent of frigid air hit him with the force of a hurricane. The temperature neared 40 below. Tears froze to his cheeks and his exposed skin had become almost completely numb.

To his right he caught a flurry of activity. A young woman in a window seat was fending off an assault from another passenger. Donovan instantly moved to help. Her mask had dropped and she'd secured it around her mouth and nose, but a man in the aisle seat, whose mask hadn't dropped, was attempting to rip it from her face. In one quick motion, Donovan restrained the man and pointed across the aisle to a vacant seat with a mask dangling from the overhead panel. But instead of understanding, the crazed passenger reached out and began to wrestle the oxygen bottle from Donovan's hands. It was a losing battle as the man's efforts finally caused him to black out and slump into his seat. The woman seemed to thank Donovan with her eyes as she leaned back and gripped the armrest.

The plane lurched and pushed Donovan hard against the row of seats. He turned his face from the icy blast and looked out the window. He was momentarily relieved to see clouds far below. They were somehow still at high altitude, not seconds away from the ground as he had feared. Donovan fought to orient himself, to understand what the airplane was doing. Everything felt wrong. It took him a moment, but he finally realized the 737 was in a steep turn to the right, heading back toward the severe weather they'd just flown over.

"What's happening?" Audrey shouted above the slipstream. Her hair and clothes whipped in the tempest.

"I don't know! We should be descending but we're not!" Donovan yelled in return. He pushed his mask back on, taking two short breaths. "I need to get to the cockpit."

"Go!" She urged.

Around him were the wide eyes of passengers who had survived the impact, yellow masks secured to their terrified faces. He saw others who had masks, but appeared to be unconscious. The panic and chaos that had filled the cabin only moments earlier had vanished. As they'd blacked out, people had dropped in the aisle and between the seats, their bodies twisted and contorted. Donovan wondered if those without masks were already dead.

He pulled his way forward, fighting the river of freezing air racing in from the massive rip in the roof. In row after row, he saw mutilated passengers. Shards of metal and plastic debris pierced their blood-soaked bodies. The gore-splattered seats and walls of the airplane gave grisly testament to the force of the impact. He saw a woman he'd spoken to briefly as they boarded. Her vacant eyes seemed to be looking in dismay at her blood covered hands.

The sight forced Donovan to move faster. As he pulled himself forward, the airplane lurched and he almost lost his balance. With careful steps he reached the forward section of the 737. All that remained were empty seat tracks. Everyone was gone. He thought of his own seat assignment in 2B, and understood that if he'd been sitting there he'd have been sucked out of the plane with the others.

Another shudder from the 737 threw Donovan into the bulkhead. He hit his head sharply and the pain brought him back to the present. He sensed the last jolt had been from turbulence. He pictured the thunderstorms, and with his head lowered, forced himself toward the cockpit

Bending down to escape the worst of the slipstream, Donovan reached the door to the cockpit. He tried to straighten up but couldn't; the roof above him was partly caved in, bundles of wires whipped viciously in the wind. The door was closed and no doubt locked from the inside. The reinforced Kevlar would be virtually impossible to penetrate. Donovan gripped the heavy oxygen bottle and brought the butt end down heavily onto the latch mechanism of the door. To his complete surprise the door flung open and slammed heavily inward. Without hesitation, Donovan guided his precious oxygen bottle through the opening, and found himself standing in the cockpit.

Oh no. Donovan tried to blink away his disbelief. He wanted to reject what he was seeing. The instrument panel was dark. Tubes that should have been burning brightly, giving precise information on the airplane's condition, were black. As his practiced eye quickly darted from one part of the cockpit to the next, he found nothing was working. No radios, no navigation, no engine gauges. Everything on the flight deck was dead. The captain sat slumped back in his seat, unconscious or worse. The copilot didn't have his shoulder harness fastened, his forehead rested against the control column. Donovan grabbed his shoulders and pulled the copilot's torso off the controls; the young man's head dangled loosely from his broken neck. In one swift motion, Donovan unfastened the copilot's harness and clutched the dead man under the arms. With all of his strength, Donovan eased him out of the seat and laid him on the floor. He took the oxygen mask from his own face and secured it around that of the captain.

Moving quickly, Donovan slid behind the controls and searched for the pressure mask. Pilots had masks vastly superior to the one he'd been using. He found it and looped the straps over his head. The seal bit hard and the pressurized 100% oxygen streamed into his lungs. He took wild gulps of the precious air as he looked out the windshield. The line of storms loomed large.

In nearly 10,000 hours of flying, Donovan had never seen such a completely useless instrument panel. He searched quickly for the two instruments that didn't need any power. All airliners had a small backup airspeed indicator and emergency altimeter. He found them; both appeared to be functioning.

Down, we have to get down, Donovan urged himself. Not knowing what to expect, he put one hand on the controls and with the other, reached for the two throttles and pulled them back. The thunderstorms were dead ahead and he was running out of time. Churning upward toward the heavens, the hard-edged cumulonimbus clouds seemed to reach out for the 737—a lightning-lit wall of angry weather directly in their path.

Donovan's mouth felt as if it were filled with cotton as he eased the nose down and tried to turn the airliner. Instantly, the damaged airplane picked up speed. The controls buffeted in his hands. He corrected the pitch and eased off on the power. The pilot in him kept searching in vain for critical flight information on the panel. Only his raw instincts could now tell him what the unfamiliar aircraft would do next. He had to tighten the turn, he knew, to get around the storm. But if he allowed the 737 to get too slow, they would go into a spin and surely crash. If he penetrated the weather they could be ripped apart. A vivid burst of lightning lit up the thunderstorms—white-hot tentacles spreading out into the sky below them. *"Come on baby, turn. Just turn and stay together."*

CHAPTER FOUR

Lauren stayed close to David Tucker as she was ushered through a heavy steel door into what she was sure must be Wayfarer Operations. There was a small lounge area. Pilots in uniform were standing in small groups talking or reviewing their paperwork. Beyond, Lauren saw a large, high-ceilinged room full of computers. One wall supported several oversized monitors, another was covered with what appeared to be a flow chart of some sort, Lauren thought it was most likely the Wayfarer schedule. Next to it was a screen that depicted the entire area of North America, it was awash with green blips that Lauren recognized as airplanes. The place seemed chaotic, and Lauren stayed close to Tucker as he made his way across the room.

"Glen! Have you seen Henry Parrish?" Tucker called out as they neared a long counter.

"I just talked to him. He's on his way in." Glen Connaghan, a heavy-set, florid-faced Irishman, glanced up from the small group of people he'd been conferring with. He spotted Lauren and immediately tucked in the front of his wrinkled white shirt that had been pulled out by his ample stomach. "Why? What's up?

"Not here," Tucker answered, nodding toward Lauren. "Someplace private."

"I don't have the time right now." Glen shot a thumb over his shoulder toward one of the monitors that showed the listing of cancelled flights. "This blizzard is killing me."

Tucker looked around to make sure he wasn't being overheard then motioned for Glen to step closer. "This is Dr. Lauren McKenna. She was talking with someone aboard flight 880 out of Dulles. She thinks we might have a problem."

Glen snapped his head from Tucker to Lauren. "What exactly did you hear?"

"Are you talking to them?" Lauren gripped the edge of the counter, her fingers beginning to turn white. "Are they okay?"

"We don't know where they are." Glen replied softly as he shook his head. "We can track every flight we have in the air—but we've lost contact with 880. Can you tell me what you heard?"

Lauren released her death-grip on the counter and pushed at her temples, trying to maintain control. This couldn't be happening. She refused to believe that Donovan might be dead, he was easily the bravest and most resilient man she'd ever known. She thought about the man Donovan used to be, and how the world believed he'd perished in a plane crash. The horrible irony was almost more than she could fathom.

"Dr. McKenna?" Glen urged. "Any information you have might be helpful."

"I'm sorry." Lauren shook away her thoughts as she collected herself. "As I told Captain Tucker, my fiancé is aboard flight 880. He called me on the airborne phone and we were having a conversation. Then, in the background, I heard screaming and all he told me was that there was another airplane. He said they were going to hit."

"He's also a professional pilot," Tucker said, adding the small detail to Lauren's story.

"How long ago was this phone call?" Glen turned toward a bank of clocks that lined one wall.

"Fifteen minutes ago, maybe a little more," Lauren replied, as a commotion sounded behind her. She turned and saw a determined-looking man sweep into the room. He was Lauren's height, no more than five-foot-nine, and looked to be in his mid-fifties. He possessed dark, serious eyes that were locked into a piercing glare. His square jaw was even more prominent due to his closely cropped hair. The man was four steps in front of a long-haired teenager in a baggy coat over a gray uniform of some kind. The young man wore a backwards ball-cap and sported an earring. Though a study in contrasts, Lauren knew from their similar facial features they were father and son.

"Henry!" Glen shifted his attention away from Lauren. "Glad you made it here so quickly. Matt. Good to see you, too."

Henry turned to his son. "Matt, I've got work to do. Why don't you go get something to drink, or go wait in my office?"

Over Henry's shoulder Lauren saw the dismissive expression on the teenager's face. He ignored his father's direction and stood defiantly, listening in on their conversation.

Henry looked at Lauren, ran his eyes the length of her body then asked curtly. "Who are you?"

"I'm Dr. Lauren McKenna," she said, bristling at his abrupt manner. She glared at him. "Who are you?"

"I'm Henry Parrish, chief pilot for Wayfarer Airlines, and I want you out of here. I don't have time for civilians right now."

"I'll leave." Lauren stepped forward until she was inches from Henry. "But after I do, I'll go straight to the press and tell them about your missing airplane."

Henry shot a furious glance at Glen. "What did you tell her?"

"I told them," Lauren continued, her intensity swelling as she spoke, "that I was on the phone with someone on board the flight. He told me there was another airplane coming at them, and then I lost the connection. I'm not going anywhere until I know exactly what's happened."

"Fine, but I want you out of the way and off the phone." Henry shifted his attention to the uniformed captain to his right. "Tucker, why are you here?"

"I'm the person Dr. McKenna found in the terminal," he quickly explained. "I brought her here."

"With this weather I doubt you're going anywhere. I'm putting you in charge of our guest. Right now we have far more questions than answers. Glen, get me the passenger manifest for the flight. I trust we're using all of our assets trying to locate the airplane?"

"Here's the manifest for flight 880." Glen handed the printout to Henry.

"Flight 880?" Matt's attention shot from Glen to his father.

Lauren watched as the young man dug furiously in his pocket and finally produced a wrinkled scrap of paper.

"Did you say flight 880 from Washington, D.C.?" Matt stammered, as all eyes turned toward him.

"Yes," Lauren answered, when it seemed as if no one else was going to.

"Look for mom!" Matt demanded, "Is she there?" It's the flight she was going to try to make to get home tonight."

"Oh Jesus." Glen held up a duplicate of the sheet he'd given Henry. At the bottom were the non-revenue names—airline personnel who were allowed to fly free if space were available.

"Is she there?" Matt said with a raised voice.

Henry pursed his lips and nodded.

Lauren immediately felt her heart go out to the young man. He suddenly shared the same terrible purgatory she herself was trapped in.

"It's your fault," Matt accused his father. "If anything's happened to her, it's your fault!"

Lauren saw a flash of anguish, or perhaps it was guilt, appear momentarily on Henry's hardened features. She looked at Matt, his hands balled up in angry fists. She couldn't help but wonder what conflict had caused father and son to have declared such open warfare on each other.

"Right now we don't have any idea what's happened," Henry said, his voice wavering.

"Call them on the radio!" Matt continued and he grew even more animated "Talk to air traffic control! You're in charge, do—something!"

"We have. We're doing everything we can." Henry offered as he shot a quick glance at Glen, who nodded in agreement.

Henry reached out to put an arm around his son but Matt instantly side-stepped the gesture.

"I know this place like the back of my hand. I can help," Matt said defiantly, once he was out of the reach of his father.

Henry's expression hardened once again. "This isn't some intern training exercise, Matt. We're trying to get this situation figured out. I can't have you getting in the way right now." He let out a measured sigh. "I have people who are trained to do these things."

"Yes sir! Captain." Matt hissed, his voice dripping with sarcasm.

"I don't have time for this, Matt," Henry replied quietly.

"There's a news flash for you! Captain Parrish only has time for himself." Matt spun away as he got in the last shot.

Henry shook his head in frustration as Matt left, then shifted his attention back to Glen, who had visibly shrunk away from the confrontation between father and son. "I'll need the emergency procedures manual as well as the current phone list for essential personnel. Tucker, like I said, look after Dr. McKenna while we try and get some answers."

"I don't need looking after," Lauren spoke firmly. "If you lose an airplane, does that mean it's crashed? Or does it mean something else? I'm a scientist and I deal in absolutes. Do you have any idea what has or hasn't happened to flight 880?"

"No, not right this moment," Henry replied, his icy tone matching hers.

"So the fact that you don't know where they are could mean that they are in fact still flying?"

"That is correct," Henry said, nodding impatiently. "Which is why I have better things to do than stand here and debate semantics."

Lauren pulled her cell phone out of her pocket and with one glance saw she barely had any signal. "I need a phone." Lauren looked around, trying to spot the closest one.

"I can't allow you to make any calls," Henry said, shaking his head.

Lauren stepped closer to Henry and lowered her voice menacingly. "Give me a phone now. I'm calling people who can help us find your missing plane. They'll need to know the situation, but I can assure you they'll keep a lid on this until it's appropriate."

"I'm sure that's your intention," Henry replied. "But until we know exactly what's happening, I'm going to have to insist that you don't talk to anyone outside this room."

"Dial this number." Lauren fought her rising anger at this impossible man. She moved to the counter and furiously jotted down a classified phone number. She ripped the sheet from the pad and held it out to Henry. "This number is for the Operations room of the Defense Intelligence Agency. Once you're convinced I'm not calling CNN, hand me the phone, and let me find the goddamn airplane!"

"Do it." Henry snatched the paper from Lauren's hand and passed it to Glen, all the while keeping his eyes locked with Lauren's.

Glen moved to a phone and moments later put his hand over the receiver. "It's who she said it would be."

Henry motioned for her to take the call.

"This is Dr. McKenna." Lauren pictured the Operations room at the DIA and the elite team of operatives always on duty in front of a multitude of display screens. The world's most sophisticated space-based intelligence platforms could be called up at a moment's notice. "To whom am I speaking?"

"Lauren, it's Steven. Where are you? What in the world is going on?"

"Steven. I have an emergency in progress. Please get Director Reynolds."

"What?" Steve stammered for a second as the gravity of Lauren's request sunk in. "Hang on. I'm notifying the Director now; I'm sure he'll be here in a moment. Are you okay?"

"No, Steven, I'm not." Lauren had worked closely with Steven for years. He was what she often described as a techno-nerd—but he was very good at what he did.

"What can I do?" Steven asked as soon as he'd put out the call for the Director. "We know he'll authorize whatever you want. Where do you want me to start?"

"I'm in Chicago." A small sense of balance and stability flowed through Lauren as she switched into scientist mode. She could easily picture Steven, hands poised over one of several keyboards spread out before him. He would be bathed in the soft glow from a bank of high-resolution screens that displayed highly classified satellite reconnaissance information. Once the Director gave his blessing, Steven could instantly pull up data from any government source that currently existed.

"Lauren, it's Calvin," came a winded voice. "What's going on and how can I help?"

"It's Donovan." Lauren battled another bout of tears. She was touched that her friends at the DIA were so quick to come to her aid. Calvin was one of her biggest champions at the DIA—almost a father figure. He was a slender, graceful man, who always came to work in his trademark tie and suspenders, one of a handful of civilians who headed up divisions at the DIA. His piercing, hawk-like gaze displayed a keen intellect and was backed up by a commanding demeanor. Calvin was easily one of the brightest men Lauren had ever met. Calvin and Donovan knew each other, and though the two strong-willed men had locked horns at first, they had eventually developed a mutual respect for each other. "He's on a commercial flight traveling from Dulles to Chicago," Lauren continued. "I was talking to him when I lost the connection. His last words were that there was another plane and it's a possibility that they collided. I'm in Wayfarer Airlines

Operations and they've lost contact with the flight as well. Can you help us find them?"

"I need an approximate position and airplane type." Calvin replied immediately.

"Donovan told me they were less than an hour out of O'Hare. I don't know what kind of plane." Lauren looked up at the expectant faces around her.

"Boeing 737," Henry answered.

"It's a Boeing 737," Lauren repeated.

"Got it," Calvin replied. "I take it they don't have any idea if these planes actually collided or if they're still flying?"

"None at all." Lauren felt her emotions waver at the grave tone of Calvin's voice.

"I think we can find them, but it's going to take a little maneuvering at this end. I want to talk to the CIA and employ their resources as well."

"I understand." Lauren knew what Calvin had in mind. The CIA's Keyhole satellites were in orbit 300 miles above the Earth and moving at twenty-five times the speed of sound. Each of them could easily identify an object as small as a license plate. She tried to picture their classified orbits, but couldn't. She had no idea if there was one in place over the United States, though if she were to hazard a guess she imagined that there would be.

"Do you want me to call you back on the phone you're on, or your cell phone?"

"Try the cell phone first. But I'd appreciate it if you would only talk to me about this," Lauren replied as she glanced at the strangers around her. She knew her connection with the DIA would ensure she was kept in the loop.

"I'll call you back shortly." Calvin's voice softened. "Is there anything else I can do? Are you with anyone?"

"Michael is on his way." Lauren was helpless to stop herself as tears formed in her eyes. "He's at Midway airport with the new Gulfstream, but now he's trying to get here."

"Very good, I'll see what I can do about helping Michael get there," Calvin replied, calmly. "We'll start working at this end, and I'll let you know the moment we have something. Call me on my direct line if you think of anything else I can do."

"Thank you." Lauren bit her lip as she hung up the phone. She wiped her eyes, then gathered herself and turned to face Henry. "Hopefully we'll know something soon."

"That's it?" Henry challenged, not bothering to hide the fact that he was annoyed. "What exactly do you think they can do to find a single missing plane?"

"Right now there are dozens of highly trained experts sifting through information from sources I'm not at liberty to discuss." Lauren glared at Henry. "On the whole, I'd say I'm doing a hell of a lot more than you are."

CHAPTER FIVE

Donovan knew he had to quickly figure out how far to push the damaged 737. Violent thunderstorms lay dead ahead, the clouds racing upward into the atmosphere. The growing turbulence pounded the airplane, like sledgehammers pummeling the thin aluminum skin. In his rush to gain control of the airliner, he hadn't fastened his harness. He cursed his lack of discipline. Any more mistakes and he knew this airplane could come raining down in a million pieces.

Donovan braced himself as the Boeing sped closer to the deadly weather. He wished he could buckle himself in, but he knew he didn't have time. He put more pressure on the controls and pulled the power back to slow the Boeing, trying in vain to decrease the radius of the turn. He'd give anything if this were a Gulfstream. He had thousands of hours in Gulfstreams, could fly them in his sleep. But a 737, even an intact one, was a mystery to him. Donovan braced himself as a seething column of clouds raced upward. The wall of the thunderstorm now filled the windshield.

Donovan held his breath as the Boeing, still in as tight a turn as he dared, punched into the side of the storm. Immediately, the turbulence punished the stricken 737. Donovan was helpless as the Boeing rushed wildly upward in the center of the storm. He struggled to focus on the tiny airspeed indicator, but the turbulence made it almost impossible. Silently, he willed the 737 to stay together. Metal screeched above him as the overhead panel buckled, then fell downward. Inches before it reached his head it slammed to an abrupt stop. Donovan jumped at the noise and crouched down in his seat. A new fear invaded his thoughts; if the panel fell away from what was left of the ceiling, he would be trapped and helpless as the 737 flew on without anyone at the controls. Donovan forced himself to ignore the lethal object hovering above him. It would either stay where it was or it wouldn't. There wasn't anything he could do about it now.

The gray world inside the clouds began to grow brighter, and Donovan allowed himself the brief hope that they might make it. All he needed was for the airplane to stay intact for a few more seconds. High above, a hint of blue sky through the swirling vapor lifted his spirits.

With one last lurch, the 737 burst from the side of the thunderstorm. And in that instant, Donovan realized the plane was flying far too slowly; the Boeing's nose was pitched up dangerously high and the plane was running out of speed. His momentary relief at still being alive was replaced with the threat of stalling the 737. If his airspeed dropped below a minimum level, there wouldn't be enough airflow over the wings to maintain sufficient lift. The airplane would simply quit flying and spin down into the storm.

Carefully, he banked the 737 and gently lowered the nose. He desperately needed airspeed, but couldn't afford to be reckless. The controls began to feel better in his hands. The airliner was slowly doing what he wanted. The sound of the slipstream began to grow louder as the small airspeed indicator showed that their speed was building. Each tick of the second hand in his head put them further away from the murderous weather.

Donovan let out a long breath into his mask, and finally dared to blink his dry eyes. He ignored the involuntary shaking in his knees. He twisted to look over his right shoulder at the line of thunderstorms. Their tops had built above the Boeing, reaching far into the stratosphere. Banking toward clear air and traveling at four miles a minute, Donovan turned his attention to the precious few instruments he had. The backup altimeter showed them at 38,400 feet. The airplane had been driven up nearly half-a-mile in just a few seconds. *Damn it!* He cursed silently into his mask, he needed to be going down instead of up. Donovan yanked the throttles back as far as they would go and forced the nose of the 737 to drop below the distant horizon. More than anything, he had to try to make up for lost time.

He checked his heading against the position of the sun. He knew he was on the north side of the squall line. Donovan gingerly turned the airplane fifteen degrees left; he used his best guess to put the airplane on a rough heading for Chicago. He really had no idea exactly how far he might be from anything, or more importantly, how he was going to be able to land the airplane with no electrical power. He momentarily took his eyes off the horizon and studied the wrecked overhead panel for some sign of life, something obvious that he might be able to correct and give himself electricity. Within seconds, the controls began to vibrate in his hands. *Be careful! Watch your pitch,* he warned himself as the airspeed built quickly due to his inattention. He made a subtle correction, silently urging the aircraft to descend.

Donovan relaxed slightly, knowing that the largest storms were behind him. He took a moment to survey the empty sky in front of the 737. Far ahead, all he could see were clouds. Carefully, using one hand at a time, he managed to secure himself in the seat harness, pulling hard on the straps.

Donovan concentrated on keeping the Boeing in a descent. The cockpit was a blur as they burst in and out of another layer of clouds, turbulence jolting the airplane and precipitation pelting the windshield. Donovan could only get fragmented glimpses of the weather ahead. The cockpit grew dark. He had done this a thousand times, but always in a fully functioning airplane, with all the information that technology had to offer.

He could hear the roar from the cabin as they quickly picked up more speed. At six miles per minute, the Boeing sped across an invisible line that marked the edge of the disturbed air. The last bit of turbulence spit them out with a final jolt, and they flew smoothly away from of its reach.

Despite the aching coldness of the cockpit, Donovan's hands were sweaty and he wiped the perspiration on the thighs of his trousers. He closed his eyes and exhaled into his mask. He prayed the more stable air would reduce the risk of the overhead section coming loose again. *Get this thing down now—before the people in back run out of oxygen.* The only way to judge his heading was to focus on the standby compass. The primitive device floated and bobbed in its case.

Donovan felt a presence at his left elbow. He turned as Audrey squeezed into the cockpit. Her eyes filled with horror when she saw the copilot's body on the floor and the unconscious captain. She touched Donovan on the shoulder, then slid her mask aside.

"Please tell me you know how to fly," Audrey demanded as she looked around in dismay at the shattered cockpit.

Donovan nodded, his eyes fixed on the distant horizon.

"Can we take these off yet?"

Donovan shook his head. "No. We're still too high." He pushed his mask back to his face and took a deep breath.

"Are you okay? You're bleeding." She pointed at his forehead.

Donovan guessed he'd injured himself in his mad rush to get to the cockpit. "I'm fine. I'm more interested in how seriously he's hurt." He looked across the cockpit at the slumped form of the captain. The 737 entered another layer of clouds. Donovan tensed his body for the turbulence but there was none. The Boeing cruised along without a bump.

Audrey moved across the cockpit and examined the captain, turning his head and inspecting his wound. She spent several moments assessing the severity, then turned to Donovan. "I don't know how badly he's injured, but at least he's still alive." She looked out the windshield, then back down at the panel. "How can you fly with no instruments?"

Donovan gave her a weak smile from behind his mask. He could see both the fear and courage in her familiar eyes. He wondered how long he could remain a stranger to her with this much contact. The two aspects of his appearance-altering surgery they couldn't address were his eyes and his voice. More than anything, he wished that he could minimize his exposure to her. "I have enough for now, but I'll need him if we're going to get this thing on the ground."

She gave him an encouraging pat on the shoulder, and quickly vanished through the doorway.

Donovan concentrated on his flying. The diffused gray world inside the clouds gradually brightened as the 737 continued its descent. He had to find clear air. He needed the distant horizon as a reference if he was going to keep the airplane straight and level. With all of the main instruments gone, he couldn't risk staying in the clouds for any length of time. The biggest danger was the potential of vertigo, which would be akin to closing your eyes on a roller coaster. In a matter of minutes he could become hopelessly confused, having no way of knowing which way was up or down. Spatial disorientation was one of the fastest ways to lose control of an airplane.

The Boeing twinjet burst from the base of the high clouds into clear sky. To the west, the sun sat low on the horizon. Below him, stretched as far as he could see, the clouds were splashed with orange and yellow in the late afternoon light. Donovan let out a slow breath into his mask. The air was smooth, and for the first time since he'd sat at the unfamiliar controls, he let his wire-taut muscles relax a little. His thighs ached, as did his hands. He flexed his fingers until some of the stiffness was gone, then loosened his harness a fraction. The aircraft was starting to respond better, thanks to the increasing air density as they descended. He dropped the nose, but within seconds the slight vibration grew worse. He eased back and it disappeared. He had to settle for the pitiful rate of descent he had. There would be no emergency descent. Normally with an emergency decompression, the airplane would be coming down at more than 6,000 feet per minute. Shaking his head in frustration, he calculated their descent at a mere 800 feet per minute.

The standby altimeter crept past 25,000 feet; Donovan needed to get the airplane down to 10,000 before he could safely breath without his mask. He again tested the controls. If he relaxed his grip, the airplane wanted to turn to the right. It took constant pressure to hold the nose straight. Donovan pushed the left throttle up an inch, and the aircraft yawed as the thrust on that side became greater. He repeated the procedure on the other side. His little test at least confirmed that both engines were producing thrust. Silently, he gave thanks for small miracles, though he still had to constantly adjust the extra sensitive pitch of the 737. When he had let the speed build too much, the vibration in the controls became dangerous. From everything he was feeling, he knew the tail section must be damaged.

Donovan once again turned his attention to the cockpit around him. Every one of the primary flight instruments was useless. Back-up systems that should have allowed at least partial power had failed. Not a single electrical component on any of the panels was illuminated.

The overhead section was what worried Donovan the most. He could only take small measured glances upwards to get a better look. But as he quickly looked back and forth, he began to get a better picture of what he was dealing with. The tremendous force of the impact with the KC-135 had pushed the metal framework down and thrust it twenty degrees to one side. A little further aft, the twisted wreckage from the roof structure nearly blocked the entry onto the flight deck. Behind the captain's seat, up near the ceiling, was more damage. Donovan knew enough about airplane design to understand that virtually all of the ship's electrical power was routed from the compartments behind their seats, through the overhead panel. He shook his head at the wire bundles that dangled above him, frayed ends swaying back and forth like severed arteries to essential organs. *This is one screwed up airplane.*

Donovan couldn't help but wonder about the people in the back. Above each row of seats were the emergency oxygen generators. They produced air for approximately twelve minutes, usually more than enough time for an airliner to descend to a safe altitude. It was taking him far longer than that; those passengers with masks would probably have run out of oxygen by now.

Donovan glanced back at the entryway. He thought he felt Audrey returning to the cockpit, but the passageway was empty. If something happened to her, he would have no way of knowing, or helping. He'd be forced to deal with all of this alone. What if he were the sole survivor?

He focused his attention back to flying the Boeing. Audrey was on her own; whatever was happening behind him in the cabin was outside his sphere of influence. His job was to keep this airplane flying—if he lost control of the 737, nothing else would matter.

CHAPTER SIX

Lauren watched as the chaos in Operations moved from the counter and was now centered on a desk away from the lounge area. Henry Parrish had turned his back on her with a silent, but dismissive expression and began issuing orders to the people around him. David Tucker was still standing next to her; Lauren sensed he was torn between watching her and wanting to join the fray.

"There's an airplane crash in Indiana. It's on CNN!" The dreaded words carried across the room to where Lauren stood.

Lauren's knees turned weak as Tucker escorted her into a different section of Operations. Moments later, Lauren stood with other members of the Wayfarer staff. They'd gathered in what she'd heard described as the war room. All four televisions were switched on, and tuned to different news stations. Henry increased the volume on the set marked CNN. The room had a complex communications system, though primitive by DIA standards. Lauren guessed they could monitor all of Wayfarer's ground and flight frequencies, as well as all of the O'Hare air traffic control transmissions. The electronics were powered up and careful notes were being written on one particular board that covered an entire wall. Flight 880's flight number had been put up, a question mark next to the word "casualties".

Lauren felt herself go numb. On the screen, a reporter in a parka stood before the camera in the driving snow. Behind him was a virtual parking lot of official vehicles, their lights flashing in a surreal rhythm.

"Live from just outside Fort Wayne, Indiana. This is Neil Hadley. I'm standing just a short distance from the grizzly crash scene of what I'm told is a Military KC-135 tanker. The four-engine Boeing aircraft is used by the Air Force for aerial refueling operations. Filled with what we can only guess is thousands of gallons of volatile aviation fuel, the jet plunged to the ground just outside this quiet subdivision approximately half an hour ago. Eyewitnesses described a loud noise, followed by a huge explosion as the plane was destroyed in a giant fireball. Unconfirmed reports suggest that the airplane was already in pieces as it fell out of the sky. Debris, we understand, is scattered over a large area and not confined to this site. Severe thunderstorms pounded this region earlier, with high winds and some reports of hail. But as you can see now, the snow is really beginning to come down. No word yet as to how many people were on board, or how many victims might have been killed on the ground. Rescue efforts are being hampered by both the rain-saturated ground and intense fire. This aircraft is said to have been enroute to Chicago's O'Hare airport. The officials on the scene have said it is too early to rule out anything—including, I'm told, an act of terrorism."

Lauren looked across the room at Henry, his jaw working furiously as he studied the images on the screen. Lauren turned back to the television as the grainy picture showed the reporter reaching up and adjusting his earpiece. He paused, collected himself and once again began talking.

"I've just been given new information. It seems there are now reports coming in, of aircraft debris, and some possible bodies, located at least a mile from here. We're also receiving unconfirmed reports of a power outage at the air traffic control center in Indianapolis, the radar facility that controls all of the air traffic in this area. We have no indication yet that these events are linked, but we do now know that the FBI has been called in to investigate. As soon as we have more details on this latest disaster, we'll get that information to you."

"It's not ours," Henry said finally, turning down the volume.

Lauren was overcome with relief, her entire body shaking. One moment she feared she was looking at the burning wreckage of Donovan's flight, only to be back where she was a few minutes ago—hoping against hope that he could somehow still be alive.

"Where are they?" she heard herself say out loud at the same moment her cell phone rang. In one swift motion she pushed the answer button and brought it to her ear. "Hello." Lauren heard nothing as she repeated herself. She looked at her phone and saw that there was no signal, but the lack of a number on caller ID told her it had probably come from the DIA. Without hesitation, she fled the room, ignoring the looks from those around her, she went straight to the phone she'd used before. She quickly punched the buttons and waited.

Lauren reached out to brace herself against a table. She feared the worst. It hadn't taken her boss very long to call her back. "It's me," she said, as Calvin answered.

"I'm glad you're still there," Calvin said. "Okay, we found one of the planes. It was a KC-135 and it's crashed in Indiana."

"I know about that one," Lauren said. "What about the other one, Donovan's plane?"

"We're still looking," Calvin began to explain. "Steven had an idea that I think is encouraging. We were able to pinpoint the exact coordinates of the KC-135 crash through the seismic disturbance caused by the airplane's impact with the ground."

Lauren's brow furrowed as she forced herself to follow what Calvin was trying to say.

"Steven accessed the United States Geological Survey's seismic array. As you know, basically, the entire planet is wired to detect even the slightest earthquake or tremor. The crash of the plane was recorded and triangulated by the sensitive earthquake detection array. The impact registered like a small-scale earthquake."

"But you told me you're still looking for Donovan's plane." Lauren's spirits soared. "Are you telling me there's only been one seismic disturbance—as in one crash?"

"Exactly," Calvin replied. "Right now we're in the process of re-tasking a Keyhole satellite. It will be above the horizon in seven minutes and we'll start a systematic scan then."

"You're wonderful." Lauren brushed her hair away from her face. "I'll pass this along and wait to hear from you."

"Hang in there dear," Calvin said, attempting to sound up-beat. "I've also put in some other calls. I'm in the process of helping Michael get to O'Hare, but I guess the roads are pretty bad right now. But we're on it."

"I appreciate everything you're doing," Lauren said, buoyed by the efforts of those closest to her. She severed the connection and took a deep breath, taking a moment to organize her thoughts.

"What did they say?" Henry moved closer the moment she'd hung up the phone.

"We'll know more in a few minutes," Lauren said as she glanced up at the clock.

"But what I can tell you, is that there has only been one airplane crash."

"How could you know that?" Henry questioned, his voice filled with doubt. "How could anyone know that right now?"

"Science," Lauren said as she spun from him, there was no way she was going to take the time to explain to this impossible man how she knew what she did.

"Dr. McKenna." Henry's stern tone relaxed slightly. "I'm sorry."

Lauren hesitated, and then faced him. He'd said the words, but somehow they lacked any real warmth, though she thought she detected a momentary softening in his demeanor. She replayed the heated exchange he'd had with his son. It was probably unfair to judge Henry Parrish under these circumstances, but she found him cold and distant.

"Dr. McKenna, I am sorry," Henry said, then paused as he measured his words. "I don't mean to be—"

"Henry, I hate to interrupt you," Glen called out from behind them. "The top-brass just arrived and they want to be briefed on the situation."

"Clear the war room, then bring them in. We'll do it there," Henry replied loudly, then said to Lauren. "I am sorry, we do need to talk, but right now I have to deal with these people. Captain Tucker will stay with you. Don't hesitate to ask him for anything at all. Interrupt me if you hear back from your friends at the DIA."

Lauren nodded. She didn't bother to acknowledge the small group of people who were waiting for the room to clear. The last thing she wanted right now was to be exposed to the top executives of the airline. In fact what she wanted most was to be alone to call Michael. Standing in Wayfarer Operations, she felt like a complete outsider.

"Where can I make a phone call and get a cup of coffee?" she asked Tucker as she walked away from the gathering of Wayfarer executives.

"This way. There's a conference room hardly anyone ever uses. How do you like your coffee?"

"Black is fine."

"I'll go get it for you, then I'll meet you in room 112. It's the third door on the left, just around the corner." Tucker cocked his head. "Promise me you're not calling anyone who might create problems. We've got enough issues to deal with right now."

"Trust me. We're all on the same side here," Lauren replied as she took her cell phone from her purse. She rounded the corner and found the room he'd directed her toward. She pushed open the solid wooden door and let herself in. The light was on and at the far end of the table she found Matt, a surprised look on his face as he hurriedly dropped his cigarette into a soft drink can he was using as his ashtray.

"Sorry." Lauren's heart went out to the young man as she studied him, she could clearly see he'd been in here alone, crying.

"My Dad's not coming in here, is he?" Matt asked, guardedly.

"No. I had to escape the Operations room. We still don't know much. Can I join you? I'd love a cigarette." Lauren rarely smoked, but right now she craved the calming effect a cigarette might provide.

"Really?" Matt reached into the inside pocket of his oversized coat and pulled out a pack. He shook out two, then handed one to Lauren. He lit hers, then his.

"Thank you." Lauren blew out the smoke without inhaling. She saw her hands shake as she held the cigarette away from her. She guessed Matt was sixteen or seventeen years old. He had brown eyes like his father. His long, stringy hair framed a handsome face, but his skin was broken by patches of acne. There was a faint blur of whiskers above his upper lip, which looked more like a smudge than a mustache. A single stud protruded from his left ear lobe and she could just make out the edge of a tattoo that crept up above the collar of his baggy sweater. By all appearances he looked like a punk, but during his earlier exchange with his father, Lauren had sensed an intelligent mind behind his anger and defiance.

"You have someone on the same flight as my mom?" Matt took a vengeful drag off of his cigarette and bitterly blew out the smoke toward the ceiling.

"Yes," Lauren said and nodded, then looked down at her cell phone, relieved to see that opposed to the war room, in this part of the building, she had a good signal. "Would you mind if I made a phone call?"

"Do you want me to leave?" Matt exhaled heavily, a crestfallen expression spread out on his young face.

"No. Not at all. I want you to stay right where you are," Lauren said quickly; she'd seen his obvious disappointment and she knew she couldn't bear to cast him away as his father had. "You're the only one in this place that knows what I'm going through. Please don't go."

"Really?" His eyes filled with gratitude at being allowed to stay.

"Yes. I didn't want to appear rude by talking on the phone without asking first. After all, you have the cigarettes." Lauren winked at him as if they were newly bonded co-conspirators. The last thing she wanted right now was to be alone, or to be surrounded by Henry or any of the other Wayfarer executives.

"Cool. Let me know if you want another one." Matt slid the soda can between them.

Tucker pushed the door open with his back as he entered the room with a cup of coffee in each hand. "Here we go." He stopped, as he looked first at the cloud of smoke, then at Matt and Lauren.

"You caught us," Lauren offered, though she didn't really care.

"This whole area is non-smoking," Tucker said abruptly. "And Matt, for God's sake, your Dad would have a hemorrhage if he caught you."

"Screw him," Matt muttered.

"Can you excuse us for a little bit?" Lauren knew she had a small window to be alone before Calvin might call back. "I need to make a phone call and then I want to talk to Matt. We'll be fine in here. Just come get us if you hear anything."

"Are you sure?" Tucker paused as if he needed to hear more.

"Positive." Lauren reached out for her coffee, then gave Tucker a dismissive look to let him know he'd just been excused.

As Tucker quietly shut the door, Lauren rose and locked it from the inside. She sat back down, dropped her cigarette into the can, and picked up her cell phone.

"This won't take long." She tried to smile at Matt, but just couldn't find one to give. The young man turned away as if to provide her some privacy, then absently picked up a nearby laser pointer and began to mindlessly click it on and off. Lauren watched as the spot of intense red light danced aimlessly around the wall and ceiling. Matt repeatedly sliced the beam through the cloud of smoke from their cigarettes. Lauren looked at Matt as she swept her phone to her ear. She very subtly shook her head in reference to the distracting light.

"Whoops." Matt shrugged an apology and thrust the device into his coat pocket

"Hello," came Michael's confident tone.

"Michael, it's me." At the sound of his voice, Lauren found it almost impossible to sort through the rapidly shifting events. The uncertainty of what had happened to Donovan was becoming harder to deal with.

"Do you know anything yet?" Michael said loudly, the sound of gale-force winds rustling through the connection.

"No," Lauren said, as a surprise sob escaped from her throat.

"I got a call from your boss," Michael said, hoping to comfort her. "Calvin brought me up to date and is trying to use some military contacts to get me to O'Hare. Hopefully I can hitch a ride on a truck or a jeep and get to you. Lauren, please hang in there, I'm coming as fast as I can, but the storm is really getting wound up."

"I'm glad Calvin called you," Lauren managed to whisper. "Hurry. Just get here. I need you."

"It's going to be all right," Michael reassured her. "Calvin told me there has only been one crash. I, for one, am hanging onto that scenario. For all we know, Donovan is sitting in first class, pissed off that the onboard phones quit working."

"I know," Lauren said, grateful for Michael's typically upbeat words.

"I'll keep you posted on my progress. Call me the moment you hear from him."

"I will. Bye." Lauren ended the call as her eyes filled with tears. Another sob escaped as she covered both of her eyes with one hand. More tears cascaded down her cheeks as she wept silently. To her surprise, she felt a hand reach out and take hers. She looked up and saw that Matt, too, had tears running down his face. She squeezed hard and they clung to each other, survivors, waiting for the answers to unthinkable questions.

CHAPTER SEVEN

Donovan pulled the oxygen mask off his head and relished the cool air on his face. They were nearing 10,000 feet and he could now breathe safely on his own. He inhaled deeply, and then wiped the perspiration from his cheeks. He massaged his face where the rubber had pressed hard into his skin. He thought of removing the mask from the captain, but decided the 100% oxygen might prove beneficial for the injured man.

Level at 10,000 feet, with a lower cloud deck still below them, Donovan leveled the aircraft and nudged the throttles forward. He had no idea how much fuel was on board and by going slow, he could conserve what they did have—plus he really didn't know where they were, or where they might be headed.

The dull roar of the slipstream decreased as the 737 slowed. A noise to Donovan's left announced Audrey's return from the cabin. His earlier fear at being alone vanished at the sight of her. "You can take off your mask," Donovan said as she slid past the mangled door. He faced forward, trying to limit his exposure to this woman from his past.

Audrey slipped free from the clumsy mask and bottle and lowered it to the floor. "God, that feels better. I was getting worried; the tank is basically showing empty. How are you doing up here? I'm sorry it took me so long, but it's truly a mess back there. The medical kit was somehow wedged in its compartment." She paused for a moment. "You saved my life and I don't even know your name."

"I'm Donovan Nash," he said warily, without facing her. He braced himself for any clue that she had recognized him.

"I'm Audrey Parrish. I'm so glad you did what you did." She put her hand on his shoulder. "How did all this..." she gestured with her hands at the obvious destruction on the flight deck. "I was walking to the restroom, then you pulled me into the seat. Right before—" she searched for the words. "Right before what? What happened to us?"

"We were hit by another plane." Donovan realized her view of the impact had been blocked, she had no idea what had happened. "I only saw it at the last second. You're not hurt, are you?"

"No. I'm not too bad, considering." Her eyes darted to his hairline. "But you have a cut on your head that needs attention."

He touched his temple and his hand came away with a trace of blood. It didn't particularly hurt. "I'm fine. Can you do something for him?"

"Right after I bandage your head." She knelt and opened the medical kit. She found the necessary items and ripped open a foil packet. "This might sting a little bit."

Donovan winced she dabbed the antiseptic on his skin. He didn't know if it was from the pain or from his discomfort at her proximity.

"Hang on, it's more of a scrape than a deep cut. I'm almost finished, just let me stick a bandage on this." Audrey tenderly smoothed out the adhesive. "How does that feel?"

"Better. Thanks." He adjusted the throttles and kept his face glued to the horizon. "Can you help him?"

Audrey didn't move. She looked at him closely. "Have we ever met?"

"I don't think so." Donovan nearly flinched as he held his breath.

"I swear you remind me of someone."

"I get that a lot." Donovan gestured to the unconscious form in the left seat. "Can you see to him?"

Audrey's gaze lingered on Donovan for a moment before she moved to the captain. She carefully pressed her fingers to his neck. "He has a good pulse," she announced. The captain's head rolled down and rested on his chest.

Donovan flew the airplane and glanced over as Audrey took another antiseptic wipe and carefully cleaned the blood from the man's head. With the blood cleaned from his face, he looked remarkably better. The captain appeared to be fairly young despite a receding hairline and a small paunch. He possessed rather soft, rounded facial features, accented by bushy dark eyebrows. The same thick hair covered his arms, which rested limply in his lap. Donovan watched as Audrey put a bandage over his wound to protect it. It looked like the bleeding had all but stopped.

"How bad is it back there?" Donovan asked about the people in the cabin and the horrible scene he'd witnessed on his way to the cockpit.

"After you left, everyone else blacked out one by one." She hesitated for a moment, biting her lip at the memory. "The flight attendant you saved is awake, but she's in pretty bad shape. I did manage to get her into a seat and cover her with a blanket, but she can't move her arm or shoulder. Besides being traumatized, I'm pretty sure she broke something when she fell."

"Has anyone else come around, anyone at all?"

"No. Not that I saw. But I was busy trying to pry the medical kit free." Audrey lowered her voice and tried to sound optimistic. "It might take them a little while."

"That's true." Despite himself, Donovan made momentary eye contact with Audrey. Her obvious anguish betrayed her optimistic hopes, as she probably held the same fear he did; no one in the back was going to wake up.

"You seem to know your way around a 737." Donovan knew she'd been around airplanes for the better part of the last two decades, but he had a vested interest in keeping up the thin charade that they'd just met.

"My husband, Henry, is the chief pilot for Wayfarer Airlines. We used to fly a lot together, so I guess it goes with the territory."

Donovan pictured the man she was talking about, though he hadn't seen or spoken with Henry in eighteen years—he'd known the man well. In fact, he'd known Henry longer than Audrey had. Seeing her had somehow released a floodgate of memories. *Be very careful,* Donovan warned himself.

"I'm going to take his mask off," Audrey said as she searched the medical kit. Moments later, she found what she wanted and broke the capsule in two. She slipped off the oxygen mask and held the smelling salts under the captain's nose until the man's head jerked and twisted to the side. She reached across him and waved the vial once again. His eyes fluttered open and he immediately flailed at the offending odor.

"Can you hear me?" Audrey questioned as she gazed at the man's face.

"What the…where are we?" The captain's words came out thickly as he shook his head to escape the pungent odor.

Audrey and Donovan watched as the captain struggled to pull himself out of the black hole he'd been in. Audrey leaned over him, trying to gauge his recovery.

Suddenly, the man jerked upright as if scalded by boiling water. His expression filled with terror. "What in the—oh shit!"

"Stop him! Get him off!" Donovan yelled as he fought to override the dangerous inputs. "Get him off the controls!"

Audrey reached in and fought to pull the captain's hands free. She lost her leverage as the airplane banked hard to the left, then climbed. She still held the capsule in her hand and forced it back under his nose. He twisted his head violently and swung an elbow toward her ribs. Audrey avoided the blow, found her balance, and used all her strength to slap him hard across the face. She'd aimed for the bandage she'd so carefully affixed to his forehead and the effect was immediate. The man cried out in pain as he released his grip, then cradled his head in his hands, rocking back and forth as he moaned.

"Captain. Listen to me. The airplane is under control." Audrey spoke reassuringly. "You've been out for a little while. Take a few deep breaths, but don't touch anything." Her voice softened. "Sorry I hit you. How do you feel? Look at me." She put her hand around his and squeezed. "Do you know where you are? Do you remember what happened?"

The captain let out another moan as his eyes tried to fix on the person in front of him. His voice was weak but clear. "God, my head hurts." His fingers went to his head and he touched the bandage. "What in the hell happened?"

"We were hit by another plane." Donovan leaned forward to assess the man's condition.

"Where's Jeff?" He asked, his voice stronger this time. "Where's my first officer?"

Audrey averted her eyes for a moment, looking behind her to where the copilot's body was still laying on the floor. "He didn't survive."

Confusion clouded the captain's face. "Jeff's dead?" He turned toward Donovan, his voice filled with bewilderment. "A midair? You saw it happen?"

"I saw the plane only a few seconds before it hit us. It looked like a military plane, maybe a KC-135. It came from our two o'clock position." Donovan pointed out the right window to indicate the angle. "It was in and out of the clouds. Didn't you get a warning from Center, or a TCAS alert?"

"Nothing. Last thing I can recall was—" he paused and fought through the pain as he searched his clouded memory. "I remember now. I was attempting to talk to Air Traffic Control, but we weren't getting an answer. That's all I remember. I never saw a thing."

"What's TCAS?" Audrey asked.

"It's a system that allows two airplanes to talk to each other electronically," Donovan explained. "It's a system designed to prevent midair collisions. Normally, there should have been multiple warnings up here in the cockpit that there was another airplane. It should have also given them the correct resolution to the conflict, told them to either climb or dive."

"You said the other plane was military?" the captain asked, as he struggled to piece together the information.

Donovan nodded. "From where I was sitting, it looked like we were shooting through a small gap in the line of thunderstorms. That's probably what the other airplane was doing, too. But if you didn't get a warning from Center, or a TCAS warning, I doubt you could have reacted even if you'd seen them." He could tell the man was processing the information. "We've lost the entire electrical system. Shouldn't the ship's main batteries be providing us with at least standby power to the essential instruments? I need your help in trying to get some of this back."

"Who are you?" the captain asked.

"My name is Donovan Nash. I'm a corporate pilot." Donovan simplified the task of explaining. "I fly Gulfstream jets out of Dulles. This is Audrey."

"What's your name?" Audrey asked the befuddled captain.

"My name is John. John Thornton."

"We were lucky Donovan was with us, John," Audrey added. "He saved all of us by managing to make his way up here and fly the plane."

John grimaced as he began to survey the wrecked remains of his cockpit, squinting from the pain. "I think I'm okay; just give me a second. How long—" his words came out muffled and strained. "How long was I out? Where are we?"

Donovan glanced at his watch. "You were out at least twenty minutes. We're down at 10,000 feet. We had an explosive decompression so we had to descend. My guess is we're about 70 or 80 miles northwest of the line of thunderstorms."

John's eyes widened as he assessed the situation.

"John, we need to figure all this out." Donovan watched as the man surveyed the cockpit. He hoped John was making sense of what he found. "Anything obvious? I don't know anything about 737s. Like I said, I fly Gulfstreams." Donovan's hopes sagged as John looked at him in confusion.

"I don't even know where to start," John said. "We must have been hit from above?"

"That's right. Can you tell if we have any power available?" Donovan urged. He started with the basics common in all aircraft. "Check the amps and the volts. Find out what we have."

John pulled his attention to the overhead panel. His head swayed slightly as he fought to understand. He reached up and rotated two knobs. A perplexed look clouded his face.

"Anything?" Donovan continued flying the airplane, but kept a close eye on what John was doing, grateful that Audrey's full attention was focused on John and not himself.

"It just doesn't make sense. Nothing. We're reading nothing. No power at all." John lowered his head and held it in both hands.

"Are you sure you're okay?" Audrey asked, hovering close. "Is there anything else I can do for you?"

John raised his head and smiled weakly at Audrey, then struggled to sit upright. "We need to check the circuit breaker panel. Are the people in back okay? What about the rest of my crew?" John tried to pivot all the way around toward Audrey, but wasn't quite up to the effort. His shoulders slumped and he exhaled heavily.

"We have some casualties. One of the flight attendants survived, but she's injured." Audrey hesitated for a moment. "I'll bring you up to date on all of that later. I think you need to help Donovan get some of the instruments back."

"Okay, right. The panel behind me, it's one of the electrical sub-panels. Can you see anything?"

Audrey looked directly behind where John sat. "I see rows of what look like little buttons. A whole bunch of them seem to be popped out."

"Okay. Good, those are the circuit breakers. Look for the ones with larger numbers written on them; they'll be the ones carrying the most amperage. Can you read them to me?"

"It's too dark to see the labels," Audrey replied.

"Here," John said, his voice came across a little stronger than before. "Use this."

Audrey switched on the flashlight John had pulled from its bracket. "That's better, I can see them now. I found some with 30 written on them. AC Bus. DC Bus. One says UNSW, the other says SW," Audrey called out after a quick search. "You want me to keep going?"

Donovan guessed she had found some of the more important ones. Thirty-amp breakers served the larger systems. The other letters probably stood for switched and un-switched, but he wasn't sure what the significance was. "John, what does that mean?"

"Uh, hang on a second." John paused for a moment as he thought. "If those are out, the power from the generators isn't getting to the main bus. We need to push all of those in."

"Not yet, Audrey," Donovan warned. "I don't think we can just start resetting breakers. We have so much damage we could easily start a fire."

"Generator Bus one." John looked at Donovan as if suddenly remembering. "We need to reset it; that's the one we want."

"Audrey, can you find that one? It's probably marked GEN BUS 1." It made sense. Donovan felt encouraged by John's small, yet significant recovery.

It took her a moment to read the small labels. "I found it. Yes, it's out."

John pulled himself upright; he clamped his jaw tightly at the pain, but only for a second. He released the air slowly from between his teeth. "Donovan. Over on your side should be the emergency checklist. Let me have a look at that before we do anything rash." He pressed his eyes shut again.

Donovan found the manual John wanted and passed it over to him. In doing so, Donovan couldn't help but notice how much John's hand was trembling.

"I'm sure that's the one we need to reset," John said emphatically, as he quickly flipped through the pages of the checklist.

Donovan was relieved that John had actually made a decision, though whether or not it was the right one remained to be seen. "Okay. I'm with you on this. Let's give it a try."

John looked up from the checklist, shrugged, and put it aside. "That's got to be it—that breaker is as good a place to start as any. To be real honest, the checklist doesn't really cover midair collisions."

Donovan grinned inwardly at John's comment, more because it showed the man was regaining his faculties than for the humor. "I think we have to give it a try. We can't do anything with what we have now. But I'll tell you, the overhead panel really worries me. It's already shifted once from the turbulence. There's so much damage, I'm worried about a fire. I'd say a major short is a very real possibility. It's probably why all those breakers popped in the first place."

"If that's the case, they should just pop out again," John explained. "Then at least we'll know."

Donovan nodded. "Okay, let's give it a try. But as an extra precaution, I think we should have a fire extinguisher handy before we do this."

"There's one right here," Audrey said, and pointed. "Hang on, I'll pull it out."

"Perfect. Set it right up here and either one of us can grab for it if we need to." Donovan looked at John. "I'm ready whenever you are, captain. Audrey, are you set?" Adrenaline rush through Donovan's body, perking his senses; if this worked, they were moments away from having functioning instruments.

"Just tell me what you want me to do," Audrey said, her eagerness accompanied by uncertainty.

"On my mark, just push in the breaker," John replied. "But don't lose sight of it; we may need to pull it out again in a hurry. Everyone ready?" John paused for a moment. "Push it in, Audrey, and then take your hand away and watch for flames or any other breakers to pop."

"It's in." Audrey did as she was instructed.

"I don't see anything happening," John said quickly. "Are you sure it's in?"

"Oh my God! We're on fire!" Audrey screamed and pointed up above them.

"Pull the breaker out!" Donovan reached for his oxygen mask. Dense white smoke began to pour out of the overhead panel. He knew that breathing even a small amount of the noxious vapor could kill him. An electrical fire could engulf the entire cockpit in minutes. He pictured being burned alive, trapped in his seat as he piloted the doomed 737.

"I got it! It's out," Audrey called, her voice a mixture of both terror and triumph.

The three of them sat, helplessly waiting for the smoke to get worse, or flames to fill the cockpit.

"We're in deep shit," Donovan said finally, as he watched the diminishing smoke drift aft toward the cockpit door. There appeared to be no residual fire. "We know we have at least one working generator, but there must be a massive short on the bus."

The very real threat of fire had served to bring John completely out of his haze. "Jesus Christ! This is so screwed up. Let me think for a moment, there has to be something else we can do."

"What about the other side?" Donovan said, referring to the opposite generator, but as soon as the words left his mouth, he knew it wasn't a very good idea.

"Same song, different verse, I'm afraid." John slowly shook his cherubic face as he studied the overhead panel, taking in the odd angle at which it hung from the ceiling. "This is just one huge electrical fire looking for a place to happen. How is it flying?"

"Not great. But then, I don't know how a healthy one flies." Donovan replied. "It's been a little tricky. I'm pretty sure the tail is damaged, but for now it's manageable."

"This whole thing is a mess." John sunk and let out a breath while he gazed out the side window. "Memphis was our alternate, so I think we need to head this plane back to the south. The weather in Chicago was going downhill fast. We'll have to find some decent weather or we're not going to get this airplane on the ground in one piece."

"We can't go back that way," Donovan cautioned. "Those thunderstorms are between us and Memphis. The storms were still building. There weren't any breaks as far as I could see, north or south. Besides, I don't think the airplane would take the turbulence if we tried to punch our way through a soft spot. We know we can't fly above them, there's probably not enough oxygen left if we even tried to climb to a higher altitude." Donovan had already thought through the scenario. "How far to the west did the system stretch?"

"Too far. It was really getting wound up. The report before we left Dulles showed marginal conditions as far west as the Dakotas."

Donovan leveled his eyes at the sun, low on the horizon to the southwest. "It's going to get dark soon. We don't stand a chance if we can't get this thing on the ground before the sun sets."

John, too, squinted at the setting sun, then quickly looked away. "We still have some time."

"Any idea how much fuel we have?" Donovan asked. The bleak expression on John's face confirmed what he was already thinking. There was no way of knowing how much was left in the tanks, or how much they were burning. At best, it was going to be nothing more than an educated guess.

"I'll have to give that some thought," John shrugged. "I put on quite a bit before we took off. We're not going to flame-out the engines anytime soon."

"What we need is a cell phone," Donovan said. "We're going to need some help from the people on the ground."

"That was my next suggestion," John said. "Audrey, why don't you go start that search. The quicker we can get help, the better."

"I know all of my things are gone, the overhead compartments and seats were all sucked out." Audrey remarked. "What about the phones in back, the ones mounted in the seats?"

"You can try," John shrugged. "But I doubt if they have power."

"Does the cockpit door have an electric lock?" Donovan finally asked. He'd been wondering how he'd made it into the cockpit so easily.

John nodded. "The lock would have failed when we lost power. Otherwise you'd have never been able to get in here. Thank God for small favors."

"I have a phone in my briefcase. It's a leather bag in row 19," Donovan said to Audrey. "It was still under the seat in front of me after the impact."

"On my way," Audrey replied. "Do you need anything else?"

"We're good." Donovan turned to John after Audrey left. "How do you feel?"

"Like I got hit by a truck. My head hurts like hell. I'm sorry. I forgot your name."

"I'm Donovan." He wished he could make an accurate assessment of the captain, to judge if his faculties were impaired. It was a difficult task even under ideal conditions.

"I want to thank you, Donovan." John made eye contact with him. "If you hadn't done what you did, none of us would be here now."

"I just did what any pilot would do. Glad I was here to lend a hand."

"Not everyone can jump into an airplane they've never flown, let alone one this messed up, and get the job done. Nice work."

"Thanks, I appreciate that," Donovan replied

John fumbled for the adjustment on his seat back. "There we go." He used the back of his hand to gingerly wipe the perspiration from his face. "Okay. I'm ready to take her."

"Are you sure?" Donovan said.

"I'm fine except for a headache." John placed his hands on the controls.

"I think I'd better brief you on how she flies." Donovan felt somewhat reluctant to hand over the controls. "Much faster than 250 knots and the buffet in the elevator gets pretty bad. She wants to turn to the right and the aileron control is pretty sloppy. A couple of times when I let it get a little slow, I had a problem getting the nose back down. I think the tail must have taken a pretty good hit."

"I'll figure it out," John said. "I've got it."

Donovan released his grip. He was poised to regain control at the slightest hint of a problem. He watched as John over-controlled briefly, then quickly developed a feel for the damaged airplane.

"I see what you mean," John said finally. "You're right. This mother is pretty banged up." John pulled the throttles back a fraction as he sorted out the damaged 737.

Moments later, Audrey came back to the flight deck, slightly winded.

"I found it," Audrey said, as she handed it to him.

Donovan flipped it open and hit the power button. He had no idea if he could even get a signal from where they were. It took a moment, but finally it located a station. Donovan looked up triumphantly. "Who should we call?"

"We need to try to contact Chicago Center," John said. "I'm just guessing, but I bet we're in their airspace by now." John nodded toward the cell phone. "Are we even sure that thing will work up here?"

"I don't know why not. It says we have a signal. As long as we're in range of a station, it should be fine. Since we're pretty low; I think it'll be able to lock on to just one station. We'll find out soon enough." Donovan thought for a moment. "Any idea what the number is for Chicago Center?"

John shook his head. "Can we just call 911? Or information? Maybe they could give us the phone number for the tower at O'Hare. I think those are listed. Might be easier than trying to get the number for Chicago Center."

"I have a better idea." Donovan quickly went through the cell phone's directory and found the number he was looking for. He pushed the send button and waited.

CHAPTER EIGHT

"Mind if I have another cigarette?" Lauren withdrew her hand from Matt's and dug in her purse for a tissue. She dabbed at her eyes as Matt produced the pack. A fresh column of smoke drifted up toward the ceiling as she tried to collect herself.

"I didn't mean to fall apart," Lauren said as she gathered her frayed emotions. The longer it took to find Donovan, the harder it was going to be to hold it together. "Thanks for being here."

"No problem," Matt replied, as he used his coat sleeve to wipe the tears from his face. "I've been thinking about my mom, too. She's all I have left."

Lauren, somewhat startled, wondered why he'd so openly reject his father. "What about your Dad?"

"I don't really want to talk about him." Matt scowled and angrily flicked at the ash on his cigarette. "There's only one way to exist in the world of Henry Parrish, and that's by the book. There will be no deviations from standard procedure! It's why my mom left him."

"Your parents are divorced?" Lauren had seen the momentary expression of anguish on Henry's face when he'd heard his wife was on flight 880. It certainly wasn't the look of someone who didn't care.

"Separated." Matt nodded sadly as he looked away.

Lauren decided for Matt's sake to change the subject. "Did I hear your father say you'd worked here as an intern?"

Matt rolled his eyes. He pulled open his bulky coat to reveal his Wayfarer issued coveralls. "Part of my father's grand plan to make me like him. He forces me to work on the ramp most summers and holidays, sometimes weekends if they get short staffed. I don't mind hanging out with all the guys and stuff. They're all pretty cool and I learned how to work every piece of equipment out there, but I hate the fact that I'm forced, you know, like slave labor. He even keeps part of the money I earn. Puts it in some sort of bullshit savings account thing I can't touch. It isn't fair."

"I take it you were working today?"

Matt nodded. "When they started canceling flights I was cut. It's why we were here so fast after Glen called. Dad had come to pick me up."

"Do you go to school?" Lauren asked, keeping one eye on her cell phone, silently pleading for Calvin to call with good news.

Matt nodded. "Yeah. I'm a junior. I hate it though. When I graduate from high school, I'm out of here and going to California. I was born there, plus I have some friends who've moved to L.A. They say it's awesome. Then I can, you know, hang out for a while until I figure out what it is I want to do."

In the short time she'd spent with Matt and his father, Lauren was starting to see why there was so much friction. Matt struck her as sensitive and forthright, Henry seemed anything but. The two men were a distinct study in contrasts.

"Where do you live?" Matt asked. "What kind of a doctor are you?"

"I live just outside Washington, D.C., in a suburb called Centreville. She quickly shifted to talk of work. "I have a Ph.D. in Earth Science. I'm a weather analyst for the government. My fiancé—his name is Donovan— is a pilot for a small, private research group called Eco-Watch."

Matt sat up in his seat. "Really? What kind of planes does he fly?"

"They have two Gulfstreams and a helicopter," Lauren replied.

"Very cool. What model Gulfstreams? They're amazing airplanes. There's nothing more boring than riding around on an airliner; they're nothing but a big bus. But flying Gulfstreams, that must be awesome. Do you know which model he flies?"

"They're G-IV SPs. Do you know a lot about planes?" Lauren tried to keep the conversation focused on Matt. Right now she couldn't bear talking about Donovan.

"Yeah, pretty much. I used to be really into it when I was just a kid." Matt lowered his head as his voice trailed off slightly. "But I don't follow it as much anymore."

"Why not?" Lauren said, she wanted Matt to keep talking.

"When I was little I used to live and breathe airplanes. A long time ago, my Dad used to fly a Gulfstream. It was before I was born, but he flew for some billionaire guy out in California. I guess my mom worked there too; it was how they met. Any way, after that guy died, we moved to Chicago and my Dad went to work for the airline."

Lauren's breath caught in her throat. She now had an idea of who the woman on the plane was. Matt's mother was the person from Donovan's past. "Sounds interesting. Do you know which billionaire your parents worked for?"

"Everyone knows about him—his name was Robert Huntington. They have shows about him on television sometimes. I even did a report on him for school. He was like one of the richest guys in the world, sort of a playboy, but kind of messed up too, I guess. His parents died when he was little, and he inherited like a billion dollars. When he grew up he ran Huntington Oil. Toward the end, his girlfriend was kidnapped in Costa Rica and she was killed. She was a famous environmentalist, Meredith Barnes was her name, we study her in school too. Anyway, everyone blamed her death on Robert Huntington. My Dad was there, and he says it didn't happen the way the media says. But everyone was convinced that he had Meredith killed. We'll never know, because not too much later, he crashed his plane and died. I think it was an accident, but some people think it was maybe a suicide, or even a murder. It's kind of sad—all that money and he got royally screwed. But that was a long time ago."

Lauren nodded as if she agreed with Matt's version of Robert Huntington, it seemed to be a topic everyone had an opinion on. But she knew what few people in the world did—that her fiancé, Donovan Nash, was Robert Huntington. She had only found out the truth several months ago. Donovan's confession had come as a complete surprise. She remembered how painful it had been for Donovan to explain himself; even though the pivotal events had taken place nearly two decades earlier.

Lauren flashed back to the events as told to her by Donovan, the real version, to which only five other people in the world were privy.

Donovan and Meredith Barnes had been in Costa Rica. They were not a typical storybook couple. Robert Huntington, the young, rich, playboy industrialist, and the breathtakingly beautiful activist, Meredith Barnes. Meredith had become the global poster-child as a leader in environmental issues. She'd also been a media darling, millions across the globe loved her and her position on the earth as not only our home, but a living, breathing entity as well. A place we desperately needed to take better care of.

Donovan had quietly admitted to Lauren that he'd asked Meredith to marry him and she'd said yes. They'd both agreed to keep their engagement a secret until after they returned from Costa Rica. They didn't want their news to overshadow the environmental issues at hand. Together they'd organized an historic meeting in San Jose, a summit that held the promise of preserving millions of acres of forests in both Central and South America. Late the first evening, Donovan and Meredith had left the security of the conference and were headed to a villa he'd secretly rented. As their car wound through the narrow streets, a truck suddenly blocked their path; gunmen had leaped out and surrounded them. Their driver was shot, and as the doors were flung open, Donovan was slammed in the face with the butt of a rifle. Meredith was dragged from the back seat, and thrown into the other vehicle, which quickly vanished into the night. It was the last time Donovan saw her alive.

The next few weeks turned into a media circus focused on Meredith's kidnapping. The conference dissolved completely as the ransom demands dominated the headlines. Donovan wanted to use his own resources and pay the ransom—anything to get Meredith back. But the government refused to give in to the kidnappers' demands and blocked Donovan's efforts at every turn. In the end, Meredith's naked, lifeless body was found in a muddy field. She was only twenty-eight years old.

What followed was the very public crucifixion of billionaire Robert Huntington. Across the continent, people were outraged that he had allowed their matriarch to be killed. Rumors began circling that he'd had her killed, that he'd done it to protect his lucrative interests in global oil production. The media ran hard with the spectacular stories, and on a global level, Robert Huntington became a pariah. So quick and complete was his guilt in the public eye, the protesters so angry, that practically overnight he went from being a member of the cultural elite, to one of the most hated men in the world. Simply put, Meredith Barnes was a martyr and Robert Huntington had been the instrument of her death.

There had been protests, riots, death threats, and boycotts against Huntington Oil. Donovan had been shunned by both Meredith's friends and family and hadn't been able to attend Meredith's funeral; in fact he'd never dared go to the small town in California that was her final resting place.

He'd tried to fight through the pain and intimidation, but finally he'd made the decision that along with Meredith Barnes, Robert Huntington needed to die. He, and all of his money, would cease to exist. Lauren had been shocked, as Donovan explained how it took him months to arrange all the details. On a dark, moonless night, he'd boarded one of his planes in Reno, Nevada. He was the sole occupant, and as he took off he left his previous life behind. He'd pointed the plane out toward the vast Pacific Ocean. Before the airplane left the mainland, he'd parachuted out and let the empty plane fly far out to sea before it crashed. All of the evidence of the accident sank beneath the waves to the bottom of the ocean.

The media pounced on the story that billionaire Robert Huntington had perished. Rumors flew as to whether the crash was an accident, a murder, or perhaps even a suicide. The public was so eager to celebrate his death, no one ever stopped to seriously consider that he might have survived. Huntington Oil released a brief statement that its beloved owner was indeed dead, and quickly named a successor from the Board of Directors.

He'd fled to Europe. Plastic surgery had altered his appearance and with a flawless set of new documents, as well as a carefully constructed past, Donovan Nash began his new life. He'd liquidated his public assets and disguised his fortune in a maze of trusts and foreign institutions. For years, Donovan traveled between continents. He loved to fly and used his passion and money to do some good in the world in Meredith's memory. He organized and flew relief flights in Asia, South America, and Africa. He employed his vast resources to help rebuild areas decimated by natural disasters. Though the world wasn't looking for a dead man, Donovan was exceptionally cautious never to reveal his previous life to anyone. At some point, Donovan became frustrated upon arriving after a natural disaster had occurred; it always seemed as if more could have been done to warn the victims. From that frustration, Eco-Watch was born. With an unlimited budget, and using the latest technology, Donovan was now helping science predict and warn of impending disasters virtually unhampered by government red tape. It was an idea that fully embodied Donovan and Meredith's shared dream. Until Donovan had reveled his secret, Lauren had only known the story from the media side. She'd been in college when Meredith had been killed; she herself had been caught up in blaming Robert Huntington for her death. To this day, Robert Huntington was linked with the worst of the billionaire robber barons, powerful people who decimated and pillaged the country in the name of their own greed. But she knew that Donovan had done everything possible to save Meredith. In her heart, Lauren also knew Donovan had lost, or given up, so much in his life, that he would always do everything in his power to try and protect those closest to him. It was one of the many reasons she'd fallen in love with him.

Lauren looked at Matt; his young, grief stricken expression begged for comfort. She tried in vain to offer him a smile but couldn't find one. "So, was your mom visiting relatives in Washington?"

Matt slumped ever so slightly in his seat. "No, she went out to interview for a job with some lobbyist or something. It's been really hard for her since my sister died."

Lauren crumbled a little inside as she heard the words. There didn't seem to be a safe haven when it came to Matt. She reached across and put her hand on top of his. "I'm so sorry."

"It's okay," Matt said, bravely. "Megan was four years younger than me and had leukemia. She was sick for a long time."

"Oh Matt. That's terrible." As a mother, Lauren couldn't imagine anything worse than losing a child She could see the wounded expression in Matt's face as he spoke of his sister. "We can talk about something else if you'd like."

"It's all right. It's been almost three years. I'm okay." Matt shrugged, then shook his head as he continued. "My mom will never be the same, though. My Dad wasn't even there when Megan died. He was out flying somewhere. The worst part is—it's obvious that my Dad thinks the good kid died, and all he's left with is me."

Lauren was both shocked and saddened at the harsh revelation of Matt's world—a world with which she was fast becoming intertwined. Matt seemed so angry, yet vulnerable. She knew from experience that at times of great stress, it was often easier to talk to a complete stranger than someone familiar. Though her connection to Matt was a potential minefield, Lauren's heart went out to the young man.

"If my Dad wasn't like he is, maybe my mom wouldn't have been on that flight. Maybe she wouldn't be—" Matt's voice trailed off and he turned his head away as he visibly fought the tears.

Lauren was about to reach out for him again when her cell phone rang. She looked at the caller ID, expecting it to be either Calvin or Michael. Her hands began shaking and the blood drained from her face when she saw the number. Unsteadily she pushed the button and raised the phone to her ear.

"Donovan," she said finally, hardly trusting her voice.

"Lauren! Are you there?"

"Donovan?"

"It's me. Where are you?"

"I'm…I'm at O'Hare, in Wayfarer Operations. Where are you?"

"I took a wild guess that's where you'd be. I'm in the airliner. We've had a little trouble but we're still flying. We need some help. I've been told to ask for Henry Parrish. Do you know if he's there?"

"Yes!" Lauren could hardly contain the sheer joy at hearing Donovan's voice. "Michael had me come to Operations after we lost touch with your flight. I'm with Henry's son Matt right now."

"Tell Matt his mother is fine. She's here with me," Donovan said. "I really need to speak with whoever is in charge down there. This airplane is pretty banged up and we're going to need some help."

"I have to get to the other room. It'll just take me a minute. Hang on!" Lauren put her hand over the phone and looked at a wide-eyed Matt. "It's them! They're still flying. Your mom is fine. But we have to get to your father, now!"

Matt burst from his chair and frantically unlocked the door. He pushed past a startled David Tucker and motioned for Lauren to follow him.

"What the hell?" Tucker exclaimed as Lauren raced past in a dead run.

"It's them!" Matt hollered as he ran interference for Lauren.

"We're going to find Henry." Lauren was so elated to hear Donovan's voice she welcomed the tears of joy that ran freely down her face. "I've been so worried."

"I know. I'm fine. Hopefully I'll see you in a little while."

Lauren could tell from the inflection in Donovan's voice that the situation was anything but fine. She followed Matt through Operations, all eyes trained on them as they rushed past. She had to stop as Matt opened the door to the war room and shoved it open.

"Matt! What are you doing?" Henry's voice bellowed as the young man held it open for Lauren.

"We're talking to them!" Matt shot back at his father.

"What?" Henry stood abruptly. The two other men at the table looked equally puzzled.

"Here's Henry." Lauren placed her phone in Henry's hand.

"Henry Parrish here. Who is this?" Henry ran his hand through his hair. "Hello…hello?"

"Are they there, or did you lose them?" Lauren asked. Henry brought the phone down and checked the connection. Lauren could see they'd lost the signal. "It was them! They're still flying!"

Henry handed Lauren her phone, then yanked a desk phone closer to them. "Use the land-line! Can you dial them back?"

Lauren nodded and quickly punched in the numbers to Donovan's cell phone. In what felt like an eternity the call began to go through. On the second ring, he picked up.

"Donovan," Lauren exclaimed with obvious relief. "Thank God! We lost you for a moment."

"Tell him we're going to put him on speaker." Henry's finger was poised above the phone. He pushed the button and turned up the volume.

"This is Henry Parrish. Can you hear me?"

"I can hear you fine." Donovan's voice was clear, despite the background noise coming through the speaker.

"Who is this?" Henry demanded.

"My name is Donovan Nash. I'm up here in the cockpit giving John a hand. I'm also with Audrey Parrish. She's the one who suggested we ask for you. As you probably already know, we've been in a midair collision. We're going to need some help to get this thing on the ground."

"Where's the copilot?" Henry glanced at the crew names up on the big board. There were five crew listed.

"He's dead. He was killed in the impact," Donovan replied. "I'll be honest, we've suffered a great many casualties. But our bigger problem is that we have no electrical power whatsoever. Everything in the cockpit is dead. The only way we can communicate with anyone on the ground is through cell phones. We've also been flying for a while now, and we have no idea where we are."

Lauren cringed at what Donovan was telling them. She'd spent enough time with pilots and in airplanes to have a fair idea of how critical their situation was.

"Have you tried doing anything to restore your electrical system?" Henry pressed.

"Yes," Donovan replied. "We tried to reset a generator circuit breaker and immediately started a fire. We were lucky to get it out before it spread."

"Hang on a second, Mr. Nash." Henry turned toward where Glen stood. "Call the tower; explain our situation. I want a dedicated phone number for the tower that I can give John and Donovan. Then tell them I'm on my way up. We're going to need their help in finding 880."

"Good idea," Donovan responded. "So far we don't have another phone except this one. We'll look for more, but nearly everything that wasn't bolted down was sucked out when we depressurized."

"Can you tell us what happened?" Henry said.

"We were hit by what looked like a military KC-135. From what I can tell, their wing sliced into us starting right behind the flight deck. It ripped a hole that's perhaps eighteen feet long by six feet wide. The overhead panel and the bulkhead directly behind us in the cockpit are destroyed. We've got exposed wire bundles and smashed equipment junction boxes. We haven't had time to do much of an inventory, but we both agree there must also be damage to the tail. The good news is both engines are working and John says we've got fuel for now, that is unless we've sprung a leak somewhere."

"As soon as you can, we'll need you to take a look at that," Henry said. "If you're losing fuel it could definitely shape some of our options."

"We'll get to that," Donovan said. "But for now, where should we head this thing? We need some decent weather. With all the damage, I'm not sure we're going to get any of these instruments back."

"Well, that's a bit of a problem," Henry replied. "The weather is down almost everywhere. How much fuel do you think you have on board, barring any leaks?"

"I don't really know. We've been down at 10,000 feet for a while. John says with what we had at takeoff, he's guessing we have a little less than two hours until dry tanks. Give or take fifteen minutes."

Henry shook his head in frustration. "The closest good weather is now south of Memphis, or as far west as central Kansas. This is turning into the biggest system any of us has ever seen. I don't think you have the fuel to make it to either place. We're going to have to figure out a solution from this end. There has got to be a way to get some of your instruments back. I think that's what we should focus on right now."

"What's the weather at O'Hare?" Donovan asked.

"Standby." Henry looked down as someone slid both the tower phone number and the latest weather report in front of him. "The weather right now is, wind 290 degrees at 18 knots with gusts to 26 knots. Visibility is a sixteenth of a mile in blowing snow. The runway visual range for 27 right is 400 variable 600 feet."

"That's not good," Donovan said after he passed the weather and the RVR information to John. "How is it to the south? Are those thunderstorms still in our way?"

"Yes, the line is solid and hundreds of miles long. I don't think you'd be able to top the thunderstorms to the south. Plus, without power you don't have any weather radar. If you have structural damage, it would be far too dangerous. Can you give us any idea as to the status of the passengers?"

"After the collision the airplane stayed at high altitude quite a bit longer than we would have liked. We lost a few people during the decompression. Some were killed from flying debris. The rest...well, the rest went without oxygen for a long time. As far as we know, there are only four people who survived."

Lauren's hand shot to her mouth. She looked at the board and saw that there were eighty-one people listed on the manifest. It dawned on her that the bodies reported outside Fort Wayne could well be passengers from 880. Only four out of eighty-one, the fact that Donovan was still alive was nothing short of a miracle.

"Did you copy that information?" Donovan asked.

"Yes, I copy." Henry cleared his throat. "So what you're saying is that the condition of most of the passengers is unknown? You think they might be—" he searched for the words. "Incapacitated by lack of oxygen, perhaps damaged in some way?"

"Yes," Donovan said as a matter-of-fact. "It would seem so at this point. But it's still possible more could be waking up now that we're finally down at a lower altitude."

"I've got a number here for the O'Hare tower." Henry said. "This should ring directly in the cab. I think we need to transfer this operation up there. With their radar, we should be able to pinpoint your position. After that, we'll start working on a way to restore some of your systems."

"I'm ready to copy," Donovan replied then waited as Henry read them off. "Got it. How long until you're there?"

"Give me fifteen minutes." Henry said. "Let's not run down the battery on that cell phone."

"I agree. Fifteen minutes it is," Donovan said, then paused. "Lauren, are you still there?"

"I'm here." Lauren focused on the lone phone sitting on the table. Donovan sounded so close it nearly broke her heart.

"Work with Henry, but don't forget about Michael, and all of our resources in Washington."

"Michael is on his way here," Lauren said. "Calvin is also in the loop."

"Good. I'll talk to you soon," Donovan said and the connection was broken.

Lauren immediately missed him. Her heartache threatened to crush her. Carefully, she looked into the drawn faces of the others around the table.

"What did he mean by resources in Washington?" Henry asked. "Who is Michael?"

Lauren took a measured breath. "As you already know, I work for the Defense Intelligence Agency. I know a great many people in Washington who would be willing to help. Michael is Donovan's business partner and best friend. He's at Midway Airport, hopefully headed this way. There are some very capable people and organizations that we can pull on if we need to."

"We'll keep that in mind." Henry gathered the papers in front of him. "Gentlemen, if you'll excuse me, I need to get to the tower."

"Not so fast," an authoritative voice said loudly.

Lauren had already started for the door, but stopped abruptly.

She turned to see who had spoken, then looked to Henry for an introduction.

"This is Cyrus Richtman," Henry said quickly, not masking his displeasure toward the man. "He's Wayfarer's CEO. The gentleman to his right is Leo Singer, founder and Chairman of Wayfarer Airlines. Gentleman, this is Dr. Lauren McKenna. Her fiancé is Mr. Nash—the man we were just speaking to from 880."

At the mention of Leo Singer, Lauren knew exactly who the elderly man was, though her only visual references were pictures obviously taken years before. The man must now be nearly seventy years old. His diminutive stature was offset by a shock of unruly white hair and intense dark eyes. Lauren easily remembered portions of the articles she'd read about him. Once revered as a maverick with the Midas touch, there were now those who felt he should step down as Chairman of Wayfarer Airlines. His upstart airline had grown so much that his hands-on business style had become ineffective. It was widely rumored he was now more of a figurehead, that he deferred much of the decision making to those around him. Lauren guessed that one of his mouthpieces was Cyrus Richtman.

"What's being done with the people who were waiting for 880?" Cyrus said, ignoring Lauren.

"Nothing yet," Henry said. "All they've been told is that the flight has been delayed."

"We need to get them sequestered somewhere," Cyrus said. "I want total containment on this situation, at which time we can choose the exact moment for any announcements. Half the battle after a crash is decided by how well we manage the press. How many crisis counselors do we have on the premises?"

"Excuse me," Lauren interrupted and glared at Cyrus. "But 880 hasn't crashed."

"Dr. McKenna. I was only speaking in terms of 'what if.' I'm sure you'll agree it's important to keep the big picture in focus." Cyrus seemed to dismiss her as he turned his attention back to Henry. "Now, how many of the crisis team do we have at our disposal?"

"We have some people on site. But Cyrus, technically, the flight isn't down; it's just delayed."

"I'm a realist, Henry. Can you look me in the eye and tell me 880 will be on the ground shortly? It sounds to me like it could just be a matter of minutes before we have a full-blown tragedy on our hands. I want those people separated from the public. The media will no doubt get a hold of this shortly, and I want total containment until we're in control of this situation. Anyone who leaks information will be fired on the spot! Do I make myself clear?"

"Cyrus, I think it's a little early for that," Henry said.

Lauren watched the disagreement in horror, as the seconds ticked off in her head marking the time until Donovan would call the tower. She looked toward Leo for some sort of input, even intervention. But the withdrawn look on the Chairman's face made it clear none was forthcoming.

"Each passenger on that flight represents a potential multi-million dollar lawsuit. It's my job to try to minimize that," Cyrus replied smoothly. "I would have thought you'd be aware of that position."

Lauren wanted to explode. Flight 880 was out there and she was trapped arguing with people who seemed more concerned with the politics of the situation than the reality.

"If you unnecessarily scare the hell out of those waiting, then you've done more harm than good," Henry nearly shouted. "But then again, you do that on a daily basis; why would I expect this to be any different?"

"Gentlemen," Leo finally intervened, he held up his wrinkled hands. "We all have different jobs here. Let's just do them. Henry, you do whatever you can from your end. We'll do what we need to from here. Now, let's get to work, and Henry, we'll expect constant reports."

"Leo, I agree completely." Cyrus glared at Henry, then turned to Leo where the angry expression quickly vanished. "I must admit to having some serious reservations about Henry's participation in this crisis, especially with his wife being on the flight. Wouldn't you agree it's just not prudent?"

"To hell with your reservations," Henry shot back. "I'm the best man to deal with this situation. I know the 737 backwards and forwards. Unless you'd like to speak with the crew yourself, give them some guidance?"

"You're on thin ice, Mr. Parrish." The CEO's words came out as almost a hiss. "Frank Devereux is on his way; when he arrives, you will turn the entire operation over to him. He'll make any decisions along with Leo and myself. Is that understood?"

"Devereux's been Vice President of Flight Operations for almost three years. I'll bet he hasn't flown the line since then," Henry said sharply. "Hell of a lot of good he'll be."

"I was right in calling him." Cyrus turned to Leo, as if to give the aging Chairman the impression he was involved in the discussion. "He said he would be here in less than half an hour."

"We're sorry Audrey is on board," Leo said quietly. "But I think Cyrus has a good point."

"Well said, Leo," Cyrus added. "It reflects how we all feel."

"Look!" Lauren's patience had vanished. "Time is running out! Henry and I are going to the tower."

"Fine," Cyrus replied, still staring at Henry. "But you will take no action that doesn't go through Leo and myself. We'll be here in Operations. Is that clear?"

"Crystal." Henry guided Lauren out past Glen, Tucker, and Matt, closing the door to the war room as he exited.

Lauren hated that the conversation with Cyrus had eaten up valuable time. She had no idea how far they were from the control tower.

"What's going on?" Matt asked excitedly.

"Glen," Henry said, ignoring his son. "Get an ID badge for Lauren. Then I want you to call the tower supervisor, tell them the two of us will be there shortly and if they could smooth the way as far as security is concerned, it would be appreciated."

"What can I do?" David Tucker quickly offered.

"Get on the phone. Find the closest military field with an up-and-running PAR approach. Then find me a systems guy. I want the best 737 engineers you can find. I want a solution to this mess—and I want it now!"

"I'm on it!" Tucker spun and headed for a phone.

"What's a PAR?" Lauren questioned. She knew she could quickly facilitate anything to do with the military.

"Precision Approach Radar," Matt said, jumping into the conversation. "The military uses a totally ground-based approach system. Two radar beams are used to direct the airplane all the way to touchdown. All it takes is a communication link with the airplane. The ground guys do the rest."

"But with all the base closings," Henry added, "I'm not sure where the closest one might be."

Lauren watched Matt's expression turn from humiliation at being ignored, to anger at being so obviously excluded from the process. She wanted to say something, anything, that might assuage Matt's feelings. But under the circumstances, she felt entirely out of place.

"Here." Glen handed Lauren an ID badge affixed to a cord, which Lauren slipped over her head.

"We're out of here," Henry said. "Glen, keep line three open for me in case I need anything more from you. If you need to reach me, call on my cell phone. Oh, and make sure Matt doesn't get into any trouble, okay?"

Lauren wished she could give Matt some encouragement. "I'll be in touch." She said, squeezing his arm as she hurried past.

Henry raced up the stairs to the main concourse level. Lauren was right behind him "We're cutting it pretty close—we're going to have to run."

"Just go!" Lauren said. Outside the window the blizzard was now in full force. Snow poured out of the diffused sky. She could barely see the snow-covered airplanes parked at the gates. The meteorologist in her knew that this storm was intensifying quickly. She wondered if this blizzard was shaping up to be far more than just the normal mid-western snowstorm. At the thought of Donovan up there somewhere, flying aimlessly in a crippled airplane, she ran faster.

CHAPTER NINE

"We're going to give them fifteen minutes and then call back." Donovan felt buoyed by the fact he'd spoken to Lauren. Thankfully, Audrey had returned to the cabin to check on the passengers. It was just he and John on the flight deck.

"I've got the airplane if you want to go—Audrey might need some help finding more phones," John suggested. "Maybe, while you're up, you could take a look around and get an idea of how much damage we have to this thing. I'm really anxious to know if we have any fuel leaks. But I'll need you up here with me when we talk to Henry again."

"My thoughts exactly." Donovan unfastened his seat belt. "If something happens, just rock the wings gently, that can be our signal that you want me."

John nodded that he understood.

As soon as Donovan stepped out of the flight deck, he stopped, staggered by the scene as he looked down the full length of the cabin. He had been in such a rush to get up to the cockpit that the extent of the damage hadn't really registered. Above him, he could see the sky through what was once the roof of the plane. The stiff aluminum ribs and stringers fluttered in the slipstream; wrinkled and torn metal jutted out at odd angles. The roar from the wind buffeted loudly, he could feel the full force of it resonate deep in his chest.

Donovan decided the first item of business was to drag the copilot out of the way. He reached down and grabbed both ankles, pulling the body from the cockpit. The young man's head twisted at an impossible angle as Donovan placed the body on the floor of what used to be first class.

Donovan straightened up and averted his eyes from the corpse. Dark stains were splattered over the gray carpet. Donovan forced himself to move aft, the icy rush of air blasting him as he ducked under the largest part of the rip in the fuselage. He needed to find a coat to stay warm or he would freeze. They all would. He momentarily lost his balance, steadying himself on one of the seats. He stiffened. Did the plane move… had John done something different? Had he rocked the wings? Donovan tensed, ready to turn and bolt back toward the cockpit. He studied the clouds out the small window. They were still flying straight and level. Had he just imagined it? He pulled his hand from the seat and recoiled at the icy blood and gore he found there. Filled with revulsion, he wiped it off as best he could on another section of the fabric chair.

The passengers seated in the first row behind the missing seats were all dead. Flying debris had inflicted massive head and chest wounds. Some were virtually unrecognizable; only their clothes hinted at whether the victim was male or female. Blood had frozen and congealed on the beige headliner and window panels. His stomach lurched as he quickly moved past the carnage.

Donovan moved a few rows, then stopped to examine a passenger near the over-wing exit. He recognized the man who had smiled and nodded at him as they'd taken their seats in Washington, DC. No oxygen mask hung above him.

All around him, people sat quietly in their seats, they looked to be asleep, but their bluish lips and gray faces told a different story. Since it was Friday afternoon, Donovan knew that most were probably headed home for the weekend. Families would be waiting for them to arrive, to walk in for dinner, or a hundred other things taken for granted. To his right a younger couple sat together. He remembered them smiling and laughing. They were probably still in their twenties. Their hands were entwined; her head was tilted over and resting on his shoulder. Sickened by the waste of life, he forced himself to move on. He had to examine as much of the airframe as he could. The dead were beyond his help.

The rip in the top of the 737 began at the cockpit, and ran aft from there. A closer inspection revealed a slight movement of the metal on each side of the gash. The stresses from flight were forcing the two sides to move in opposite directions. Donovan shook his head in near disbelief. It was a miracle the airplane was still intact. As an afterthought, he looked at his hands. A small amount of blood remained. He reached up, fighting the wind rushing along the roof and made a red smudge on the aluminum where the crack ended. He now at least had a reference to where the split stopped. Hopefully, the tear in the metal wouldn't expand.

"Donovan!" Audrey yelled against the noise of the wind.

He turned to see Audrey and another man. Donovan was at first startled, then thankful, that someone else was up and around, maybe the first of many who would wake up. Carefully, Donovan stepped around the bodies of passengers who had collapsed in the aisle.

"Here." Audrey handed him a coat. "You're going to freeze."

Donovan gratefully slipped on the heavy wool garment and was happy to discover that it fit him fairly well. He studied the newest member of their small group of survivors, and guessed the man was in his mid-to-early-forties. He was husky, about six feet tall, with a full beard and longish blonde hair. At first glance he appeared to be a little on the rough side, but upon closer inspection Donovan could see small refinements. He wore an expensive gold watch and shiny cowboy boots peaked out from beneath precision creased slacks.

"This is Keith." Audrey made the hurried introductions. "Keith, Donovan."

"Are you okay?" Donovan nodded at Keith as he quickly buttoned up the heavy coat in an attempt to retain his body heat. He hadn't realized how cold he was. The effect was almost immediate. He felt in the pockets for gloves but found none, only some matches and half a roll of breath mints.

"I'm fine," Keith said. "How bad is all of this?"

Donovan brushed off the question and turned toward Audrey. He hated that he had to have this much contact with her, but hopefully the situation they were in would divert her thoughts from the past "How many more survivors are there?"

"I don't know yet; so far Keith's the only one." Audrey lowered her head and removed some strands of hair that had blown into the corner of her mouth. She pulled up the collar on her coat to ward off the freezing blast of air. "It's too early to tell, but I do think we need to get these people out of the aisle. It's hard to go back and forth to the cockpit."

"Keith?" Donovan pointed to the people who lay on the floor. "Let's see if we can untangle these guys."

"This one first." Keith moved toward a man in a business suit. His face was contorted in a mask of fear. They had to pry his dead hand from the wrist of another passenger. "Let's get him up and put him in that empty seat."

Donovan recognized the corpses; they were the men who had attacked the young flight attendant who had come to help them. They'd ripped her mask away, and had paid for their panic with their lives. He grasped the first one by the collar and pulled him into a sitting position.

"There's a pilot up front, right?" Keith ventured as he kneeled to grasp the dead man's twisted legs.

"Yes," Donovan replied. He was thankful Keith was a big man. "Ready, lift." Both men groaned as they heaved the corpse into a vacant seat. Audrey pulled the victim's hands into his lap, and then strapped him in with the seat belt. "Now him," Donovan said, indicating the next casualty. They wasted no time in clearing the aisle. Donovan's revulsion at handling the bodies diminished as they worked.

"How long before we land?" Keith cupped his hands together and blew into them for warmth.

"I'm not sure." Donovan said, vaguely. "But trust me, we're going to land as soon as we possibly can."

Audrey inspected several of the other passengers. Donovan watched as she felt for pulses and lifted their eyelids. She turned to him and shook her head. He could tell from her hopeless expression that all of these people were dead.

She looked up to where the oxygen masks should've dropped, but for some reason didn't. "They never had a chance."

"We were up at high altitude too long," Donovan said to no one in particular. He knew he wasn't responsible, but the fate of the passengers still weighed on him.

"You saved us all by getting up to the cockpit," Audrey said. "We'd all be dead if it weren't for you."

"What about those people?" Keith tilted his head toward a section where the masks had dropped; rows of people sat motionless with yellow rubber cups still fastened to their faces.

"I only checked a few of them," Audrey said. "Some are alive, but I don't think all of them are. I tried to wake them up—but couldn't. I don't know what to think."

Donovan shook off his feelings of helplessness and decided he should get back up to the flight deck with John as quickly as he could. "We need to organize a search for more cell phones."

"I tried the phones back here," Audrey offered. "John was right; they're worthless."

"We figured as much," Donovan forced himself to tune out the bodies as he decided what to do next. "We'll have to do this the hard way. I think we should start in the back of the plane and work our way forward. That way we'll keep it organized and not have to do this more than once."

"I have a cell phone in my briefcase," Keith said. "Why do you need it?"

"The radios in the cockpit are damaged. They don't work."

"You've got to kidding!" Keith exclaimed. His eyes grew wide. "I'll have to go look for it; I couldn't find my briefcase after I woke up."

"Donovan, are you coming?" Audrey had started aft with Keith.

"I'll be right there." Donovan knelt and used the back of his hand to wipe away the frost that had formed at the edges of the plastic. He carefully studied the right wing, and then moved to several different windows to get a complete view of both the wing and engine. With a single-minded effort, he ignored the bodies and focused his attention outside. He found nothing out of the ordinary, which was a relief. But when he moved across the aisle to the left side, the damage was obvious. The leading edge of the wing, out by the wing tip, was smashed. The outer six feet looked like someone had taken a sledgehammer to it. It was no wonder the airplane flew so poorly. Thankfully, he found no fuel leaks.

Donovan finished his appraisal of the wing and moved aft. He passed another section of the cabin where the masks had dropped. As before, the passengers sat in their seats, eyes closed, perfectly still. The rubber jungle created by the dropped masks swayed and danced in the wind. It gave Donovan the impression of some sort of bizarre hospital room. He spotted the woman he'd helped before he'd gone to the cockpit. She was sitting with her head against the side of the plane, the male passenger who had tried to rip the mask from her was slack-jawed, his face gray and lifeless.

Donovan could almost picture the scene. Those passengers with masks would have had a minimum amount of oxygen at first. But after the canisters depleted, they simply passed out. Audrey was right; some of them were probably still alive, but perhaps in body only. There was every possibility that they'd suffered brain damage. He turned away and tried not to think about the fact that the damage was most likely permanent. With a good idea of the damage to the Boeing, he joined the others at the back of the 737.

"Find one yet?" The wind was less of a factor back here. Donovan had to raise his voice only slightly above the slipstream. It also felt warmer. He guessed that the normal hot air used to heat the cabin wasn't affected by the electrical system. They wouldn't be able to adjust the temperature, but at least there was some heat.

"I'm still looking." Keith was down on all fours, searching.

Audrey leaned in close so Keith couldn't hear her. "How's John? Do you think it's a good idea to leave him up there alone?"

"I think it's okay. He seemed to be pulling himself together." Donovan hated the proximity with Audrey and moved away from her to help Keith look for a phone. "I found it!" Keith held his phone up in the air as he got to his feet. He flipped it open and checked that it still worked. "Sorry. I'm afraid there isn't much battery left. I used it a bunch before we took off from Washington."

"It'll get us started," Donovan said. He looked over Audrey's shoulder, surprised to see a figure moving in the rear of the plane. The small frame was covered with a blue blanket. As he moved closer, Donovan could see that it was a young woman. She turned and looked at them, it was the flight attendant he'd saved earlier. Donovan could still picture the brutal assault she'd suffered at the hands of the crazed passengers.

"She's hurt pretty badly," Audrey offered as she turned to see what he was looking at. "I think maybe her collar bone and shoulder are both broken. She can't move her arm at all."

Donovan was unsettled by the pain-filled expression on the flight attendant's face. She couldn't be a day over twenty-five. She looked up at him; and struggled to focus. The fat lip and the swollen bluish marks on her young face testified to the trauma she'd endured. Donovan moved back to where she sat, Audrey following close behind.

"Christy," Audrey began. "This is Donovan. He's the one who saved you."

"Thanks," Christy mumbled through swollen lips, blinking as tears overflowed and raced down her face, her pretty features nearly hidden by her tousled blonde hair. "I don't remember much of what happened."

Donovan frowned, he wondered if she'd simply blacked out or if she'd suffered a concussion. "What you tried to do after the impact was very brave."

"I'm all that's left of the cabin crew? Maria and Susan are gone? What about John and Jeff, are they still flying the plane?"

"John is fine but Jeff didn't make it." Donovan answered her question truthfully. If it were him, he'd want to know about the people he worked with.

Christy pursed her lips bravely at the news. "I can't believe the passengers attacked me." She winced as she tried to move, then put her head back and surrendered as the pain overwhelmed her. Quietly, she closed her eyes and began to sob.

Donovan's heart went out to her, she was not only injured, but trying to grasp the fact that her coworkers were dead. He hadn't lost anyone aboard the plane that was close to him, but Donovan knew all too well about losing friends and loved ones to tragedy. It was a feeling he wouldn't wish on anyone.

"I'm going back to the cockpit." Donovan saw Audrey nod in understanding. A part of him wanted to stay and help the survivors. But his job right now was on the flight deck with John.

As Donovan made his way through the wrecked cabin, he jammed his hands in his coat pockets and lowered his head against the cold. He bent down to avoid the worst of the air pouring in from the outside, his teeth began to chatter and his shoulders shuddered as he drove against the wind. Another thought occurred to him. Usually there was no way to see the rudder of an airliner from the inside. But if he could look out through the rip in the roof, he might be able to check the condition of the vertical stabilizer. Positioned against what remained of the forward bulkhead, Donovan looked aft. It was so unnatural to be seeing through the top of the plane. From his angle he could only examine part of the tail, though it didn't look right. He quickly decided that a mirror might allow him a better view.

Donovan thought for a second. The closest mirror was in the forward lavatory. He pulled open the door. On the floor of the small compartment lay the body of a passenger. Donovan, surprised, stepped back at the sight of the corpse. The man had been nearly decapitated. It wasn't hard to picture how violently he had met his end. The bulkhead had caved in from above and the sharp aluminum had cut him down. Donovan briefly considered that this man probably saved Audrey's life. If he hadn't have occupied the forward lavatory, she wouldn't have been forced to go aft. This could easily have been her body he was looking at. Donovan turned away and surveyed what was left of the small enclosure. The impact had destroyed virtually everything. He spotted a soda-can size piece of the mirror that he thought might work.

He closed the door reverently, then positioned himself and mentally prepared himself for what he wanted to do. He moved directly into the worst of the wind and held up the mirror. The sleeves of his coat snapped tight in the rush of wind, the fabric fluttered wildly, making it difficult to hold the mirror steady. It took him several seconds of adjustments to find the correct angle. He blinked as he tried to orient himself to the reverse image, his tears instantly froze onto his skin and he found it difficult to draw a full breath. Despite the dangerous cold, he processed the reflection, at first not believing what he'd found, but he quickly realized the mirror wasn't playing tricks. The damage to the vertical stabilizer was no illusion. Part of the fin had been sheared off.

Donovan ducked out of the slipstream and immediately cupped his hands to his mouth and exhaled warm air onto his frozen fingers. He finally caught his breath, flexed his hands several times and then gently peeled away the ice from the corners of his eyes. He fought off the lingering effects of the cold and collected himself. Once he felt as if his joints worked, he moved under the sharp metal and headed forward. The good news was that he hadn't seen any fuel leaks. The bad news was that the damage to the Boeing was so severe, that this airplane could rip itself apart with little or no advance warning.

CHAPTER
TEN

Lauren followed Henry as they ran up the last few steps to the tower cab. She'd managed to catch her breath in the elevator as they rose seventeen floors above the terminal.

Lauren checked her watch. They had a few minutes to spare before Donovan was scheduled to call them back. They burst into the cab and all eyes turned toward them as they moved into the small compartment. Lauren took in the scene around her. Instead of a panoramic view of the surrounding area, the world outside the windows was an opaque, gray nothingness as snow beat mercilessly against the thick glass. She'd expected the place to be teeming with activity; instead, it was eerily quiet. The few people who manned their stations looked up expectantly at her and Henry. There was no conversation.

"I'm Henry Parrish, this is Dr. Lauren McKenna. Has 880 called yet?"

"No. Not yet. I'm Wayne Koski, tower supervisor."

Lauren shook Wayne's hand. He was a short man with a slight build. He sported a sparse beard and wire-frame glasses that made his brown eyes appear too large for his narrow face. Lauren quickly took in the scene around her. She'd never been in a control tower before and some of what she saw was a mystery, but she easily recognized the radar screens and radio equipment. Other instruments and screens were stationed in clusters at what she guessed were different duty positions. Lauren understood that there was probably a highly organized system at work here, but at the moment it made no sense to her at all. With an emergency in progress she fully expected more commotion, but the only sound was that of the wind and snow howling against the broad expanse of glass that surrounded them on all sides.

"We do think we have them on radar." Wayne moved over to where a woman wearing a small headset was intently watching the never-ending sweep of her scope.

"This is Kate." Wayne gestured to a pear-shaped woman with curly brown hair. Kate glanced up and nodded at the visitors. She wore a serious expression that seemed incongruous with her cherubic features—a face more cute than beautiful. "She's been tracking a primary target since we got your call. It's the only plane out there. Everyone else has finally departed the holding patterns and diverted to their alternates. We're usually in the middle of our Friday, late-afternoon push about now, but due to the storm everything has ground to a halt. We haven't talked to an airplane in the last twenty minutes. The visibility is so low right now no one can land or take off."

"How do you know it's flight 880?" Lauren leaned over and tried to find the tiny blip on the green backlit screen.

"I don't, for sure," Kate explained. "But it doesn't have a working transponder; otherwise I'd be getting a data block from the airplane. I'd be able to read its speed and altitude. This is just a raw return, the radar energy bouncing off the metal of the plane. If it's not them, then someone else is out trying to fly in this mess, and I highly doubt that."

Lauren finally saw the target Kate was watching. It seemed so small and insignificant. Henry's cell phone sounded and he moved away to take the call. Lauren tried to orient herself but couldn't. "Which way is North? In fact, how can you guide the airplanes if you can't see out the windows?"

"It's pretty easy, actually. North is this way," Koski said, pointing. "We have the new digital radar system for airplanes on the ground. It's over there. That's Andy, he's in charge of all the snow removal efforts. He's in contact with the dozens of vehicles on the field right now. Once the airplanes start to move again, we track each one using the same radar. We just see them electronically instead of looking out the window."

Lauren could just barely hear Andy as he spoke quietly into his headset.

He paced back and forth softly as he stared at the surface radar. He turned at the sound of his name and nodded. Lauren saw tired, red eyes framed by a thin face. His longish hair was the same color as his goatee. She immediately got the impression he'd been at work for hours. Despite her rising anxiety, Lauren took a small measure of comfort that the blip of his airplane was still visible, and also from the quiet professionalism displayed by the people in the tower. "Excuse me," Lauren said, as her cell phone rang. She backed farther away when she realized the call was from Calvin.

"Lauren, we found them," Calvin's soothing voice said. "They're still flying."

"I know. I'm in the tower cab at O'Hare. Donovan called a few minutes ago. It's what we thought; their airplane was hit by the KC-135 we saw on television. About all we know right now is that they don't have any electrical power on the airplane."

"Thank God he's alive," Calvin replied. "I'm not surprised to hear they're without power. We have some high-resolution photos of the plane and the damage is significant. Do you know what they're doing to get him down?"

"Donovan is supposed to call us back any second," Lauren said excitedly. "All the wheels seem to be in motion at this end."

"You said you're in the tower cab at O'Hare?" Calvin said. "We're going to send you the photos we have." Calvin paused as he gave someone the order to transmit the images. "We're sending them now, addressed to you. You'll have to use your encryption password to access the pictures. But it might help in judging what you have to work with."

Lauren knew Calvin could instantly pull up the e-mail link of any government installation in the world.

"I also spoke with someone at the National Transportation Safety Board," Calvin continued. "He's highly placed, and he gave me an off-the-record update on exactly what they think happened. There was some maintenance being done at the air traffic control facility in Indianapolis. A worker fell on the main power feeds leading into the building and was electrocuted. When they shut off the main power, none of the back-ups came on and the building went dark. No one could talk to any of the airplanes they were working at the time. When the power was finally restored, they were two airplanes short."

"I'll pass that along," Lauren replied, angry that such things could happen in this day and age of high technology.

"Good. I've also been talking to Michael. The roads are virtually impassable right now due to all the snow. We're still trying to find a way to get him to O'Hare. We reached the Army and are trying to get a Hummer or something to get him there. I'll keep you posted as we know more."

"Thank you." Lauren wished Michael were here already. She could use his soothing presence to help her deal with what amounted to a gathering of strangers.

"Is there anything else I can do?" Calvin said in a softer voice.

"I don't think so right now. You've been wonderful. Thank you, for everything." Lauren saw Henry get off the phone and turn to say something to her. "I have to go now. We'll talk later."

"Who were you talking to?" Henry said.

"The DIA," Lauren replied, then she addressed Wayne. "I have an e-mail we need to retrieve."

"An e-mail?" Henry asked.

"It should have been sent here addressed to me." Lauren followed Wayne as he stepped up to a terminal. With Henry standing behind her, Lauren waited impatiently as Wayne located the message. She ignored their quizzical looks as she typed in her code and quickly downloaded the first of two images. Moments later the first picture materialized on the screen.

"Oh my God!" Henry slid in closer to get a better look.

Lauren focused on the high-resolution satellite image. The somewhat grainy image of an airliner filled the frame. It took her a little longer than Henry to grasp what was wrong with the airplane. Starting just above the cockpit a giant gash was visible in the aluminum skin. Lauren put her hand over her mouth as she saw how the fuselage had been ripped open and peeled back.

"Is there another one?" Henry asked.

"Yes." With shaking hands, Lauren clicked the mouse to open the next file. It appeared on the screen and was a much tighter shot. Though it lost some detail due to the enlargement, Lauren could make out individual shards of metal that bracketed the wide opening. It seemed unreal that she was looking at an airplane that Donovan was aboard.

"Unbelievable." Henry stepped away from the monitor.

"What part?" Lauren asked. She wanted some concrete assessment from Henry about what they'd just seen. "That we were able to get these shots, or the damage to the plane?"

"Both." He looked up at the clock, then leaned over and searched for the solitary blip on the radar screen.

"Who were you on the phone with?" Lauren asked Henry. "Do we know anything else?"

"I was talking with Tucker." Henry looked up from the radar screen. "He made some calls. The military option is out. The only base we think 880 could reach is up near Duluth. The PAR system is down for maintenance and the required personnel are off duty. Though he did tell me he spoke with the local phone company. An engineer there explained that as long as 880's no more than 20 miles from an antenna the cellular link should work. But he warned that the direction the airplane was traveling and the altitude could have a bearing as to how long the connection holds. Something about the switching logic."

"That makes sense." Lauren nodded as she processed the physics involved.

"Also," Henry said, then paused as he thought. "Tucker, and one of our 737 instructors have unearthed a few theories about how to restore power to 880's instruments. Once we talk to John we'll have a better idea of how to proceed."

The shrill sound of the phone caused Lauren to jump.

"O'Hare Tower," Koski spoke excitedly as he swept the instrument to his ear. He listened for a second then gave everyone a thumbs-up to indicate it was indeed flight 880. "I'm putting you on speaker." Koski punched a button. "880, you still there?"

"We're here." Donovan's voice poured through the speaker. "Though I'm not sure where here is. Do you by chance have us on radar?"

"Turn thirty degrees to the right," Kate said from the radar position, then she waited as she stared intently at the scope.

An avalanche of emotion threatened to choke Lauren as she heard Donovan's voice. She desperately wanted to talk with him privately—but couldn't.

"Wayfarer 880, radar contact," Kate said calmly. "Your position is forty-five miles southeast of O'Hare. Turn to a 330 degree heading and say your altitude."

"We're level at 10,000 feet," Donovan reported. "Is Henry Parrish there?"

"I'm here," Henry said, stepping nearer the phone. "Can I talk to John?"

"Stand by." Donovan's voice could be heard in the background as he and John exchanged duties.

"Hey, Henry," John said finally. "What do you have in mind for us?"

"The early consensus is to try again to restore the power to your primary instruments. But we're going to have to be careful to eliminate the possibility of fire. Everyone down here is brainstorming on the best way to make that happen. Is there anything else you can tell me about the damage to the cockpit? We've seen some pictures of the outside of your plane."

"How did you do that?" John said.

"Seems we have some pull with the military, we looked at some impressive satellite photos," Henry replied. "What does the inside look like?"

"As you no doubt saw, the point of impact was from above, directly behind the pilot seats. The wing of the other plane made a complete wreck out of not only the overhead section, but the junction boxes as well. Both sides are equally messed up."

"So all you have right now are the standby altimeter, airspeed, and the wet compass?" Henry said.

"You got it. Nothing else. Is there any place else we can fly this thing and land? Hell, I'd take a stretch of interstate highway at this point."

"We're still working on that." Henry rubbed his face in frustration. "We're trying to make sure we don't miss a single detail. I should have that weather information for you shortly."

"I understand." John's dejected voice registered with everyone in the cab.

"John, hang in there buddy. We know where you are and what we have to work with. Did you get a chance to check for fuel leaks?"

"Yeah, Donovan went back and took a look. He didn't see anything venting."

"That's great news, it buys us some time. I want you to give me twenty minutes to sort out some things. If this works the way I envision it, you'll be on the ground inside the hour."

"I'm going to hold you to that," John replied.

"Before you go, 880," Kate said, "I need you to turn to a 310 heading. There's a lot of wind up there and I want to keep you in my airspace."

"We copy," John said. "And Henry, twenty minutes."

Lauren had so wanted to say something to Donovan but she'd lost her chance when John had taken over on the phone. Now that they were gone, she felt the familiar tug at her heart—wondering if she'd heard Donovan's voice for perhaps the last time. Her eyes shot to the engagement ring on her left hand as she wrestled with her emotions. Her thoughts took her to Florida and the wedding that was scheduled for the following weekend. In a moment of fragility she pictured herself standing alone at the altar— Donovan ominously missing from the image. She fended off the morose image and turned toward Henry. "Now what?"

"I have an idea." Henry reached for his phone.

"Me too," Lauren said. "I'm your best chance at finding that stretch of interstate they spoke of."

"Do it." Henry nodded and dialed his phone.

"Give me some idea of how far they could go," Lauren said, as she thought of the parameters she was going to need to set up the search.

"Two hundred miles, three hundred if we really stretched it," Henry said.

"Is there a land line I can use?" Lauren turned toward Koski. "My cell phone battery is getting a little low."

Lauren once again dialed the direct line to the DIA command center. Calvin answered before the second ring.

"Calvin," Lauren said, "we've talked to them again and studied the damage to the airplane. The first thing we need to do is to try to find them some good weather where they can land. I'm told they could go 200, maybe 300, miles from here with the fuel they have. The captain said it doesn't even have to be an airport; he'd settle for a stretch of road if he could see the ground."

"We've been looking into that since you called," Calvin said. "This could take some doing; as you've no doubt guessed, the storm is really intensifying. We've re-tasked a satellite to focus on your area. Give us a second to make some adjustments. In the interest of time, we'll scale down the search from the usual 1,800 mile swath down to 600."

"That works," Lauren pictured the activity in DIA Operations. The Defense Meteorological Satellite Program, or DMSP, had been the backbone of military weather forecasting for the last twenty years. High above, in a polar orbit, some 450 miles above Earth, the nearly two-ton satellite was always peering down on the planet's surface.

"Lauren," Calvin said. "We're getting the analysis now. It'll take a few more seconds and we should have something for you."

Lauren listened as a vicious blast of wind rattled the tower windows behind her. Through the phone she could hear the murmur of voices and what sounded like papers being shuffled.

"Lauren, I have the data," Calvin said. "I'm afraid the news isn't good."

CHAPTER ELEVEN

"Henry Parrish is about as good as they come. I, for one, am glad he's the guy working on this," John said as he gestured at the destroyed cockpit. "I have faith he and the airline will find some way to get around all this. Henry's not the most emotional guy you'll ever meet, but I'd want him in my lifeboat every time."

Donovan nodded absently at the accurate description of his old friend. Henry was a serious man, one of the most talented and meticulous pilots Donovan had ever known. His attention to detail was a textbook study in the art of being prepared for every eventuality. It had taken Henry a long time to loosen up from when Donovan had first hired him. But once Donovan had demonstrated that he himself was indeed a serious pilot, and that he could fly equally as well as Henry, they'd gotten along famously. In the years they flew together, Donovan discovered that Henry was a private, yet highly emotional man. Henry's natural state was to put up a wall against the outside world. So, it came as no surprise that John had described Henry as someone who came across as being somewhat distant.

"What do you think our options are if we can't get the power back?" Donovan asked; he wanted to keep John talking as much as possible. Every now and then John seemed to drift off, and Donovan didn't know if it was the result of his injuries or if he was simply thinking about the situation.

"I don't know what we'll do." John glanced anxiously at his watch. "I do know that twenty minutes is going to feel like an eternity."

"I was just thinking the same thing. What are we missing?" Donovan inventoried the decimated cockpit. "Is there something else we should be doing?"

"I'm hesitant to start pushing in circuit breakers again. I'd rather not torch this airplane with us inside. Let's wait a few minutes and see what Henry has for us before we get desperate."

Donovan shook off the image of being burned alive in the wrecked cockpit. "If you have the airplane, maybe I'll go back and check on things. It would be great to have at least one more phone. Unless you want to go?"

"No. You go. I'll stay here," John replied.

"Can I get you anything, maybe something for the pain?"

"I'm fine. You might take a quick look around back there. See if anything has changed. I don't know if it's my imagination or not, but I'm starting to feel a little different vibration in the ailerons. It might be nothing. This thing seems to have a different feel at every speed."

"I'll look everything over again and be back as soon as I can."

Free of the cockpit, Donovan stopped in the forward galley. Alone in the purgatory between the decimated cockpit and the rows of dead people, he surveyed the huge hole in the roof. He couldn't see the tail without the mirror, but he knew if the vertical fin failed, it would all be over in a matter of seconds. If John was feeling something different in the controls, it would most likely be something with the wings. Donovan stopped and leaned up against the side of the plane and pulled his phone out of his pocket. With freezing hands he carefully typed a short, concise, text message to Lauren. He hoped when she received it, no one else would be close enough to read what he'd written. Just as he finished, he looked up to see Audrey coming toward him, a concerned expression on her face. He hit the send button and stuffed the phone into his pocket.

"Donovan? Is everything all right?" Audrey called out above the roar of the wind.

Donovan nodded. "I spoke to your husband again. He's working on a solution."

"I'm sure he is," Audrey said, nodding. "Did he say anything about Matt?"

"I'm sorry." Donovan shook his head. "There wasn't really time. John and Henry did most of the talking."

Audrey forced a smile as she lowered her head.

Donovan searched for the right words, but found none. He didn't know what to tell her, or any of the other people aboard this plane. "If I get a chance, I'll ask him next time we talk."

"Thank you. It's just hitting me all the sudden. Sitting back here waiting is awful. Henry knows this airplane as well as anyone. He once told me he thought he could assemble a 737 from a pile of unmarked parts."

"I'm sure they'll come up with something." Donovan tried to sound reassuring but knew he'd failed. "Did you find any other phones?"

"So much of the luggage in the overhead compartments was sucked out." Audrey pulled up the collar on her coat. "We found six phones, some had dead batteries and a few were smashed. Keith is taking them apart; he's hoping he might be able to swap parts and repair at least one."

Above the noise in the cabin, Donovan heard what sounded like a scream and whirled around. A figure in the aisle moved with an unsteady gait toward the rear of the plane. Christy screamed again, putting her good arm over her face as if to protect herself from the approaching passenger.

Donovan raced down the aisle and grabbed the man by the shoulders. With more force than he'd intended, he spun the man until they were facing.

"Let me go!" came the panicked shriek of the man Donovan had seized. "What are you doing?"

"Relax. I'm not hurting you." Donovan eased his grip and studied the man's face, trying to assess his condition. He had no idea if the man posed a threat or not, no idea if any of the oxygen-deprived people might be dangerous.

The man yelled again, "What's going on? What happened to us?"

Donovan moved slightly to allow Keith to join him. "Calm down," Donovan said, attempting to reassure the frightened man. "How many fingers am I holding up?"

"Four," he responded correctly. "Who are you?"

"He's one of the pilots," Keith replied.

"What's your name?" Donovan asked, his tone firm and controlled. The confused man turned his head to look at the others and Donovan winced at the sight of him. The left side of his face and scalp looked as though it had been sanded away. Though not a deep wound, it had to be painful.

It took a moment for the man to reply. He seemed transfixed by the interior of the wrecked plane; a look of disbelief further contorted his bloody face. "I remember a noise. The plane lurched." His expression clouded as he tried to remember. "Then I woke up." His English was slightly accented. "What's happened to us?"

"It's a long story." Donovan guided the man toward the rear of the plane. "We were hit by another plane. We need to get you looked at."

Donovan could still see the alarm in Christy's eyes, though she seemed to have settled down once Donovan and Keith had the situation under control. Donovan turned to the man. "Sit here. Keith, find him a coat to wear."

Keith returned, reached in, and wrapped a heavy coat over the injured man.

"My name is Rafael," he said finally, his hands went to his face; he winced at the pain as his fingers gingerly explored his wound.

Keith knelt down with the medical kit and some damp paper towels from the lavatory. "I'm not sure where to start." Keith hesitated as he studied the injury.

Rafael pulled away and stopped Keith from touching him. "Do you have a mirror?" Rafael asked. "I'm a medical student. I need to see."

"I saw one earlier," Keith said, raising himself up. "Be right back."

Keith returned with a small mirror he'd found in a passenger's purse. He handed it to Rafael who in turn examined his own injuries.

"It's just superficial," Rafael announced finally, then looked down at the medical kit. "Are there any other injured people?"

"Christy, the flight attendant is banged up pretty bad," Keith answered. "But besides her I think it's mainly just a few scrapes and bruises."

"Donovan!" Audrey called from where she sat with Christy. She pointed at something across the aisle. Donovan stood—someone else was awake. Donovan took several steps closer and spotted a man in a suit and tie seated in a center seat. He looked to be in his late fifties, his bald head and weathered features were marred with dried blood. He'd pulled off his mask and was jostling the arm of the woman seated next to him. She still wore a mask but her eyes were closed.

As Donovan moved in, the man spun in his seat and leveled a look of desperation at him.

"I need—" the man stammered. "Someone do something! Help us!"

"Try to calm down and relax. We'll help you," Donovan said soothingly.

"Get us out of here." He spoke to the woman seated beside him. "Mary, wake up!"

"We have a doctor on board. Let him look at her." Donovan lied, but he wanted to get the man out of the way so Rafael could see if his companion was among the living.

"Wake up!" The man was growing more agitated. He raised his voice to the inert woman as he ignored Donovan. "Mary, wake up!"

Donovan reached in and gripped the man by the upper arm, trying to ease him up from his seat.

"Leave me alone!" The man jerked his arm upward at Donovan, then tried to twist free but was held firm by his seat belt, which he savagely released. He then began to shake the woman. "We have to get out! Now!"

Donovan's patience evaporated. He knew how dangerous it was to shake an injured person. He once again gripped the near-hysterical man, but this time he did so with far more force. With one swift tug, he dragged the agitated man from his seat and propelled him into an empty seat a row behind. Rafael quickly went to the aid of the woman.

"Sit there and don't move," Donovan said with authority. He examined the gash on the man's head and nose and decided the wounds weren't dangerous; in fact, most of the bleeding had already stopped. No doubt it was an injury from flying debris. "Tell me if you're hurt."

"Go to hell!" the man sputtered. "You have no right to accost me!"

"I need you to settle down," Donovan said calmly, as he switched tactics. He didn't want this to escalate into a shouting match. He shot Rafael a quick glance, hoping to get a clue as to the woman's condition. Rafael shook his head almost imperceptibly.

"Sir. My name is Donovan. Can you tell me your name?"

"What difference does it make?" The man began flailing in his seat, fighting against Donovan's iron grip. "Get us out of here. We've been in a plane crash!"

"We haven't crashed," Donovan said. "We're still flying."

At the words, the man blinked his eyes as if trying to awake from a bad dream. He turned and gazed out the small window.

"Sir," Rafael said. "Your wife is alive, but not responsive."

"What?" He stared forward. "She's not my wife. She's my secretary. You're a doctor. Do something!"

"I've done all that I can." Rafael said.

"I don't understand." He looked around at other people sitting quietly in their seats with their eyes closed. "What happened?"

"Tell me your name first," Donovan urged, finally feeling like he was making some progress.

"I'm Norman Wetzler," he said. "Mary is my secretary."

"We've been hit by another airplane," Donovan began, hoping to make Wetzler understand that he was lucky to be alive. "There are only a few of us conscious. Can you tell us if you're injured?"

"No! I'm fine." Wetzler touched the top of his head and his hand came back dry. "How could we be hit by another plane? How could this happen?" He looked around, still unable to make sense of his surroundings. He shuddered against the cold and wrapped his arms around his chest in an effort to try and warm himself.

"We'll find you a coat in a minute. Where are you from?" Donovan asked, noting Wetzler's deep tan.

"I live in Mexico City." Wetzler said. "Why?"

"Keith," Donovan said. "Where do you live?"

"Aspen, Colorado."

"Rafael?"

"La Paz, Bolivia."

"I think the three of you are alive because you live in high-altitude cities." Donovan continued with his theory. "Your bodies have more red blood cells than those of us who live at sea level. It's what saved you."

"Yes, of course." Rafael nodded in agreement. "It makes perfect sense. But how did you and the others survive?"

"We managed to make it to the portable oxygen bottles. We had enough supplemental oxygen to breathe until we made it down to a lower altitude."

"You let the others die?" Wetzler sneered as he looked up at Donovan.

"Shut up!" Keith snapped. "This man has been doing everything he can to help us survive, and you'll treat him with respect, or you'll have to deal with me."

Wetzler started to get up out of his seat but Donovan's firm hand forced him back down quickly. "Sit down!"

"Don't you threaten me," Wetzler seethed. "When I get finished suing this airline into oblivion, I'll start on you, for assault and intent to inflict bodily injury!"

"I'd suggest you shut up," Donovan said, then paused for effect. "As one of the pilots in charge, I have the authority to come back here and personally handcuff you to a chair. So don't press your luck."

"And I'll be right here to back him up," Keith said, making a fist for emphasis, and his eyes left no doubt he'd follow through if need be.

Wetzler's face contorted as he fought his growing rage.

"Now that we've reached an understanding," Donovan continued, "Do you, or Mary, happen to have a cell phone? The airplane radios aren't working and we need cell phones to communicate with the ground."

"I don't have one. I don't know about Mary."

"Audrey is in charge back here and I'll expect you to follow each and every order she gives." Donovan and Wetzler made eye contact. "Do we understand each other?"

"Yeah," Wetzler said with as much displeasure as he dared. "We understand each other."

"Perfect." Donovan turned to Keith. "We might need an extra pair of hands up front. I'm going to want you with me when I go back to the cockpit." Donovan felt a small measure of relief that he had just hit upon the perfect way to keep Audrey out of the cockpit. If Keith stayed up front, Audrey would need to be in the back with the survivors. "Rafael, if you can, take a look at Christy. Audrey thinks she might have broken something. Also, maybe you can figure out who is alive and who isn't back here. If you could wrap the survivors in a blanket, or find some way to identify them, it'll make it easier for the emergency medical people to know who's who once we're on the ground. Audrey, how many phones do we have that work?"

"Two." Audrey reached into her pocket and handed them to Donovan. "The batteries are pretty low on both."

"Thank you." Donovan took the phones. "Rafael, if you have any problems with our Mr. Wetzler, come get us."

"Yes, sir."

"You ready?" Donovan turned to Keith.

"What is it you think I can do?" Keith asked with a measure of skepticism.

"I'll explain it to you once we get up front." Donovan led Keith to the cockpit. Halfway to the front of the plane, Donovan stopped, then leaned over a row of seats to take a closer look at the left engine. A thick dark fluid seeped back in the slipstream. The liquid danced and vibrated as it worked its way free from a seam in the aluminum.

"What is it?" Keith asked. He maneuvered next to Donovan, looking out the window.

"It's oil," Donovan replied once he'd studied the color and viscosity of the liquid. "We're leaking oil."

Keith pursed his lips and his eyes turned serious, though there was no sign of panic. "Will it run without oil? We can still fly on one engine, right?"

"It can run a long time without oil," Donovan said, twisting the truth a little. "And yes, we can fly with just one engine."

"I thought so," Keith said and nodded knowingly. "Jet engines are different than piston engines in that regard."

"It'll either run or it won't." Donovan quickly looked at both wings. There was no visible difference than from before. He once again led the way up to the front of the plane. The cockpit was just ahead. "Be careful, some of these edges are really sharp."

"Wait. Hang on for a second," Keith called out in a strangled voice.

Donovan stopped. Keith had bent over, hands on his knees. "What's wrong?" He could see the big man fighting for gulps of air.

"Just a little lightheaded or something. Give me a second, I'll be all right."

Donovan put his hand on the man's back. "Deep breaths. In and out. Do you think you're going to be sick?"

Keith gurgled a reply. Then, before Donovan could stop him, Keith rose up and opened the door to the forward lavatory. The grisly sight of the dead passenger instantly pushed Keith over the edge. Donovan did his best to support the man while he emptied his stomach. Donovan felt his throat constrict at the pungent smell of vomit. It took a moment for Keith to try to regain his composure. Donovan closed the lavatory door and thought about the effects of stress, how it was affecting everyone aboard. Christy was not only hurt, but traumatized by being attacked. Wetzler was angry and combative. Keith was having what amounted to a major physical response. Ongoing stress could manifest itself in many ways. He wondered what it was doing to John, Audrey and even himself.

"I'm okay now," Keith gasped, as he brought himself back up to his full height. He ran his hand across his mouth. "That caught me by surprise. I'm sorry."

"Don't worry about it. Are you better?" Donovan studied Keith's watery eyes and drawn face. "You feel well enough to start this, or do you need a little more time?"

"I'm ready. Anything to get us on the ground and out of this thing."

"I like your attitude." Donovan was relieved to see a flicker of resolve in Keith's expression. "Follow me." They both ducked down out of the icy blast of air and carefully negotiated the narrow pathway.

"I've never been in the cockpit of a commercial jet before."

"You still haven't. There isn't much of one left on this plane." Donovan slid into his seat and motioned for Keith to come forward. "John, this is Keith. I thought maybe we could use some help up here."

"Come on up." John turned slightly in his seat. "Thanks for giving us a hand."

Keith squeezed into the area just behind the two pilots, careful not to bump anything. "No problem." He stiffened as he saw the lifeless instrument panel. He slowly let his eyes play over the twisted overhead panel; the severed wire bundles dangled near his head. "Holy shit!" He looked directly at Donovan. "I can't believe it! How are you going to make any of this work?"

"We only need a little bit of it to work," Donovan explained. "We've talked to some people on the ground and they're working on a way to get some of this back online."

"I'm a building contractor. I know a little bit about electrical systems—at least the ones in homes. Are there any gloves?" Keith asked. "I'd like to wearing something nonconductive if I'm going to be touching anything that might have current running through it."

"Behind my seat should be a pair. They're insulated," John said. "See if you can pull out the jump-seat. It'll give you a place to sit."

"Okay. I found the gloves. They'll work fine." Keith slid the jump seat out and sat down.

"How is it back there?" John asked as Keith was trying to find his seat belt.

"Not good," Donovan began. "Besides Keith and Audrey, we have Rafael, a medical student, a Mr. Wetzler, who wants to sue the airline, and one of the flight attendants, Christy, who's hurt and maybe in shock. Everyone else is either missing, dead or unconscious. I asked Rafael to try to somehow identify the people who are alive, so the emergency people will know whom to evacuate first. He also said he'd take a closer look at them when he had a chance. We also have another small problem—we're leaking oil out of the left engine."

"There are only seven people awake?" John's shoulders visibly sunk at the news.

Donovan knew a captain felt responsible for each and every passenger who'd boarded his airplane. From the devastated expression on John's face, he knew the news was taking a heavy toll. Donovan glanced at his watch. They still had a few minutes before they were supposed to call the tower. As he scanned the carpet of clouds that stretched as far as he could see, it occurred to him that his wristwatch was by far the most sophisticated instrument on the flight deck.

CHAPTER
TWELVE

Lauren gently replaced the receiver and stared out the window. Even before Calvin's assessment she'd felt that the weather was going to get worse before it got better. But the briefing she'd just received from DIA Operations had staggered even her expectations. She looked around for Henry. She needed to bring him up to date, but he was still on the phone. Her cell phone beeped in her hand and she looked down to see she had a text message. She quickly ran through the menu to display the text. Her heart soared when she saw it was from Donovan. She held the phone close as she read his words.

Henry from the past
be careful. Love D

"More news?" Kate asked as she looked up from her position at the radar scope.

Lauren shook her head and erased the message.

"I'm not sure I heard what position you have with the airline," Kate probed as she tried to read Lauren's temporary security badge.

"I'm not with the airline actually," Lauren said. "My fiancé is one of the people on 880."

"I'm sorry," Kate said solemnly. "You seem to be holding up pretty well. I promise we'll do everything we can to help them."

Lauren suddenly wished there wasn't this time to stop and think. If she stood around much longer she knew she wouldn't be doing nearly so well. She both wanted and needed to stay in motion.

"Do you have the number for Wayfarer Operations?" Lauren asked.

"Yeah, sure." Kate stepped to the phone and looked at a laminated sheet. "Want me to dial?"

"Yes, please." Lauren moved closer and jotted her cell phone number down on a sheet of paper. She lowered her voice as she handed it to Kate. "In fact, I'd like you to ask for a David Tucker. I want him to give this number to Matt Parrish. Have Matt call me as soon as possible."

"Sure," Kate replied.

Lauren once again wished Michael were here. Whatever Henry and Wayfarer were planning, she knew she'd feel better if Michael were somehow involved. A gust of wind rattled one of the windows as a reminder of how terrible the conditions were outside. She wondered if Michael was stranded and if he'd even be able to make it to O'Hare.

"Done." Kate hung up the phone and handed the paper back to Lauren. "I also gave him the direct line to the tower; I jotted it down for you, too. If you need anything later, please call me. I'm the only Kate in the tower."

"Thank you so much." Lauren tried to smile but instead felt hot tears try and push themselves to the surface.

"We're all family here," Kate said and reached out and put her hand on Lauren's. "This whole airport is one big family. We'll do whatever it takes to get them down safely."

Lauren jumped as her cell phone rang. All eyes turned as Lauren answered.

"Hey, it's Matt. You called me?"

"Yes." Lauren shook her head at the others as if to say it wasn't Donovan or Calvin. "Okay, sorry. I'm back with you. Hey, I wanted to share a few things and then ask you for a favor."

"Okay," he replied tentatively.

"First of all, I want to tell you your mother is fine. Your father is working on a way to get them down. So hang in there, okay?"

"If you say so," Matt replied weakly.

"What I need to ask is, I'm waiting for a friend of mine to show up. His name is Michael Ross. He's trying to get from Midway to O'Hare, but the roads are terrible. If he shows up, can I trust you to get him from Operations to wherever I am?"

"No problem," Matt said swiftly. "But I doubt if he's coming anytime soon. I've been watching the weather. It's just getting worse out there."

"I know. But he's a pretty resourceful guy. All I ask is for you to keep an eye out for him."

"Can I do anything else?"

"That's it for now. Where are you? What have you been doing?"

"I'm in my Dad's office. I opened up some of the intercom lines, it's something I do sometimes, you know, when I'm bored. I've been sitting here listening to everything that's been happening. Hey, if you leave the tower can you give me a heads up so I can get the hell out of here?"

"Do you have a cell phone?" Lauren wasn't surprised at all by Matt's ingenuity at finding a way to monitor the situation.

"Yeah." Matt rattled off the numbers. "Cool. Now we can stay in touch."

"Thanks Matt." Lauren saw that Henry was now off the phone. "I've got to go. If you need me, call the tower number. My cell phone battery is getting low."

"Will do," Matt said. "Thanks."

Henry quickly stepped over to where she was. "You have a weather briefing for us?"

Lauren collected herself, glad to finally be back doing something other than thinking about Donovan. Lauren quietly cleared her throat as she became the center of attention. "As I'm sure you're aware, you in the aviation community have the ability to request weather information from each and every airport you fly to. I, or should I say we, at the DIA have the resources to calculate the weather at each specific latitude and longitude. We just finished a detailed satellite analysis of the surrounding 600 miles. We're in the middle of what I would describe as a classic Colorado low pressure system, but with a few twists I don't think anyone has ever seen before."

"Such as?" Henry said impatiently. "How soon until this thing blows past?"

Lauren shook her head gravely. "It's not as simple as that. There is a huge dip in the jet stream—it digs way south, then up along the front range of the Rockies, from there it runs just along the low. That's what's fueling the huge line of thunderstorms to our south. Behind the front, all along the trough, is the worst snow event I've ever seen. In fact, with the trough where it is, this system isn't about to blow over quickly. In my opinion we've only seen the first half."

"Oh no." Henry pinched the bridge of his nose. "So this thing could dump another foot or more?"

"Some are calling this the fifty-year blizzard. I say they've missed it by half. Right now we're seeing as much as five to six inches per hour of snow accumulation. We could get another two feet of snow before it's over. There are going to be drifts in excess of ten feet with the strong surface winds. Personally, I don't think a meteorologist alive has ever seen anything like this."

"What about any breaks in the overcast?" Henry asked, his expression seeming to indicate that his estimation of Lauren had just risen.

"We scanned a 600-mile radius around Chicago and the only partial break in the overcast is right here." Lauren paused as she calculated how to explain what she knew. "Are any of you are familiar with the term *heat island*? It's a phenomenon associated with large urban centers. The heat from these cities impacts and alters the weather downwind of the source itself. In this case, the heat from downtown Chicago and the temperature gradient from Lake Michigan has created a hole in the weather. It's not big, and it's constantly changing as the temperature fluctuates due to the snow accumulation, but it's there. The only opening for 600 miles is just southeast of the Loop over Lake Michigan."

"Show me," Henry said as he processed the information.

They gathered around the radarscope. "We're right here." Kate pointed to the system of runways depicted on her screen. "These are the buildings downtown. We have that area permanently marked on the scope so we can help planes avoid them."

"The opening in the clouds is east of them—right about here." Lauren pointed with her pencil. "It's entirely off-shore—out over Lake Michigan."

"I think we have a plan that will put them right here at O'Hare," Henry said. "I don't think we have to worry about them trying to land in the lake."

"Really?" Lauren embraced the words and the confidence in Henry's voice. "How?"

Behind Henry, another man pushed through the door into the cab. She wasn't sure who it was until Henry addressed him by name.

"Frank. Over here," Henry called out half-heartedly.

Lauren could tell from Henry's tone that Frank was a Wayfarer employee, but wasn't a welcome addition.

"Cyrus briefed me on what's happened," Frank, winded, said as he drew near.

"I'm Dr. McKenna," Lauren said.

"This is Frank Devereux," Henry said without emotion.

Lauren nodded as she recalled Henry's disdain for the man in the earlier, rather heated exchange with Leo and Cyrus. She tried to size up Devereux. He looked to be in his early sixties, a slender, short, nervous-looking man with thinning reddish-gray hair and quick darting eyes. His mannerisms gave Lauren the impression of a small nervous bird—a distinct contrast to the authoritative, decisive characteristics of all the other pilots she knew, including Henry.

"What have you come up with?" Frank exclaimed as he clasped his hands together. "Tell me what you're thinking in terms of getting them down."

"In just a second." Henry looked past Frank and sought out Koski. "Right now I need to know which runway we can use and what the field conditions are."

Lauren listened as Koski addressed the one person in the cab who had been quietly working with a determined fervor since they'd arrived. She saw Andy hold up a finger as he continued to pace as far as the cord on his headset would allow. He stopped from time to time and glanced at the surface radar. Lauren had the impression Andy choreographed the events in his head and didn't really need the information on the scope.

"Andy. Got a minute?" Koski repeated.

"You looking for an update?" Andy called out over his shoulder. "One second. Standby Snow One, I'll get right back to you. You've got time for at least one more pass down 32 Left." Andy studied the screen for a moment before he turned and faced Koski. "What do you want to know?"

"Which runway is in the best shape?" Henry asked.

"Usually you can take your pick, but right now I'm struggling to keep 32 Left as well as 27 Left open. I'd say with the wind, 32 Left is your best bet."

"What about emergency vehicles?"

"Already making sure they can get out of the fire stations to their staging areas." Andy keyed his microphone and began talking rapidly. "Yeah, Snow One. Make one more pass on the parallel taxiway for 32 Left. Yes, sir. All the way down taxiway Tango. We'll get back to 27 Left in a bit. Let's get this 737 down first, then worry about that, okay?"

"Who is he talking to?" Lauren whispered to Kate.

"Andy talks to the person designated as Snow One. He's in a truck and is the supervisor down at field level. Snow One in turn issues orders to the fleet of plows and blowers. Right now on 32 Left, a staggered line of vehicles, one blower truck just behind one plow, is making his way down the runway. A 200 foot-wide-swath is being cleared with each pass. It's amazing to watch. These guys are the best in the world."

"How much snow have we had?" Frank asked no one in particular.

"We went code black almost two hours ago," Andy adjusted his headset. "It's the highest level we have, meaning this is as bad as it gets. With the wind blowing like this, some of the drifts are already as high as five feet. I think the official total is 16 inches so far, and it's still coming down at five inches an hour. It's worse than the storm in '79. In fact, from where I'm sitting, it's by far the worst blizzard I've ever seen."

Henry nodded. "We're going to set up for 32 Left then. They could be here inside the next half hour. Is that going to be a problem?"

"Don't worry," Andy replied confidently as he ran his hands through his dark hair. "I'll make sure 32 Left is plowed full length and width. There are patches of wet snow and ice. It's coming down so fast there could be another three inches of snow or more by the time your guy gets here. We're having trouble with the drifting, but we'll handle it. Touchdown zone lights are visible, but some of the runway edge lights are buried. It'll be as good as we can possibly make it."

"Thanks," Henry said sincerely. "Keep up the good work."

"Any time." Andy gave Henry a small nod of appreciation, then resumed his task. "Snow One, I hear you. If you want to, stagger the group and hit several of the high-speed taxiways onto Tango. That would be great. When I give the mark, I want all vehicles to reposition to the emergency assembly locations. We're about to have an emergency landing and I want everyone to stay sharp!"

Henry turned to Devereux, "32 Left it is. But right now the runway is the least of our problems."

"What do you mean?" Frank nervously shifted his weight from one foot to the other. "What is it you plan to do? You know, of course, we'll need to run everything past Leo and Cyrus before we commit to any specific action."

Before Henry could answer, the shrill sound of a phone sounded from the middle of the room. Koski looked at the incoming number and took a deep breath. He glanced at Henry as if to say that the call was probably 880. He picked it up and put it on speaker.

"O'Hare Tower."

"It's 880," Donovan said. "What have you folks got? We could sure use some good news up here."

"I think we've got some," Henry said, ignoring Frank and stepping nearer the phone. "Donovan, can you put John on the phone?"

CHAPTER THIRTEEN

"Henry wants to talk to you." Donovan handed the phone over to John, then took over the task of flying the 737. He wished he could hear both sides of the conversation, but it wasn't his airplane, or his airline.

"Henry. What's the weather now?" John said quickly as he placed the small receiver to his ear.

Donovan knew from the grim expression on John's face that the weather hadn't improved.

"Okay, I see." John then examined the circuit breaker panels. "About half of them, maybe more. Okay, I follow you so far. That makes sense." John's face was a study in concentration. "We tried that. The smoke was almost instantaneous."

The suspense for Donovan was unbearable as John rolled his eyes in disbelief at what he was hearing.

"I'll need to talk this over with Donovan." John gave the overhead panel a disdainful glance while shaking his head. "Okay, I know what you're saying. It's worth a try if that's all we have." He listened further. "It'll take us a little bit to get everything situated. How about we call you back in a couple of minutes." After a moment, John disconnected the line. He let out a long breath. "This is going to sound totally insane— but it could actually work."

"What are they saying to do?" Donovan asked.

"They want us to pull out every last circuit breaker. After we've done that, we push in a select few—try and reinstate the power we need to shoot an approach. They think it will minimize the risk of fire."

"But the breakers will just pop out again," Donovan said.

"Not if we hold them in."

The flesh on the back of Donovan's neck tingled. Holding in a circuit breaker that wanted to pop was against every sound principle of safe flying. They were asking for a major electrical fire. The current draw would be enough to weld metal to metal, after which a fire could rage out of control. The cockpit could be engulfed in flames within minutes. "You're right, that is insane. What about the runway conditions and the weather? What's the visibility?"

"Henry said the snow removal crew is now concentrating on runway 32 Left. It's into the wind and 13,000 feet long. They're trying to get the snow off all the lights so we'll have something to see. The weather is still the same, we'll only have 600 feet of visibility."

Donovan knew that was far below the usual minimums needed for an approach, but what choice did they have? "What else? How do we get the gear down on this thing?"

"We're not going to bother. With all our structural damage, Henry recommends we do this gear up. I agree with him. If we drop the landing gear we'll never get it back up without a full hydraulic system, which would compound our problems if we have to go around. Stopping isn't going to be a problem in all the wind and snow. No gear and no flaps. This is going to be one fast approach."

"If we're on fire, coming in fast might not be a bad idea," Donovan said, as he pictured the scenario.

Keith's eyes widened as he listened to the two pilots talk and realized the implications. "Excuse me. It doesn't take an engineer to figure out how dangerous that could be. How much voltage are we talking about?"

John twisted in his seat to look at the Keith. "It's 115 volts, going down to 28 volts to power the few instruments we need to land. It shouldn't be too bad."

"How big are the generators on this thing?" Keith asked, curiosity momentarily taking the place of fear.

"45KVa generators, 400Hz," John explained.

"That's enough power to light up a city block!" A frown came over Keith's face. "Or weld metal."

"I know." John nodded his head. "But like we said, it's not going to be for very long." John addressed Donovan. "Why don't you go back, brief Audrey and the others. If Christy is out of commission, we'll need Audrey to get the cabin ready. They'll need to get out of this thing fast once we're down. When you finish, come back and we'll go through this step by step. Maybe you should grab an extra fire extinguisher while you're back there. It might come in handy."

Donovan threw off his harness and squeezed past Keith. His mind was filled with reasons why they shouldn't do what Henry had suggested, but as hard as he tried, he couldn't see any other alternative. As he ducked away from the jagged shards of aluminum into the rush of freezing air, it served as a grim reminder that the time for playing it safe was probably long gone. He saw the expectant faces of the survivors as he made his way toward them.

"Everyone! I need you to listen very carefully," Donovan said loudly and looked at everyone except Audrey. "I don't have much time to explain. We've talked to the people on the ground, and they've outlined a plan that should get us down. The method we're going to use has some risks, mainly the threat of fire. We already know that the smoke, if there is any, will be sucked out the rip in the fuselage. It shouldn't pose a problem for you back here."

"Oh for Christ's sake!" Wetzler exploded. "You're going to risk starting a fire on this plane?"

"That's exactly what I said," Donovan replied.

"It's not enough you crash us into another plane, now you want to burn us all alive!"

"Wetzler!" Donovan raised his voice while trying to keep his temper in check. "Knock it off!" Donovan glared at him, then continued with his instructions. "Audrey will be in charge of the emergency evacuation. Listen to her, and do exactly what she tells you. Rafael, I want you to be ready to open the aft doors when we come to a stop. Everyone will need to go out one of those two exits."

"I need something for my pain," Wetzler announced. "I want some liquor. Something to take the edge off."

"The answer is no," Donovan said. "It's for your own safety. Just do what you're told and we'll be on the ground as soon as we can." Donovan turned his attention back to Rafael. "Did you get a chance to look at

Christy and the others?"

"You were right about Christy, she has a broken collar bone. I also think her shoulder is separated and possibly fractured. There may also be some vertebrae trauma. She's in a great deal of pain but there's nothing much I can do." Rafael lowered his voice. "I also looked at the people who are… unconscious. It's called anoxia. They didn't get enough oxygen to their brains. Some died, probably in conjunction with other circumstances. Others are still alive, but only in the most basic sense."

"What do you mean?" Donovan was afraid he knew exactly what Rafael meant, but he needed a moment for the permanence of the diagnosis to sink in.

"They are brain dead. All higher function is most likely gone forever."

"Can we help them? Is there anything we can do?" Donovan asked.

Rafael shook his head. "No. They are what they are."

Donovan glanced at Audrey and found she was staring at him. He tried to convey with his eyes for her to be ready for anything. "Audrey, when we go into the clouds, that'll be the signal that we've started the approach."

"We'll be ready back here. What about them?" Audrey gestured at the passengers who were still alive. They'd secured them in their seats and wrapped them in what few blankets they'd found.

"Once we come to a stop, there will be emergency personnel all around the plane. I want each of you to evacuate as fast as you can. Once you're out of the plane, go toward any emergency person or vehicle you see. They are highly trained and are aware of our situation. We're going to inform them about the other survivors. Let them get those people out; it's much safer that way. I'll see everyone on the ground."

Donovan moved to the back of the cabin and opened an overhead compartment. He quickly unlatched a fire extinguisher and pulled it from its rack. As he closed the overhead door, he felt Audrey at his side.

"You know what? I think I hate you more now, than I did back then." Audrey glared at him.

"I don't know what you're talking about." Donovan looked at her and not only found anger, but maybe even a small measure of perverse delight at figuring out who he was. Her expression burned with both triumph and resolve. He tried to anticipate what she might say next.

"It bothered me from the first moment I saw you. It was impossible, wasn't it? You're dead. But the eyes, mannerisms and of course that voice."

Audrey whispered so only he could hear what she was saying. "You goddamned son of bitch!"

"I have no idea what you're talking about." Donovan knew his protestations were extremely weak—he'd spent far too much time with her. He picked up the fire extinguisher and prepared to leave without saying another word.

"Fine, Donovan. Or should I call you by your real name, Robert? As in Robert Huntington?"

Donovan felt crushed; as if his chest were caught in a vise. It was a name he'd buried long ago. "I have to get up front," Donovan finally managed to say, his grip still on the fire extinguisher. "This isn't the time or place. When we're on the ground we'll talk. But right now I want you to focus on getting out of this airplane. Do you understand me? Don't worry about anyone else."

Without waiting for a reply, Donovan hurried back up the aisle. His mind raced as his worst nightmare was unfolding. If Audrey wasn't willing to keep his secret, then the entire life he'd built would vanish overnight. He ducked down to avoid the sharp metal and was reminded that if they failed at this attempt to land the crippled 737, then it might not matter what Audrey knew.

Donovan handed the extinguisher to Keith and slid into his seat.

"Everything set in back?" John asked.

Audrey's words echoed and reverberated in Donovan's mind. After twenty years, how could she still be so angry? A bigger question might be exactly what was she so mad about? For a split second he wished he were still back there, trying to run some kind of damage control. How would he deal with this furious woman from his past—a woman who now held his fate in her hands.

"Donovan? Everything set in back?" John asked again

"Yes. Audrey and Rafael know exactly what to do." Donovan angrily cinched his harness tight around his lower body, pulling the straps over his shoulders until he was locked down firmly in the seat.

"Let's get rigged up." John followed suit and tightened his own straps. "I've been thinking about this. There should be three sets of smoke goggles. Everyone needs an oxygen mask."

Donovan helped Keith get strapped in, the mask and goggles organized. Keith secured the thick insulated gloves.

"Everyone set?" John asked.

Keith swallowed hard. "I guess so."

"Good. Keith, I want you to find all of the electrical panels behind us and pull out every one of the breakers. We'll point out the ones you'll need to push back in once we're ready to start. Any questions?"

"A bunch, but they can wait until we get on the ground," Keith said. "You want me to start now?"

John nodded. "Make sure they're all out." He then said to Donovan, "Let's run through the approach itself, what our speed should be, and what we can most likely expect. We'll need to put on our headsets. That will be the only way to communicate when we have our masks on—providing we get power to the audio panels."

"What about Keith?" Donovan asked. "Do we have a headset for him?"

"No." John shook his head. "His job is simple. He has to hold in the main breaker no matter what."

Donovan was impressed with the way John was handling the situation. He was calm, in command and businesslike. Together they began to review the approach procedure.

"We'll be coming in from the southeast," John explained. "As soon as we have power, the VHF radios should work. I'll need you to set up the frequencies. We can talk to the tower on 120.75. It will take a minute or so for the emergency gyro to spin up. Once it does, we'll start the approach. We won't descend into the clouds until everything is stabilized." John let out a breath. "Have I missed anything?"

"I think you covered it all." Donovan thought about everything that had been said. "This should work. As long as we have power."

"I'll have to fly this thing by hand." John gave Donovan a solemn look. "We're not going to get the autopilot back. I don't have to tell you what a 600 RVR approach looks like."

Donovan nodded that he understood. John would have to fly a perfect approach; they would see the runway at about the same time they touched down. The margin for error was small. "It'll be a piece of cake," Donovan said, trying to reassure him. "I'll give you all the input I can."

"Thanks. I'll need every bit of it."

Donovan glanced over his shoulder at Keith, who was now wearing insulated gloves, smoke goggles, and holding an oxygen mask. He seemed out of place in the cockpit of a modern jet. A fire extinguisher was at his feet. "Are you ready? Do you have any questions?"

Keith nodded. "The others in the back—is the rear of the plane the safest? I've always heard that, but never knew if it was true."

"In this situation it's by far the best place," Donovan replied, but wondered to himself how the 737 would stay together with all the structural damage. He guessed it wouldn't take very much to snap the weakened fuselage in half and end up skidding down the runway in pieces. Donovan wished he could shake off his thoughts of Audrey, but one simple phrase ran through his mind: *Hell hath no fury like a woman scorned.*

"Keith, you do exactly what we tell you," John reiterated. "Nothing more, nothing less. Is that understood?"

"I understand," Keith said.

Donovan took a moment to watch John. He could almost see and feel the captain's tension rising. He was aware of his own adrenaline surge, though at this point he didn't know which he dreaded more. The upcoming approach—or Audrey Parrish.

CHAPTER FOURTEEN

At the sound of the phone, all conversation in the cab abruptly ceased. Koski quickly punched the button. "Tower."

"This is 880," Donovan's voice announced over the speaker. "We're ready."

"Donovan, this is Henry. I take it John is going to be doing the flying and you and I will talk?"

"That's the plan. All the breakers have been pulled. What we need now is the exact sequence in which you want us to reset them. We've got someone up here to help us do all of that. But before we start—what's the weather, any improvement?"

"It's about the same, Donovan. RVR is pretty steady now at 600 feet." Henry fingered the notes he and Tucker had created, checking them for the umpteenth time. "Okay. Are you ready for the sequence?"

Lauren could feel the tension in the cab rising. She crossed her arms and her fingernails dug painfully into the palms of her hands. She'd listened quietly as dozens of fire trucks and ambulances were positioned strategically along the runway. Kate had tried to explain what was happening, while at the same time offering comfort. Lauren was deeply thankful for the woman's efforts.

"Go ahead. I'm writing it down," Donovan replied. "We'll want to locate all the breakers before we start this, make sure we have them identified."

Henry ran down the list, then stopped and waited as Donovan read everything back. "You've got it. That's the exact sequence we've figured out. Within sixty seconds, you should have the instruments you need to start the approach. Radar will have you positioned to intercept the approach course before you push everything in. We're estimating the time from start to landing at a little over six minutes. That will minimize your exposure to fire."

"You won't mind if we try to make it a little faster than that," Donovan said.

A nervous grin flashed across Lauren's face. Right now, more than anything, she needed to hear that Donovan sounded confident. It was a sharp contrast to the apprehension that was building within her.

"I understand completely," Henry said. "I look forward to meeting you."

Lauren's attention was drawn across the cab to Devereux. His eyes darted nervously around the room as if he were measuring something. He moved slowly in their direction.

"Let's have a current altimeter setting, then give us a vector for the intercept," Donovan said. "And just to make sure, we'll be able to talk to you on 120.75 when we get everything powered up."

"That's correct." Koski gave them the altimeter setting, then looked at Kate seated at the radarscope, her face focused and determined. He gave her a quick nod.

Kate responded with a practiced professionalism. "Wayfarer 880, turn right to a heading of 150 degrees. This is for a downwind leg to ILS 32 Left," she explained. "I'm going to turn you on a 25 mile final."

"Roger, turning to 150 degrees," Donovan said. "I think 25 miles sounds good. We're still several thousand feet above the clouds here. What altitude do you want us at when we turn all this on?"

"Eight thousand feet, Wayfarer 880," Kate said.

"Okay, we're out of ten thousand for eight thousand now."

"Consider yourself relieved from this operation." Frank Devereux spoke in a hushed voice to Henry. "You can stay and observe if you like."

Though Lauren suspected this was coming, the words cut deeply. Frank Devereux had sat back quietly while Henry had both organized and accomplished all that needed to be done. In her mind it was a completely chicken-shit move on the part of Devereux. She watched as Henry's expression drew taut.

"You can be in charge," Henry said, as he shot a look of hatred at Devereux. "Just let me get 880 on the ground."

Devereux recoiled. "You are relieved as of this moment. I have my orders from the top. We both know it's best."

"We do, huh?" Henry made no attempt to either lower his voice or hide his anger.

"Fine. It's all yours. I hope you know what you're doing."

"You're too emotionally involved right now to be running this," Devereux sneered, echoing Cyrus' words.

Lauren glanced around at the personnel in the cab. They had all heard the heated exchange. She could see everyone's general discomfort at being exposed to what was obviously a political issue.

"If you weren't being manipulated by Cyrus," Henry said, pointing his finger at Devereux, "Honestly, would you still be doing this?" Frank looked away, stung, the words producing their intended effect.

"What's going on down there?" Donovan said over the speaker.

"Donovan, this is Frank Devereux, Vice President of Flight Operations. I've just arrived and I'm taking over at this end. Nothing for you has changed. We'll be turning you shortly for the approach."

Lauren closed her eyes, shaking her head in frustration. The fate of Donovan and the others was now officially out of Henry's hands—and with it perhaps her own input. She wondered where Matt was, and if he'd overheard the orders that had led up to this action. Inwardly, she cursed Cyrus and wished Michael had somehow arrived in time to help her with this deteriorating situation.

"I don't really know who you are. But I was kind of getting used to Henry," Donovan said. "I think he was doing an outstanding job."

"Let's just get back to the task at hand; Henry is still here, but only as an observer," Frank stated.

"Wayfarer 880, turn right to a heading of 340 degrees," Kate interrupted. "You will roll out on the final approach course, 25 miles from touchdown." She had just made the perfect vector; 880 would be positioned exactly where it needed to be.

"In the turn now," Donovan reported. "We're getting ready to push in the breakers. Tell us when we're one minute from intercept."

Lauren moved away from Devereux, her anger and frustration barely under control. She looked over Kate's shoulder at the blip on the screen. It was hard to imagine the green shape was an airplane—an airplane with Donovan on board. It struck Lauren as almost surreal.

"One minute from intercept." Kate glanced at the second hand on her watch. "Wayfarer 880, you are cleared for the ILS approach to runway 32 Left."

CHAPTER FIFTEEN

"Okay, Keith, now!" Donovan listened and counted the seven distinct clicks as each specific circuit breaker was reset in sequence. They were just skimming the tops of the clouds at 8,000 feet. John was flying the airplane beautifully. Donovan switched off the cell phone and set it beside him. The lights on the VHF radio blinked to life. He slipped his oxygen mask on and faced the instrument panel as more lights began to flicker. It was working. Donovan was relieved to see the instruments powering up. He quickly tuned the radios to the appropriate frequencies.

"Okay, I'm getting some action here." John shifted in his seat as systems began to return. "We're on the localizer."

Donovan could hear John clearly through his headset. The microphones in the oxygen masks were working. He watched as electronic indicators settled into position. It showed them lined up perfectly with the distant runway. The signals would guide them down an invisible path to the airport. As long as John flew the 737 so that the two needles were precisely centered, the aircraft would touch down on the centerline of runway 32 Left. "Looking good, John." Donovan turned to Keith, who gave him a thumbs-up.

"The gyro appears to be stable." John focused on the standby attitude indicator. Its information was vital; without it, he could become instantly disoriented. "Here we go. I'm leaving eight thousand feet. We're on the glide slope."

The Boeing descended toward the tops of the clouds. Light turbulence buffeted the 737 as they sped through the wisps of vapor. Donovan's muscles tightened; they were committed, heading into the raging blizzard that lay between them and the ground.

The world outside the cockpit went from blue to gray. Donovan keyed the microphone. "O'Hare Tower. This is Wayfarer 880. We're out of eight thousand feet. On glide slope and localizer. Great vector."

"Roger 880, we read you loud and clear," Kate said calmly. "The snow removal equipment is clear and we have emergency vehicles standing by. All of the approach lights are on full intensity."

"Tower. What's the wind and RVR," Donovan said. He felt as though the world was going by in slow motion, but his senses were moving at the speed of light.

"Wind is 290 degrees at 15, gusts to 25. RVR is 600 variable to 800 feet. Altimeter is 28.92. Runway surface is plowed 125 feet wide, full length."

Growing turbulence pounded the Boeing. Each jolt threatened to displace the aircraft from its required position in the gray murky sky. John rode out each series of bumps, and corrected their glide path to keep them on course.

"I show us 19 miles from the airport, on localizer, on glide slope. Airspeed is 220 knots." Donovan knew how difficult John's job was and was relieved to see he was handling the plane expertly.

"It's going to get rougher as we descend," John said. "I'll want call-outs of any deviation at all."

"You're 17 miles from touchdown." Kate's voice came over the speaker loud and clear. "Wind is now 330 degrees, at 17 knots with gusts to 28 knots. RVR is holding steady at 700 feet."

"We copy O'Hare." Donovan held his breath as a powerful gust tipped the 737 into a 20 degree bank. John fought the controls, trying to bring the wings of the Boeing back to level. They had drifted slightly out of position.

"We're a little right of course, and a little bit low," Donovan called out. The sensitivity of the course needles would increase as they got closer to the runway.

"Correcting," John said.

Donovan scrutinized the strain on John's face. His eyes never left the precious few instruments in front of him. The tendons in his forearm flexed as he battled both the elements and the damaged 737.

"Uh, something is getting pretty hot back here." Keith pulled his mask aside. He had one glove off; his bare hand pressed to the gray metal panel, his gloved hand held in the crucial power breaker.

Donovan spun around in his seat. His eyes scanned each panel for smoke. He found none. He nodded at Keith, then directed his attention back to John, who was fighting yet another onslaught of turbulence.

"Any smoke?" John asked, his eyes riveted to the panel.

"None," Donovan said. "We're almost halfway there. I'm showing us a little high on the glide slope."

"Wayfarer 880, the RVR is now 800 feet." Kate's excited voice announced the news of the improving visibility.

"Just keep it coming John. We might pull this off yet," Donovan said. "We copy O'Hare; just hold the weather right there."

"We'll try, Wayfarer."

Donovan felt a hand on his shoulder. He turned and saw the first wisps of smoke beginning to seep from the panel behind John's seat. Keith's eyes were wide and unblinking.

"What is it?" John said.

"Just a little smoke," Donovan said. "Don't worry about it. I show us a little right of course and low."

"Where's it coming from?" John asked, his voice filled with apprehension.

"There's not very much. Far less than the first time," Donovan reported, but he knew John's stress level was rising fast. John couldn't do anything but continue to fly the plane while something behind him began to burn. Donovan looked back over his shoulder as Keith pointed at the overhead panel. More smoke was starting to drift from it also. "Just keep flying, John. Check your glide slope; we're still a little low."

John added power. He struggled with the turbulence and the added distraction of an unseen fire. He steadied the 737 and brought the two needles back into place. "How bad is the smoke now?"

"It's okay. We're only 15 miles from the airport. Less than five minutes. You're looking good, John. Just keep flying this thing the way you've been doing. We'll be on the ground shortly." Donovan could sense John's apprehension getting the better of him. Donovan needed to keep John's attention on flying the plane. "Stay with it, John. You're a little right of course, slightly high. Speed is good."

"Oh Christ. We've got a fire!" Keith cried out through his mask. His terrified voice filled the cockpit.

Donovan spun around. Bluish flames flickered from the edge of the panel. Smoke poured from the seams. "Keep your mask on! Don't let go of the breaker!" Donovan shot a look at John. "You fly! We'll handle this."

"What do you want me to do?" Keith yelled.

For an instant, Donovan was afraid Keith might try to bolt from the cockpit. But the man bravely held his position. "Just keep holding in the breaker!"

"How bad is it?" John's voice was clipped and tense, his breaths came in ragged gulps.

"Manageable," Donovan said as calmly as he could. "We'll make it. I'm going to use the extinguisher."

More turbulence battered the 737. Donovan held on tightly as they rode through the worst of it. Without warning, as if a volcano had decided to let go, a plume of gray smoke erupted from the overhead panel. It poured out thick as liquid. Within seconds, visibility in the cockpit was near zero.

"Wayfarer 880, we show you drifting right of course," Kate announced.

"Jesus Christ! I can't see anything!" John yelled, pushing both throttles to maximum power. "I'm getting us out of here!"

Donovan could hardly see the panel in front of him. He turned to Keith, "As soon as we're in the clear, pull all the breakers!" Keith, wide-eyed, nodded in agreement.

Donovan grabbed the extinguisher. He didn't need to watch John anymore. He could hear the whine of the CFM engines as they spooled up to full power. Any second and they would be in a massive climb for the clear air above. He pulled the pin on the extinguisher, gripped the handles and fired the bottle directly into the flames. The white vapor streamed from the nozzle and swept the flames away. Donovan then aimed at the overhead panel. He emptied the bottle as the smoke continued to pour out.

Through the dense smoke, Donovan watched in horror as another sheet of flames erupted behind John. Donovan squeezed the handle but the extinguisher was empty. He let it drop and reached through the smoke to try and find the second one.

John twisted violently in his seat, shrieking in pain. "Oh Jesus, I'm on fire!" He released his grip on the controls. "Help me! I'm burning!" He screamed helplessly into the microphone.

The flames shot up from the left arm of John's uniform. The synthetic material had ignited. Donovan pointed the fresh bottle and fired. John writhed in agony, his screams filling his headset, as his hands frantically beat the flames away. Donovan dropped the bottle—no one was flying the airplane.

Donovan grabbed the controls, fighting to see the instruments through the dense smoke. Their speed was building. Donovan knew they desperately needed to climb, but when he pulled back on the controls they didn't move. He tried again but nothing happened. He felt them jerk in his hands as John tried in vain to escape the flames. Ignoring the fumes, Donovan pulled his mask aside. "Keith! Get him off the controls! I can't fly!" Keith's muscular arm reached around and tried to subdue the pilot. Donovan hoped it would be enough. Keith could only use one arm if he was going to keep the breaker in. John's cries of agony dissolved into nothing more than a pitiful moan. Donovan forced his mask back into place, took a breath, and then recoiled as a small amount of smoke shot into his lungs. He threw his head from side to side trying to escape the caustic fumes, gagging and coughing. His throat and nose were burning. He resisted the urge to rip the mask away. Donovan focused on the panel, while at the same time attempting to force clean air into his tortured lungs. The instruments before him flickered once, and then went black. The electrical feeders had finally burned through and now they were flying completely blind.

CHAPTER SIXTEEN

Lauren had flinched then stiffened, when the first screams had sounded through the speaker. Now there was nothing but silence.

"Wayfarer 880. This is O'Hare Tower. I show you drifting right of course. Do you copy?" Kate transmitted for the third time.

Lauren stood over her and watched the blip continue in a right turn. With each successive sweep of the scope, it was obvious they were headed wildly off course. The radar was still picking up information from the 737's transponder, indicating that they were in a rapid descent. Lauren traced 880's path and a new horror filled her. On their present heading, rising up into the clouds, were two of the tallest buildings in the world. The Sears Tower rose to over 2,000 feet above sea level. The Hancock and Amoco buildings were nearly as tall. The 737 had turned directly toward them and had been picking up speed.

"Wayfarer 880 do you read O'Hare?" Kate gave Lauren an expression of helplessness. "880, please respond!"

Frank put both hands to his temples. "Keep trying. We have to reach them!"

"Wayfarer 880 this is O'Hare. Turn left now. Repeat. Turn left now. Wayfarer 880 how do you read?" Kate kept transmitting. She looked up. "They're below 2,000 feet and descending."

"Tell them to turn," Devereux pleaded. "They need to turn!"

"I've just lost their transponder," Kate said. "Now I don't have any altitude information on them."

Lauren steadied herself on the console. She knew a fire must be engulfing the cockpit, and she felt ill. The screams she heard from 880 were almost inhuman. She had no idea who they came from, but she knew they would be etched in her mind forever. Every sweep of the radar put Donovan closer to the buildings. She could see the small circle on the scope that warned where the skyscrapers were. 880 was now less than a mile away. It was only a matter of seconds.

"What's their altitude?" Devereux shouted.

"We have no way of knowing," Henry shot back at his boss.

"Wayfarer 880. If you read me turn left or right. Turn now, please!" Kate implored the blip to alter course.

The blood drained from Lauren's face and her legs threatened to buckle. It was incomprehensible that the airplane might crash in moments. The 737 and all the people aboard 880 would be strewn across the streets of downtown Chicago. She thought of the densely populated Loop, all the buildings that reached up into the sky. She could see the helplessness on Henry's face. She thought of him losing a daughter; now his wife was in mortal danger. And Lauren thought of Donovan and their life together, all of the plans they'd made for the future. On the radar screen the ghostly green image of 880 and the warning area merged.

CHAPTER SEVENTEEN

"Forget the breaker—grab his arms!" Donovan yelled into his mask, the words muffled by the rubber seal. Donovan hoped that Keith would hear him. "Pin him back against his seat!" The sound of the slipstream grew louder. Donovan yanked as hard as he could, doing everything possible to regain control of the jet. He felt Keith bang against him; the larger man had unbuckled himself and moved toward John. In the smoke-filled cockpit, Keith braced himself to counter John's pain-driven frenzy. Keith measured his point of attack, then leaned forward and wrapped John up with both arms. He forced the captain away from the controls, ignoring his distorted cries of distress.

With a lurch, the controls in Donovan's hands became free. He instantly felt the dangerous high-speed vibration. He pulled back. The altimeter needle crept slightly higher; the noise in the cockpit changed. It sounded like they had accelerated even more. He felt as if he were spinning. The deadly warnings of vertigo raced through Donovan's mind

The smoke began to diminish, pulled out of the cockpit by the tremendous vacuum created from the rip in the airplane. Donovan could barely see the tiny altimeter. He was shocked to find they were down to 1,600 feet. Their speed was almost 280 knots. Donovan had never felt so helpless. With the loss of power, the emergency horizon gyro had spun down. There were no instruments to tell him which way was up. All he could feel were conflicting G-forces. He had no idea where they were in relation to the ground, or if they were even right side up. The gyro that had moments ago been giving reliable information was spinning wildly. Donovan was filled with uncertainty; if he did the wrong thing it might be fatal. If he did nothing, it would absolutely be fatal. He held his breath and pulled back on the shaking controls, terrified of the result. If they were in a bank, the turn would tighten and they would simply stall. The 737 would roll upside down and slam into the ground.

In a flash, two rows of red lights filled Donovan's side window. Just below, a vibrant fluorescent glow reached out to him. Donovan fought to orient himself. There were confusing rows of lights falling away beneath him, dissolving in the driving snow. He caught a fleeting glimpse of people seated near a window. The dark gray walls, the glass and the people inside seemed near enough to reach out and touch. The twin red-and-white spires that soared up from the top of the John Hancock building flashed past and melted into the clouds behind them. Donovan put it all together, the split-second reference gave him what he needed. The 737 was in a steep bank to the right. Donovan leveled the wings and pulled on the yoke as hard as he dared, images of the damaged airframe flooding his mind. With the other hand, he pushed both throttles all the way to the stops. The seconds ticked off in his head as he pictured their climb away from the concrete and steel mountains below them. He tried his best to hold their attitude steady. He pleaded for the cloud tops to show themselves before becoming hopelessly disoriented once again. It slowly became brighter. The airspeed bled off to less than 200 knots. He was running out of speed.

"I can see blue sky!" Keith pointed out the windscreen. "Right above us."

The 737 burst out of the clouds and into the clear air of the winter afternoon. The airplane was banked to the left, the nose pitched up almost 25 degrees. Donovan carefully brought the Boeing to a stable position and pulled back the power. The buzz in the controls subsided. He sat for a moment, stunned, amazed that they were still flying. The massive suction behind them pulled the smoke out quickly. He slid his mask over his head, then turned to Keith. "Is the fire out? Can you see if anything is still burning?" Donovan recoiled at the stench of burned insulation mingled with the more pungent smell of charred flesh and hair.

"I think it burned itself out." Keith relaxed his grip on John and took a closer look. "Just some residual smoke."

"You can let him go," Donovan said. "Check the panel for any signs of fire." Donovan fixed his gaze on the overhead section; the smoke looked to be dissipating.

"I don't see a thing," Keith said, wrinkling his nose. "I think whatever was burning lost its electrical source. We're damn lucky."

Donovan peeled his goggles off. His legs and arms shook uncontrollably. He knew it was the after-effects from the massive amounts of adrenaline that had just been pumped into his body. He looked out the window at the clouds below. It was pure luck that they'd missed the Hancock building. He couldn't stop his legs from shaking as the image replayed in his mind. They had been well below the top of the building. He guessed they had missed it by only a scant few feet. A little more to the right and they would've plowed into the side of the massive structure. Images of an airliner striking a skyscraper were a horror he and everyone else in the world were all too familiar with.

"John, can you hear me?" Donovan said as he reached over and put a hand on John's shoulder. "Keith, go back and get help; bring the medical kit." Keith nodded and raced from the cockpit. "John, we're back on top of the clouds; we're in the clear."

John rolled his head side-to-side. Tears streamed from glazed eyes; they trickled out from under his goggles, his mask was still secured. He made a weak gurgling noise.

Donovan saw John's right hand; he must have burned it while trying to sweep the flames away. It was bright red, the blisters rising; the cuff of his shirt was black and singed. "Hang in there, John. Help is on the way."

Audrey was the first onto the flight deck, her hands shot to her mouth. "Oh my God!"

"John's been burned." Donovan said.

Audrey leaned over John and quickly tried to inspect his injuries. He pulled away. She turned to Donovan, shaking her head. "It's not good. We need to get him in back."

"Coming through," Rafael announced from the door.

"Give us a second, Rafael. We're coming back to you," Audrey called out, then turned to Donovan, her face filled with revulsion at the sight of John's burns. She pointed to the goggles and oxygen mask. "We might have to cut these off him. The straps look melted to his skin."

"Do whatever you have to. Just keep him off the controls," Donovan said, frustrated at not being able to help. He caught partial glimpses of John as Audrey stood over him and studied the best way to remove the partly melted gear. He was moaning into his mask, still conscious. Donovan wondered if it might be a blessing if John were to just black out.

"John. I think I can remove your goggles. Hang on to the seat," Audrey instructed.

A muffled shriek filled the cockpit. John's body jerked, then went rigid. Donovan shuddered at the painful cries and looked away.

Audrey dropped the smoke goggles on the floor. The strap had melted; clumps of burnt hair clung to the crinkled elastic.

"Breathe, John. Take deep breaths." Audrey squeezed his good hand. "It's not as bad as I thought. We'll take the mask off in a second." Audrey said to Donovan. "How do I do this?"

"There are two red tabs underneath his mask. When you squeeze them together, the straps around his head will inflate; then you slide the whole thing up and over. But be careful. If you let go, the straps will contract again." Donovan could clearly see the hesitation in her eyes; her face had gone white from the strain. "Just do it one quick sweeping motion."

"Okay," she nodded. "Here it goes."

Donovan's muscles tensed as he heard the straps inflate on John's mask. Without the rubber seal over his mouth, John's wail of agony, now clearly audible, cut Donovan to the core. John flailed against his harness as he reacted to the blinding pain. The controls bucked momentarily in his hands, but Donovan was able to hold the 737 steady.

"It's okay John. It's over." Audrey held him tightly, her voice wavering. "When you're ready, we'll try to get you up. Do you think you can walk?"

John gasped through clenched teeth.

"Keith!" Audrey yelled back to the cabin. "Are you there?"

"Yeah, I'm here. What can I do?"

"There's not enough room in here for both of us. I'm coming out, then I want you to help John back to the cabin."

Keith moved into the small space. He took a moment to decide where it would be best to grasp the injured pilot. "This is going to be a little awkward."

"I'll lean over to give you more room." Donovan gave Keith as much space as he could, gripping the controls firmly. "I'm ready when you are."

Keith put one hand under John's right arm, then reached out to support his unburned left hand. John groaned as Keith lifted him out of his seat. "I've got you."

John swayed slightly. His face was drawn and colorless. He held his burned arm away from his body. Tears trickled from his bloodshot eyes.

"We're coming back through," Keith yelled. "Rafael. Get ready to take him."

Donovan had to look away. He saw where the material of John's uniform had burned through, leaving fabric melted onto his skin. The hair on the left side of his scalp was almost completely burned away, except for a dark strip where the elastic from his goggles and mask had been. He had no idea how John could function. It took Keith several careful moments to lower John through the opening to the waiting arms of the others in back.

Alone on the flight deck, Donovan banked the plane to the west and could see the setting sun, the orange colors playing across the tops of the clouds. Far to the south, the same thunderstorms that he had fought so hard to avoid towered brilliantly in the subdued light. The distant lightning flashed white and blue. It was a beautiful sight. He found comfort at witnessing the magnificent vista. He wondered how many vivid sights like this he had witnessed during his career in the sky. Would this be his last?

"Coming up," a voice called from the door to the cockpit.

Donovan's peaceful moment vanished at the sound of Audrey's voice.

Audrey slid into the space between the pilot seats. "Rafael didn't need me. I thought I'd come and see how you were doing."

"I'm okay, considering." Donovan could still taste the bitter smoke in his mouth. "How is everything in the back?"

"We're all fine." Audrey wrinkled her nose at the burned smell.

"You can sit right there if you want to." Donovan knew he wasn't going to get rid of her anytime soon. She'd figured out his true identity and wasn't going to let it rest. He gestured to the jump seat.

Audrey carefully slid into the seat. "I don't know when I've been more terrified. I can't believe how close those buildings were."

"I need you to do something for me."

"What is it?"

Donovan found the cell phone they'd been using and handed it to her. "Can you redial the last number?"

"Who am I calling?" Audrey pressed two buttons and put it to her ear. "It's ringing," she announced, handing the phone to Donovan.

"O'Hare Tower!" Koski's anxious voice sounded loudly through the speaker.

"Well folks, that didn't work very well." Donovan didn't know what else to say.

"What's your situation?" Henry demanded. "What happened?"

"Henry, is that you? Good, you're still there. I've got to hand it to you, it was working. We were doing great until a fire broke out. John's been burned pretty badly. I have a sneaking suspicion that the main feeders burned through. When we lost everything, it all went out at exactly the same time. We were lucky to get back on top."

"Donovan, this is Frank Devereux. I'm glad you're okay. Can you give us a status report?"

"How badly is John hurt?" Henry jumped in. "Tell me exactly where the smoke started."

"Guys, I'm only going to talk to one of you—and that person is Henry. So Frank, just listen up." Donovan paused for a moment. "Okay, the fire started in the panel behind the left seat. It ignited John's clothing. His neck, hand, and the side of his face are all burned. They're still working on him in the back."

"That doesn't sound good," Henry said. "How's she flying right now?"

"About the same." Donovan said. "Any improvement in the weather?"

Devereux spoke loudly, clearly ignoring Donovan's wishes. "The weather at the moment is holding steady. We're still trying to figure out exactly what our next step should be. We're tracking a weak spot in the weather with the Doppler radar. We're hopeful that the area will expand."

"Where is this area now?" Donovan asked, sensing Devereux's uncertainty. "Is Dr. McKenna still there? If it's about the weather, I want to hear it from her."

"I'm here," Lauren said immediately.

"Good to hear your voice." Donovan closed his eyes briefly as he soaked up the image of her. "Talk to me."

"I spoke with Calvin. We searched a 600-mile radius and the only break in the overcast is a heat island event. The area is stationary, about a mile downwind of the Loop. That's the good news. The bad news is, it's over Lake Michigan."

"We're hoping the area will widen," Devereux said, jumping into the conversation. "Which might let you land at one of several smaller airports. Unfortunately, we don't think it will reach O'Hare. But it might work for Midway, or perhaps Gary, Indiana."

"Ignore him, he's an ass," Lauren said. "He doesn't have a clue what he's talking about. It's a small, localized phenomenon. It's not going to expand or move. In fact, as the snow cover lowers the surrounding temperature of the Loop, the area should actually begin to contract."

Donovan knew he'd been right about how tentative Devereux sounded. He didn't seem to possess a fraction of the drive that Henry had demonstrated. And now he'd tried to lie to him about the weather. "Lauren. What do you and Henry think?"

"Excuse me," Devereux interrupted. "Henry's wife is on board your flight. We don't feel he's the best one to be giving advice right now. That decision has been made."

"Well, Frank." Donovan's irritation increased. He knew every institution possessed a number of ineffective, bureaucratic, political creatures, and he had just placed Devereux in that category. The fact that Lauren had called him an ass, spoke volumes. "I'm not sure how you do things at your airline, but despite the fact that Henry's wife is on this plane, he is exactly who should be working on this. Use the best resources at your disposal. Now as the pilot of this airplane, I'd prefer to keep working with Henry."

"I'm sorry you feel that way, Donovan," Frank replied. "But it's not going to happen. I can assure you, even with Henry's dismissal, we're still doing everything we can to find a solution."

"I'll tell you what—prove it then!" Donovan made no effort to hide the anger in his voice. "I'll call you back in twenty minutes. We're running out of cell phones, daylight and fuel. You get with Henry, or the engineers who designed the Boeing 737. I really don't care. But I want less posturing and more results! Do you understand me?"

"880. This is the Tower Chief. You're 25 miles northeast of the airport. Keep flying the same pattern you've been flying; it will keep you in our airspace."

"Roger." Donovan terminated the call.

"What did they say?" Audrey asked.

"Not much, I'm afraid."

"Did I hear you say Frank, as in Frank Devereux?"

Donovan nodded.

"Oh, God. Henry hates him, thinks he's totally inept, and you know what happens when Henry Parrish gets agitated."

Donovan knew the question was a loaded one. He looked at Audrey, into a face that had been deeply affected by his actions so many years ago. It felt so strange to be close to her as Donovan Nash, instead of Robert Huntington. In so many ways it felt as if the ensuing years had suddenly evaporated. She was probably right; he did owe her an explanation. And right now it probably wouldn't make any difference. If he was forced to ditch this airliner into the storm-tossed waves of Lake Michigan, there was little chance either one of them would survive. His secret would probably sink with them.

"Yes—I know what Henry Parrish is like when he makes up his mind," Donovan confessed, turning and looking into her knowing eyes. "If my memory serves me correctly—I'm the one who introduced the two of you."

CHAPTER EIGHTEEN

The howling wind rose and fell, whipping snow against the windows. Lauren needed a moment to try to gather herself, to blot out the image of the 737 merging with the skyscrapers. Her hands were still shaking, her nerves frayed. The solitary aircraft on the radar screen was Wayfarer 880, circling offshore.

Henry was on the phone, as was Devereux. Lauren wished she knew what was being said, what plans were being made to try to save Donovan and the others. She kept thinking of how business-like Donovan had sounded. He was easily the most capable man she'd ever met; his bravery had made a difference in countless lives over the years. She hoped the people around her were half as capable. Her thoughts were interrupted by the sound of her cell phone ringing. She pulled it out of her coat pocket.

"Hello?" Lauren answered.

"Hi. It's Matt. I tried the tower number but it was busy."

"Did you hear what happened?" Lauren eyed Henry, making sure he was still on the phone and not listening in on her conversation.

"Yeah," Matt replied. "Most of it anyway—Uh oh."

"What's going on?" Lauren said as she heard some odd background noise.

"Lauren," Matt said finally, his voice barely a whisper. "Someone just went into the conference room we were in earlier. I have the intercom open; hang on a second."

"Matt, what are you doing?" Lauren put a hand up and covered one ear. "I can hardly hear you."

"Can you hear this?" Matt said softly.

Lauren listened intently as the voice became audible, only it wasn't Matt, it was someone else. Lauren strained until she could make out the words. Only then did she realize she was listening to Cyrus Richtman.

"I can hear him," Lauren said, matching Matt's conspiratorial tone. "What's he saying?"

"He just made a phone call. He must be on a cell phone—none of the lines from the phones in that room are lit up. I'll try to jack up the volume a little, but I can't let him know I'm listening or I'll be in tons of trouble."

Lauren wondered why Cyrus would sneak off to make phone calls in the deserted conference room. She eyed Devereux, wondering if he was privately talking to the CEO. She waited as Matt increased the volume. She could now easily hear Cyrus Richtman as he spoke.

"Look!" Cyrus hissed. "This is the opportunity we've been waiting for. When this is over, Leo will be history. The old man should have stepped down years ago. I'm just as concerned as you are that somehow these people will get that airplane on the ground in one piece and Leo will get the credit. I'm doing everything I can to make sure that what does happen makes Leo look like a confused old man."

Lauren's anger rose. She wondered who he might be talking with.

"Trust me, I'm going to put maximum pressure on Leo to get this airplane to ditch in the lake. The last thing I need is for this airplane to miraculously end up safe. The minute flight 880 is down, I'm going to call a board meeting and do everything I can to vote Leo out. After all, he was foolish enough to sign off on allowing a civilian to fly the plane. For god's sake, they nearly crashed into the Hancock building. After I make an example of Leo's spineless hand-wringing, and then point to the body-count from flight 880, I'm certain the board will elect me acting chairman. On Monday morning, Wayfarer stock is probably going to plummet dramatically—that's when you make your move. With Leo gone, your group needs to make its tender offer for controlling interest in Wayfarer. I'll of course recommend to the board that we accept the offer."

Lauren had to suppress a scream. She looked at Henry who was still on the phone, oblivious to A Cyrus' maneuverings.

"Our deal is still intact? I have your word that I'll stay on as Vice-Chairman until your management team is in place? At that point the final payment will be deposited to my account." Cyrus paused as he listened. "Excellent, I need to get with Leo and finish things at this end. I'll be in touch."

"Lauren?" Matt said in a normal voice the instant Cyrus had left the conference room. "Are you there? Did you get all of that?"

"I'm here," Lauren said, livid at what Cyrus was doing. "Yes, I heard."

"What are we going to do?" Matt nearly pleaded. "He's trying to kill everyone."

"Don't breathe a word of this to anyone," Lauren urged. "They won't believe either one of us. Let me talk to your father."

"Like he can do anything," Matt said.

"Cut your father some slack," Lauren said, abruptly, then immediately regretted her words. The battle between father and son wasn't hers to fight.

"Whatever." Matt's wounded tone was clearly evident.

"I'm sorry," Lauren said as she watched Devereux answer his cell phone. "I shouldn't have said that, but your father is all we have right now to fight this. I promise your father and I will do whatever it takes."

"Henry," Devereux called out as he lowered the phone from his ear and ended the call. His face had drained of color. "We need to talk. It's been decided."

"What's been decided?" Henry shot back. He terminated his own call and quickly crossed to where Devereux stood.

"Based on Dr. McKenna's assessment of the weather situation, and the amount of daylight left—" Devereux's voice was low and guarded. He shifted his weight and cleared his throat. "It's been decided that 880 needs to take advantage of the heat-island event and ditch in Lake Michigan."

Lauren felt as if she'd been physically punched. Cyrus had already put his plan into motion. "I have to go. Your father and I are probably on our way down," Lauren whispered to Matt, and then quickly disconnected the call.

"Not yet you're not!" Henry raised his voice. "We've still got other options."

"There are no other options, Henry. I'm sorry," Devereux said.

"You're crazy!" Henry exploded. "This is Cyrus' idea, isn't it! I can't believe you'd be a party to this madness. There are always other options. We just need to figure out what they are!"

"I don't really care what you think," Devereux said, his hands shaking. "It's the only thing we—or they, have left."

"You might as well just pull the trigger and kill all those people yourself!" Henry said loudly. "They won't survive a ditching in Lake Michigan. Are you out of your mind? It's certain death for every one of those people. Even if they manage somehow to stop in one piece, which I doubt will be the case, how long do you think they'll stay alive in the freezing water? How fast do you think the rescue boats could be on the scene? You've seen how big the waves get when the wind is blowing like this. I can't believe you'd even think about this!"

"What else would you have them do?" Devereux countered. "We're running out of time, Henry. A controlled ditching is the best option. When they run out of fuel, that's exactly what they're going to be doing anyway. Don't you think it would be better to have them do it while they still have some control, some daylight? We'll have ships standing by to get to them as soon as they're in the water. It's their only hope."

"What about trying to get power back to the other side of the electrical system? We only tried the number one generator. What about number two?" Henry's face grew red; his control seemed to be slipping away.

"They were almost burned alive trying to get power to the instruments; for God's sake, John may not even be able to fly the plane now. They almost crashed into the middle of downtown! Now you want to try it again? You're the one who has lost his mind."

"We can figure it out," Henry said. "There are still the batteries. Maybe it's possible to route the power in another direction. There are still options we haven't explored yet!"

Lauren knew that Henry was fighting a losing battle. She moved toward him to get him to leave the tower, get him someplace where she could explain what she knew. Their only chance now was to find Leo Singer.

"We can't take the chance that we'll kill more people. It's a tragedy, Henry. We didn't cause this horrible chain of events, but we have a responsibility to try to minimize the deaths of innocent people. Can you imagine the public outcry if 880 had crashed on Michigan Avenue?"

"Jesus." Henry shook his head, looking at Devereux with total disgust.

"You sound just like Cyrus. I hope you can sleep at night knowing you took the easy way out, that you didn't explore every option to save them."

Lauren looked around at the solemn faces of the tower crew. They had stood by and watched as Henry and Devereux argued. The only person who had a task was Andy. Lauren envied his focus, how removed he was from the scene crashing down upon her.

"I'd prefer if the two of you went back to Operations," Devereux said quietly. "They're expecting you. Henry, I'm sorry, but this is out of your hands and things will work more smoothly if you and I don't argue at every turn."

"I'll leave you to orchestrate this—this act of murder." Henry angrily spun away from Devereux.

Lauren gave a silent nod of thanks to both Kate and Wayne. She could see in their grim faces that they, too, were stunned at what had just transpired. Henry fell in behind Lauren and the door to the tower slammed shut behind them. Lauren went down one flight of steps and stopped on the small landing. She waited for Henry to catch up.

"What is it?" Henry asked as he joined her.

"We have a bigger problem." Lauren's tone was dead serious—from the expression on his face she knew she had Henry's undivided attention. "I need you listen very carefully to what I have to tell you."

CHAPTER NINETEEN

Lauren was still in step with Henry when they barged through the security doors that led to Operations. All eyes turned at the commotion of their entrance, then were quickly averted as their identities registered. Lauren could almost feel the negative atmosphere of the room. It was apparent that everyone already knew that Henry had been relieved and were keeping their distance. She was beginning to hate the political minefield that existed at Wayfarer Airlines. To her left she saw Tucker with Matt. The young man was gesturing for her to join him.

"Where are Leo and Cyrus?" Henry called across the room.

Glen hustled to where Henry stood. "Henry. I'm sorry. I've been instructed to keep you out of the way and not to disturb them until this is over."

"That's no surprise." Henry's jaw worked as he battled his anger. "How much time do we have until they're in the water?"

"Right now we're trying to organize all the rescue assets. It's going to be at least forty minutes before we have everything in place."

"Keep me advised," Henry replied, and then lowered his voice to Lauren and Matt. "We've got to find Leo."

Lauren had her hand on Matt's shoulder, as if to offer some small measure of comfort. Once again she wondered if he'd been crying.

"Matt," Henry said as he slowed. "Try not to worry. I'm doing everything I can, but right now I have to find Leo."

"You're going the wrong way." Matt shook his head in obvious frustration at his father's paper-thin encouragement. "They're not in a conference room, they're in Devereux's office."

Henry stormed down the hallway, his shoes silent on the carpet. Lauren followed close behind.

As they neared the office, Lauren heard Cyrus through the closed door. Henry put his hand on the doorknob, but before he could open the door Lauren reached in and stopped him.

"I know you don't like this, Leo." Cyrus raised his voice. "Neither do I! But we've made the best decision, now let's not second-guess ourselves. It's the best option. We can't risk any more lives with this fiasco. If they can get it down in the lake then we've solved all our problems. The brain-dead people will die. It's probably best for them anyway, don't you think? We can dodge that public relations bullet. Do you have any idea what the press would do to us? The public is desensitized to airplane crashes; the sight of body bags on the evening news only stays with them until their favorite reality show starts. But can you imagine the public's reaction to the images of those people being led off our airplane? You've poured your guts into this airline, Leo. The crash isn't our fault! We'll be absolved of any wrongdoing. We might also be able to point our finger at the guy from Eco-Watch. We can't be responsible for civilians who think they can fly our planes. The casualties will be the victims of an outdated air traffic control system." Cyrus softened his tone. "Leo, I can picture us spearheading the move for some meaningful policy decisions in Washington. It could go down as the Singer Aviation Safety Bill. You could lead the way for decisive action that makes our skies safe into the next century. We have the connections to get that ball rolling."

Lauren was both horrified and sickened at what she'd heard. Cyrus was talking about trying to pin part of the blame on Donovan and Eco-Watch. She felt for her cell phone.

"What are you doing?" Henry whispered.

"This is bullshit!" Lauren struggled to keep her voice low. "I have to reach Donovan. These people are trying to kill them. He needs to know."

"Not yet! Give me a second to think," Henry said, trying to calm her down. "There has to be a way to get Cyrus away from Leo. He's like some of deranged seeing-eye dog and Leo is being led to slaughter."

Lauren started to say something, but hesitated as a vague idea sparked to life. She tilted her head to one side and looked at Henry. "What did you just say?"

"I have to create a diversion, something to get Cyrus away from Leo. Then I can try to convince Leo he's being manipulated."

"You called Cyrus a seeing-eye dog," Lauren said, letting the words hang as her scientific brain began to hastily connect the separate pieces of the puzzle.

"Yeah, so what," Henry replied. "It's the truth. Leo's blinded by the crap that Cyrus feeds him."

"That's it!" Lauren began, then quickly ushered Henry away from the door and around the corner. She looked up and down the hallway to make sure they were alone.

"What are you trying to say?" Henry said impatiently.

"We can be 880's seeing eye dog." Lauren locked eyes with Henry. More than anything she needed for him to hear what she was about to say. "If we get another airplane, we could go up and get them—lead them down to the ground. It's possible—right?"

Henry stepped back as if her words had some sort of tangible force. His eyes narrowed as he processed what she'd just said. "How good is this flyboy fiancé of yours? Was he ever in the military?"

"No. He's always been in the private sector." Lauren saw the flash of disappointment that crossed Henry's face. "Why?"

Henry shook his head. "The problem is your boyfriend doesn't have any flight time in airliners, or military formation experience. With John out of the picture, I don't know if it could be done. Flying formation in this weather is harder than you can imagine. I just need to get to Leo."

Lauren watched as Henry Parrish seemingly dismissed her idea and turned to leave. Desperate, Lauren reached out and grabbed Henry by the arm. "Wait."

"Let go," Henry said, pulling his arm out of her grasp. "I have to get in there and break up that meeting."

"What if the Donovan had the skills—would you do it?"

"I'm sure you think your fiancé is a wonderful pilot, and all of that, but what you're asking would be almost impossible for someone with no military background."

Lauren bit her lip as she fought with herself. Henry was starting to leave and she knew she only had one shot at this. "What if you *did* know the man at the controls of flight 880?"

Henry stopped. "What do you mean?"

"A long time ago…and you have to promise me that what I'm about to tell you will go with you to your grave."

"What are you trying to say?"

"Do I have your word?" Lauren said. She didn't have time to measure all of the repercussions of what she was about to say. But it didn't matter at this point. She needed Henry to see that Donovan was more than capable of pulling off this plan.

"Sure." Henry held out his hands as if he had nothing to lose.

Lauren trembled as she thought about the solemn promise she'd made to Donovan—a promise she was now about to break. "The man flying 880 is someone you used to know, but you knew him by another name—Robert Huntington."

Henry opened his mouth as if to speak but no words escaped.

"Does that change your mind?"

"That son-of-a-bitch!" Henry whispered, his anger clearly evident. "You're trying to tell me he didn't die all those years ago? I can't believe this!"

"Forget everything that happened back then. What I want to hear is that now that you know—tell me he's good enough for what we have in mind."

"You're telling me he faked his death, then left me to answer all the questions about why his plane crashed? That he had the unmitigated gall to hang me out to dry and clean up the mess he left behind."

"What are you talking about?" Lauren was truly shocked at the furious expression on Henry's face. "Henry, will this plan work?"

"The bastard wanted the world to think he died in a plane crash—I should grant him his wish!"

Lauren was blindsided by Henry's fury. "Look, I don't know everything that happened back then, but we've got bigger issues at stake here. Put all that behind you and think of the people on flight 880—what Cyrus is trying to do."

"I can't believe he betrayed me." Henry's voice dripped with anger.

Lauren recoiled at not only the force of the words but the implications. She tried to gather herself; whatever had gone on between Donovan and Henry was ancient history as far as she was concerned. She leveled a dead-serious glare at Henry. "I asked you a question. Is Robert Huntington good enough?"

"Yeah. He's good enough." Henry nodded, his face red with bitterness and resentment. "But we need to move fast. Stay close, you're the only way I can talk to that S.O.B. I'll try and save his ass—but I'll never forget everything he did to me." He lowered his voice and pointed his index finger at Lauren. "And trust me, if we do pull this off and I get him on the ground—I might decide to kill him for real."

Lauren sidestepped Henry as he stormed down the hallway toward Operations. As they rounded the corner, Lauren saw that the door to Devereux's office was wide open. A sick feeling lodged in her stomach as she realized that at some point during her and Henry's conversation, Cyrus and Leo had left. Had they heard any or all of what was being said?

Henry waved her forward. "Forget it. If they heard about our plan we'll know shortly, trust me, we won't get very far. Once we get to Operations, we're going to have to find some help. Do what I say and don't ask questions."

Lauren, angered at Henry's words, nevertheless stayed close as they hurried to Operations. She scanned the room but didn't see either Leo or Cyrus. Henry immediately went to where Matt and Tucker stood.

"What's going on? What happened?" Matt said, reacting to the grim expression etched on his father's face.

"We're going to take an airplane and go get 880," Henry said, quietly but with conviction. "I'm going to need some help."

Lauren felt galvanized by his words

"I need to find a plane." Henry lowered his voice and glanced warily around him as he spoke. "One that's already been fueled, and hopefully not buried in snow. Once we know which gate, we need to get there as fast as we can."

"I take it Leo didn't sign off on this?" Tucker whispered.

"I didn't even ask," Henry said in a rush. "For some really screwed-up reasons—Cyrus wants this airplane in the lake. I don't have time to explain it all right now, but trust me, this is the right thing to do."

"I'm in," Tucker offered. "John's a good friend of mine. You're going to need another pilot."

"I was hoping you'd say that." Henry clinched his fist. "Matt, once I get a gate number, I want you to go there and start getting the plane ready. Move any ground equipment that might be in our way."

"Sure." Matt nodded as if it were no big deal. "What about the security cameras? Someone in Operations might see what we're doing."

"I forgot about them," Henry said. "Hopefully it's snowing too hard for anyone to notice."

"What can I do?" Lauren's hope surged as Henry began to set things in motion.

"You need to call 880 and tell them we're coming. But let's wait a few minutes before we do that." Henry paused as he thought. "Tucker, you and Matt start toward the H concourse. We'll call and give you a gate number as soon as we have one."

"See you shortly." Tucker and Matt quickly made their way as instructed.

Henry stepped over to a computer terminal and began typing on the keyboard. Lauren moved closer and used herself to shield the rest of the room as to what Henry was doing. Several minutes later Henry logged off and looked around.

"H-18," he said quietly. "It was fueled to go to Dallas and was one of the last flights cancelled. It should have less snow on it than some of the others."

Lauren pulled out her phone and sent the information as a text message to Matt's cell phone. A few moments later, her phone beeped that he'd received the information.

"Let's go." Henry took her by the arm as he scanned the busy room. He grabbed a two-way radio and shoved it into his back pocket.

"Do you think we can get airborne before anyone notices we're stealing an airliner?" Lauren was relieved that the others in the room were too preoccupied to be listening. Without knowing where Leo and Cyrus were, or if they had any inkling as to what she and Henry were trying to do, they slipped out of the room into the nearly deserted concourse.

Lauren led Henry into a deserted gate. "We need to let them know we're coming." Safely away from anyone who might eavesdrop, she pulled out her cell-phone and dialed Donovan.

Henry looked expectantly into Lauren's eyes as they waited for 880 to answer. "I just hope Robert Huntington is as good a pilot as he used to be."

CHAPTER TWENTY

Donovan braced himself for Audrey's reaction. She was the first person from his past that he'd had to confront face to face. The first person from his previous life to whom he'd admitted his deepest secret.

With her left arm Audrey swung an open hand toward Donovan's cheek. Donovan, reacting even faster, grabbed her wrist mid-flight and held on as she expended her fury.

"Let me go!" Audrey cried out as she squirmed to free herself.

"Only if you promise to talk—not hit," Donovan said calmly. He knew she probably had the right to be angry, though he wasn't sure what she might be most angry about—that he'd deserted them all—or that she'd tried to seduce him and he'd turned her down.

Audrey massaged her wrist after Donovan released her. "You bastard, you had that coming."

"Did I?" Donovan needed to select his words carefully, he needed to let her calm down and do the talking. He recognized that this might be most important conversation of his life.

"I can't believe you faked your death," Audrey said, visibly upset. "You let the entire world—including those closest to you, think you were dead. Then what? You simply run off to some deserted tropical island. What do you think you accomplished?"

Donovan said nothing as he thought back to the night she'd showed up at his hotel room on some flimsy pretense that there were some papers for him to sign. For several months after Meredith's death he'd been living in various hotels. He felt isolated and lonely in his own house, plus the protesters and reporters were always gathered outside. Audrey had come over late and knocked at the door to his suite. He'd been surprised at her arrival and as he looked at the papers she'd brought, he realized there was no real reason his signature couldn't wait until morning. When he gazed up at her, the seductive expression on her face told him she was there for something else. He finished signing the papers and was putting them back in the folder when she moved in and closed the distance between them. She'd openly asked him if he wanted her—if so, she'd stay the night. He knew she was seeing Henry. Though her affair with Henry was supposed to be hush-hush, it was really not a closely held secret. Donovan had been appalled by her arrogance; that she had essentially barged in on him with the intent of screwing him. He was even angrier that she would do that to Henry. In retrospect, he might have handled it a little better than he did. But he'd gripped her by the upper arm and escorted her firmly toward the hallway. Without a word, he'd shoved her and closed the door.

"You had the world in the palm of your hand. Rich, famous, and talented—I don't get it? Why?"

"You remember the death threats, the private security that I had to employ to make sure no one close to me became another kidnapping target. There were almost daily threats to the people around me. You knew all about that, you were there—why are you so upset? The minute I died all of that insanity stopped."

She looked at Donovan, her head tilted slightly as if sizing him up. "You don't think I'm angry because you wouldn't sleep with me are you? Don't flatter yourself. I was a young woman back then, you were a wounded man, but the chance to bed the famous billionaire Robert Huntington was just too good to pass up. Trust me, it would have been my prize, not yours. I know what you're thinking, yes, Henry and I had been seeing each other, but it wasn't that serious yet. And to answer your next question, no, Henry never knew."

A hundred questions flew through his mind. Despite her words he knew every woman hated to be told no, especially attractive, intelligent, aggressive ones.

"Are you still wondering why I'm so goddamned furious at you? I'll tell you why—you nearly killed Henry," Audrey said as she sought out his eyes with her own. "After your accident, the months rolled by and you left him holding the proverbial bag—it nearly did him in. He and I had become very close by then, and I swear, you'd be hard pressed to find anyone who took your death harder than he did."

"I know," Donovan replied as he remembered back to that time. To how, in the end, he was finally forced to orchestrate Henry's termination.

"They kept coming at him, the Federal Aviation Administration, the National Transportation Safety Board, the media. The same questions over and over, how had the plane you were flying crashed? Was it an accident, murder, suicide? Henry, as your chief pilot, was the go-to-guy as far as anyone cared. God knows he felt responsible. He was devastated, and you're accountable for that."

"I didn't expect it to happen the way it did," Donovan said honestly, but he also knew he'd never in a hundred years be able to explain it to her satisfaction. Why he'd done what he did.

"Was it really so awful back then? Was leaving your only option?"

"I've asked myself the same question for the last eighteen years," he answered firmly, his voice filled with conviction. "The answer is yes."

"You and Henry shared a bond the rest of us didn't have. You both loved your goddamned airplanes. After you died, he tried to mourn with the rest of us, but he was sucked into the post-crash investigation. I don't think I've ever seen him more troubled, or lost, but he was forced to delve into every painful aspect of the disappearance of your plane. I honestly think at times, he felt like he'd somehow had a hand in your death."

"I understand that," Donovan said quietly. "It wasn't fair...none of it was. But it had to be that way. It was my hope that Henry would stay on with Huntington Oil, but as he became more and more entrenched into the investigation of my death, he became a liability. If you remember, at one point he wanted the FAA to recover the plane, which would have been a disaster. Post-crash analysis would have raised plenty of suspicions as to whether or not I was on board when it hit the water. I had no choice except to let him go." Donovan stopped talking, there was probably no way he could explain everything that had happened back then. He also doubted that she'd be receptive to hearing the other side of the story, how he'd helped Henry rebound from being let go from Huntington

Oil. All of the behind-the-scenes maneuvering he'd accomplished on Henry's behalf. He hoped there would be time for that—later.

Audrey swallowed hard "There is so much to ask, so many things I want to know." She paused, her curiosity finally overcoming her anger.

Donovan was about to answer when the cell phone in Audrey's hand sprang to life. She looked down at the caller ID, then back up at Donovan. "It's someone named Lauren."

"Give it here," Donovan said quickly and took the phone. "Hello."

"Donovan, can you hear me?" Lauren's voice was scratchy but audible.

"Are you still in the tower? Did you find someplace for us to go?" Donovan knew she didn't call to chitchat.

"I can't talk long." Lauren kept her voice low. "I'm with Henry. We're on our way to get another airplane ready to go. We're going to take off, fly up and rendezvous with you. We think it'll be possible for you to fly in formation with us, follow us all the way to the runway."

Donovan sat straight up in his seat as he processed the words. "Tell Henry he's a genius!"

"It was my idea, actually," Lauren said. "The down-side is the airline doesn't know we're doing this—in fact, I overheard one their executives, Cyrus Richtman, he's the CEO, saying that he wants you to crash in the lake. There's a lot of ugly corporate maneuvering going on here. But the bottom line is Cyrus wants you to crash so he can oust Leo Singer and takeover the company. I also heard him say that he thinks he can place part of the blame on you and Eco-Watch."

"You and Henry do whatever it takes."

"I hope you mean that," Lauren replied. "I'm sorry, but I had to tell Henry who you are, that you could do this, otherwise he wouldn't even have attempted it. It worked, but he's not too happy you're alive."

"I understand," Donovan said, then took a deep breath and looked at Audrey. He understood enough about human nature to know that it would be a miracle if his long-held secret would remain in this small circle of people.

"Henry says to sit tight, no matter what Devereux says, and we'll be there inside the half hour."

"We'll be here." Donovan squinted at the setting sun. Henry was pushing it if they were going to get this thing on the ground before it was completely dark.

"I love you, Donovan," Lauren said, her voice full of warmth.

"I love you, too," Donovan said, then the connection went dead.

"Who was that? Who is Lauren?" Audrey probed. "What's going on?"

"Lauren is my fiancée." Donovan turned and smiled for the first time in what felt like days. "Seems she and Henry are stealing a jet to come up here and lead us home."

"They're what?" Audrey shook her head as if she hadn't heard correctly.

"It's brilliant. Once they get here, we'll join up with Henry's plane and follow them all the way through the storm to the runway. We'll use his instruments to make it to the runway."

"And Lauren? She's your fiancée? How is it possible she's with Henry?"

"She was waiting for me at O'Hare. They found each other." Donovan wondered what Audrey was thinking.

"Did you ever marry?"

Donovan shook his head solemnly. "No, but I finally found Lauren, and she's wonderful, well worth the wait. I can't imagine my life without her."

"Does she know who you are?"

"Yes, I finally had to tell her," Donovan said, then paused. "We also have a daughter, Abigail. She's almost a year and a half old."

"Good for you." Audrey's wistful smile dissolved quickly into a heartbreaking expression of pain and sorrow.

"What's wrong?" Donovan asked, perplexed by the haunted look on her face. In the last few minutes she'd gone from white-hot rage, all the way through the emotional spectrum to quiet desperation. Donovan knew it went far deeper than just being in this airplane and coming face to face with him.

"Henry and I had a daughter. Her name was Megan. We lost her to leukemia," Audrey said, her voice choking as she spoke. "It been almost two years now."

"I'm so sorry." Donovan lowered his head.

Audrey smiled bravely. "Thank you, but I shouldn't have brought it up. When Megan died is when I lost Henry."

"I don't understand." Donovan replied, he waited to see if she would continue.

Audrey averted her gaze and looked out the window. "No, I didn't lose him in the literal sense, but it was the beginning of the end for our marriage. The day Megan, passed, was also the day I think our relationship died. It took a long time for our marriage to die, it takes a while for a marriage to die from neglect. Anyway, a few months ago Henry finally moved out and I don't think we're getting back together—it's over. That's why I'm on this flight, I was out in D.C. interviewing for a job. Matt and I might try to start over on the east coast."

Donovan wished there was something he could say, but he was now an outsider. He'd given up that right long ago. He thought about Henry and wondered about the impending confrontation, how would his old friend react when they were finally face to face. That is, if they got that chance.

"Permission to return to the flight deck, Captain." John's voice sounded weak as he inched his way into the cockpit. Audrey quickly got out of the seat and slid sideways, allowing the injured pilot to get past her.

"John. Are you sure about this?" Donovan eyed his bandages; his right hand and most of his left arm were covered in plastic. Blisters on the side of his head had already formed. Clumps of burnt, matted hair stood out in stark contrast to his brown locks.

"I'm sure. I don't know how much help I can be, though." John eased himself down slowly into the left seat. He let out a stifled moan, beads of sweat glistening on his brow. "There. I'm okay." He turned to Donovan, his breath coming in shallow, rapid gasps. He wiped his forehead with his good arm. "I always knew I'd hate being on fire," he said, forcing a grim smile.

Donovan studied John carefully. "I can't believe you can even move."

"Rafael's pretty clever. He wrapped most of this in plastic, he then taped it tight at each end. He says with burns, it's the oxygen that causes the worst pain. Believe me, it still hurts and my right hand isn't good for much. But I can use this one." John fastened his harness, and then triumphantly rested his left hand on the controls. He tested his abilities by flexing his joints. "I don't think I can do much more than fly straight and level. But I'd sure like it back for a little while."

"You've got it then." Donovan let him take the controls of the airliner. "We just got a phone call from Henry. We're going to have company soon."

"What?" John shot Donovan a questioning glance.

"Seems Henry is borrowing another airplane to come up and lead us home. He wants us to sit tight."

"I'll be damned!" John said. "You're talking about our flying in formation with Henry's plane—all the way to the ground?"

"Exactly." Donovan tried to measure John's reaction.

John lowered his head in defeat. "I'm afraid it's probably beyond what I can do—one handed."

Donovan nodded grimly—he'd already accepted the fact that he'd be the one who'd have to do the delicate flying.

"I've been watching you though; you're a natural. From coming up here in the first place, to flying us back on top of the clouds after our first approach." John arched his eyebrows. "How do you feel? Do you think you can fly what's left of this plane?"

"You bet," Donovan said with more confidence than he felt. He knew it was difficult to fly in tight formation under ideal conditions. In this blizzard, with this 737, the task was far from ideal.

"Then we'll wait here for Henry." John turned to Audrey, and forced a lopsided grin. "Your husband is now officially my favorite person."

"There's one other small detail." Donovan could feel the cloak of doom evaporating from the cockpit. They now had a new, legitimate chance to survive. "Henry is stealing the airplane. For whatever the reasons— management, or whoever is in charge down there isn't behind this plan. Someone named Richtman wants to use our crash to oust Leo Singer. So, we need to keep this under wraps from Devereux."

"God, I hate Richtman," John said angrily. "But it sounds about right for the total idiots we have running this airline. No balls—and no imagination."

"Donovan!" Rafael's excited voice called out from behind them. Moments later the young student stuck his head into the cockpit.

"What's the problem?" Donovan glanced at both John and Audrey.

"Keith caught Wetzler breaking into the liquor. Wetzler attacked him and now he's barricaded himself in one of the lavatories and won't come out."

"John, can you fly the plane without me for a little bit?" Donovan asked, abruptly.

"Yeah, sure."

"Audrey, you stay here," Donovan said. He threw off his harness, hoping she understood he wanted her to stay up front and watch their injured captain.

"Go! I'll be fine," John said, and shrugged painfully. "If I need you I'll rock the wings back and forth like we talked about before."

"After you take care of Wetzler, we could use another phone," Audrey said. She gave Donovan a discreet nod that she understood her job. "Your phone is nearly dead, as are the other two we have."

"I'll see what I can do." Donovan rose from his seat. "Where's the crash ax?"

John pointed out the ax's location. "You're only going to use that on the door, aren't you?"

"We'll see," Donovan said, grabbing the razor sharp tool. "Trust me. This won't take long."

"I guess not," John added.

Donovan was livid. He ran down the aisle toward the rear of the plane. Sitting on the floor in the aft galley, Keith held a compress to his forehead. Donovan ignored the alarmed expressions of both Christy and Rafael as he positioned himself outside the lavatory. Above the wind noise he could hear Wetzler talking to someone. Donovan stood back and tested the weight of the ax. He measured the point of impact, then with one fluid motion, drove the razor-sharp edge into the thin metal of the door, severing the latch. He yanked the door open and grabbed a terrified Wetzler, and with as much force as he could generate, jerked the man out of the lavatory.

"What the—!" Wetzler blubbered. In his surprise the phone he was using dropped from his hand and clattered to the lavatory floor.

Donovan immediately shoved Wetzler backward into the galley and slammed him hard against the bulkhead. Wetzler's head crashed against the wall, but he quickly gathered his wits and tried to resist the assault. Donovan reached down for the phone, but before he could grab it, Wetzler, screaming obscenities, propelled himself forward.

"You asshole! You can't push me around. I have my rights!"

Wetzler's sudden attack forced Donovan backwards. He put his arms up to ward off the poorly aimed blows as he tried to regain his balance. The stale smell of alcohol enveloped him. He was about to retaliate when Keith's massive arms reached around Wetzler, holding the frenzied man motionless.

Donovan picked up Wetzler's phone. His anger grew when he realized it was smashed. He tossed it to the floor and spotted the half-dozen empty vodka miniatures that Wetzler had pilfered from the galley. He turned and glared at the pathetic, red-faced Wetzler, struggling in vain against Keith's grip. "You had a phone the whole time we were looking for one and didn't say anything?"

Keith tightened his hold until Wetzler cried out in pain.

"I would've given you mine, but you found one!" Wetzler sputtered.

"You're useless!" Donovan resisted the urge to strike the man.

Wetzler tried once again to squirm free. "I'll make you pay for this!"

Donovan shook his head. "No you won't. If we live through this, I'm having you charged with interfering with a flight crew—it's a felony."

"Go to hell!" Wetzler screamed, twisting and flailing. He kicked his legs and caught Donovan on the shin just below the knee.

Donovan looked at Wetzler, staring into defiant, crazed eyes. He inspected Wetzler's injured face; the cuts and abrasions barely scabbed over. Donovan picked a spot and hit him hard. With a loud pop that signaled at least a severely broken nose, Wetzler's pupils rolled back and he went limp in Keith's arms.

"Good shot," Keith shouted triumphantly as he tossed Wetzler like so much rubbish into an empty seat. "If you weren't going to, I was. What a piece of shit."

Donovan massaged his stinging fist as the pain dissipated.

"I can't believe he attacked me," Keith said as he touched the fresh gash on his forehead.

Donovan leaned down and cinched up a seat belt around the unconscious man. "I don't think he'll cause any more problems."

Donovan felt everyone's attention riveted on him, he saw their scared faces, waiting for him to say something. "Just so everyone is on the same page, I need to bring you up to date. In about half an hour we're going to be joined by another airplane. The plan is for us to fly in close formation with the other plane and follow it down and land at O'Hare. Audrey will come back and be in charge of the emergency evacuation. It might be smart to gather up all the pillows you can find and use them to brace yourselves for an emergency landing. When all of this happens—and I mean this—save yourselves first. Don't worry about Wetzler, or the others. Just do what Audrey tells you to do, and get out of the plane."

"Could this really work?" Rafael furrowed his brow, his expression one of guarded optimism.

"Yes," Donovan replied quickly. "Formation flying is done all the time in the military. Have you ever seen the Blue Angels, or the Thunderbirds? They do it with up to six airplanes at a time. Two is a piece of cake."

"In the middle of a blizzard?" Keith asked.

Despite the legitimate concern, a small glimmer of hope began to etch itself on the faces of the survivors. Donovan didn't want to even contemplate what it must be like for them to sit back here—with the dead and near-dead—waiting.

"Yes," Donovan said, to reassure them. "We'll be able to see the other plane in the clouds."

"Keith?" Christy called out weakly.

"I'll be right there," Keith answered, then turned back to Donovan and lowered his voice. "She's in pretty bad shape. If I leave for more than a minute or so, she's like that. She's in a great deal of pain and every now and then she goes to sleep—or passes out. I'm not sure which. But I have to keep waking her up if she's suffered a concussion. I do know she feels safer if I'm there with her when she's awake."

"Then stay with her," Donovan said, thankful that Keith was helping to hold everything together. "Once we start this, there won't be anything to do until we come to a stop. All you have to do is open either of the aft doors and get away from the plane. We'll be surrounded by emergency personnel within seconds."

"I was wondering…" Keith lowered his voice. "I've been kind of keeping tabs on the engine we looked at earlier. It's still leaking oil. Maybe more than before."

"Don't worry about it." Donovan had almost forgotten about the oil-streaked cowling. "To begin with, these engines hold a lot of oil. If it hasn't shut down yet it'll be fine. If everything works the way I think it will, we'll be on the ground in less than an hour. It's not a problem."

"What if it doesn't work?" Rafael asked.

"If the engine shuts down?" Donovan wasn't exactly sure what Rafael meant.

"No. What if flying in formation doesn't work. Then what?"

"Then we'll go back to plan B, which is to ditch in Lake Michigan."

"Oh." Rafael's eyes went wide and unblinking. "I'm sorry—it's just that I can't swim."

"Rafael, we'll get this airplane down on the ground." Donovan had no intention of explaining that he doubted that the ability to swim would make any difference if they did indeed end up in the lake. "But what might help is if we could find at least one more phone. Is there any place you haven't searched yet?"

"We stopped at row 15," Keith said. "After we found the first few phones, we figured it was enough. Forward of there it gets pretty gruesome, no one wanted to go much further. Those people are pretty messed up. And to be honest, that wind up near the front is nothing short of brutal. Living in Aspen I always hear people talk about how dangerous frostbite and hypothermia is, I know it doesn't take long for it to do major damage."

"Keith, you stay here with Christy and keep an eye on Wetzler. Rafael, I'm hoping you don't mind helping me search those people?" Donovan had seen the carnage, and Keith was right, it wouldn't be pleasant. But he also knew they couldn't afford to lose contact with the outside world.

"I can do that." Rafael held up a finger for Donovan to wait as he kneeled and pulled two sets of surgical gloves from the medical kit. "Probably be safer if we wear these."

Moments later, Donovan had his gloves on and slowly walked up the aisle toward row 15. It was the row with the woman he'd helped earlier. Rafael started on the other side. He noticed that she had her arm through the strap of her purse, which was why it hadn't been sucked out of the airplane. She was next to the window, so he was forced to lean over before putting his fingers around the slender leather strap. He was momentarily startled when he tugged on the purse and the woman fell over on her side, her disheveled red hair parted to reveal a delicate face. Though she appeared to be sleeping peacefully, he knew better, the lack of a blanket marked her as one of the dead. Donovan gently freed her purse. He opened the main compartment and quickly searched the contents. He pulled out a large wallet that was on top and was rewarded as his hand closed around a small cell phone. As he attempted to gently replace the wallet, it fell open and exposed the woman's Virginia driver's license. Her name was Patricia Wheeler. She lived in Centreville, Virginia. Donovan gave it a closer look; he saw her address and knew it wasn't far from where he and Lauren's new home would be. Thoughts of Lauren and Abigail hammered him as he glimpsed a picture of a younger Patricia, in her wedding dress. The groom was tall and handsome; they both seemed to radiate happiness. *Till death do us part.* Donovan thought of his own impending wedding. Would he get the chance to make that same pledge to Lauren?

Donovan considered what Lauren had told him a few minutes ago, how Cyrus Richtman wanted this plane to crash. He was suddenly tired of death, sick and tired of the human destruction around him. He glanced over at Rafael who was going through the passengers' possessions a few rows ahead of him. Donovan slipped Patricia's wallet into her purse and carefully put everything back where he found it. He knew he'd made a mistake by connecting with one of the victims. At some level, deep inside him, he knew the carnage around him had just become personal.

CHAPTER
TWENTY-ONE

"Are we almost there?" Lauren felt like they'd been running forever. There were fewer and fewer people the further out the concourse they'd gone.

"Just around the corner." Henry stopped and waited for her to catch up. As he did, he cocked his head to one side, as if trying to listen to something in the distance. "Quick. This way!"

Lauren, startled at the dramatic shift in Henry's tone, was momentarily confused until she, too, heard the voices. He grabbed her arm and pointed toward the security door that led to the jetway. Henry pulled out his card, swiped it and frantically punched in his code. He threw open the door and motioned for Lauren to follow. Henry then eased the door closed behind them.

"What's going on?" Lauren asked. "Who are they?"

"I think they might be airport police," Henry whispered, he held his index finger to his lips to signal her to be quiet also. "It sounded to me like they were giving voice commands to their dogs."

"Are they looking for us? Or are they just making the rounds?"

Henry shrugged. "I don't know. We're well past the initial security checkpoint. I have a bad feeling. This way." Henry walked softly, yet quickly down the jetway toward the small landing that was connected to the airplane. "Stand here. You should be able to look out this window and see inside the terminal. Let me know how many guards go past that bank of windows to your left."

Lauren positioned herself as instructed. Through a dizzying amount of falling snow she could just make out a sliver of the terminal window Henry was talking about. Behind her she heard a soft click, followed by the unmistakable static of Henry's hand-held radio. He adjusted the frequencies until he found the one he wanted. Lauren finally sorted through the nonstop chatter on the radio.

"That's what I was afraid of." Henry turned the radio off and hung his head. "The fact that 880 narrowly missed the buildings downtown has set off a full-scale security alert. They're shutting down the airport."

"That doesn't change what we're doing does it? I mean we were stealing an airplane anyway—right?" Lauren kept her eyes on the terminal, waiting to catch sight of the security guards.

Henry stood beside her and joined in the vigil. "It does complicate things. We not only have to keep our secret from the airline—but from everyone else as well."

"There they are!" Lauren watched as the two-man security contingent with a German shepherd passed the window. "Now what?"

"We probably need to go the rest of the way outside. They might hear us if we slip back inside the terminal." Henry put his hand on the door. "I wish I'd brought a heavier coat. Are you ready?"

"Let's go." Lauren turned up the collar on her jacket and waited as Henry pushed the door open. Together, they carefully maneuvered down the snow-covered steps to the ground. The snow dampened all sounds except the howl of the wind above them. Henry waded through the knee-deep snow, plowing a path for her as they continued their trek. It felt like an eternity before Lauren could finally make out movement around one of the airplanes. As they neared, she heard the low muffled roar of an APU. She knew enough from all of her experience flying on the Eco-Watch jets, that the auxiliary power unit was needed to get everything else running. Through the heavy snow cascading down from the sky, she understood they'd reached the airplane they were going to steal.

"Go up those stairs." Henry pointed at the jetway. "Get to the cockpit and tell Tucker we're here, explain to him about the security issues. I'm going to try and get us some help de-icing this thing."

Lauren nodded and with frozen toes began to climb the steps. Halfway up she stopped and looked at the airplane's left wing. It's polished metal surface was buried under a thick blanket of snow. Where the wing joined the fuselage, the drifts had risen up to the windows. She stomped up the remaining steps and let herself into the narrow jetway. A moment later, she passed through the main cabin door and into the cockpit where Tucker was seated.

"We're here!" she called out and blew into her hands to get rid of the chill. She stamped her feet to shake loose the melting snow that was beginning to seep into her shoes.

"About time." Tucker said, never taking his eyes from the checklist. "I've got us ready to start engines. Where's Henry?"

"He's outside trying to get us some help de-icing." Lauren scanned the cockpit of the airliner. It was bigger than the Eco-Watch Gulfstreams, but surprisingly, the layout was very similar. The glowing tubes had the familiar blue and brown display that would give the pilots their information about which way was up and down. In the center were the engine and various system read-outs. The center console housed the throttles and radios. She quickly felt at home in the 737.

"I've got the heat all the way up." Tucker adjusted a knob, then peered out the side window for any sign of activity.

"Henry wanted me to tell you that Homeland Security has shut down the airport. He thinks it's from 880's near miss with the buildings downtown. We just saw some security men with their dogs patrolling the concourse."

Tucker gestured to the small headset that he had in his right ear. "I've been listening. I figured out which runway we're going to have to use. We won't have far to taxi, which will help. If this is going to work, we've got be airborne before anyone knows what we're doing."

Lauren nodded, it had been nearly ten minutes since she'd spoken with Donovan. She couldn't imagine what must be going through his mind right now. Was he angry with her for telling Henry his secret, or did he understand that it was the only way Henry would even attempt this? She also wondered if Cyrus and Leo had overheard any of the conversation. She thought of how devastated Donovan would be if the world once again knew who he was. In some ways, the attention would be worse than before—his guilt in the public's eye would now be absolute.

"Does 880 know we're coming?" Tucker asked.

"Yes. I talked to them a little bit ago. They're waiting for us." Lauren hesitated as a different noise invaded the cockpit.

"De-ice fluid." Tucker said as a fine mist blew past the windows on the right side of the jet. "Shouldn't be long now."

Lauren left the cockpit and hurried out to the jetway. She opened the door just as Henry was coming up the stairs. He was covered with heavy, wet snow. Over his shoulder she saw another de-ice truck pull up behind the left wing. Soon, there would be two streams of heated fluid spraying down on the airplane.

"Who's in the trucks?" Lauren asked as Henry stopped and brushed the snow from his shoulders and head.

"Matt is on the right side and Raymond, our field service supervisor, who is an old friend of mine, is on this side. Thank God he was willing to help; he just shaved precious minutes off of the job. How's Tucker doing up front?"

"He says we're ready to start engines." Lauren reached out and removed the last of the snow off Henry's jacket.

Henry glanced down at his watch. "I'm worried about the ramp. The snowplows have made some pretty big ridges out there. I hope the tug can push us back through that mess; otherwise, we're not going anywhere."

"Dad!" Matt came barreling through the door, nearly running over his father.

"What is it?" Henry stepped back to make room for his son in the cramped space.

"I'm out of fluid. Raymond is still shooting. I checked the level on his tank and he's down to less than fifty gallons. We used a lot earlier, before the flights started being cancelled. The nearest trucks are six gates down."

"Damn it!" Henry slammed a fist into his open hand. "We don't have that kind of time. How much snow is still on the wings?"

"I managed to spray the entire surface. It's a slushy mess. I was just starting to blast it off when I ran out."

"It'll have to work. Hopefully it'll just slide off when we start our takeoff roll." Henry moved Matt out of the way and opened the door. He squinted against the driving snow as he surveyed the condition of the wing. "It's probably as good as it's going to get. Tell Raymond to stop. I want him to shoot the rest of his fluid under the plane, so the tug will be able to get enough traction to push us back."

Matt nodded his head that he understood. "Dad, you can go up front. I'll move the jetway back and close the door for you."

Henry leveled his eyes at Matt. "You close it from the outside. Then go with Raymond. You're not coming with us—I don't want you on this plane."

Lauren watched as Henry's words sunk in. Matt looked shocked, then just as quickly he converted it to anger.

"What do you mean—I'm going with you!" Matt said in disbelief.

"It's too dangerous," Henry said. "You're staying here. I'm not even sure I'll be able to get this thing off the ground."

Matt's face contorted into an expression of anger, wordlessly he spun and fled back out into the blizzard.

Henry started to say something else but the door slammed shut. He held out his hand to Lauren. "Give me your phone. Like I explained to Matt, this is dangerous and you'd be better off staying here."

"And getting arrested?" Lauren said as she held her ground. "I'm coming with you."

"Fine. Get inside. I'm going to get the jetway pulled back away from the plane."

Lauren stepped into the galley area. She watched as Henry went to the jetway controls located just inside the large accordion-like opening. First, the canvas of the awning retracted, then the entire steel frame began moving away, but it immediately ground to a halt only inches from where it'd started. Above the howl of the wind, the heavy electric motor strained noisily against the drifted snow. Henry slammed a lever back-and-forth, attempting to coax the structure away from the plane.

"The snow is too deep. I can't get it to move!" Henry cried out, "I have to get us some more help. I'll be back."

Lauren's frustration grew as Henry vanished down the stairs—it seemed like everything was taking far too long. Moments later, he reappeared and jumped across the small chasm between the jetway and the door of the plane.

"Stand back!" Henry ordered as he began to pull the door shut.

A massive crash and the sound of bending, twisting metal assaulted Lauren's ears. The jetway crumpled and lurched away from the plane. Henry latched the door.

"Let's go," Henry said.

"What happened to the jetway?" Lauren asked as Henry peeled off his sport coat and threw it on a seat in first class.

"Matt took the tug and bulldozed it out of the way. We're clear. He's getting hooked up to the tow-bar to push us back. I'd prefer you up front in the jump seat in case we hear from Robert."

"His name is Donovan," Lauren warned. "You can't make that mistake again!"

"I'll try," Henry said, as he headed for the cockpit.

Lauren followed, and within moments the three of them were settled into their seats. Lauren strapped herself in the small jump seat, as Henry and David rapidly went through their checks.

"Give him the signal to start pushing," Henry instructed.

The plane jerked sharply as it began to inch backward. It gained momentum, but just as suddenly it stopped completely. With agonizing slowness, Matt pulled it forward then reversed directions. Once again it started backward, but instantly bogged down in the deep snow.

"Damn it!" Henry slammed his fist on the controls. He leaned forward and gave Matt the signal to disconnect the tug. A long minute passed before Matt was clear of the Boeing.

"What are you thinking?" Tucker ventured.

"I'm going to start the engines and back us out of here with the reverse thrust." Henry settled himself into his seat as he mentally calculated the distances he had to work with.

"That'll be a first," Tucker replied. "I don't think anyone's ever done that before."

"All kinds of firsts today," Henry said.

Lauren leaned forward until she could see Matt out of the side window. He was still sitting in the tug. Her heart went out to him. He'd done so much. She had no doubt he was numb from the cold. He'd wanted to go with them. Henry's words had made sense, though she chafed at the harshness with which they were spoken. As a father, Henry would no doubt do everything he could to protect his only remaining child. For reasons unknown, Henry still viewed him as just a boy, but Lauren couldn't help but consider Matt as someone more man than child.

Lauren was still watching Matt when she spotted at least two security guards, guns drawn, race past a terminal window. A moment later more security people flashed by.

CODE BLACK

"Henry! They're coming. I saw guards coming our way!"

"Shit!" Henry pivoted and scanned the terminal to gauge the threat.

Without thinking, Lauren unfastened her seat belt and ran back to a window in first class. Guards came running down the wrecked jetway. One was jockeying the controls and the other was on his radio while keeping his pistol trained at the main door of the Boeing.

"Henry! They're at the door!" Lauren's control was slipping away. She and Henry weren't terrorists; they weren't a threat to anything but the carnage that Cyrus wanted to inflict on flight 880. Behind her, near the rear of the plane, a door opened loudly. She spun around, expecting security personnel to begin storming the plane to arrest them. Lauren wanted to scream for them to stop—to let her and Henry explain what they were trying to do.

"This way!" a voice shouted from the rear of the plane. "Hurry!"

Lauren tried to make sense out what she was seeing. Somehow, Matt was in the back of the plane—motioning frantically for her to follow.

"They're coming! We don't have much time!" Matt yelled.

In a near panic, Lauren raced for the cockpit. "Henry! Matt's given us a way out! Come on!" As she turned to lead the way, a series of loud reports sounded just outside the door.

"What was that?" she yelled at Henry.

"They're shooting the tires!" Henry shouted as he scrambled out of the cockpit, Tucker was ten feet behind him.

The metal handle on the main door began to turn; Security was seconds away from bursting into the cabin.

"Jesus!" Tucker ducked out of the cockpit as Henry and Lauren fled toward the rear of the plane.

Shouts erupted and Lauren's panic rose to levels she didn't know existed. She'd never been shot at before. She felt as vulnerable as she'd ever been in her entire life. Behind her a vividly bright light flashed—followed by a deafening explosion. The concussion wave nearly pushed her to the ground as it ripped through the cabin. Tucker cried out as he fell heavily in the aisle.

"Go!" Henry yelled through clenched teeth.

Lauren reached the back of the plane with Henry close behind. She held her breath, wondering if at any moment a bullet was going to find its mark. She careened heavily into the aft bulkhead, then pushed herself

171

to the left and bolted toward the open door. Matt was standing below on the hood of the tug, arms outstretched. Without a moment's hesitation, she jumped. Behind her she felt Henry make the same leap.

"Where's Tucker?" Matt yelled.

"Get us out of here!" Henry shouted. "He's not coming!"

Matt expertly swung himself behind the wheel. He waited impatiently as his two passengers piled into the cramped cab—then tromped on the gas pedal. At least for the moment their actions had gone unnoticed by the horde of security people in the jetway. Lauren hung on with all of her strength as they lurched away from the bullet-riddled jet.

The tug wasn't made for speed; Lauren guessed they were only going twenty miles per hour. Matt did his best to keep equipment and airplanes between them and the security forces. They ran without lights as they vanished into the raging blizzard. Matt kept his foot on the gas as they rumbled under jetways, airplane wings, around scores of baggage containers and other equipment. They powered through a small tunnel beneath the concourse as they made their escape.

Lauren's ears were ringing from the explosion in the airplane. She turned to Henry. "What in the hell was that?"

"I'm not sure," Henry said, shaking his head. "I think it's what they call a flash-bang grenade. It's used to both blind and disorient people in a closed space. We were lucky we were as far away from it as we were."

"What about Tucker?" Lauren swallowed to try to clear her ears.

"They have him. But I'm pretty sure those things don't cause serious injury." Henry sat up straighter and focused his gaze out the window. "Hopefully, we'll be able to do something for him later. Matt, pull over under that 767."

"What now?" Lauren said as Matt stopped the tug under the wing of the wide-bodied jet.

Henry was shivering. All he had on was his shirt and a light sweater. In their rush to escape, he'd left his coat in the airplane. "Where are we?"

"We're two gates from the main terminal," Matt said, confidently. "Tell me where we need to go and I can get us there."

Henry wiped at the frost that was forming on the window. "I don't know what to do. They'll be watching every airplane at the terminal, we'll never have a chance." He turned to Lauren. "You said earlier you have a Gulfstream at Midway airport?"

"Yes, but if my friend Michael can't get to O'Hare—what chance do we have of getting to Midway?"

"Dad, in the maintenance hanger there's a Boeing 737. It's been signed off for flight status. We were about to go reposition it when the flights began to cancel, I'll bet it's still there."

"Son, are you sure?"

"Yeah, I can't imagine anyone moved it. We were going to bring it over to H-20, but that gate was still occupied by another plane. It still has to be there!"

"Let's go!" Henry said.

Without another word, Matt stepped on the gas and once again they barreled from under the parked jet into the full force of the storm. None of them spoke as Matt carefully threaded the tug through the maze of parked airplanes and ground support equipment.

"We need to try to stay under the terminals," Matt yelled over the roar of the tug. "They won't be able to see us and there's no snow there, no tracks for them to follow."

"How far away is this hangar?" Lauren asked as Matt pulled to a sudden stop near an American Airlines gate.

"It's across the airport. Up on the north side," Henry replied, then turned to Matt. "Why are we stopping?"

"This thing is too slow. We'll never get anywhere." Matt put the tug into park and pointed straight ahead. "Let's trade this in for that."

Matt was pointing at a blue, dual cab Ford pickup truck with an American Airlines logo painted on the side. It was tucked under the concourse and was relatively free of snow.

"The keys are always in these things." Matt threw open the door to the tug.

Lauren thought it made perfect sense and followed Matt without waiting for Henry's approval. She briefly entertained the idea that they might be able to bluff their way through Security in another airline's vehicle. But in her heart she knew the entire airport was probably looking for a man, a woman, and maybe even a teenager. They would need to get to where they were going without being spotted.

Henry slid behind the wheel, found the keys in the ignition as Matt had promised, cranked the engine, and gunned the accelerator. He put the truck into gear and carefully maneuvered away from the Wayfarer tug.

"Matt, what's the best way to Terminal One?" Henry found the windshield wipers and switched them on to clear the snow that was quickly covering the glass.

"Go under there and make a left on the other side of that MD-80," Matt said immediately. "From there we can stay close to the terminal and hopefully no one will be able to see us."

"Matt, do you know how to work this thing?" Lauren gestured to the two-way radio that was jammed up against her knees in the middle of the cramped bench seat. "Maybe we can hear what's going on."

"Cool. Good idea." Matt reached down and brought the unit to life. "It's set to the ground control frequency. I wonder if we could use this to give them some sort of fake report of where we've gone."

"I love it!" Lauren called out and handed the microphone to Henry. If there were a transmission it would have to be from an adult male; neither she nor Matt would be believable.

"Let's wait and listen." Henry pushed the microphone away as he drove the stolen truck through a tunnel and came out on the north side of Terminal Two. Dead ahead, nearly obscured by the snow, lay United Airline's two gigantic concourses.

Lauren had no idea how O'Hare was laid out. She only knew that they were running out of time.

"If we could go straight across from here, it would only take us five minutes," Henry explained. "The problem is that we have to cross this large expanse of ramp, plus two runways. Someone in the tower will surely see us on the surface radar, but I think that's a risk we'll have to take."

"Wait! What if we see how many friends we have in the tower?" Lauren reached into her pocket for the slip of paper Kate had given her earlier. "This is the direct number to the cab. It might be worth a try."

Henry took a deep breath as he thought.

"If they're no help, we'll just hang up." Lauren brought out her cell phone and began to dial.

"Sure. Why not?" Henry put the truck into park. "Go ahead. But be careful what you say until we know what side they're on."

"Don't worry." Lauren put the phone to her ear and held her breath as it rang through.

"Tower. Koski here."

"Hello, Wayne," Lauren said, remembering his first name. "My friend and I were in the tower a little while ago. I'm sure you remember us."

"Yes. Go ahead." Wayne replied, guardedly.

"Have you figured out what we're trying to do?" Lauren could picture the scene. Devereux was no doubt standing close, waiting, and watching all of the activity in the tower.

"I have a fair idea," Wayne said, again using his business voice. "All I can say at this time is the airport is shut down due to security concerns. I'm going to give you another number for that. Maybe they can help you."

Lauren memorized the number that Wayne gave her. She hung up and quickly dialed. Moments later a female voice answered.

"Hello," Lauren said, tentatively. "Wayne gave me your number, said we should talk."

"Is this who I think it is?" Kate replied, an air of caution in her voice.

"Yes." Lauren wasn't going to use names.

"I'm on a quick break," Kate explained. "Wayne knows I always take my cell phone. What can I do for you?"

"I guess you know we're in a bit of a bind?" Lauren wasn't sure how much to divulge.

"That's putting it mildly," Kate said dryly. "I would have thought you'd be in custody by now. Though I do have to hand it to you two, it was a pretty bold plan."

"We're not finished yet. Please tell me 880 is still flying."

"Yeah. Last I heard they're getting everything settled before they go for the lake. They're going to call in ten or fifteen minutes so we can start. It's why I'm on a quick break. Wayne wants me back before—."

"I'm going to level with you. We have one more option, but we need to somehow get from the main terminal to Wayfarer's maintenance hanger. There's another airplane there we can use to go get 880. What we need to know is, will we be seen as we try to cross the runways?"

"Yes," Kate said as a matter of fact. "But it will be Andy who sees you first. If you give me three minutes, I'll get up there and have a word with him. I can't guarantee anything."

"I owe you so much," Lauren said. "If there's anything I can ever do..."

"You can forget we ever had this conversation." Kate's tone turned serious. "I'm sticking my neck out a mile here, and I can't promise this will even work. They've shut down the entire airport and I know they're looking everywhere for you. I believe in what you're trying to do, but I can't be a part of it. Especially if it's on our landlines, or the open frequencies. Everything is taped and saved. The procedures are very strict and I'll abide by them at all costs. Do I make myself clear?"

"Perfectly," Lauren said.

"Give me three minutes—then make a run for it. It's the best I can offer."

Lauren was about to thank her, but Kate was gone. She turned to Henry as she looked at her watch. "In three minutes we go. There are no guarantees, but we might not get thrown to the wolves."

Matt cranked up the volume on the truck's radio to see if the three of them could piece together all of the chatter. For the most part it was Andy talking to the snow-removal teams from the tower. Each seemed to have a different designation, but there was someone with the call sign "Snow One", who seemed to be in charge of relaying the results of the team's efforts. Lauren watched anxiously as the second hand slowly ticked across the face of her watch.

"Snow One," Andy said, his voice transmitted from the tower. "I'm thinking we should give runway 32 Left one more pass, then we can start worrying about runway 27 Left again. Before I forget, remind me to get some people up toward the north maintenance hangars."

"That's the cue! He's doing it!" Lauren cried out. "Henry. Go!"

Henry threw the truck into gear and stepped heavily on the accelerator. The wheels spun and the tail end fishtailed as the tires sought, then gained purchase and propelled them forward. Drifts on the inner ramp stood almost two feet deep in places, but Henry never let up as he plowed through them. The truck slid and skidded as they raced across the ramp to the large expanse of concrete that separated them from their destination.

Lauren put one hand on Matt and used the other to brace herself against the ceiling as the truck bounced and jumped over the ridges. Henry seemed to know where he was going as he yanked the wheel first one way then the other. The world outside was nothing but snow. In a matter of seconds, she became hopelessly disoriented.

"Dad! Look out!" Matt yelled as a huge snow bank appeared out of nowhere.

"Hang on!" Henry said through clenched teeth as he slammed the brakes and tried to steer away from the obstacle.

Lauren was thrown against Matt as the truck swerved to the left and careened sideways into the mountainous drift. In an instant they were airborne, followed by a jarring impact as they rolled over on their side and slid to a stop in two feet of fresh powder. The engine revved, then died. At first all she could see was snow coming down from the sky, then the powerful flashing lights of a vehicle bearing down on them. Lauren struggled to get her weight off of Matt. Henry threw open his door and crawled out. He in turn reached in and grabbed Lauren's hand and helped her climb from cab. Matt followed close behind.

"Everyone all right?" Henry asked as he desperately put his full weight against the cab as if he could somehow right the vehicle.

"We're fine," Lauren replied, and Matt nodded that he, too, was okay. The snow had softened the impact. If the accident had happened on the bare tarmac, there might have been far greater consequences. Matt joined his father in pushing against the truck, but the heavy vehicle wouldn't budge. Closing in fast were two other vehicles, both coming from behind. Another sound invaded her ears and Lauren searched the snow-obscured sky above her. Out of the gloom and mist the unmistakable outline of a helicopter appeared. Its olive-drab color told her in an instant it was an Army chopper. As it hovered closer, she recognized it as a Black Hawk; she'd ridden in them before with her duties at the DIA. Her heart sank at the sight. It was no use running. They were caught. She resisted the impulse to throw her hands up in surrender; instead she put her arms protectively around Matt. As the Black Hawk settled gently into the snow, she thought of Donovan circling in the sky somewhere high above her. She had no way of telling him they weren't coming—they wouldn't have that last phone call she knew they were both counting on. She so wanted to talk to him one more time, to say how much she loved him. But now that was all lost.

CHAPTER TWENTY-TWO

The airplane moved abruptly beneath Donovan's feet. The wings of the 737 rocked back and forth, signaling him to return to the flight deck as fast as possible. In his headlong dash for the cockpit, Donovan glanced up at the ceiling where he'd marked the split in the aluminum; the rupture had advanced at least eighteen inches farther aft from his impromptu smudge. The airplane was continuing to split apart as they flew.

"What is it?" Donovan said as he burst into the cockpit. His practiced eye quickly scanned the horizon outside; the airplane seemed to be under control. He then glanced at John who also appeared to be fine.

"Someone wants to talk with you." Audrey held up Donovan's phone as if it were somehow tainted.

Donovan swept the phone to his ear; from the expression on Audrey's face he doubted this call was good news. "Hello."

"Mr. Nash. This is Cyrus Richtman. We need to talk."

"I'm a little busy right now," Donovan said warily, sensing an ominous tone in Richtman's voice. "What do you want?"

"I'm going to go on the premise that right now you're in a better position to listen than talk." Cyrus paused. "You know, it's not often I get the chance to talk to a dead man—especially such a famous one."

Donovan's anger began to burn, but he remained silent.

"There have been some developments down here that I need to make you aware of. Your friends' little attempt to come to your rescue has failed. Henry and Dr. McKenna are in custody—no one is on the way."

The words hit Donovan hard. "They're not coming?" he said, his thoughts shifting from success to failure. "How? Why?"

"They tried to steal an airplane and were discovered," Cyrus continued. "My guess is they'll be in jail a long time."

Donovan hated the underlying self-confidence Cyrus used as he spoke.

"I want you to get on with landing your airplane in the lake." Cyrus said firmly. "Don't expect any help from me or the airline. Just get it over with!"

"Henry's idea was a good one. Why wouldn't you help—why would you condemn the people aboard this airplane?"

"Interesting choice of words," Cyrus said, chuckling as he spoke. "I would have thought you understood condemnation. If I remember my history correctly, you condemned Meredith Barnes to death all those years ago."

"You son-of-a-bitch!" Donovan snapped before he could reign in his anger. "The two events we're talking about have nothing in common." Donovan ground his teeth and stepped further away from John and Audrey. Somehow Cyrus knew about his past. Frantically, he searched for some edge, some way to get Cyrus to help them. "What is it you really want?"

"If you're thinking about trying to bribe me, forget it," Cyrus said. "What I want is for you to land that goddamned airplane in the lake."

Donovan was about to reply when a beep sounded in his ear. He pulled the phone away and saw the low-battery symbol. He had less than a minute left to talk. "What's to stop me from telling the world what you're trying to do? Leo could still overrule you and launch another airplane."

"He'll do no such thing," Cyrus stated evenly. "The entire city is terrified at the reality of a damaged airliner circling overhead. You almost flew it into the side of the Hancock building. Trust me, no one, especially Leo, will sign off on risking another accident. If you make an attempt to go around me, I'll simply announce to the press who you are, and that you have a daughter in Virginia. Yes, I know about that too, seems in all the excitement, Dr. McKenna left her purse behind."

Thoughts of clutching Cyrus' throat flashed through Donovan's mind. If the world knew Robert Huntington was still alive, the response would no doubt be swift and sure. He made a fist and squeezed hard as he tried to think. His phone beeped a final warning.

"You have no options. Get that airplane down—now," Cyrus whispered, then the connection was lost.

Donovan saw that Audrey was near tears. John kept looking back as he flew, his face a mixture of sadness and resignation. Donovan slid his dead phone into his pocket, then dialed Lauren's number with the phone he'd just found. He listened as it rang, until it went to voice mail.

"They're not coming, are they?" John lowered his head in defeat.

"Let's think this through." Donovan put his hand on Audrey's shoulder as he moved past her and sat down in the copilot's seat. He thought of Michael and the *Galileo II* sitting at Midway, then he remembered Lauren telling him Michael was headed to O'Hare. It would take far too long for them to return to Midway and launch the Gulfstream.

"I hate to say it," John said, his voice far more strained than before. "Maybe they're right. We can't sit here much longer boring holes in the sky, waiting for something that's not going to happen."

"How much fuel do you think we have at this point?" Donovan hated the thought of giving in to Cyrus. But in the face of the facts, and what he'd just heard, they had precious few options.

"We can't have much." John shrugged as he looked at the lifeless fuel gauges. "Plus it's going to be completely dark inside the hour. We need to do something soon."

Donovan gazed out the window as the 737 wheeled in the deserted sky. Below them was the spot that marked the heat island phenomena Lauren spoke of. Through the scattered clouds and driving snow was Lake Michigan. He pictured the maneuver he'd have to perform, the spiraling descent through the opening. He'd have to stay in the tight turn until they were almost to the water. Then at the last second he'd have to point the 737 into the wind, level the wings, and hope they stayed in one piece as they crash-landed. Donovan hated the water; a phobia that stretched back to a near drowning as a teenager, but he remained calm. Their chances of getting out of the airplane were virtually zero. The 737's engines were mounted under the wings and would hit the whitecaps first. If the engines touched the surface of the lake at exactly the same instant they would decelerate quickly. The engines might even shear off from the impact, if they were lucky, it would give them a smooth underbelly with which to skip along the surface until they came to a stop. But in reality, one engine would undoubtedly hit first, and the energy from that would probably cartwheel the airplane. The end would be quick as the 737 broke up around them and sank.

Donovan shook off the thoughts and focused on the job at hand. He knew they were going to have to do something now, or all of their options were going to evaporate. He considered the helpless people in back. If they ditched in the water, they would all drown strapped into their seats. They, out of all the survivors on 880, had no hope at all.

"Donovan?" Audrey leaned forward. "Are you all right?"

"Yeah," Donovan replied. "I'm just trying to figure out what's best."

"It's the damnedest thing," John remarked, solemnly. "Just circling here, waiting to do something that has so little chance of working. I liked Henry's idea; it was a gutsy move. But it doesn't look like that's going to happen."

Donovan slowly nodded as he looked across the cockpit at the injured man next to him. The blood from the wound on his forehead had seeped through the bandage. Despite the wrapping over his burns, John still cringed each time he was forced to move. But whatever injuries the man had incurred, John was still the captain.

"Tell me what you guys are thinking," Audrey said, breaking the silence. "What options are left?"

"You're the captain." Donovan deferred the question to the man in the left seat.

"I'll listen to anything at this point." John waited, but nothing was forthcoming from either Donovan or Audrey. "That's what I was afraid of. I think we should get on with it then. What I don't want to happen is for us to run out of fuel. Then we'd be trying to ditch one really big glider. I don't think I need to remind you what a crappy glider an airliner makes."

"It's decided then," Donovan said. "I should probably go back and break the news to the others. I'll get everyone briefed on what to expect."

"There should be several life jackets in the overhead compartments," John added as Donovan rose to leave. "We don't carry very many, we're not required to in the 737, but find what we have and hand them out."

"Will do." Donovan started to get up.

"Audrey," John said as she, too, started to leave. "Could you stay here for a minute? I need to have a word with you. It won't take long, then you can go back and join the others."

"Sure." Audrey sat back down and let Donovan slide past her.

"Go on," John urged a puzzled Donovan. "She'll be there shortly. I think she should be in back when we do this. It'll be safer."

Donovan exited the cockpit. He had no idea what John could want with Audrey. Carefully, he made his way through the wrecked entryway and slowly walked aft. As he neared the survivors, it became evident that the continued strain was taking its toll. Rafael sat in one of the last rows looking fiercely up at the ceiling, motionless except for the muscles in his jaw, which were working overtime. Across from him sat Keith and Christy; Keith a direct contrast to Rafael. The big man sat with his head lowered, all emotion drained from his face. Christy's hair, fully undone, hung over her eyes, as if she needed one more barrier to separate her from the horror of the cabin. Wetzler was still strapped unconscious in his seat. Donovan knew that they would have to try and rouse Wetzler before they ditched. Like him or not, the man deserved a chance to survive.

Without stopping, Donovan glanced over at Patricia Wheeler. The woman was as he'd left her, eyes shut, still clutching the valuables in her purse. The image of her and her husband served as a grim reminder of the wedding Donovan was supposed to attend, and now most likely wouldn't. He thought of the chance he'd missed to say good-bye to Lauren. He'd make one last attempt before they started, but if she and Henry were in custody, it would probably be in vain.

"Are they here?" Rafael shot to his feet and began looking out the windows, trying to find the other jet they'd been told to expect.

Keith too, began to search the empty sky for the airplane that they hoped would lead them home.

Donovan shook his head as he approached. "It's not going to happen. There were problems on the ground and they're not coming. We're on our own."

Rafael sat heavily, as if a huge weight had pressed him into the seat. He kept his eyes on Donovan. "Does this mean we're going into the water?"

"I'm afraid so." Donovan hated to crush their hopes. "But there is a spot where we can make it all the way to the water without our instruments. We're told that the Coast Guard, as well other rescue elements, will be on the scene. They should be able to get to us quickly after we've come to a stop."

"How do we get out of this thing? Are there life vests, or are we going to have to use the silly seat cushions?" Rafael's eyes darted nervously around the cabin as if he were already imagining being trapped inside a sinking plane.

"Audrey will be back here in a minute or two. Together we'll explain what needs to be done. There should be several emergency flotation vests in the overhead compartments."

"When you open the aft doors," Christy said, raising her good arm and brushing the hair from her bruised face. She pointed toward the rear of the plane; her voice wavered as she tried to be heard. "After the slides inflate; they can be detached from the airplane and you can use them as rafts."

"I'm here." Audrey came running down the aisle toward them. "Did you find the vests yet?"

In a flash, Rafael was up out of his seat as he began to search for the life vests.

"Okay." Donovan pointed at the two aft exit doors. "Before we start, I want each of you to go back and study how to open the door. Memorize it. It's going to get darker as we descend."

"I found three!" Rafael displayed the yellow pouches. He held one close to his chest and dangled the other two out for the others.

"Audrey, you take one, and Keith, you take the other. I trust both of you can swim?"

"I can." Keith grabbed the bag and ripped it open. He gently pulled himself free of Christy, slipped the rubbery fabric over his head, and with some effort fastened the strap around him. Once he'd secured it, he sat back down next to her. "Don't worry, I'll be right here."

"Thank you," Christy said, turning painfully and looking at the others. "Good, you found them all. I'm sorry I can't help much…"

"Like this?" Rafael had mimicked Keith's actions and slid his vest over his head. He fumbled for the straps that hung loosely at his side.

Audrey moved in and helped him secure it properly, then donned her own vest. "What about him?" she asked, motioning toward Wetzler.

Donovan didn't give the unconscious man a second glance. "Once we start our descent, wake him up. Throw water in his face if you need to. But don't let him get in your way. Keith, if he becomes a problem—take him out. I won't have one half-drunk obnoxious passenger jeopardize the rest of you. Are we clear on this?"

"Perfectly," Keith replied as he eyed Wetzler.

"You're all set then." Donovan wanted to say more but found he didn't have the words. He turned to Audrey and it suddenly seemed as if they'd left so much unsaid.

"How will we know when we've started?" Rafael kept pulling at the straps of his life vest, cinching them tighter and tighter. "I mean, when should we brace ourselves?"

"You'll hear the engines get quieter as we reduce the thrust. Then we'll go into a fairly steep bank. We'll be making a series of turns as we spiral down through the opening in the clouds. Once we level the wings you'll be able to see the water. At that point I'd advise you to assume the crash position. I'll expect we'll hit and skip a few times before we come to a full stop. Stay strapped in until you're convinced we've stopped moving. Then get out—fast."

"What about you and John?" Audrey asked.

"We're going to be doing the same thing you are. Once we've come to a stop, John and I will be out the front exit. We'll use one of the emergency slides as a raft." Donovan stretched the truth. He'd already calculated the force of the ditching against what was left of the damaged forward section of the Boeing. He figured the cockpit would shear away from the main fuselage once they hit. It was anyone's guess where he and John would end up in relation to the others. But there would most likely be no emergency slide to get to. He seriously doubted they'd survive the crushing impact.

"Anything else we should know?" Rafael asked nervously.

"I think that covers everything." Donovan guessed that each of them was silently considering their odds of survival. "I'm going back up to the cockpit. Again, once you feel the airplane start a sharp bank you'll know we're starting down. It'll be ten or fifteen minutes from now. John and I will need some time to get things ready up front."

"I'll walk you up," Audrey said as she followed Donovan away from the small band of survivors. They'd gone four rows when she stopped him. He wasn't sure what to expect.

"You know better than I do—but, I'm guessing that our chances really aren't very good, are they?"

Donovan shook his head slowly. He couldn't lie to her.

Audrey bit her lip and stared at the ceiling, fighting back her tears. "If—if somehow you make it and I don't." She took a moment to wipe her eyes. "Tell Henry I'm sorry. I'm sorry that things worked out the way they did. If I—we, could do it differently, I would. Tell him to take care of Matt, I so hope they can somehow find each other again."

"Hopefully you can tell him yourself,"

"I would have liked to meet Lauren," Audrey said, drying her eyes and collecting herself. "I'd like to think maybe we could all be friends— someday."

"Maybe we'll get that chance." The second he said the words he knew they sounded empty and hollow.

"Thank you, Robert." Audrey pulled away. "You'll always be Robert to me—and Robert was nothing if not a survivor."

Donovan watched as she joined the others in the back of the plane. He stood there for a moment as he replayed Audrey's words and wondered if he should have countered her last words with some of his own. He thought of his daughter who might never know him, and Lauren, the woman he'd leave behind. Despite his fatigue and frayed emotions, a small sense of renewed purpose emerged in Donovan as he made his way forward to the flight deck. He negotiated the sharp objects and pulled himself through the opening. To his complete surprise he found John strapped into the right seat. The captain's chair was waiting for him.

"John, are you sure about this?" Donovan said as the wounded pilot turned to greet him. He understood now why John had asked Audrey to stay behind. She'd helped the injured man switch seats.

"I'm in no shape to do what needs to be done," John explained. "I figured you'd be able to fly better from that side."

"You might be right." Donovan slid into the seat and for the first time since he'd charged up to the cockpit, felt an inkling of being at home. He adjusted the seat and his senses took in everything around him. He always flew the Gulfstreams from the left seat; it was where the Captain on a jet was supposed to be. He scanned the horizon. They were headed south. Ahead of them and far below, the small indentation in the clouds marked their destination.

"You got it?" John asked as he prepared to relinquish the controls.

"In a minute," Donovan replied. "Hand me one of those cell phones. I think we should call the tower and let them know we're about to start."

CHAPTER
TWENTY-THREE

As the helicopter's rotor wash enveloped her, Lauren turned away and waited for the intense blizzard created by the spinning blades to subside. She expected a small army of soldiers to leap from the helicopter, guns drawn, to arrest them. Instead, one figure jumped out into the knee-deep snow. Behind them, a snowplow and a four-wheel-drive pickup came to a stop near their overturned vehicle. She glanced at Henry, who appeared as confused as she was.

"Lauren!" the lone figure from the helicopter called but the words were nearly swept away by the wind.

Something seemed familiar as the soldier approached. Was she crazy? Had he called her by name? Lauren squinted as the heavily bundled man closed the distance between them. People were shouting out to them from the other vehicles. Lauren didn't see a single weapon.

"Lauren! Thank God!" Michael Ross pushed up his goggles and swept her into his arms. "I thought I'd never find you!"

In shock, Lauren wrapped her arms fiercely around Michael's neck. His blonde, Southern California good looks and ready smile were always such a comfort. "How did you—?"

"We don't have much time." Michael pulled away. "The tower only let us land because they thought we were part of the security response team here to arrest you three terrorists. Unless you want to meet half the policemen in Chicago, I'd suggest you get into the helicopter!"

"What in the hell is going on here?" a large black man shouted out as he trundled from the truck marked Snow One. With powerful legs, he quickly made his way to the small group. The immense man stared at Henry, the snow falling and lodging in his dark beard and eyebrows. Before he pulled on a thick wool cap, his shaved head reflected the flashing lights from his truck. Intense brown eyes surveyed the scene around him as he slid on his heavy gloves. "Somebody better explain what this is all about. We're standing here in the middle of one of my goddamn runways!"

"We need to get to the Wayfarer hanger," Henry said as he scanned the taxiways to see if they were about to have more company.

"Wayfarer?" the man from Snow One asked, as he leveled his gaze at Henry. "Why?"

"We're with Wayfarer, we borrowed the truck from American Airlines, we're trying to help flight 880," Henry explained, hurriedly. "There's a 737 up there that's running out of time."

"Michael," Lauren said jumping into the conversation as she thought about Eco-Watch's Gulfstream. "How long would it take us to get to Midway and launch the *Galileo II?*"

"Forever," Michael said. "Midway is closed and the Gulfstream is probably covered with at least a foot of snow by now. I gave up trying to keep it ready to fly."

"I have an idea," Lauren said. "But we're going to have to act fast."

"If you have a way to save those people; I'll help get you to the hanger," the man from Snow One said as he stepped closer and listened to what amounted to a conspiracy. After Lauren finished outlining what she thought they should do, he simply nodded his approval, and turned to the driver of the snowplow and barked a series of orders.

"You're brilliant! I'll be right back!" Michael whirled around and ran to the helicopter. "God, I hope this works," Henry said as he whisked Matt and Lauren away from the overturned truck.

The first faint warble of sirens in the distance was drowned out by the noise of the helicopter powering up to depart. Lauren held out her hand to Michael as he fought the downwash from the helicopter. The rotor wash obliterated their footprints as the Black Hawk clawed skyward and vanished into the blizzard.

"Get up there now!" Henry yelled as he, too, heard the approaching sirens.

Quickly, Lauren, Matt, Henry and Michael hoisted themselves up and over the sides of the snowplow and settled heavily into the load of sand that nearly filled the hopper. Lying flat, they were invisible to anyone on the ground. The wail of sirens drew close, followed by the slamming of doors, there were shouts from what sounded like at least a dozen security personnel.

Lauren listened as their savior from Snow One began to explain what he'd seen to the leader of the security force.

"We got here just in time to see some soldiers pile three men into that helicopter and leave," Snow One explained loudly. "It was a Black Hawk. There were guns drawn and everything!"

"Did you say three?" came the heated response.

"It looked like it to me. Whoever they were, the Army has them now. What in God's name is going on around here? And what are you going to do about this truck? I can't have it laying here in the middle of my runway!"

"I'm not at liberty to explain that to you," the voice of the security officer said loudly, full of authority. "This is a crime scene and I'll need you to clear the area."

"Whatever you say. This runway was closed anyway," Snow One said, then yelled to his man. "Get this plow up to the north side and finish what you were doing!"

Lauren lay motionless the security man keyed his radio and asked the tower where the helicopter was headed. They all heard the response. The helicopter was headed south, but they had no idea what its destination was. Lauren held Michael tightly. She couldn't believe he was here with her. Moments later, the snowplow lurched and began to move beneath them. The sounds of the security men faded in the distance as they sped away. Lauren glanced at her watch and gave Henry an expectant look. He could only shrug his shoulders. He, like Lauren, had no idea what was happening in the sky above them.

"Hurry up and call them!" Henry finally said above the rising noise from the truck. "We've got to tell them we're still coming!"

Lauren nodded and felt for her phone. A wave of alarm came over her as she found only an empty pocket. Frantically she searched her other pockets, only to come up empty. "I can't find it! It must have fallen out when we flipped over! Give me yours!"

"It's in my coat, back in the airplane," Henry replied as he shivered in the cold. "Does anyone have a phone?"

"Mine's dead." Michael held out his empty hands. "I used it up talking with Calvin and the Army. It took us forever to get the helicopter launched."

"I have mine." Matt rolled over and dug in his pocket. He handed the phone to Lauren.

"Thank you, Matt." Lauren smiled warmly at the young man. Lauren dialed Donovan's number, her heart soaring at the thought of talking with him. But just as quickly, her hopes plummeted as her call went straight to voice-mail. She left him a message not to ditch—that they were still coming to get them. But deep down, something told her that it would be a miracle if Donovan ever heard her message.

"No luck?" Michael asked, as she hung up. "Is there another number we can call? Is there any other way to reach them?"

"I can keep trying." Lauren started to hit the re-dial sequence.

"Not yet," Henry said, stopping her. "That's the only phone we have left. Wait a few minutes. Maybe they're just in a bad spot. We've got some other problems to solve before we get to the hangar."

"What are we up against?" Michael asked. "Explain to me exactly how we're going to get this airplane off the ground without all those cops charging out to stop us."

"I understand you're a pilot?" Henry asked Michael.

"Yeah. I'm ex-Navy. I flew fighters," Michael replied.

"Perfect, because I'm one pilot short to help me fly the 737. Do you have any flight time in Boeings?"

"Nope." Michael shook his head. "But I'm a fast learner."

"You're going to have to be." Henry looked at his son and hesitated as he tried to formulate the right words. "Matt, if it weren't for you, we'd be in custody right now. That was quick thinking back there. Once we get inside the hangar you'll know what to do. We're going to have to work fast to get that airplane out the door. You're in charge of making that happen."

"Sure. What are you going to do?" Matt said, unsure of what else might be needed.

"I'm going to have to convince the people on duty to let us have the airplane," Henry said. "I imagine the people at the hangar have already heard about our first attempt, they might even have figured out what we're trying to do. Hopefully they'll be sympathetic to our cause. I know one of the shift supervisors on duty; he and I go way back."

The snowplow ground to a halt and Lauren and the others hastily piled out of the hopper.

"What can I do for you folks now?" the big man said as he pulled his pickup truck next to the plow and rolled down his window.

"We don't even know your name." Lauren went to where the man sat. "Or how to ever thank you."

"The name's Emmett. Now, I'd love to sit here and chat, but my guess is we don't have time. So, what else can I do to help you get out of here?"

"I can probably taxi the airplane out to about here," Henry said, pointing to an area on the ramp. "But from here on out to runway 14 right, I'm going to need some assistance."

"You going to take off downwind?" Emmett frowned. "It's blowing pretty hard."

"I'll never make it down to the far end without Security getting in my way," Henry said. "The runway is 13,000 feet long and the airplane is going to be pretty light. It'll work."

"Gotcha," Emmett said, nodding. "I'll get started right away on taxiway Yankee. Trust me, you'll have a way to the runway."

"Won't you draw attention to yourself?" Michael looked up and down the deserted section of the airport.

Emmett thumped a thick finger into his chest. "You leave that to me."

"Thank you so much." Lauren wanted to hug the man who had pulled them back from the brink of failure.

"Go on." Emmett rolled up his window.

Henry went to a side door of the hangar and tested that it was open. It was. He opened it a crack and peered inside. He then motioned for the others to follow.

Lauren was thrilled to see a Boeing 737 sitting in the middle of the hanger. Only the auxiliary lights were on and the place looked deserted. All the better, she thought.

"There should only be a handful of people on duty. It's Friday, plus we've downsized our maintenance base here in Chicago. Most of our mechanics were transferred to Dallas," Henry whispered. "I'm going to go find the crew. Matt, help Michael get to the cockpit, then pull all the gear pins and covers. I'm going to find the switches to kill all these inside lights. I want a dark hanger when we start."

"I'm on it." Matt leaned in and pushed a large red toolbox out from under the wing of the Boeing.

"When I was in the helicopter, I heard some chatter that led me to believe there might be Air Force fighters on their way here," Michael said. "I'd hate to get shot down after all the trouble we've gone through."

"You help Matt. I'll make a phone call." Lauren still had her hand around Matt's phone. "Maybe Calvin can take care of the fighters." Lauren punched out the number to reach Calvin. As she waited, she thought of Donovan. She prayed that he was still flying. She watched as Henry sprinted toward the offices across the hangar in search of help.

"Reynolds here."

"Calvin, it's Lauren."

"Lauren, what's going on? How are you doing?" Calvin said warmly. "I'm told Michael is probably somewhere on the airport by now. He's most likely trying to find you in Operations."

"He's standing right next to me, but we've got a little problem we need your help with."

"Name it."

"Michael thinks there might be Air Force jets on their way to our area. Do you know anything about this?"

"No, but it wouldn't surprise me. I can make a call and see what's going on." Calvin hesitated. "I will tell you that the media is all over this story. There are all kinds of conflicting reports from Chicago. The most worrisome, is that an airliner narrowly missed the Hancock building. The Office of Homeland Security has set up shop in the White House situation room. What exactly is going on there?"

"It's complicated and I don't have much time." Lauren surveyed the hangar and found that Matt had already cleared most of the equipment from around the 737. "We're getting ready to take off from O'Hare. It's not authorized, so I guess you can say we're stealing a jet. The authorities managed to shut down our first attempt, but we found another plane and we're going to get Donovan. What we need from you, is to make sure we don't get shot down before we can help them."

"I'll make a call to the Secretary of Defense. He's the highest-ranking official I can reach right now," Calvin said. "I'll do my best."

"Thank you." Over Michael's shoulder Lauren saw Henry sprint from the distant door followed by two men. "I have to go!"

"Lauren. Do whatever it takes," Calvin said quietly, reinforcing what she'd already heard from Donovan. "I'll try to intervene with the Air Force."

"I've got to go."

Henry began to shout orders, his voice echoing through the high-ceilinged space.

"I'll call when I know more," she said, and turned off the phone.

"Let's go!" Henry yelled in Lauren's direction.

"Fighters taken care of?" Michael asked as they hurried to the metal stairs that would take them up into the 737.

"I don't know. Calvin's working on it." Lauren reached out and took Michael's hand. "I'm so glad you're here. I've felt so alone since all of this started."

"I might not have gotten here as quickly as I'd have liked. But you were never alone." Michael squeezed back. "When I was in the helicopter, I was listening in on one of the radio frequencies. Did someone really shoot at you?"

Lauren nodded.

"Wow, Donovan is going to be so pissed when he hears about that."

Lauren smiled. If anyone could soften a moment with his sense of humor, it was Michael Ross. She'd seen it a million times.

"Michael!" Henry commanded as he drew closer. "Get up in the right seat and start familiarizing yourself with the cockpit. When we go—we're going fast. I'll need you to keep up."

"What about the doors? How do we pull this thing outside?" Michael asked as he took the steps.

"I've got two men who are going to kill the lights and open the doors behind the jet," Henry said. "Once we start the engines, they'll open the front doors. I'm hoping we'll be airborne before anyone knows what we're doing."

"Beautiful," Michael said as he bounded up the stairs two at a time.

"Did you find another phone?" Lauren was about to follow Michael into the plane.

"Yes." Henry held out the proof in his hand. "We need to get going. Did you talk to your people at the DIA?"

"They're working on it, but we've created a security nightmare. I guess we'll know soon enough."

"You didn't by chance talk to 880, did you?" Henry signaled to the two men across the hangar. The overhead lights immediately winked out, their elements glowing red-hot in the dark hangar. At the same time, the massive doors behind the 737 began to rumble open. He motioned for Lauren to go up the steps.

"No. I'll keep trying though." Lauren climbed up into the Boeing as fast as she could.

Henry reached out and swung the door closed and latched it firmly. He squeezed past Lauren and slid easily into the left seat. His hands flew expertly around the flight deck and within seconds the high-pitched whine of the APU filled their ears. With electricity from the generator, instruments came to life. Henry quietly guided Michael to assist and they settled into an even, but hurried cadence of activity.

Lauren pulled down the jump seat and untangled the seat harness. She strapped herself in and then leaned forward to hear what was being said.

"Okay." Henry's eyes darted around the cockpit. "Once we get both engines started, I'll give the signal to open the front doors. I'm hoping there's a snowplow waiting outside to lead the way. If not, I'm not sure we'll make it to the runway."

"He'll be there," Michael said confidently. "I'm a big fan of Emmett. What about the tower? What are we going to tell them?"

"Nothing. We don't want to hear anything they have to say until we're airborne."

"Works for me," Michael said. "Better to beg for forgiveness than ask for permission?"

"Something like that." Henry put a finger on the start button for the right engine. "Ready?"

"Do it." Michael began calling out engine rotations and temperatures.

Lauren found herself holding her breath as the two pilots methodically started both engines and quickly ran through a series of checks. Michael read as Henry completed each task. Moments later, Henry gave a thumbs-up to the men outside and the steel doors in front of them parted. Snow began to billow inside the hanger the wider the doors opened. Through the murk Lauren began to make out a vague shape, then two. Slowly the dark objects became visible. Lauren's heart soared at the sight of three snowplows, each lined up in position to lead them out to the runway. The yellow flashing lights on top of each cab were turned off, their huge steel blades were down, and black diesel exhaust poured out of their stacks.

"Would you look at that!" Michael leaned forward to gauge when their wingtips would be clear of the doors.

Henry nudged the throttles and the Boeing inched ahead. Instantly the plows began to pull forward. The 737 rocked gently as they passed over the door tracks and settled into the snow.

"Turn the anti-icing on," Henry reminded Michael.

Michael reached up and selected the switches Henry had shown him earlier. His hands then went down to the center console and rested on the flap selector.

"I can see the runway," Henry said as he added power to keep pace with the plows. "In about 500 feet we'll have to make a sharp right turn followed by another left turn. Then we'll be there."

"Aircraft on taxiway Yankee. This is O'Hare Tower. Stop and hold your position. The airport is closed."

The sudden intrusion from the overhead speaker startled Lauren. She didn't recognize the voice. She first looked at Henry, then Michael, to see if their having been spotted by the surface radar made any difference. Henry added more power and the 737 picked up speed.

"Unidentified aircraft on taxiway Yankee. This is O'Hare Tower. You are in violation of TSA directives. Stop your aircraft and hold your position!"

"We might need to hurry a bit." Michael pointed. "I see someone coming up fast."

"Shit," Henry said, as he, too, saw a vehicle roaring down the parallel taxiway they were headed toward.

"This is going to be close." Henry touched the brakes as they neared the ninety-degree bend in the concrete. "I've got to slow down to make the turn."

"I think it'll work." Michael struggled to keep the vehicle in sight. "Keep going and I think we can cut him off."

"Unidentified aircraft! This is O'Hare Tower. Hold your position. I repeat. Hold your position and stop your engines!"

"This must be killing them," Lauren said, regarding the frantic calls from the tower. "They know what we're trying to do, they're on our side, but their hands are tied."

"Holy shit!" Michael shouted as a blaze of flashing lights swept under their right wing. He braced himself when Henry smashed on the brakes to avoid hitting the truck.

Lauren stifled a scream as the security vehicle came skidding to a halt between them and the snowplows—blocking their path. The Boeing slipped and jerked, the anti-skid brakes fighting for purchase on the snowy taxiway. Lauren couldn't believe they'd driven the truck directly under the Boeing's wing to stop airplane. They nosed down heavily, grinding to a halt with no more than ten feet of space between the nose of the 737 and the security vehicle.

"Wayfarer Boeing! This is O'Hare security. You are ordered to shut down engines or we will open fire. I repeat. We will open fire."

Henry's shoulders slumped. He put his hands on two levers under the throttles. Lauren had watched Donovan shut down the Gulfstreams and she knew it began with the same action. She lowered her head. It was too much. They'd come so close.

CHAPTER
TWENTY-FOUR

"Everything's ready." Donovan snapped the phone shut. "The tower says all of the rescue boats are in position. I guess it's time to do this."

"Once we're in the water—" John had just finished securing the cockpit. There was now nothing left that might fly around and injure them when they hit. "I want you to get out. I don't know how mobile I'm going to be."

"We'll make it out together." Donovan gave John a reassuring nod, then looked out the window to gauge their distance from the starting point. The hole in the storm lay just beneath their nose. Donovan banked the airplane to the left and stared down through the haze at the barely visible waves. The strong winds created long foam streaks in the dark green water. The angry lake seemed to taunt him, daring him to succeed. On the western edge he caught sight of the rock wall that served as a breakwater for the harbor. He knew the margin for error was small. He'd have to slow the Boeing as much as he dared and spiral inside the small opening in the tempest below. He would have to level out and ditch while still in the relatively clear air. If they went too far, the visibility would probably drop to near zero. He'd have no choice but to set it down anyway—far away from the rescue boats. They then ran the risk of the Coast Guard not being able to find the sinking airplane in the blinding storm.

"Donovan?" John said. "Are you ready?"

"Yeah." Donovan refocused on the job at hand. "I'm going to swing around and begin the descent. Once we start, I want you to give me constant altitude call-outs. It'll give me a rough idea of where we are in relation to the water. We're going to have to do this right the first time."

John used his good hand to pull his harness as tight as it would go. "I've seen you fly; you're good. You can do this."

"I appreciate the vote of confidence." Donovan took one last moment to steady the airplane. He thought of his daughter, Abigail, both sad and angry that he might never see her again. He thought of Meredith, Michael, and Eco-Watch. But his final thought before he rolled the 737 into a steep bank was of Lauren. He wished they'd had one last chance to talk to one another. Donovan pulled both throttles back and slowed the crippled plane. He locked his eyes on the turbulent waves below and started down.

CHAPTER TWENTY-FIVE

"Henry, wait!" Michael shouted. He reached out and used one hand to grab the throttles, with the other he grasped Henry's wrist, stopping him from shutting down the engines.

Startled, Lauren strained to see what Michael was looking at. In an instant, the security truck was swept away by what appeared to be an avalanche propelled by a huge snowplow. The security truck's flashing red lights cast an eerie glow from beneath its tomb of snow as it careened sideways off into the grass.

"Go! Go! Go!" Michael yelled, as their path was once again clear. "Standing by on the flaps."

"Wayfarer Boeing! This is O'Hare Tower. You are not cleared for takeoff! You are to hold your position!"

Henry added power and they started to move. As the Boeing rounded the final turn, the runway lights suddenly increased to full intensity to help guide them through the raging blizzard.

"Somebody up there likes us." Henry settled in his seat as he lined up on the brightly illuminated runway. "Give me takeoff flaps and hang on. This could get ugly."

"Flaps set," Michael called, as the snowplows split off from each other, clearing a path for them to begin their takeoff roll.

Henry keyed the microphone. "O'Hare Tower. This is Boeing 31 Whiskey Alpha. We're declaring an emergency."

Lauren wasn't sure why Henry had called the tower, or why he'd used the number painted on the tail of the airplane instead of a Wayfarer call sign. But moments later, he stood the throttles up and the powerful engines began to surge beneath them. Lauren was pressed backward as Henry released the brakes and the Boeing lurched forward and began to gather speed. From where she sat, she could only see two runway lights at a time and the lateral movement of the blizzard gave her the impression that the plane was slipping sideways. The snow-covered surface turned into a blur and pounded the airplane; the Boeing accelerating, then slowing as they plowed through eighteen-inch drifts.

"Eighty knots. We're not accelerating very fast," Michael shouted.

"Give me ten knot call-outs!" Henry battled against the wind. Each time the Boeing began to accelerate, they hit deep piles of snow that killed their speed. They needed at least 150 knots before the wings could generate enough lift to pull them off the runway.

"Ninety knots!" Michael called out, his voice steady.

Lauren gripped her seat and watched helplessly. A curtain of blowing snow momentarily blocked their vision.

"One hundred knots," Michael called.

Every muscle in Lauren's body was wire-tight as she could once again see the faint centerline lights. The 737 passed over a section of the runway with less snow and the Boeing surged forward.

"One hundred ten," Michael yelled.

Lauren had no idea how much pavement remained. She was terrified they would run out of runway. If they did, they would careen into the multiple rows of metal stanchions at the far end.

"One hundred twenty," Michael called out, his voice more hopeful. "One thirty! One forty! Rotate!"

Lauren sensed the sudden acceleration. In what seemed like slow motion, Henry pulled back on the controls. The nose of the 737 lifted off and pointed into the obscured sky, the main gear slamming loudly into drift after drift.

"Come on baby—fly," Henry muttered as he struggled to get them airborne.

At 150 knots, the Boeing hit another section of ridges on the plowed runway. The impact shot up through the landing gear and rocked the airplane. Lauren winced. It sounded as if the undercarriage was being ripped away. Outside, the wings flexed and whipped at the structural assault.

Without warning, the horrific pounding abruptly ceased. They were flying. Free of the snow and producing maximum lift, the sturdy wings of the Boeing gripped the thick atmosphere and pulled the 737 upward.

In a flash, Lauren saw the glowing approach lights. She closed her eyes, anticipating the impact.

"Keep climbing!" Michael shouted.

"Gear up." Henry fought the growing turbulence as the 737 clawed its way into the storm.

Michael's attention was glued to the instruments. "Gear coming up."

"We might get the shaker!" Henry inched the nose up as high as he dared. "It's climbing. We're accelerating. 200 feet, 500!" Michael leaned back and shot a quick look at Henry.

"God, that was close." Henry carefully lowered the nose. "Flaps up."

"Gear up and locked," Michael reported. "Flaps are moving."

Henry left the throttles at full power. Out of 800 feet he banked the airplane toward the east. He pushed the 737 to its limit. They quickly accelerated to 300 knots. The speed limit in this airspace was only 200 knots, but he didn't care.

The storm battered them violently around the sky. Lauren could picture the 737's wings and tail bucking under the strain. She prayed the airplane could take the punishment. The cockpit was silent except for the roar of the wind as it whipped past. Waves of snow lashed against the windows.

"Call the tower," Henry said as they climbed. "See if they'll help us now. Use our tail number; we can't use a Wayfarer flight number today."

"O'Hare. Boeing 31 Whiskey Alpha is airborne. We're out of three thousand climbing," Michael radioed.

"Roger 31 Whiskey Alpha," Kate replied. "Understand you have declared an emergency. Radar contact. Turn to a 090 degree heading and climb to and maintain 8,000 feet. We're standing by to assist."

A shrill sound erupted in the cockpit, then ceased. Lauren froze as she searched the instrument panel for warning lights. A bell or buzzer was always the prelude to major trouble in the cockpit of a sophisticated jet.

"What's that?" Michael also snapped his head at the noise.

"It's the phone!" Lauren realized as she reached for Matt's cell phone in her pocket.

She pushed the answer button and swept it to her ear. "Hello." She paused for a second. "This is Lauren McKenna. Who's this?"

"Lauren? This is Audrey Parrish. I was looking for Matt."

Instantly Lauren put it together. "We're on our way! We're coming to get you! Tell Donovan not to ditch!" Her voice was a mixture of urgency and anguish. There seemed to be a thousand things that she needed to say.

"What do you mean? Where are you? They told us—." Audrey sputtered.

"We're in another plane!" Lauren could plainly hear the fear in her voice. "Tell Donovan to wait for us!"

"Lauren—we've already started. I don't know if there's time!"

"Get to the cockpit now!" Lauren screamed. "Go as fast as you can! You have to stop them!" Lauren tried to ignore the raw fear that threatened to unhinge her as both Henry and Michael turned, searching for some kind of confirmation that they weren't too late.

"I'm on my way," Audrey called out. "Oh my God! We're in a steep turn! Tell Matt and Henry I love them."

"I will." The sting of tears burned Lauren's eyes, as at the same time a wave of hope began to build inside her. It would only take one sentence from Audrey to stop Donovan from ditching. He'd understand immediately. Seconds ticked by. She silently urged Audrey to get to the cockpit. But then a muffled explosion was followed by Audrey's scream.

CHAPTER TWENTY-SIX

Donovan jumped, startled by the loud noise from the cabin. It sounded as if something had exploded just beyond the cockpit door. They were in a tight spiral, just about to enter the small hole in the clouds. Donovan felt the controls for some sign that the damaged plane had somehow come apart, that the dangerous rip in the fuselage had let go and they would start a helpless tumble to the water below.

"Jesus Christ, what was that?" John twisted painfully in his seat.

"What happened?" Any moment Donovan expected to loose control of the 737.

"Can you hear that?" John cocked his head.

"No. What is it?" Donovan thought it might be the tearing of metal, the first sounds of the Boeing ripping itself to pieces. He kept the 737 in its tight spiral downward through the column of clear air.

"They're shouting!" John said. "Donovan, it sounds like Keith!"

"I can hear them too." The indistinct sounds finally registered. Someone in the back was yelling at them. It made no sense—why couldn't they get to the flight deck? Donovan added power and pulled the 737 up sharply. "I'm going to level off. John, find out what in the hell is going on!"

Someone screamed from just beyond the bulkhead.

John put his hand on Donovan's shoulder. "Something's happened. I think they're saying Audrey's been hurt."

"John. Can you take the plane? Keep doing 360s if you need to, but keep us in this clear air."

"I've got it." John gripped the controls with his good hand. "Go!"

Donovan squeezed out of the cockpit and saw immediately what had taken place. A solid yellow wall blocked his path. The twenty-foot long emergency escape slide had somehow inflated. Donovan knew that they inflated with near explosive force, he could tell that as it expanded inward, it folded over on itself twice and filled the forward cabin. On the floor, a delicate hand protruded from under the yellow material.

"Get something to puncture it with!" Donovan yelled to the other side of the barrier.

"I've got the crash ax," Keith shouted. "Stand back!"

Above the wind, Donovan heard the hiss of air rushing from the tube. The slide deflated rapidly, whipping savagely in the wind before finally crumpling to the floor. Donovan pushed the rubber fabric aside and reached for the motionless form that lay underneath.

"Oh my God! Rafael!" Keith screamed toward the back as he saw the carnage.

Donovan recoiled. Blood was everywhere. Audrey's coat was soaked, a puncture plainly visible in her life vest. Donovan knelt and pulled the vest aside. He hesitated, then tugged at her coat. They had to stop the bleeding. He looked at Keith. "What was she doing? Why was she up here?"

"The phone, where's the phone?" Keith began looking frantically around them. "Donovan! We got one of the phones to work. She called her son, then she ran to the cockpit. We've got to find the phone!"

"Let me through!" Rafael charged forward, medical kit in hand. He knelt down, a grave expression clouding his face.

Donovan opened Audrey's coat and began unbuttoning her blouse. Her blood was warm and sticky on his hands. Rafael reached in and ripped the saturated fabric away, exposing her flesh. Blood oozed from Audrey's chest. Rafael immediately pressed his palm on her wound. Donovan turned away, helpless.

"I feel something sharp. It's hard, like metal." Rafael tried to explore the wound without letting up on the pressure. He took one quick look and blood poured from under his hand.

"Help me find the phone." Keith was still down on his knees, his hands groping wildly under the mountain of deflated rubber.

Partially hidden under the folds, Donovan saw a black object. "I found it!" He picked it up. "Hello." Instead of the static he expected, he heard an excited voice. "Don't ditch! We're coming to get you!" The words swirled in the chaos. With a sudden burst of understanding, Donovan whirled and ran to the cockpit. "Climb John! Climb! Get us out of here!"

CHAPTER TWENTY-SEVEN

Lauren slumped in her seat, her entire body had gone numb. The hand holding the phone fell limply into her lap. "We're too late." Her throat tightened as her eyes clouded with tears. "Oh dear God." She pictured Donovan and the others disappearing into the icy depths of Lake Michigan.

"Lauren, what happened? What did you hear?" Michael reached out to her.

All Lauren could do was shake her head in utter defeat.

"Boeing 31 Whiskey Alpha, this is O'Hare Tower. Fly heading 030 degrees. Traffic is another Wayfarer 737 at eleven o'clock 20 miles."

Michael's brow creased, as if he'd not heard correctly. "Tower, say again. Understand 880 is still flying?" Michael reached down and eased the cell phone from Lauren's hand. "Hello? Is anyone there?" Michael lowered his head as he listened. "I hear something. I still have a connection. They're still there, but no one's on the phone."

Lauren wiped her tears. "Are you sure? What can you possibly hear? Audrey was running forward and I heard an explosion—then she screamed."

"O'Hare Tower," Henry said, keying the microphone, his fingers shaking. "This is Boeing 31 Whiskey Alpha, say position of Wayfarer 880? What's their heading?"

"Wayfarer 880 is now in a left turn heading northwest, altitude unknown. At your two o'clock and 18 miles." Kate's voice was strong and confident over the speaker.

Lauren was confused. She looked at Michael for answers.

"Don't ditch! We're coming to get you!" Michael shouted into the phone. "Someone answered! They heard me. It's Donovan! Yes! He's yelling for them to climb! We did it! We stopped them!" Michael pumped his fist in victory.

Lauren wouldn't let herself believe it. She held out her hand for the phone. How could there be someone on the other end? She'd heard the sound of impact and Audrey scream. "Who is this?"

"Lauren? It's Donovan." His voice sounded tired and strained.

"What happened to Audrey? Are you still flying?" Her words came out in one breath. "I thought you'd crashed."

"We're almost back on top. John is climbing as we speak. Where's Henry? Was that Michael?" A hundred questions needed to be asked. "Audrey's injured. They're working on her now. One of the forward emergency escape slides deployed inside the plane."

"Oh my God! How badly is she hurt?" Lauren began to understand what it was she heard.

"I don't know. It just happened."

Two rapid beeps sounded in Lauren's ear. She looked at Matt's phone—the signal had been lost.

"Did they make it on top?" Henry asked. He'd turned to the new heading, leaving the throttles at maximum power.

"Yes. Donovan said they were climbing," Lauren said, her voice trembling.

"We'll have the tower vector us in closer when they get stabilized," Michael said.

"What happened to Audrey?" Henry asked.

"All Donovan said was that she was hurt." Lauren lowered her head. "He said an emergency slide deployed inside the cabin. It was the noise I heard."

Henry winced. "Did he say anything else?"

Lauren shook her head. "All he said is that she was hurt; it was too early to tell anything about her condition. Then we were cut off."

"We'll get her on the ground as fast as we can," Michael said. "At least they're not in the water. We can still help them."

"You're right." Henry straightened up in his seat as he collected himself.

Climbing steeply, the Boeing raced for the clear air above. The murkiness of the clouds diminished as they approached the top of the overcast. The airplane burst into the waning orange sunset. The sky to the east had already turned a shade of purple; to the west it was still light, but the winter sun would vanish in a hurry. Henry could fly by outside reference now. He leveled off and the 737 rapidly gained speed.

"Boeing 31 Whiskey Alpha," Kate transmitted. "I need to separate you from another emergency in progress. Say your intentions?"

Henry picked up the microphone. "O'Hare Tower, this is Boeing 31 Whiskey Alpha. We're VFR on top. We'd like to cancel our instrument clearance at this time."

"Roger one Whiskey Alpha. Understand canceling IFR at this time. You are free to maneuver. Would you like to stay with me for advisories?"

"That's affirmative O'Hare," Henry continued. "We'd like updates on the traffic ahead if you don't mind."

"Roger that." Kate's voice gave just enough inflection to let the pilots know that she understood what needed to be done. "Traffic is at your twelve o'clock and ten miles, appears to be maneuvering."

"We're looking," Henry replied.

Lauren scanned the clouds below and the empty sky ahead of them where 880 should be coming into view. She leaned forward, searching for the other 737. Beneath them, a glimmer of sunlight caught her eye. Another flash and she found 880, a small dark shape against the lighter colored clouds. "I've got them," she said. "Straight ahead, moving left to right."

"I see them too," Henry said. "Tower, this is 31 Whiskey Alpha. We have the traffic in sight."

"Roger, Whiskey Alpha." Kate sounded relieved. "Maintain visual separation."

"Here we go." Henry pushed the nose down slightly and pointed the Boeing to intercept 880. He flew as fast as he could; daylight was disappearing in a hurry.

"Which side are you going to approach from?" Michael asked.

"I want them to see us, but I also want to take a quick look at the damage. I think I'll come in from the left. We'll be hard to miss. I'm bringing us in real close."

What had been a sparkle on the horizon turned into the vague silhouette of an airplane as they rapidly closed the distance. Henry held the 737 just below the red line of 320 knots.

"Look at that!" was all Michael could say, as 880 began to take a definitive shape.

"I see it too," Lauren said. Starting just above the flight deck, the entire roof section of the aluminum fuselage was ripped away. "My God, I can't believe the damage. It looks far worse than the satellite image we saw earlier."

"It's no wonder they don't have anything left in the cockpit." Michael moved aside slightly so not to obstruct Lauren's view. He affectionately gripped her hand and squeezed while flashing his winning smile. "Hang in there."

Henry surveyed other parts of the stricken airliner. "Part of the vertical stabilizer is missing." Henry reduced power as they descended even lower toward flight 880.

"How are they even flying?" Lauren said, as she released Michael's hand and pointed. "Is that smoke I see?"

"You're right. I see it," Henry said. "It's white. I'll bet it's coming from one of the engines. I'm going to swing underneath, then up around the other side. Let's try to get a quick look at the damage." Henry guided his jet below flight 880. The belly appeared to be intact, except for the white smoke streaming a narrow trail behind the number one engine.

"The smoke is from the engine burning oil," Michael said as they pulled underneath Donovan's 737. "I wonder how long it's been doing that?"

"How bad do you think it is?" Lauren asked.

"I don't know. They don't have any warning lights or gauges to tell them the status of the engine. Let's hope it holds together for a little while longer."

"I pray it does," Michael said. "Flying that thing on one engine, with that much missing from the rudder, might be too much to ask."

"I hadn't thought of that," Henry remarked. "I doubt they could do it. The asymmetrical thrust would be tremendous. Unbelievable. I never would have thought an airplane could take that much damage and still fly."

"What's that?" Michael pointed. "Right there behind the left engine. It looks like something is hanging."

Henry eased the Boeing closer. "I'm not sure. It's got to be part of the flap, or the housing for the flap actuator."

"I think you're right," Michael said. "I don't see it fluttering, but it's definitely out of position. If that piece lets go, it could create a control problem."

Henry nodded. "If they put the landing gear down, that section could snap off. Good call. We'll warn Donovan and John."

Henry slid the airplane around to the right side of the other Boeing. Lauren couldn't see anything obviously wrong. "It looks to me like the military airplane must've come from this side."

"That's my guess too," Henry said. "On impact, the top of the fuselage must've peeled back, with flying debris damaging the tail and the left wing."

With a smooth combination of rudder and aileron, Henry passed over the top of the mangled 737. Lauren's stomach dropped as she caught sight of the yellow emergency slide through the hole in the roof of 880. Where was Audrey? Was she still alive? Lauren wanted so badly for Audrey to survive. Not only for both Henry and Matt, but she wanted to meet this woman from Donovan's past.

Henry allowed them to drift back 100 feet above and behind 880. All of them could see the decimated rudder, as well as the extensive damage to the tail section. Streaks of hydraulic fluid flowed from the vertical fin. The left horizontal stabilizer was twisted slightly in relation to the other.

As they gradually moved up the left side, the damage to the left wing tip became evident. The hole just aft of the cockpit was enormous, and Lauren understood how those unfortunate passengers had been sucked out at impact.

"Come on Donovan. Call us back," she said aloud.

Henry motioned to the waning light in the western sky. "We're running out of time."

CHAPTER
TWENTY-EIGHT

"It all happened so fast," Keith tried to explain, his face white and drawn. "We were all going to make one last call. You know, call our loved ones. Audrey went first. She called her son."

Donovan put his hands on Audrey to keep her steady while Rafael worked on her. "Her pulse is getting weaker. There's nothing I can do." Rafael gestured to the airliner's medical kit. "I just don't have anything to help her."

"What do you need?" Donovan asked. "What would you do for her if we were on the ground?" Audrey had held things together. She had made clutch decisions that had perhaps saved them all. He thought of her last wishes for Henry and Matt.

"She needs fluid, she needs to stay warm to help fight off the shock. We need to somehow replace the blood she's losing," Rafael said. "I think her spleen has been punctured. It's an area of high vascularity. It's only a matter of minutes before she bleeds out completely."

"Would a transfusion work? Can one of us give her blood?" Donovan asked. "It might be a long shot, but it's worth a try."

"I don't know what blood type she is, even if we could figure that out, trying to locate an artery and run a line under these conditions well, well it would be too little too late I'm afraid. She could have a reaction that would kill her." Rafael turned to Keith. "Go get as many blankets as you can find. I'll have to stay up here with her, we don't dare try to move her."

Donovan was growing impatient. He couldn't stand the sight of Audrey just lying there, dying in front of him. "How long can she hold on?"

Rafael lowered his eyes. "Hard to say. She could die any minute, or she could hold on longer—but if we don't get on the ground fast, I think we'll lose her for sure."

Donovan rubbed some warmth into his hands and noticed that some of Audrey's blood had already frozen in the brutal cold. He eyed the hole in the roof, his mind trying to wrap itself around something that had been said earlier.

"Keith said something earlier about hypothermia and how quickly it takes effect. What if we let her freeze?" Donovan said. "I've read stories about when people drown in ice water, their brains survive longer than usual—right?"

"I have the blankets." Keith announced. He slid to the side, avoiding the worst of the slipstream. He unfolded them and began fighting the wind to cover her and try to keep her warm.

"Does what I said make sense?" Donovan desperately needed to hear what Rafael thought.

"I hadn't thought of that," Rafael slowly began to nod his head as the idea began to take hold. "It's very clever actually. In heart transplant surgery they often cool the patient to minimize the risk of brain damage when they stop the heart. It could work. Do it—get her out of her clothes right now."

"Pull the blankets off!" Donovan shouted. Ignoring the numbing cold, Donovan moved next to Keith and began removing Audrey's clothes. Despite fingers that felt more like stubs than anything useful, Donovan and Keith pulled off her clothes until Audrey was lying in her bra and panties, her bare skin exposed to the harsh elements of the cabin. Her hair blew in the wind, nearly covering her shock-white face. During the entire procedure, Rafael kept one hand planted around her shoulder to steady her, the other hand was placed firmly on her wound, trying to staunch the flow of blood.

"Pack as many blankets as you can between the two of us and the bulkhead. I have to stay with her to keep pressure on the wound. What I want is for neither one of us to slide forward when we land." Rafael placed his free hand on her neck. "Her pulse is slowing rapidly. We may have bought her some time—but not much."

Donovan looked from Rafael to Keith then down at Audrey. She seemed so small and fragile; he could just make out the bluish tinge that began to discolor her lips. Rafael and Keith had identical helpless expressions locked onto their faces. Each of them knew that Audrey had probably saved their lives, yet they couldn't do anything but lay her out in the arctic blast pouring from above.

"I'll be right back." Donovan ran up front and stuck his head into the cockpit. He was relieved to find that John had the 737 back on top of the clouds. "Audrey's hurt, she's in bad shape. I just need a few more minutes back here. You okay?"

John turned and nodded. "Hurry Donovan. I'm serious, we're losing our light."

"Hang in there. We're about to have company." Donovan noticed one of the leftover portable oxygen bottles behind the seat and quickly grabbed it. With no time for further explanation, Donovan hurried back to where Rafael was waiting.

"Here's what little 100% oxygen we have left. Is there anything else we can do for her?" Donovan knelt and opened the valve on the bottle. "Should we try CPR, try to keep her blood moving?"

Rafael shook his head as he carefully placed the mask over Audrey's nose and mouth. A faint wisp of condensation blurred the clear plastic as Audrey exhaled, welcome evidence that she was still alive. "We're doing what we can. It would take two of us, and we don't really have the room up here to do it right. Her core body temperature is going to drop fast. She gave us a chance to get to the airport instead of crashing in the water— the best thing you can do for her is to get us on the ground—now."

"What the hell?" Keith pointed a bloody hand up toward the gap in the roof.

Donovan turned to see what Keith was talking about. Coming in fast from behind was another 737. He could just make out the blue-and-gold paint scheme of Wayfarer Airlines. He didn't think he'd ever seen a more wonderful sight.

"What are they doing?" Keith asked, as the other plane moved closer.

"They're here to help us." Donovan headed for the cockpit. "Keith, you're in charge back here. Assist Rafael. Do whatever needs to be done for Audrey and get ready for an emergency landing."

"What's going on back there?" John said the moment Donovan entered the flight deck. "Is Audrey all right? Why in the hell was she up?" John gasped at the sight of Donovan's coat and hands. "Good lord, you're covered with blood!"

"It's Audrey's," Donovan said, sliding into the left seat. "It's too soon to know if we got to her in time. She was running up here when we were in the steep bank. I saw the debris she probably stumbled over. Something hooked the bar and deployed the emergency slide inside the cabin. The force of the inflation threw her into the shards of metal. Rafael thinks her spleen is punctured."

"Oh my God, that's awful."

Donovan looked across at John. "She may have saved us. She managed to call her son. It's why she was trying to get up to the cockpit."

"She made a call?"

"We have company." Donovan pointed out the left side of the plane. The other Boeing seemed to float there. Its speed was perfectly matched to their own.

"What?" John leaned over to see the twin of their own aircraft positioned above and off to the left

"It's Henry Parrish. They made it. You were right about his being a fighter. I was talking to them when we were cut off. We need to get him back." John rocked their wings gently to let them know they were in sight. The wings on the other 737 rocked in return. Donovan exhaled slowly. Their problems were far from over, but at least they weren't alone.

"Coming up," Keith called from the passageway. "Rafael is keeping up the pressure on Audrey. He says we've bought some time, but not much."

Donovan nodded. He grabbed the phone, the one Audrey had used. He studied it for a moment until he figured out how to re-dial the last number. A moment later it rang.

"Donovan? Is that you?" Lauren said the moment she answered.

"Hi there," Donovan said softly.

"Oh, thank God," Lauren said in return. "Are you okay? How's Audrey?"

"Not good," Donovan answered. "We need to hurry and get this thing on the ground. Let me see if I have this right. You're with Henry and Michael?"

"Yes. We stole a plane."

"I can't tell you how glad I am to see you. Let me talk to Henry. He and I need to get a few things figured out before we start." Donovan wished he had time to say more.

"I'll talk to you later?" Lauren framed it as a question.

"You bet. We have a date for next weekend. I promise I'll be there, but we might have a little problem," Donovan said, then lowered his voice so John couldn't hear. "Cyrus knows—he mentioned Abigail. Whatever happens, make sure she's safe."

"How? Oh no," Lauren said, her voice breaking. She instantly pictured the open office door right after she'd told Henry who Donovan was. Cyrus had overheard their conversation. She'd truly opened up Pandora's box. It was no doubt how he knew to send security in search of them. "I'm so sorry."

"We'll deal with him later," Donovan said. "Let me talk to Henry."

"Here he is," Lauren replied, sick to her stomach at the growing implications of her mistake.

"Donovan," Henry said sharply as he came on the line.

"Let's get this thing on the ground," Donovan said to the man who used to be his friend.

"That's the plan. You ready to do this?"

"I want to go over everything once, just to make sure we're on the same page."

Henry dispensed with pleasantries, challenging the pilot directly. "I'm counting on you to fly that thing in perfect formation with us, all the way down to the runway."

"Exactly what I was hoping you'd say," Donovan said.

"Hang on for a second, we're talking with the tower."

Donovan could hear both Henry and Michael in the background as they coordinated with the tower.

Henry once again spoke into the phone. "Donovan, the RVR is up a little, but we're still going to have to shoot a Category III approach. Most likely runway 14 Left."

Donovan carefully constructed the scene in his mind. The CAT III approach would be flown by Henry's autopilot. The sophisticated lighting system on the ground was twice as visible as the regular ILS instrument approach. There was a massive array of lights that stretched out far before the runway threshold; high-energy strobe lights fired in sequence to help lead an aircraft to the touchdown zone.

"But that means landing downwind," Henry cautioned.

"John and I discussed this earlier. The only CAT III approaches at O'Hare are to the parallel runways 14 Left and Right. We ruled it out because the wind would be directly on our tail."

"I know, but we just took off from there, and I can tell you I think it's the only way we have any hope of seeing the runway," Henry countered.

Donovan once again heard some garbled conversation in the background.

"I'm back," Henry said. "We've also decided you can't risk putting the landing gear down. We can see part of the flap assembly that's out of place. The airflow from the main gear might rip it off."

"Shouldn't be a problem. We were going to land gear-up the first time, glad we made the right decision."

"Now, if you land on 14 Right, which is the one we just took off from, I don't think it'll work very well. It's rougher than you can imagine. I think you'd be sliding all over the place and hitting the drifts at odd angles. I think if you landed on that runway, the airplane would break up for sure from all the pounding it'll get."

"Go on, I'm listening," Donovan said, relieved that Henry was all business. He guessed there would be time for a long-awaited confrontation—later.

"Okay, that leaves us with 14 Left, on the other side of the airport. They're telling us it's got at least a foot or more of snow on it. They quit trying to keep all the runways open and it hasn't been plowed. All the better, don't you think?"

"I like it, Henry. The snow will cushion our landing and help slow us down. It might even counteract the effect of coming in with a twenty-five knot tailwind."

"Exactly."

"Let's get on with it then. From where I'm sitting, anything sounds better than dropping this thing in Lake Michigan." Donovan watched as Keith came up and spoke softly to John. Just as quickly, he vanished into the rear of the plane.

"What's going on?" Henry asked.

"Henry, I'm ready when you are—but we really need to hurry. Audrey needs to get to a hospital. I'm moving into position now."

"I'm handing the phone to Lauren. We'll relay through her."

CHAPTER TWENTY-NINE

Lauren was relieved to once again have the phone. Henry and Michael had sprung into action, setting up the cockpit for the approach. "You there?"

"I'm here," Donovan said.

"Tell tower we're ready, Michael," Henry said. "And tell them we're a flight of two."

Michael followed Henry's directive. He then looked out and tried to spot flight 880. "I don't see them. They must already be in position behind us."

"Where are you?" Lauren asked as she too searched for his plane.

"Right behind you, about 50 feet," Donovan answered.

"Boeing 31 Whiskey Alpha," Kate transmitted, "the snow removal crew is still working on getting the snow off the lights and taxiways. It'll be a few minutes before we can begin the approach."

"Tell them we need to start the approach now," Henry shot back at Michael. "We'll just have to take it as is. We need to go now!"

"Tower," Michael said, "get them out of there! We need to start this."

"Roger. Boeing 31 Whiskey Alpha. Turn left heading 240 degrees. Descend pilot's discretion to four thousand feet. I'll turn you on a twenty mile final. That should give us time to clear the runway of men and vehicles."

"Donovan, we're turning to a 240 degree heading," Lauren relayed over the phone. "We're also cleared down to four thousand. Stay with us no matter what. Henry says this is going to be a very fast approach."

"I understand," Donovan replied. "Tell Henry not to get slower than 190 knots. This thing just turns to mush. I'll need the extra speed to stay responsive."

"Donovan says no slower than 190 knots," Lauren said and Henry nodded he understood.

"Let me say one more thing to him." Henry held out his hand for the phone. "It's Henry. Listen, when I see the approach lights, I'll be going around. My autopilot will be flying this approach. It should provide the most stable platform for you to stay in position. When you see the lights, don't worry about us, just get your airplane on the runway. I'll be accelerating and climbing. Any questions?" Henry waited for a reply. "Donovan? Any questions?" He looked at the phone in his hand. "Shit! I've lost them."

"I wonder if our own airplane interrupted the signal." Lauren tried to judge their position relative to where Chicago lay beneath the clouds.

"Boeing 31 Whiskey Alpha, this is O'Hare Tower. Turn left, heading 170 degrees and intercept the 14 Left localizer. You are cleared for the CAT III ILS approach. Stay with me."

"It doesn't matter if they call back now or not." Henry passed the phone to Lauren "He just needs to do what he's supposed to do."

Lauren focused on Henry. The news that his wife was injured had hit him hard. She sensed he was fighting his way through the mental agony and she wondered if he might be losing that battle. She turned and looked at the remaining light. It would be dark soon. She had no idea how much daylight Donovan needed to hold his position relative to their plane. As they descended there was nothing to do but watch the clouds come closer and closer.

CHAPTER THIRTY

"We were cut off." Donovan gave the phone to John. He put both hands on the controls as he began to maneuver closer to the other 737. "No need to call them back. Henry said when we see the lights he'll be accelerating and pulling away. We're going to set it down right behind him. The snow-covered runway should slow us quickly, absorb much of the impact." Donovan closed the distance between his and Henry's planes. The other Boeing seemed to hover just a few feet away. It felt so unnatural to be flying this close to another aircraft. The entire airspace system was designed to keep airplanes apart. Now he was going to guide their 737 as close to the other Boeing as he possibly could. "This is pretty unorthodox. But God, is that airplane beautiful."

"How close do you—how close are we going to get?" John asked.

"As close as I can. It's going to be hard as hell to see them in the clouds. I want to be able to count every rivet." He glanced at John. Donovan knew firsthand how difficult it was to sit and let someone else fly. He turned his attention back to the other Boeing. Henry, Michael and Lauren were only 50 feet away. He delicately began to guide them in even closer.

Donovan's tension mounted. Part of Henry's plane was distorted from the super-heated exhaust coming from Henry's engines. He had to avoid getting too close to the jet blast. Another danger would be the vortices from the other Boeing. The lift from Henry's plane created small tornadoes of disturbed air just behind each wing tip. Donovan carefully calculated how to avoid each of these risks. The biggest threat, though, was not staying close enough. No matter what happened, he had to keep them in sight. His leg muscles tightened. In theory, it was easy. All he had to do was follow Henry down through the storm until they spotted the runway. In reality, it was going to be the most difficult flying Donovan had ever done.

"Okay," Donovan announced. "I'm going to slide in above their horizontal stabilizer, just to the right of Henry's rudder. I can move in close, and it should keep us out of trouble, well away from the jet blast. John, when we get near the ground, I want you to keep your eyes open for any sign of the runway lights. We need to spot them as soon as possible. What we can't afford to do is to follow Henry back up into the clouds. I don't think we have the daylight or the fuel to make that mistake."

"I'll do my best," John said.

Donovan took another quick look across the cockpit. John's eyes were fixed on the Boeing as it gradually filled the windscreen. "We'll be all right. If we somehow get separated, we'll fly back out over the lake." Donovan said, wishing he had something more to offer.

John nodded, then shifted uncomfortably in his seat, helpless to do anything but sit and watch.

"Just a few more feet and we'll be there." Donovan nudged the 737 into a shallow bank to bring him within twenty feet of the other plane. The controls shook briefly in his hands as he passed through the edge of Henry's wake turbulence. "So far so good." He offered a silent thanks that the ride was still smooth. If he could just stay locked in formation like this, they had a chance. "They're in the turn," Donovan said. He took a deep breath and his chest felt tight. He knew it wasn't just from the harness. Donovan looked away for just a fraction of a second. To his right, John's hands were poised to grip the controls.

"Careful!"

"Damn it!" Donovan yelled as he looked out at the other plane. They had drifted a few feet out of position. He corrected quickly, knowing he had just been given his first and perhaps last warning. One moment of inattention—one wrong move, and the situation would turn deadly.

"It's okay," Donovan said. With their speed matched once again,

Donovan guided their wounded Boeing to within twenty feet of the other plane, and despite the cold a wet trickle of perspiration raced down his rib cage.

Donovan pictured the area below them. He'd landed in Chicago many times over the years. The closer to O'Hare, the more dense the population. Scores of people would be consumed by the fiery impact if he made even a slight miscalculation. A wave of turbulence lifted the two 737s, rocking them in unison as they entered the clouds.

"Have you still got them?" John called from the right seat.

The aluminum skin of Henry's plane was now nearly invisible, engulfed by the dense vapor of the storm. Donovan made constant control inputs to keep in position. He jockeyed the throttles in the rough air. He concentrated on the small white navigation light and the dull outline of the other aircraft as they raced toward the snow-covered ground. "I have him," he said. Every movement required yet another subtle correction to keep Henry's 737 in sight. They were constantly shifting back and forth in relation to the other airplane.

"I can hardly see them," John said.

"I can. Just enough," Donovan said, his voice tight. He jammed the throttles forward as their host nearly disappeared into the clouds, then back again as the silver object filled the windshield. He overcorrected and the 737 faded from view.

"Power, Donovan, we're losing him!" John cried out. Henry's plane had vanished. "Add power!"

Donovan pushed the power levers all the way up; the 737 surged ahead. "Where is he?" His stomach fluttered with fear. He was playing high-stakes blind man's bluff with another airliner.

"There!" John yelled. "He's right there. Do you have him?"

"I've got him." Donovan reduced the power. He had gained too much speed and had pulled almost even with the other plane. He could see the row of cabin lights through the small windows that ran the length of the Boeing. Donovan lowered the nose and used the rudder to reestablish his position. The controls became even harder to manage in his wire-taut hands.

"Easy," John said.

"Something's wrong!" Donovan clenched his teeth and poured more power to the twin CFM engines. The left wing dropped and a different vibration reverberated through the airframe. "John, we're in trouble." Donovan slammed the throttles as far as they would go. A helpless feeling enveloped him as the other Boeing disappeared in the murk.

CHAPTER
THIRTY-ONE

"Boeing 31 Whiskey Alpha, this is O'Hare Tower," Kate said over the speaker. "I show flight 880 has separated and is now on a 170 degree heading."

"Son of a bitch!" Henry reached up and disengaged the autopilot. There was no need to continue if 880 had broken off. He slammed the throttles forward and pulled back on the controls. "Tell them we've missed the approach and are climbing back on top!"

The fear in Henry's words took Lauren by surprise. In an instant, she understood that 880 could be anywhere in the column of clouds, headed up or down, or right at them.

"God damn it! What happened? Why couldn't he do it?" Henry looked at Michael. "If he couldn't hold formation through that, what chance do they have down lower where it's rough as hell?"

"Are we sure they were in position before we went into the clouds?" Michael said in a manner meant to calm Henry down. "We have no idea what went on back there, Henry."

They broke out of the clouds and leveled at 8,000 feet. The dark orange sky to the west was all the daylight that remained. Lauren silently urged the phone in her hand to ring. What she dreaded most was to hear a report from Kate that 880 had vanished from her screen. Lauren squeezed her eyes shut and forced the unthinkable from her mind.

"He had plenty of time to move in close. The son of a bitch can't do it.

I was wrong about him—he's nothing more than a rich, spoiled amateur, that's probably all he ever was." Henry slammed his fist on his thigh, a look of defeat etched deeply on his face.

Lauren was horrified at Henry's reference to Donovan's past. She prayed that the comment would go by the wayside.

"Do you know Donovan?" Michael asked, an edge in his voice.

Henry turned toward Lauren, then Michael. "Yeah, a long time ago. It's nothing, forget it."

"Well I can tell you one thing." Michael leveled a dead-serious stare at Henry. "There aren't many pilots alive that can do what Donovan Nash can. I've seen most of it firsthand. So, what I want from you—is to get your head back in the game, and we'll try this again. Do I make myself clear?"

"Try again?" Henry shot back. "We might not get another chance! They might not even make it back on top! They could've already crashed for all we know!"

Lauren wanted to jump in the middle of the debate. She hoped that Michael wouldn't give Henry's comment any more thought. She began to scan the ragged cloud tops for any sign of the other plane. The longer 880 stayed in the clouds, the worse their situation would become.

"Oh God. I need this to work." Henry massaged his temples.

Lauren reached out and put her hand on Henry's shoulder. "We didn't come this far to fail."

"I know. It's just that if they'd stayed with us, they'd be on the ground by now. Audrey could be—" Henry closed his eyes as he said the words, then fought to pull himself together. "We might not get another chance."

Lauren jumped, surprised at the sound of the cockpit door opening behind her.

"Where'd they go?" Matt's words came in a rush as he burst onto the flight deck.

"Jesus Christ, Matt!" Henry yelled. "What in the hell are you doing here?"

"I saw the whole thing!" Matt chose to direct his words at Lauren instead of his father. "Where are they now? Are they all right?"

"What did you see, Matt?" Lauren asked.

He pulled up right next to us. I could see everything. He was all over the place trying to stay with us in the turbulence," Matt said. "Then, there was a flash, then a huge trail of fire came blowing from their left engine. That's when they peeled off."

"How close were they?" Henry asked. "How long did they stay up with us?"

"They moved in real close just before we went in the clouds. It was getting pretty dark and kind of murky, but I could still see them the whole time. Then the engine went, just like that." Matt snapped his fingers. "There was smoke, some sparks, then a flash of fire."

"It was the left engine?" Henry asked. "Was the fire just momentary?"

"Yeah, it was the left one. That's the only one I could really see. The fire was still burning when they went out of sight. They were so close I could see the pilots. I wonder if Mom could see me."

Matt's words delivered a final blow. The pain registered clearly on Henry's face. Lauren turned away, masking a similar heartache.

"What?" Matt said. "What is it? What's going on with Mom?"

"Your mother was hurt." Henry struggled to find the right words. "We don't know much more than that."

Matt shook his head. "What happened?"

"She fell," Lauren said, jumping in to help Henry explain. "They're taking care of her." She turned as if to scan the empty sky; the helpless look on Matt's face was too much to bear.

"Where are they?" Henry said, searching the clouds.

Michael picked up the microphone. "Tower. Say 880's position."

"They're at your two o'clock position and three miles," Kate replied. "Altitude unknown."

All four of them swiveled their heads to look out the right side of the plane.

"I don't see them," Matt said.

Lauren tried not to think about the earlier conclusions Henry and Michael had reached about 880's left engine, and attempting to fly on one engine with their damaged rudder. She was terrified that Kate's next transmission would be to tell them she'd lost radar contact with 880.

Henry reached for the microphone. "Tower. One more time, say 880's position."

"Wayfarer 880 is now one o'clock and two miles."

But all they could see in the fading light was empty sky.

CHAPTER
THIRTY-TWO

"John! Help me! I need more right rudder!" Donovan cried out. Slowly, the controls became more effective as their speed began to build. Donovan knew he could very well be pushing the airframe beyond its limits; but he'd had little choice except to point the nose of the Boeing down at a dangerous angle. He needed the speed to build as rapidly as possible. The right engine was at full power, and Donovan was using all of his strength to push the right rudder, to compensate for the loss of thrust from the left engine. He waited as long as he dared for the speed to build, then smoothly raised the nose and held the 737 steady.

"We're almost there. It's getting brighter!" John strained to look out the forward window.

Abruptly, they soared from the top of the overcast. Their wings banked and the nose was pointed up nearly 30 degrees to the horizon. Donovan carefully allowed the nose to drop, then leveled the wings. He released the pressure on the controls, making minor corrections as the 737 once again flew straight and level above the clouds. He tried to sense how much maneuverability he had lost with the engine out. The partial rudder was all he had to help hold them straight. It was enough for now—he hoped it would be enough for later.

"Do you see them anywhere?" John searched for Henry's plane.

Donovan took a quick peek outside. "I don't see a thing." He wanted to pull the throttle back to conserve fuel, but instead was forced to leave the right engine at full power. They needed the speed. "Get on the phone. Tell Henry what happened. We need to get positioned for another try."

"I'm on it."

Donovan let the Boeing accelerate. With more air flowing over the rudder, the 737 was a little easier to fly. He'd come close to losing control of the airplane. He waited impatiently for John to reestablish the connection with Henry.

"We're on fire!" Keith yelled. He was out of breath. "The engine on the left side of the plane is burning!"

"We know." Donovan wasn't surprised at the news. "That engine seized. It'll be okay. We won't blow up," he said calmly. "We're going to try this again, Keith. Nothing's changed."

Reassured by Donovan's relaxed demeanor, Keith could only nod his head.

Donovan searched for the other 737. He found only vacant sky. "Where in the hell did they go?"

"I've got him." John handed him the phone. "It's Henry."

Donovan grabbed the phone. "Where are you?" He craned his neck to locate the gold and blue Boeing.

"We've got you in sight." Henry's voice came in loud and clear. "We're behind you, we'll be there in less than a minute. We know about the engine; it's still burning. How's it flying?"

"Not great. It was touch and go there for a while," Donovan said. "But I think I've got enough to work with." He hesitated for a moment. "How did you know?"

"My son was in the back. He saw it let loose," Henry replied. "We're coming up on your left side."

Donovan turned to find Henry's aircraft, above and slightly behind. "I've got you now. Henry, we need to do this a little differently." Donovan glanced at his airspeed indicator. "I don't think we can fly this thing much slower than what I'm doing right now. I know it's fast, but we're going to need to shoot this approach at 225 knots."

"You're calling the shots," Henry said. "If you want 225, that's what you'll get. You ready to do this again? O'Hare wants us to make a left turn back toward the final approach course."

Donovan could still feel Keith behind him. He turned around. "What's happening in back? How's Audrey?"

"It's not good. Rafael doesn't think she'll last much longer. We need to get on the ground now, or she probably won't make it."

Donovan clenched his jaw and a fresh wave of confidence flowed through him. A new intensity burned behind his tired eyes. He looked at Henry's airplane, drew a deep breath, and started to move his 737 into position again, taking great care to measure his closure rate. "I want 225 knots. Nothing less." He began to close the final distance to the other airplane, deftly countering the vibrating controls.

"Here we go then," Henry said.

"Keith. Go back and get ready to land. Tell Rafael we'll be on the ground in less than ten minutes." The man turned and hurried toward the rear of the plane. He banked the airplane to match Henry's movements. John sat silently. "Not much longer, John."

"I know," John replied, weakly. "I promise, I'll call the approach lights the second I see them."

Donovan took one last look around the cockpit. He met John's eyes briefly. They both knew that they were running out of time—so many things could still go wrong.

CHAPTER
THIRTY-THREE

Henry once again handed the phone to Lauren. "Let me know when they're in position. Hopefully we can keep this connection open for the entire approach," Henry said, and then asked quietly, "If you get a chance, can you ask him how she's doing?"

Lauren asked Donovan the question that was on everyone's mind.

"Tell Henry she's about the same," Donovan said. "Honey, I need both hands to fly. I'm going to have to give this to John. We can relay through him. With a little luck I'll see you shortly. How about a late dinner?"

"It's a date." Tears welled up in Lauren's eyes.

"What did he say?" Matt asked. "How's Mom?"

"He said she was doing about the same."

A wounded expression formed on Matt's face.

"They'll be on the ground in a few minutes," Lauren said.

"Pull out the jump seat, Matt, and strap in tight," Henry ordered.

"Hello?" John's voice sounded over the phone.

"This is Lauren. We're here, how are you doing?" Lauren heard the sound of buckles next to her as Matt cinched himself up.

"Donovan's got us situated. We're moving into position. Give us another twenty seconds and we'll be there." John paused. "Tell Henry we can't have very much fuel left. If we can't stay with you and have to break it off, I think we should probably just head this thing for the lake."

"I understand," Lauren said.

"Boeing 31 Whiskey Alpha, this is O'Hare Tower. Turn left to a heading of 170 degrees and intercept the localizer. You are cleared for the CAT III approach to 14 Left," Kate said. "All vehicles are clear, centerline and touchdown zone lights have been plowed. Emergency vehicles are in position and standing by."

Henry turned the plane toward O'Hare, and Michael verified the clearance. Only a trace of light was still visible to the west. Henry glanced at Matt. "You all buckled in? You already know how rough it's going get."

"Are you sure I shouldn't be in the back of the plane—watching what's going on?" Matt said.

"No. You stay right here." Henry said.

"John says they're in position," Lauren relayed.

"I hope we have enough light left for this," Henry muttered.

Lauren wondered how much more difficult the growing darkness made it for Donovan to see their airplane. The autopilot began a gentle turn to the left. She couldn't shake John's words about heading for the lake if they failed.

"Localizer's alive," Henry called out to Michael "I'm showing we've captured both the localizer and glide slope. Speed set. Tell them we're starting down."

Lauren held her breath as the first wisps of vapor flew by with alarming swiftness. At 225 knots, they plunged into the diffused world of the raging blizzard.

"Lauren." John's strained voice sounded far away. "Donovan wants Henry to kill the strobe lights. They're blinding us."

"Kill the strobes," Lauren said.

Henry reached for the switch, then double-checked that all the other external lights were on. Turbulence began to shake the 737. All the powerful lights on Henry's airplane shone forward; there were precious few in the tail for Donovan to see. "Do they still have us?"

"Yes, just barely," Lauren said.

"When we get closer to the ground, there should be some light from the city filtering up through the clouds; it should help silhouette us. But it's going to get worse before it gets better."

"Boeing 31 Whiskey Alpha, O'Hare Tower. RVR for 14 Left is 600 variable 700. Wind is 330 degrees at 22 knots, gusts to 32."

Lauren relayed the information to John, and then listened. She put her hand over the receiver and turned to Henry. "John doesn't sound good; they can hardly see us."

"There's nothing we can do about that!" Henry said.

In a flurry of motion, Matt unlatched the belts and threw off his harness.

"Goddamnit Matt, sit down!" Henry yelled, but his son ignored him and bolted headlong from the cockpit.

Lauren started to say something—but Matt was already gone. A barrage of turbulence pounded them as they descended lower into the storm. It was getting even darker.

Lauren gazed at the glowing instruments before her. The autopilot reacted instantly to each new disturbance in the atmosphere. It had grown eerily quiet on the flight deck. Suddenly, John began shouting something to her but she couldn't make out what he was saying.

"There's a what?" Lauren snapped her head toward Henry. "John, slow down, I can't understand you."

"What's happening?" Henry asked.

Lauren's eyes grew wide. "John says there's a beam, a laser of some kind coming from our airplane. He's ecstatic! He's saying that they need for it to stay in a fixed position."

"How can that be?" Henry shook his head, and then glanced at Matt's empty seat.

"It's Matt! He has one of those laser pointers; I saw him with it earlier." Lauren listened to what John was telling her and then relayed to Henry. "Donovan says for us to fix the beam just above the tip of the right horizontal stabilizer!"

Henry's focus never left the instruments as he picked up the handset for the cabin announcement system. "Matt. They want you to keep the laser beam pointed out into space, just above the tip of the right horizontal stabilizer. Son, do your best to hold it still."

"John says keep it right there," Lauren reported, her voice filled with exhilaration. "Matt's got it perfectly. Donovan can't believe how much of a difference it makes!"

"It's working, Matt," Henry said. "No matter how rough it gets son, just keep it steady!"

CHAPTER THIRTY-FOUR

Donovan fixed his gaze on the red, pencil-thin beam of light that reached out into the darkness from Henry's plane. The sharp contrast of the laser gave him a constant point of reference back to the other 737. "John, it's a stroke of genius!"

"Incredible," John muttered.

"I'll keep the beam out in front of us. It's so damn perfect." Donovan could just make out a face in the rearmost window. He knew it was Matt holding the laser steady. He remembered Audrey's words, her desire for Henry and Matt to reconnect. Donovan wished she could see this, her husband and son working together.

Donovan guided the 737 within 20 feet of the other plane. As before, he stayed slightly behind and above the other Boeing—the sleek vertical stabilizer rose almost level with their cockpit. Wayfarer's logo was bathed in a soft light, a stark contrast to the piercing red beam. He reacted to each small movement of the other aircraft, aided by the small point of laser light from the Wayfarer jet. He felt as though he could reach out and touch the painted aluminum.

As the turbulence grew, Donovan's control adjustments became more aggressive. His body tightened; the tendons in his hands and wrists twitched as he battled to stay in formation.

"Lauren says it's going to get a lot rougher the lower we go," John relayed.

"No kidding." Despite the unstable air, Donovan remained in perfect position. "How high are we?" He didn't dare risk even a quick glance at the altimeter.

"We're going through four thousand feet. We're twelve miles from touchdown," John said. "At this speed, we'll be there in three and a half minutes."

The tailwind hurtled them over the ground at almost 260 knots. Donovan hoped he'd be able to bleed off some of that speed, but the touchdown might still be as fast as 200 knots—a staggering difference from the usual 125. He pushed the power up slightly as the other plane pulled several feet in front of them. Donovan marveled at how steady Matt was able to hold the laser despite the turbulence. The aching fatigue moved from his legs to his shoulders and arms. His eyes burned, unblinking, as he constantly judged his distance from the tail of the other 737. The laser beam glowed brightly in the murky sky.

"Outer Marker," John relayed, as the planes sped over the final approach fix. "One minute and fifteen seconds until touchdown."

Donovan nodded. The 737 reacted sluggishly in his hands and he added a fraction more power. His legs throbbed painfully; his calves began to cramp. He wriggled the numbness from his toes. "John, I need a little more help with the right rudder. I'm having trouble holding it." The pressure applied by John was only a slight relief. A dull orange glow reflected off the polished metal of Henry's Boeing. It took Donovan a moment to realize it must be from the fire in his left engine—it was still burning.

"One thousand feet above the ground," John said.

Donovan's right leg trembled involuntarily from the strain. He was tapping into the last of his physical resources. The ache in his shoulders crept down his arms and into his hands. He desperately wanted to shift in his seat, but the risk of creating some small control input made it far too dangerous.

"I saw some lights straight down!" John said. "Just a flash, but I saw them."

Donovan knew that forward visibility would be the deciding factor. Often you could see directly down in the fog or snow, but the view straight ahead was the one that mattered. He was about to ask John how far they were from the runway when a massive wave of turbulence pummeled both Boeings.

"Look out!" John yelled, as they skidded and rocked dangerously close to the other airplane.

Donovan tried to turn away, but they lurched toward the tail of the other plane. He could see Matt in the window; the laser pointer fixed exactly where he wanted it. The young man never so much as flinched at what seemed like certain impact. Donovan was so close he could recognize individual rivets on the paint-chipped tail.

He put both hands on the controls and tried to roll away. He held his breath as a second jolt hit the 737. The aircraft grazed the side of Henry's plane, and the shudder and sound of scraping metal almost made Donovan duck. He fought the controls. If he corrected too far, he would lose them. Not far enough and they would hit again. The rudder and elevator of Henry's airplane fluttered for a moment, correcting for the forces of the two planes having touched.

"Oh shit! We hit them," John's voice cried out. "We're still here, we're okay. Are you?" He listened for a moment on the phone, then turned toward Donovan. "They're all right!"

Donovan struggled as he tried to regain control of the plane. The instability had eased momentarily, but still pounded the planes. He knew they had entered an area where two different rivers of air collided. The turbulence was bordering on severe. Scraped paint and a small indentation in the smooth metal marked the point of impact on Henry's 737. Matt gave a thumbs-up from the window, the laser beam a rock-steady red line in the near darkness. "Just a fender bender. Tell Henry his son is magnificent!"

"Will do, five hundred feet to go," John said. "Keep going Donovan. We're almost there!"

Donovan nodded, swallowing hard. His tortured muscles ached and screamed in protest as he continued to match the other 737 move for move.

"Two hundred feet. Ground contact straight down!"

Again, turbulence tore at the two airplanes. John reached out and grabbed the glare-shield. The blurred yellow glow of streetlights flashed past. Donovan strained through his burning eyes to see the first section of the approach lights.

"One hundred feet. I see the strobes! Right below us," John cried out.

"I've got them." The array of approach lights flashed directly beneath them, their rhythmic white pulses leading to the runway. At this rate, they'd be over the concrete in seconds. Donovan's muscles tightened even more. He had no way to get to the runway—Henry's plane was still in their way.

The lights that marked the touchdown zone raced past. Donovan yanked the good throttle all the way back, trying desperately to fall away from the other plane. He knew he was eating up runway at an alarming rate.

"Go around!" John screamed into the phone at Henry. "We have the runway!"

Donovan watched in horror as the other 737 plummeted even lower. Full thrust from Henry's engines raised a giant plume of snow as he struggled to go around. In what seemed like slow motion, the other 737 clawed and lifted its way out of the wind shear, moving ever-so-slightly out of their path. Donovan held the controls tightly as the jet blast from Henry's plane buffeted his aircraft. When the right wing tried to come up, Donovan forced it level. If he let a wing tip dig into the snow, they would cartwheel and die in an instant. Donovan used all of his strength to raise the nose. They were still going 190 knots. He managed a few more degrees of pitch before the Boeing finally plunged heavily onto the snow-covered runway.

Donovan's harness dug deeply into his shoulders at first impact, then eased as the 737 skipped. He caught a glimpse of Henry's airplane as it struggled to climb upward into the night sky. Donovan pulled back on the elevator with everything he had to kill some more of their speed. The tail hit the ground and the force rammed the nose heavily into the snow. He caught one last glimpse of the other 737 lifting up and away from 880.

The next impact threw him even harder against his straps. Above the roar of the plane, Donovan heard John shriek in agony. From behind him, the sound of tearing metal filled the cockpit. The rudder pedals slammed against his feet. He tried frantically to keep the Boeing's nose pointed straight ahead. Without warning, the 737 began to skid sideways. Donovan used every last ounce of his strength to hold it straight, but the airplane spun hard, and Donovan was hammered against the wall of the cockpit. Everything outside vanished under a wall of snow as they careened off the runway. Seconds later he was catapulted into the control column—and the world went black.

CHAPTER THIRTY-FIVE

Lauren had come out of her seat as the wind shear pushed them down almost to the runway. Henry jammed both throttles to full power and the engine noise resonated through the airframe.

"They've got the runway!" Lauren called out "Henry, get us out of here!"

Fifty feet above the ground, they began to accelerate. Henry eased back on the controls. One tiny mistake and they would hit the runway and crash in front of the other plane. The 737's wings bit hard into the cold air; the huge turbofan engines were screaming.

Lauren felt the first subtle sensation they were picking up speed. She knew that 880 was somewhere close behind them and she steeled herself for the first tremor of a collision. Henry forced the 737 away from the runway, straining against the onslaught of turbulence as they climbed back into the heart of the blizzard. Below them flashed the long-term parking lot lights and broad expanse of the International Terminal.

"John! Can you hear me? Are you down? Talk to me!" Lauren cried out over and over into the phone.

The powerful Boeing pounded through the turbulence. Henry finally pulled the engine thrust back a fraction. They were now hurtling out of 3,000 feet for the smoother air above.

"Tower. This is Boeing 31 Whiskey Alpha," Michael said, breathless as he spoke into the microphone. "We're going missed approach. Did they make it? Is 880 down?"

"Surface radar shows they're down. We can't see anything. We're waiting for reports from the emergency crews. You are cleared to climb to 10,000 feet." Kate stopped for a moment. The background noise in the cab increased as reports from the crash landing poured in. "31 Whiskey Alpha, you are cleared to climb to 10,000 feet and say your intentions."

"Stand by." Michael waited for Henry. They'd finally flown above the worst of the storm.

"I've lost the connection." Lauren lowered her head, as she slowly closed the phone. The 737 plowed through the occasional rough air currents as they continued to climb

"Tell Kate we want to hold at 10,000 feet." Henry leveled the wings as another jolt buffeted them. "Any word yet at all?"

Michael keyed the microphone. "Tower, we'll level at 10,000 feet. Can you tell us anything about 880?"

"Boeing 31 Whiskey Alpha, you're cleared to 10,000 feet. Turn left to 090 degrees. I'll give you vectors to keep you in my airspace. I have no official word I can relay over this frequency. O'Hare is officially closed at this time due to an accident."

Lauren slumped in her seat.

"It worked!" Matt exploded into the flight deck. "They made it down. Is Mom okay? Do we know yet?"

"Not yet. We'll know soon." Lauren turned toward the young man. She leaned over and gave him a huge hug. "You were amazing," she whispered, before she let him go.

"That guy was incredible!" Matt said. "You should have seen how close he held the airplane. I could almost see right inside the cockpit." He held his hands together to illustrate how both airplanes had been positioned. "I thought we were done for when he bumped into us. The turbulence was so bad! I could see his wings flexing up and down. His left engine was still on fire; the whole time we were flying, that thing was burning. But he stayed right there. Man, it was something! I could even see the scratch on his nose where he ran into us."

Michael looked back and smiled. "What made you think of the laser?"

Matt shrugged. "I just remembered screwing around with one on a really foggy night. It's pretty intense."

"What else did you see?" Henry said, with more than a trace of anguish in his voice. "What did you see when we went around? Could you tell what happened to them after they touched down?"

"I saw the lights rush past us. The other plane dropped back slightly but then we slowed down, too. He raised the nose and I was scared we were going to hit again. But somehow he got his plane on the runway. I swear I could see down through the hole in the top. Then everything went white as we pulled up."

"They touched down flat? Like a normal landing?" Michael asked. "Yeah," Matt said, and shrugged. "Pretty much."

"Sounds like a survivable landing to me." Michael forced a smile, then turned toward Henry as his smile subsided.

"Is there any way we can find out about Mom?" Matt said to Lauren. "Will they call us or something when they know?"

"The tower can't give us any information on the open frequency." Lauren began searching for Kate's cell phone number. "Maybe Kate will talk to us on the phone."

"Tower," Henry said into the microphone, "this is Boeing 31 Whiskey Alpha. We have a phone number. We're calling it now."

"Roger 31 Whiskey Alpha," Kate responded. "It's on."

"Her name's Kate," Lauren said to Michael. "God, she did a great job." Lauren switched her attention to the ringing cell phone.

"Kate here."

"Kate. It's Lauren. What can you tell us?"

"Okay—" Kate said quietly, then took a long breath before she started to speak. "Thanks for using the phone. As I explained before, all the communications in the tower are recorded, and as it sits right now we've bent the rules pretty far today. I'm not sure how much trouble we're going to be in at this point." Kate continued. "What we know right now is that 880 is down, but not on the runway. The visibility dropped and the rescue elements had to follow the marks in the snow to get to the aircraft. We don't think there's a fire, but we're not sure of much else. I'm sorry, but we're not going to know anything for a little while."

"Kate, thanks again. Can you let us know on the radio if we need to call you back? If you hear anything more we'd sure appreciate it."

"I'll do as much as I can," Kate said. "I don't know how much longer I'll be here though. The facility chief is on his way and I'm going to be put on standard administrative leave pending an investigation."

"Once we get on the ground we'll do anything we can to help you," Lauren said.

"I appreciate that. I need to go."

Lauren severed the connection. "They're down. There's no report of fire. I'm afraid we're not going to know much else for a while—but we got them down."

The 737 emerged from the clouds into the clear air above the storm. The last traces of the sunset burned deep purple steaks across the western sky. A heavy silence pressed in on them as each person on the flight deck pondered what lay below in the raging blizzard—and there was nothing more they could do except circle above.

CHAPTER
THIRTY-SIX

Donovan tried to move, to say something, anything. After hours of howling wind, the silence was palpable in the absolute darkness of the cockpit. He fought for a breath. He struggled to turn but his harness held him firmly in place. With a painful gasp he managed to get some air into his lungs, then gradually his breathing became easier. He'd had the wind knocked out of him. He called blindly, "John, talk to me." He reached toward the copilot's seat and felt for John. Donovan found an arm and gently shook it. It flopped limply in his hand. Donovan fumbled for his own harness release and threw off his restraints.

He could see nothing. The windows were completely covered with snow. Only the residual light from the airport filtered through, and as Donovan's eyes adjusted he regained a measure of vision. He knew they needed to get out. The risk of fire was very real.

On shaky legs Donovan pulled himself out of his seat. He knelt beside John and carefully raised his head. "John. Can you hear me?" With a relief he could feel John's warm breath on his hand.

A small moan passed through John's lips; a crease formed on his forehead.

"John. Wake up. We have to get out of here!" His voice was firmer this time. As Donovan's eyes adjusted further, he could see John's chest moving. The faint lights from outside began to flash red as emergency vehicles arrived on the scene. The silence was broken by the deep roar of diesel engines and wailing sirens.

"Help!" a voice called from just aft of the cockpit. Donovan recognized it as Rafael's. He slid past John and squeezed out into the cabin.

"Rafael," Donovan called. "Where are you?"

"I'm right here," came the feeble reply.

Donovan turned and could just make out Rafael, still huddled over Audrey. They were squeezed into the small floor area of what was left of the forward galley. Donovan dropped to his knees. "How are you? Is she alive?" He saw Rafael had somehow held her in roughly the same position through the entire approach and crash landing.

"Yes, but just barely. Get help."

Donovan stood and looked for the others. It was too dark to see into the back of the plane. He wasn't even certain if there was a back of the plane. Above him, a flashlight pierced the darkness through the hole in the roof.

"In here!" Donovan yelled. He shielded his eyes from the harsh light. "Help us."

The sound of rescue vehicles grew, along with muffled shouts and voices yelling from outside the 737.

Another beam of light hit him from the rear of the Boeing. Dressed from head to toe in a fireproof suit, a man raced down the aisle. "Please help them," was all Donovan could say. The rescue worker put his hands around Donovan's shoulders and moved him gently into the arms of another fireman who was right behind him.

"There's one more in the cockpit," Donovan called out as he was escorted toward the rear of the plane. They passed the seats where Christy, Keith and Wetzler had been. They were empty. He marveled that the aircraft was somewhat still intact. Swiftly they reached the aft emergency exit. Donovan was helped the short distance to the snowy earth. The solid ground had never felt so sweet.

The biting wind served to erase the cobwebs. Donovan accepted a blanket that was thrown around his shoulders. From behind him a piercing scream rang out. Rescue personnel sprinted toward the commotion. As Donovan moved closer he could see two paramedics restraining Keith. Wetzler was down on his hands and knees, emptying the contents of his stomach onto the ground.

"That son of a bitch had it coming!" Keith yelled as he struggled against the men holding him. "He's lucky I don't kill him!"

Bathed in the flashing lights, a fresh gash glistened on the side of Keith's head, and part of his face was streaked with blood. Donovan rushed forward. "Let him go!" He stepped behind the still retching Wetzler, and turned to Keith. "What happened?"

"Donovan. Oh, thank God you're safe!" The paramedics released Keith immediately and he wrapped one unsteady arm around Donovan and pointed the other at Wetzler. His eyes burned with hatred. "This miserable little piece of shit!"

"What happened after we landed? Where's Christy?"

"After we finally stopped, I got the door open and was carrying Christy out, when Wetzler tried to get out first. He pushed me into the bulkhead." Keith gulped large quantities of air as he touched the fresh blood on his face. "I almost dropped Christy as Wetzler ran screaming from the plane. First chance I had, I knocked the crap out of him!"

Wetzler raised his head and tried to speak. He only managed a weak gurgling sound and heaved again.

"Where is she?" Donovan asked the paramedics. "Where's Christy. The flight attendant?"

"We already loaded her into an ambulance. She's on her way to the hospital," one of them said.

"Take care of this man," Donovan said, gesturing at Keith, then he knelt down to make sure Wetzler could hear him. "When the dust settles, your name is going to be synonymous with the word coward. And, if I have my way, you'll be brought up on a multitude of felony charges. Good luck with all of that."

"What about the others?" Keith asked as Donovan stood. "Audrey?"

"We all survived the landing. I don't know much more than that." Donovan watched as Wetzler, gasping, was pulled to his feet, then he turned back to Keith. "Let them take care of that wound. It looks awful."

Keith nodded. "Thanks—for saving us."

"I couldn't have done it without your help," Donovan said, knowing the last thing he needed was to be in the spotlight. He already had enough problems; in fact, his problems were just starting. "I'll try to find you later."

"You're not coming to the hospital?"

"Not yet." Donovan put his hand on Keith's shoulder. "Like I said, I'll be right behind you."

The paramedics led Keith away. Donovan looked back at the 737. It was completely surrounded by emergency vehicles. The flashing lights cast an eerie red glow in the blizzard. Thick foam covered the left engine. Steam rose from the battered CFM turbofan. The huge inlets of the engines had served as massive brakes, which slowed the 737. The outer ten feet of the left wing was missing. He wondered where it was. He let his eyes carefully trace up the tail. The damage to the rudder was far worse than he'd thought—twisted and sheared off at the top. It was a miracle it had stayed in one piece.

"Right this way," a voice sounded. A paramedic tried to guide him to a waiting ambulance.

Donovan pulled away, ignoring the order. Finally, he made out the forward section of the Boeing. A blanket of snow concealed the cockpit. Different lights caught his attention. He scanned beyond the wreckage. Fifty feet in front of the 737, stood twin rows of streetlights. He realized that they'd come to a stop just short of the taxiways that crossed over I-190—the main road into O'Hare. The pile of snow they'd created had saved them from plunging down onto the highway. Landing as fast as they did had used every inch of the 10,000-foot runway, plus a little more.

"You need to come this way, sir," the paramedic at his side said again.

Donovan yanked his arm from the man's grip and spun around. "The other airplane. What happened to the other airplane?"

"I don't know, sir. My job is to get you to safety. Please come with me."

"I'll go with you when I'm good and ready." Donovan patted the EMS technician on the back. "I'm the pilot of this plane and I'm fine. So until I'm sure everyone's okay, let me do what I need to do."

The roar of a powerful engine caused Donovan to turn away from the paramedic. A snowplow approached the front of the plane. The driver raised the blade and skillfully inched the huge truck forward. When the signal was given, he lowered his blade. Black smoke poured from the exhaust as he slowly backed away from the fuselage, dragging the mountain of snow from the cabin door. Within seconds the entryway was open and the paramedics rushed inside.

Donovan moved closer as the first stretcher was carried out the forward door. Rescue workers huddled close, paramedics carefully holding IV bottles in the air. It was Audrey. Someone was squeezing a round rubber bladder to force air into her lungs. Another person was pushing rhythmically on her chest even as they rushed her into the back of the ambulance. Right behind her, supported by two paramedics, came Rafael.

"Rafael. How is she?" Donovan's eyes pleaded with someone to tell him something—anything. The grim faces of the rescue workers spoke volumes as they ignored him and hurried toward an ambulance.

"We did all we could do." Rafael said weakly, his hands and shirt covered with blood. "She's in good hands now. They're doing everything they can."

"You did an amazing job," Donovan couldn't help but imagine how difficult it had been for Rafael to do what he had. He could see Rafael's teeth were chattering uncontrollably, his hands tucked up under his armpits for warmth. He instantly understood that the brave young man needed to get someplace warm. "I can't go with you right now—but I'll come as soon as I can. I'll find you later."

Donovan stepped out of the way. Rafael nodded that he understood as he was helped into the back of the ambulance. The door slammed shut and the vehicle drove away and vanished in the blizzard. Donovan wished he had gone with Audrey, but he had things he needed to do.

More stretchers emerged from the rear door. They would be the people in back, the passengers who would never wake up. A deep sadness for their families moved through him. He thought of Patricia Wheeler; at least her family would get her body back. He thought about how lucky he'd been today. A bittersweet joy filled him as he took another long look at the crumpled Boeing. He'd made a promise to Lauren that he'd be there for their wedding, and miraculously he was still alive. He looked up into the blizzard and wondered where she was. Would they be able to land here, or would they end up in a distant city until the storm passed?

Donovan turned to the man who hovered a few steps away. "Is there a VHF radio in one of these vehicles?"

"They all have them, but I can't allow you to tie up the frequency.

There's a lot of official business going on."

"It's okay. Trust me." Donovan stepped through the snow to a nearby crash truck. He hoisted himself into the cab. The engine was running and the interior was warm and comfortable. He located the radio and from memory dialed in the frequency for the control tower. He thought for a moment about what to say, then keyed the microphone. "O'Hare Tower, this is Wayfarer 880. I just wanted to say thank you for a terrific job."

"Wayfarer 880." Kate's surprised voice came in loud and clear. "You're welcome. Just so you know, there's also a Boeing 31 Whiskey Alpha on the frequency."

"Hello 880, good to hear from you." Michael transmitted over the radio. "You doing okay? Do you know anything about the others?"

"I'm fine. Audrey's been taken to a hospital. She was still alive after we landed. I think most everyone else is in one piece."

"No one else was hurt in the landing?" Henry said through the speaker.

"We're all a little banged up," Donovan said. "But for the most part, everyone is intact."

"Nice job," Henry said, then paused. "I've got to tell you, that was a hell of piece of flying. I'm impressed."

"The person who was impressive was Matt Parrish. I'm looking forward to shaking his hand."

"You don't know the half of it," Henry said. "Someone else wants to say hello."

"Hi there." Lauren said, brimming with emotion. "You're okay…?"

"I'm fine, a little tired," Donovan admitted.

"Me too. But I'm not sure when we can land. Henry thinks we may have to divert. I might not see you until morning."

"That would be a shame." Donovan hated the thought of not seeing Lauren until tomorrow.

"I'll find you when we land. We need to talk privately. Do you still have the phone you were using?"

"No. But I'll get it." Donovan could tell by her tone that it was important. "Call me in ten minutes. Did you by chance make any friends down here?"

"Ask for Emmett," Lauren said cautiously, remembering what Kate had said about all the frequencies being recorded. "He drives Snow One. He seems to know his way around."

"Thanks. I'll see if I can find him. Stay safe. I hope to see you soon." Donovan put the microphone down.

He continued to ignore his escort and turned back toward the wreckage. The paramedics were still bringing people out from the rear of the plane, so Donovan stepped through the snow to the front of the 737. He entered through the open door, and the headlights from the firefighting vehicles illuminated the interior of the mangled fuselage. Clumps of red slush spotted the floor. It was Audrey's blood mixed with snow that had been tracked into the plane. He ducked and made his way to the cockpit. It took him a moment, but finally he located the phone that he and John had used during their final approach. He snapped the cover down and took one last look around the shattered cockpit. He couldn't help but consider how close he'd come to dying in this cramped space. He breathed in the cold, crisp air. He was truly thankful to be among the living, but his joy was mixed with sadness and anger. He clenched his jaw and walked out of the Boeing for the last time.

He stepped out of the plane just as a man in a pickup truck pulled up and stopped.

"Are you Nash? You looking for me?" a heavyset black man called out as he rolled down the side window.

Donovan realized this was Emmett. The man had overheard the transmission on his radio. The two shook hands warmly. "I'm Donovan Nash."

"What is it you're looking for?"

"I have to get to the main terminal. Can you drive me to Wayfarer Operations without having to go through a lot of red tape? I understand there might be some security issues."

"Sure." Emmett shrugged his huge shoulders. "I can do that."

"Uh, Mr. Nash," the paramedic spoke up. "You can't leave the accident scene unless it's to get medical attention. I can't allow you to go anywhere."

"That's fine." Donovan patted the man on the shoulder. "I'll get medical attention at the main terminal."

"Jump in." Emmett motioned to the truck. "I'll radio a plow to come make us a path."

Donovan trudged through the snow, opened the door to Snow One, and threw himself onto the bench seat. In seconds, a snowplow moved into position in front of them.

"You ready?" Emmett put the truck into gear and flashed his headlights at the plow.

"Yeah." Donovan held the phone in his hand and wished Lauren would call him back. As they began to pull away from the crash site, Donovan sat back in the seat and tried to relax, but his muscles were still wire tight. As they continued he could just make out the dozens of parked airplanes half-buried by the blizzard. He didn't think he'd ever seen a major airport this paralyzed by the weather.

"I wanted to thank you for what you did back there." Emmett gestured behind them toward the crash site. "You brought those people home and that means a lot."

Donovan studied Emmett. In the yellow glow from the snowplow's flashing lights, Donovan caught a sadness in Emmett's eyes, dampness on his cheeks. Donovan was about to ask Emmett if he'd known someone on the flight when the cell phone in his hand sprang to life.

"Hello," Donovan answered, but he made a mental note to ask Emmett later about his comments. He also wanted to find out how instrumental Emmett had been in their being safely on the ground. Judging by the conditions and the fact that Lauren hadn't hesitated in bringing him up, Donovan had a hunch that Emmett had played a key role in getting Henry and Michael into the air.

"It's me." Lauren breathed a sigh of relief. "Okay, I'm in the back of the airplane where no one can hear me. Where are you now?"

"I'm with Emmett. He's taking me to the terminal. What you and I need to discuss is this phone call Cyrus made. I know he wanted us to crash—do you have any idea who he might have been talking to?"

"Not a clue, but it had to be someone from another airline. Oh, Donovan," Lauren said, her voice trailing off. "I'm so sorry I allowed this to happen. It's all my fault."

"Don't worry about it." Donovan checked the time on his watch. "Did you by chance call and let anyone know that Abigail might be in danger?"

"Yes. Just now. Without going into a lot of detail, I called William and told him what might be happening. Knowing him, he's probably already putting an escape plan into motion until this blows over."

"Good." Donovan nodded his approval as he thought of William, his closest and most trusted ally. The elder statesman knew every facet of Donovan's life and had been by his side since he was a boy. William was almost like a father to him. "Hopefully, I can persuade Leo to act on this, but the fact is, this is just our word against Richtman's. We're holding a pretty weak hand."

"If it doesn't work, if somehow Cyrus can't be convinced to stay quiet, you know I'll support whatever it is we need to do. You and Abigail mean everything to me. I'm with you whatever happens."

"I feel the same way." Donovan loved her more right now than he ever thought possible. "I need to go. I'll do what I can to get us past this."

"I know you will. I hope to see you soon."

Donovan ended the call and studied the keypad on the phone, trying to decide what he could do with what little evidence he had. He glanced over and saw Emmett studying him.

"I couldn't help but hear what you were saying. Let me see if I got this right. The reason your friends had to steal a jet was because there was someone at Wayfarer who wanted you to crash?"

"You heard right," Donovan said, and nodded. "He was going to sacrifice a lot of good people in the process."

"He threatened someone named Abigail?"

"My daughter." Donovan thought again about Emmett's earlier reaction as they left the crash site. He lowered his voice. "Emmett, did you know someone on board the plane?"

Emmett's jaw tightened and he banged his hand on the steering wheel. All the big man could do was tip his head forward and back as his thick chest shuddered.

Donovan reached over and put a hand on Emmett's shoulder. "I'm sorry."

"Not your fault," Emmett managed to say after he gathered himself. "He was my nephew, coming home from Georgetown University. I didn't even know he was on the flight until a little while ago. My sister called when she heard about the emergency on television. I found him before I came over to find you. He didn't make it."

Donovan pictured a young man who'd been seated near a window, close to the rear. He was about college age, and hadn't been wearing a mask. He was among the dead rather than the near-dead.

"This whole thing is pure bullshit!" Emmett once again slammed his huge fist against the steering wheel—this time with far more force, and the reverberation rippled through the entire vehicle. "Who is this guy?"

"His name is Cyrus Richtman," Donovan said calmly. "From what little I know, he's going to try and oust the chairman of Wayfarer Airlines and take over the top spot."

"So he was doing this for money?" Emmett asked, his voice filled with rage and grief. "Is he going to get away with it?"

"Maybe. Right now I don't have any proof. It's a long shot, but if I can get Leo Singer, the chairman, to listen to me, then maybe I can intervene before it's too late."

Donovan caught Emmett mumble something beneath his breath. He was about to ask him to repeat himself, but stopped. The cold look in Emmett's eyes told him whatever it was, it was private.

CHAPTER THIRTY-SEVEN

Lauren sat down in one of the aisle seats. It occurred to her that she'd never before been the only passenger on a commercial jet. The empty airliner made her feel isolated and alone. The more she thought about what she'd done, the worse she felt. She'd let Donovan's deepest secret fall into the hands of someone despicable. Cyrus had already used the knowledge to threaten them. What would come next—blackmail, or a public announcement that Donovan was actually the late Robert Huntington? What would happen to the three of them if that happened? Lauren gazed out the small window. To the east, the first star of the evening hung brightly in the heavens, and she wished she were doing anything besides sitting here, helplessly circling above Chicago. She raised herself up to join the others in the cockpit, when a faint idea glimmered in her mind. She sat down and tried to put it all together. Moments later she fumbled for her cell phone while staring at the distant star. She hoped what she had in mind was possible, and more importantly, that she wasn't too late.

"Calvin. It's Lauren. Donovan's on the ground, he's safe, but I need a huge favor." It only took her a few minutes to outline what she needed. She was careful not to divulge the real reason she was asking Calvin for his help.

"What you're asking is extremely difficult," Calvin said, finally. "I don't need to remind you that the political, as well as the legal implications are pretty much off the chart."

"I know. But this man needs to be stopped," Lauren said, waiting for Calvin to decide what he could or couldn't do.

"This individual, the one you overheard, you're positive he was conspiring with another party in regard to the outcome of today's events?"

"Yes, he was not only going to use the crash to gain control of the airline, but he was going to place as much of the blame on Donovan and Eco-Watch as he could."

"If I do this—and believe me when I tell you I'm not sure I can even pull it off," Calvin said. "There is no way this can ever be made public, and it could never be used in a court of law."

"I understand." Lauren prayed that Calvin had heard enough to help.

"I'll see what I can do," Calvin said, as he exhaled heavily. "But I'm going to need a few things from you first."

Lauren returned to the flight deck and ignored the questioning expressions of both Henry and Michael. Calvin had promised he'd do his best, but he'd offered no guarantees. It remained yet another item on her growing list of uncertainties.

"How soon can we land?" Matt asked, turning the attention away from Lauren. "Are we going to be able to land at O'Hare?"

Henry shook his head. "The airport is closed. We've got some fuel left. We can hold here for a little while longer, but we'll have to divert somewhere else if the weather doesn't improve."

A frown crossed Matt's face. "But if we divert we wouldn't be able to get home until later tonight or even tomorrow. We have to land here. Mom needs us."

"We'll hold here for as long as we can. Trust me, son. I'm just as frustrated as you are. We have to be patient."

"You don't care, do you?" Matt muttered under his breath.

"What was that?" Henry snapped his head in Matt's direction.

"You did this for your precious airline, didn't you? Mom's right, it's all you've ever cared about, isn't it?"

"Matt! Knock it off. This isn't the time or the place."

Without another word, Matt flew up out of his seat and stormed from the cockpit.

Lauren resisted the urge to confront Henry, to get in the middle of this escalated dispute between father and son. She rose from her seat and went back to find Matt. She walked down the aisle in the empty cabin until she reached the very last row of seats. He had his head buried in his hands.

"Matt, I'm sorry all of this is so difficult." Matt turned further away from her as she spoke. Not to be ignored, Lauren continued. " I want to thank you for everything you did today. From helping us escape from the first jet, to recognizing there was another airplane we could use, to the laser idea. You made the difference. Everything you did gave your mom a fighting chance."

Matt raised his head. His eyes were filled with tears and he took in a deep breath to try to hold them in. He shrugged and looked away.

"I won't make excuses for him, but your father is just as stressed as you are." Lauren wasn't sure what she could do to make the young man feel better. "Everything that we did today happened amazingly fast, and you are a huge part of why we succeeded. You should be very proud of what you did. I know I'm proud of you."

"It doesn't matter," Matt said, then sniffed. "We're stuck up here and I need to be on the ground. I have to get to my mom."

"I think it matters a great deal." She wanted to keep Matt talking, try and diffuse his frustration and rage. "If it weren't for you they would have been forced to land in the lake. You gave everyone on that airplane a chance to survive."

"Yeah, well." Matt shrugged wistfully as he looked down at the floor. "I wish it were him down there. Not her."

Lauren crumbled a little inside at Matt's sad disclosure.

"I wish it were me, too," Henry said. "I'd trade places with your mother in an instant."

Lauren turned, startled by the sound of Henry's voice behind her.

"I'll leave the two of you alone." Lauren slipped past Henry.

"No. Stay here," Henry, said quietly, as he put his hand on Lauren's arm to stop her. "You're a part of this. I need you to hear some of what I have to say."

Lauren looked into Henry's eyes. She expected to see the same angry expression to which she'd become accustomed. But instead, she found a softening around the edges, as if the tremendous weight he'd been carrying had finally caved in a small part of the facade.

"Matt." Henry waited to see if his son would turn and face him. When it didn't happen, he continued anyway. "I'm sorry, son. You didn't deserve to be yelled at, and I want to apologize."

Matt sat rigidly in his seat, his attention focused somewhere outside the gently turning Boeing.

"I know we've had some problems lately." Henry lowered his head. "I'm sorry if you feel as if you've been caught in the middle of the issues your mother and I are having. You know we both love you, and we want only the best for you. But when you came aboard this airplane, you were putting yourself in harm's way, which, as a father, is the last place you want your child to be. Can you understand that, can you understand why I was angry?"

"I'm not a child," Matt muttered. "You treat me like I'm a little kid. You've never bothered to notice I'm not ten years old anymore."

Henry started to say something in return but no sound escaped his lips. A look of profound sorrow flashed across his face, as if he'd been charged and found guilty by his own flesh and blood. At that moment, Lauren didn't know which of the two of them was the more wounded.

"I know you're not a child anymore. Which is the hardest thing imaginable for me right now."

"Why is it so hard?"

Henry took a slow measured breath as he searched for the right thing to say. "You might be right." He shook his head sadly. "I've already lost one child I couldn't protect. I couldn't bear to go through that again. Which is why I wanted you to stay out of this today—it's why I was angry about your putting yourself at risk."

Matt wiped at his tears. "Why did you do it?"

"Do what?"

"Why did you risk everything to save Mom?"

"I did it because it was the right thing to do. Leo and Cyrus couldn't see it—but I felt in my heart it was what had to be done."

"So Mom wasn't part of it?" Matt said, a wounded tone in his voice. "You were just doing your job?"

"Of course your mother was part of it. She's always been a part of what I do. We may be having our problems—but I still love her. If I'd only focused on her, I wouldn't have been able to function. I can't bear the thought of losing either one of you. What if something had happened to you today? What would that have done to your mother—or to me? It's why I tried so hard to keep you out of all this."

"You weren't going to lose me," Matt said. "I knew what I was doing. So did you."

"I don't know son." Henry shook his head slowly. "There were a few times today I wasn't sure of anything."

"No way."

"Really," Henry said, and nodded. "Today was nothing but one big gamble. If anything had hiccupped, if one set of events had turned out differently, we might not be sitting here having this conversation."

"So what happens now?"

"Well, we can circle for a little while longer," Henry began, but Matt cut him off.

"No. I mean what happens now. With you, Mom—and me?"

Lauren slid sideways and let Henry get past her to be closer to Matt. She moved forward as Henry sat down next to his son. She loved this new beginning, words spoken in honesty instead of anger. She sensed it was time for her to leave them alone.

"Come get me if you need me," Henry said, then tilted his head in Matt's direction. "And thank you."

Lauren smiled and made her way forward. She went through the open cockpit door and sat heavily in the jump seat.

"How's it going back there?" Michael asked as he joined her. "You get them calmed down?"

"I hope so." Lauren pulled a stray hair away from her eyes. "Anything happening up here?"

"Nothing. Kate keeps giving me the latest weather, but so far nothing much has changed."

"What do you think our chances are of making it back into O'Hare?"

"Not great." Michael leaned forward and in the waning light looked down at the carpet of solid clouds beneath them. "It might not be a such a bad idea for us to go somewhere else. I don't think they're all that happy with us down there. What do you think about us diverting to, I don't know, maybe an airport where a bunch of high-powered attorneys could meet us. Or, what if we arranged our own little press conference from up here? Then we could go somewhere and find legal counsel. We're not far from Canada, maybe they'd take us?"

Lauren smiled at Michael's scheming.

"No wait! I have a better idea!" Michael turned and smiled. "Let's go to Florida. We can lie on the beach and wait for everyone else to arrive for the wedding. I can work on my tan. Maybe even play a little golf."

"I'd love that." Lauren let out a small laugh. "You have no idea how much I'd love that."

"Boeing 31 Whiskey Alpha, this is O'Hare Tower."

Lauren's smile dissolved at the ominous tone in Kate's voice. She braced herself for bad news, word that something terrible had transpired.

"Go ahead tower." Michael, too, frowned as he replied.

"Uh. There's been a slight change in plans. You're about to be joined by two Air Force fighters. You are now under their jurisdiction. I'm officially out of this loop. Contact them on 121.5. They're using the call sign Blackjack Zero-One."

"Michael!" Lauren put her hand on Michael's arm as she peered out the left side of the airliner. The dark silhouette of a fighter was visible alongside them, missiles hanging menacingly under its wings.

"We see him," Michael radioed to Kate. "We're switching frequencies now."

"What in the hell is going on? When did they get here?" Henry burst into the cockpit. Matt followed close behind.

"We're about to find out." Michael keyed the microphone. "Blackjack Zero-One, this is Boeing 31 Whiskey Alpha. What can we do for you?"

"Boeing 31 Whiskey Alpha, this is Blackjack Zero-One. Be advised we have new instructions for you. You are to change course and divert immediately. We will escort you to Scott Air Force base."

"Let me talk to them." Henry slid into the left seat and found his microphone. "Blackjack Leader, we prefer to wait here until the weather at O'Hare improves."

"Negative," the fighter pilot replied sharply. "You will turn to a 220 degree heading at this time and leave the area. Any deviation and we are under orders to open fire. Do you copy?"

"This is Cyrus' work!" Henry slammed the microphone into its cradle. "The son-of-a bitch is behind this, I can feel it!"

"I see his wing-man." Michael had turned and found the other fighter poised above and behind them. "I think they're serious."

"Dad. We can't leave—do something!" Matt cried out.

"I'm afraid we don't have any choice." Henry shook his head in defeat. "We have to do what they say."

"Start your turn now," the F-16 pilot said firmly as he banked away to give them room to maneuver. "I repeat. Start your turn now."

Henry reached up and put his hand on the knob that controlled their heading. With one angry twist, he commanded the autopilot to turn the Boeing to the new course.

CHAPTER THIRTY-EIGHT

"This is the closest entrance to Wayfarer Operations." Emmett pulled the truck up to a steel door near Wayfarer's concourse.

The phone in Donovan's hand rang. He pushed the button and put the phone to his ear. "Donovan Nash."

"Donovan. This is Calvin Reynolds. Lauren gave me this number if I needed to reach you."

"What's going on?" Donovan couldn't imagine why Calvin would be calling.

"Here's the deal," Calvin said. "Lauren explained a little of what's going on there and asked me for a favor. It's not something I can do legally and I'll deny it came from this office. Do you understand?"

"Yes."

"Lauren wanted me to recover a certain conversation that took place earlier today. Because this particular call was made from a cell phone, during what was believed at the time to be a terrorist attack, certain intelligence elements were activated. There exists classified technology that records virtually every broadcast communication in the world. Once a transmission is recorded, computers key in on certain words and phrases consistent to a given threat. In today's case it was your flight number. The phone call in question has been retrieved."

A small smile crept across Donovan's face. He eyed Emmett, who was watching him. "Very clever."

"It's Lauren you have to thank for this," Calvin said. "But before we go any further, I need you to understand a few important details. This information cannot be used in any legal process. You can do what you need to do, but again, I am not involved. If the information is used publicly, this office will never be mentioned."

"Of course. You have my word."

"Your phone is going to ring again. Let it go to voice mail."

"I don't have any way to access the messages on this phone," Donovan said. "Why don't you leave it on our machine at home?"

"I'd rather this information be on a random cell phone. It gives me another level of deniability. I don't want what I'm sending you to be traced back to me, or this office. Do I make myself clear?"

"I understand. Do you have the code I'll need to listen to the message?"

"We just tracked it down," Calvin said, then paused. "It's 5599."

Donovan ended the call. The moment he did the phone rang again and continued to ring until it went to voice mail.

"Who was that?" Emmett said.

Donovan held up the phone triumphantly. "I think we now have what we need to go in there and cause some serious trouble." Donovan waited for the beep that would announce a new voice message had been received. He dialed the sequence to retrieve what Calvin had sent. What Donovan hadn't been prepared for, was the emotional response he had at the sound of Patricia's cheerful voice asking him to leave a message.

Donovan tried to blot out the image of her lifeless body as he followed the prompts. He pushed in the code Calvin had given him and listened intently. He recognized Cyrus' voice as the CEO clearly outlined his plan for flight 880—and his bigger plan for Leo and Wayfarer Airlines.

Donovan was livid, he clenched his jaw and ground his teeth together. He carefully saved the message, glanced at his watch, and looked over at Emmett.

"Is it what you needed?" Emmett asked, his dark eyes smoldering.

Before Donovan could answer, the door to the concourse burst open and six armed security men quickly encircled the vehicle, their automatic weapons pointed dangerously at the cab. The closest man yelled for Donovan and Emmett to raise their hands.

Donovan did as he was told. Moments later, both doors flew open and he was pulled out of the warm truck and roughly forced against the side of the vehicle. Donovan was quickly searched and cuffed, his wallet unceremoniously yanked from his back pocket, as was the phone that held the crucial message. On the opposite side of the truck Emmett was subjected to an identical process.

"Inside!" yelled one of the men.

"Where are we going?" Donovan asked as he was propelled forward. They climbed a flight of stairs and proceeded out into the deserted concourse.

"Where are you taking us?" Emmett said as the barrel of a gun pressed into his ribs.

"Be quiet! Get in the cart," the leader said and he pushed his gun in harder for emphasis.

A guard ordered Donovan and Emmett to sit down on the bench seat of an electric cart. The security officers positioned themselves in front and behind them, then they sped down the empty concourse. Two minutes later, they were shepherded into an elevator. Once the door opened, they were marched toward double security doors. Following a quick exchange on the radio, the doors swung open from the inside. The entire entourage swept through the entryway, into a large room.

"Stop here!"

Donovan and Emmett stopped. Donovan studied his surroundings and deduced that they'd been brought to Wayfarer Operations. A man in a tie approached them, with TSA emblazoned on the front of his dark blue coat. He looked to be about Donovan's age, though far smaller in build. He sported a familiar government-issue crew cut, and from the scowl on his face, Donovan could tell the man wasn't at all happy.

"Did you search them?" he asked as he drew close. One of the men nodded, and handed over Donovan's and Emmett's wallets. "My name's Preston. I'm the head of Transportation Security Administration here at O'Hare."

Donovan watched patiently as Preston pulled out the driver's license and studied Donovan's picture. He repeated the process with Emmett, noting the airport identification around the large man's neck.

"You're under arrest for conspiracy," Preston said to Emmett, then turned to one of his men. "Read him his rights."

"He didn't do anything wrong," Donovan said calmly.

"Mr. Nash." Preston snapped his attention toward Donovan. "If I were you I'd keep quiet."

Donovan's eyes narrowed into slits as he glared at Preston. "This man did nothing more than bring me to you. In case you're a little behind in your information—I'm one of the pilots of flight 880. As you no doubt already know, you're in the middle of a very high-visibility event. If I were you, I'd be very careful where I got my information and whose toes I stepped on."

"You're Nash?" a voice called out from behind Donovan.

Donovan bristled as he recognized the voice. He maintained his composure as the speaker came into view, and answered the question. "I'm Donovan Nash. You must be Richtman."

"Mr. Preston," Cyrus said, turning immediately to the TSA agent. "This is the pilot who just crash-landed flight 880."

Donovan glared at the man who had wanted him to crash-land the airplane in Lake Michigan, and had threatened his daughter to get what he wanted.

"What about him?" Preston pointed at Emmett.

"I don't know who he is," Cyrus said.

"I work for the airport," Emmett stated angrily. "I responded to the crash and was asked to drive this guy here. What in the hell is all this about?"

"Release them both." Preston sighed heavily. "I apologize. I'm in the process of locking this airport down tight. We're in the middle of a full-blown terrorist alert."

Donovan massaged his wrists where the metal handcuffs had dug deep, and eyed Preston. "I take it you're still under the assumption that there were terrorists?"

"That's right," Preston said, nodding emphatically. "I've been working closely with Wayfarer management to try to contain the situation."

"What situation is that?" Donovan was growing impatient, but he understood he needed to get through this man to get to Leo Singer.

"The attempted theft of one airliner, followed by the theft of another aircraft," Preston replied, as if everyone knew what had taken place.

"Who told you they were stolen?" Donovan asked.

"I'm afraid you've been out of the loop," Cyrus chimed in smoothly. "After what you've been through, I think it would be best if you let us get you to the hospital."

Preston ignored Cyrus and addressed Donovan. "Of course they were stolen. I've been working with Mr. Richtman and the top management of Wayfarer Airlines. Airport security wounded one of the suspects in the first attempt. What do you know about all of this?"

"Was this suspect, or terrorist as you call him, perhaps a Wayfarer pilot?" Donovan ignored the flash of anger that crossed Cyrus' face.

"My job right now is to lock this airport down," Preston shot back. "We can sort out all the details later."

"Would you be interested in sorting out a great deal of it right now?" Donovan asked as calmly as he could. "I propose we go talk to Leo Singer. I have a feeling he'll be able to straighten all of this out."

"That's impossible," Cyrus replied. "Mr. Singer is currently unavailable. I'm sure you understand the demands on him at a time like this."

"Mr. Preston!" a member of Preston's security crew called out from across the room. "I have confirmation that the Air Force has intercepted the jet. They're being escorted from the area. The terrorist response team will be in place at Scott Air Force base by the time they arrive."

"The moment they land, I want everyone on board that plane separated and locked up," Preston said without taking his eyes off of Donovan. "Nothing leaks to the press, no local agencies are to be involved. Is everyone clear on this?"

"That's unnecessary," Donovan said. He hated the thought of Lauren and the others being met by what would amount to a federal SWAT team. "If I were you, Mr. Preston, I'd be very careful about where I was getting my facts."

Cyrus stepped forward as if to cut Preston off. "Let me take care of Mr. Nash. He's clearly uninformed about today's events."

Donovan bristled at the superior smirk that lingered on Cyrus' portly face. To his left he caught a glimpse of Emmett's barely concealed rage.

"I don't really have time to debate all of this right now. You two stay where you are. I'll deal with you later," Preston said as his cell phone rang. He answered and then stepped away to speak privately.

"Mr. Nash." Cyrus glanced at his watch. "We have so much to discuss, but I'm sure you'll understand when I tell you I have a great deal to do at the moment."

"Oh, don't worry. I'm not going anywhere."

"Wise choice." Cyrus buttoned his suit coat and pulled smartly at his sleeves. He then spun on his heel and walked away.

"What now?" Emmett whispered. The big man nervously cracked his knuckles.

"I need that phone, then we have to somehow get past Cyrus and the TSA and find Leo Singer."

Donovan studied the three TSA agents positioned around the room, they were each eyeing him cautiously. Donovan shot a sideways look at the table where Preston had placed his and Emmett's possessions. The all important cell phone was in plain view. Donovan with a slight tip of his head motioned for Emmett to follow as he began to walk toward the table.

"Where do you think you two are going?" Preston called out as he put a hand over the receiver of the phone.

"Mr. Preston!" Donovan said, ignoring the armed men around him "It's essential that I speak to Leo Singer. In fact, I'd even go so far as to suggest that your career is hanging in the balance."

"He's in a meeting." Preston's eyes darted toward a closed door across the room. "What I want is for you to sit down somewhere and wait."

Donovan shook his head, then stepped forward and yanked his arm to shrug off the agent's hand that had grabbed his shoulder. He clutched the cell phone, pushed Preston aside, and started for the door that Preston had looked at a moment before. "Not going to happen."

Preston and his men attempted to intercept Donovan, only to find Emmett blocking their path. It was the narrow window of opportunity Donovan needed. He threw open the door. Behind him, Preston shouted as Emmett kept the TSA agents at bay. Inside sat Leo Singer and Cyrus.

"Can I help you?" Leo remarked politely, as if the intruder must be lost.

"Hello, Mr. Singer." Donovan approached the aging CEO and shook the surprised man's hand. "I'm Donovan Nash."

"I'm sorry," Preston shouted as he barged in and grabbed Donovan from behind to remove him from the room.

"Let him be," Leo ordered, then put both hands on the table and rose to his feet. "If you'll excuse us, Mr. Preston. I'd like to talk to Mr. Nash."

"What?" Preston said, recoiling.

"Leo, this is not the time for this!" Cyrus, too, had stood at the sudden intrusion.

"It's fine." Leo nodded, and waited as Preston backed out of the room and gently closed the door.

Leo's hawk-like eyes looked Donovan up and down, sizing up the man he'd only heard about until now. "Mr. Nash. It's a pleasure to finally meet you. Though I must admit I'm a bit surprised to see you so soon after the crash. I trust you're uninjured?"

"I'm fine, thank you," In his life as Robert Huntington, Donovan had dealt with a great many powerful men, some with class, some with very little. Leo Singer certainly belonged in the former category.

"Leo, I really must insist that Mr. Nash is in no condition to be here." Cyrus moved toward where Donovan stood.

Donovan put a hand on Cyrus' chest, shoving the agitated man back into a chair. "Sit down and listen."

"I'll do no such thing! I'm calling security!"

"We'll call them shortly," Donovan promised, then turned his attention back to Leo. "Mr. Singer, I know you're surprised to see me. I'm supposed to be in Lake Michigan—where Cyrus tried to land us—despite a legitimate rescue effort by your own people."

"We felt the lake was best," Cyrus said.

"I'm sure you did." Donovan moved to a phone on the table. "Mr. Singer, I have something I think you need to hear. Do I need to dial nine for an outside line?"

"You need to leave!" Cyrus yelled as he sprang to his feet.

"Mr. Singer," Donovan said, barely keeping his anger contained. "The future of Wayfarer Airlines depends on your listening to this."

"Cyrus," Leo said firmly. "Sit down and let's humor Mr. Nash for a moment." Cyrus' face contorted as Donovan put the phone on speaker and went through the same prompts as before. Moments later, Cyrus' recorded voice filled the room.

"Look. This is the opportunity we've been waiting for. When this is over, Leo will be history. The old man should have stepped down years ago. I'm just as concerned as you are that somehow these people will get that airplane on the ground in one piece and Leo will get the credit. I'm doing everything I can to make sure that what does happen, makes Leo look like a confused old man."

"You do what you need to do. I don't really give a damn about Leo or his legacy."

Cyrus' face went shock-white and his hands began to tremble.

Trust me, I'm going to put maximum pressure on Leo to get this airplane to ditch in the lake. The last thing I need is for this airplane to miraculously end up safe. The minute flight 880 is down, I'm going to call a board meeting and do everything I can to vote Leo out. After all, he was foolish enough to sign off on allowing a civilian to fly the plane. For God's sake, they nearly crashed into the Hancock building. After I make an example of Leo's spineless hand-wringing, and then point to the body count from flight 880, I'm certain the board will make me acting chairman. On Monday morning, Wayfarer stock is probably going to plummet dramatically—that's when you make your move. With Leo gone, your group needs to make its tender offer for controlling interest in Wayfarer. I'll of course recommend to the board we accept the offer."

"We're not paying a penny more than $33.00 a share for the stock. Whatever happens, the price had better sink down into the low-twenties."

"Our deal is still intact? I have your word that I'll stay on as vice-chairman until your management team is in place? At that point the final payment will be deposited to my account."

"You have my word. We'll be ready at this end."

"Excellent, I need to get with Leo and finish things at this end. I'll be in touch."

When the recording ended, Donovan once again saved the voice mail.

He waited a few seconds, measuring the devastation etched on Leo's face. The aging man's expression slowly turned to anger. He raised his hand and pointed a trembling finger at Cyrus.

"Explain yourself," Leo said in a hushed voice, his temper seemingly barely under control.

"Wait just a minute! This is highly out of order!"

"I said explain yourself!" Leo slammed his hand down on the table, and Cyrus jerked.

"That—that tape. It's fake,"Cyrus said. "This is a ploy by Nash to get us to stay quiet about who he really is. Leo, this is blackmail!"

"I recognize the voices, you fool! It's you, talking to that bastard Tipton, at Atlantic International. There is no way Mr. Nash could have fabricated what I just heard. I'll deal with Tipton later."

Cyrus leaned back in his chair, and a defiant look spread slowly across his cherubic face. "I have nothing to say. All you have is what I'd describe as an illegal wiretap. Nothing you have will hold up in a court of law."

"Cyrus." Leo leaned forward as he began. "The level of betrayal you've displayed here is morally and professionally reprehensible. I don't need a court to deal with you. You're fired—and you will stay quiet regarding this matter. If you fail to do so, and decide to make use of any public forum, then I will make sure that the Securities and Exchange Commission is made aware of your actions. Legal or not, I will destroy you and everything you have. Do you understand what I'm saying?"

"I'd like to add a caveat of my own." Donovan stared at the devastated CEO. "If you go public with anything you learned today, then I will release the tape to the media myself."

"You can't threaten me!" Cyrus cried out weakly.

"It's not a threat," Donovan countered. "It's a promise. I have more resources that you can imagine. If you force my hand, I will wreck havoc on you at every level imaginable."

"Now go," Leo said, dismissing Cyrus with a flip of his wrist. He pushed the intercom button and quietly instructed someone to relieve Cyrus of his security credentials and escort him from the building.

"Thank you." Leo held out his hand to Donovan after Cyrus had left the room. "Well done, Mr. Nash. It would seem I am deeply indebted to you. You're a brave and resourceful man—your father would have been proud of you."

Donovan was stunned. He searched Leo's face for any sign that the words held anything other than the meaning they implied.

"Yes, I know who you are. I, too, overheard Henry and Dr. McKenna. Though until you walked into this room, I'll have to admit I didn't believe it." Leo smiled as he reflected. "I knew your father fairly well before he and your mother died. I watched with more than a passing interest as you grew up. I was deeply saddened by your own death, so you can imagine my surprise when I learned the truth today. Now, here you are—like some kind of avenging angel come back from the dead."

"That wasn't exactly my intention," Donovan confessed as he shook his head solemnly. "I would have preferred that none of this happened. But hopefully, everything has worked out the way it was supposed to."

"Nothing much I did today worked out. I foolishly listened to Cyrus instead of Henry. I had a hand in stopping Henry from taking the first airliner. If I'd listened and helped, then Audrey wouldn't have been hurt. Her injuries are my responsibility. God forbid, she dies. I've made so many mistakes today, been naive and gullible at the hands of someone who I thought was a trusted advisor."

"You didn't know," Donovan said. "What's done is done; the important part is what you do next."

"I fear I must finally listen to my critics and step down," Leo said in a strained voice. "In the face of all that has transpired today, perhaps I don't deserve to be at the helm of this company any longer."

"I disagree. You have a chance to make amends. I hope you can see that right now isn't the time for a change of leadership. Wayfarer is in the middle of its first fatal accident since you started the airline. Your firm hand is what's called for. Later, perhaps, you can quietly step down and name a successor."

Leo studied Donovan, the stress seemed to momentarily lift itself from his heavily lined face. "You might be right. As I recall, you were quite the business leader in your day, as was your father. If you were in my place what would you do? I'd love to hear the thoughts of the late Robert Huntington."

Donovan allowed himself a brief smile as he calculated his response. "You really want to hear what I have to say?"

"Of course,"

"I've watched you and this airline since it's inception. You started out as a crop duster in west Texas. From those sparse beginnings you started one of the most successful startup airlines in history. Why do you think you made it while so many others failed?"

"Luck, hard work." Leo's eyes narrowed as if he'd remembered something, a fragment from a long-forgotten past.

"And good people," Donovan added.

"Yes, good people are key. You know, after I started this airline, I was fortunate to receive a great deal of funding from a west coast venture capital entity. All I ever managed to discover was that it was hinted to have originated from Huntington Oil money. I always assumed that it was someone who knew of my past relationship with your father, but I was wrong, wasn't I?"

"Over the years, I made various investments, and one of those was Wayfarer Airlines."

"Then I'm even more indebted to you than I thought."

"Not at all," Donovan said. "My initial investment paid off handsomely. It was a very beneficial transaction."

"I remember now. It was at one of the venture capital meetings. Someone handed me Henry Parrish's resume. With the none-too-subtle suggestion that Henry should join the team."

Donovan smiled at that small detail he'd orchestrated. "It was a favor I owed him. Which brings us back to the earlier question," Donovan continued, secure with where he was taking this conversation. "You can't really leave this airline. Even as a figurehead your presence is invaluable to your employees and customers. But you can promote yourself. If it were me, I'd make myself chairman emeritus, sit back and turn over the day-to-day operations to someone else—someone who has the same maverick spirit you showed for so many years. Someone who would go to extreme lengths to do what's right, for not only the company, but for the passengers as well."

"Are you suggesting who I think you are?" Leo arched an eyebrow as he processed what Donovan had said.

"Years ago he worked for me," Donovan said. "I can't think of another person who would work as hard for you as Henry. He reminds me a little of you, once upon a time, don't you think?"

"Well I'll be damned."

"Later, after you deal with all the post-crash damage control, you can simply announce that Cyrus Richtman has resigned, and that Henry Parrish has been named the new CEO. Since he's the hero who saved flight 880, I think it would work beautifully. I'd bet the board of directors would gladly sign off on any scenario you might recommend."

"I'll have to give all of this some thought. But I will admit what you're proposing has some merit." Leo slowly brought himself to his feet. "But speaking of damage control, I think I have a certain TSA agent I need to speak with. I'd also like to make a copy of that tape."

"I'll make sure you receive a copy." Donovan said. "I'll be making one for myself also."

"What else can I do for you?" Leo asked.

"I have one simple request."

"Don't worry," Leo said, and placed a fatherly hand on Donovan's shoulder. "Your secret is safe with me. But I don't have any idea what Cyrus might do. His thirst for revenge might be more than we can anticipate."

Donovan nodded that he understood. If Cyrus was going to act, it would probably happen very quickly. The fallout would be swift and unyielding. He needed to get with Lauren and make preparations. "Do you think you could convince Agent Preston to allow Henry and company to land here at O'Hare? I think we've determined that there were never really any terrorists."

"Yes," Leo said firmly, a new energy charging through the old man.

Donovan could only watch as Leo had a private word with Preston. He had no idea what was said, but afterwards Preston jumped on his radio and began to issue a barrage of orders.

"Done," Leo said as he rejoined Donovan. "What else can I do for you?"

"Have we heard anything yet from the hospital?" Donovan asked. "Do we know anything about Audrey or John?"

"Nothing yet," Leo replied, his voice full of concern. "If we'd have heard anything, I'd be the first to know."

Both men turned as Preston walked up to them.

"I've spoken with my superiors in Washington. In light of what I've just been told, the fighters have been recalled," Preston announced, a different, more reverential disposition in his voice. "Your airplane is free to return. But I'll need to interview each of the people on board before they're released. I'd also like to have a word with Mr. Richtman. There's a possibility he's facing federal charges of obstructing justice."

"Let's deal with him later," Leo said.

"Has the weather come up any?" Donovan asked to no one in particular. "Can Henry's plane land back here?"

"I've spoken with the tower," Glen said, walking over and joining Donovan and Leo. "Technically, Henry's aircraft is still an emergency in progress. They can pretty much do what they want. The weather has improved slightly. I think they could make it in."

"If they can land here, can we have them taxi to Wayfarer's hangar facility?" Donovan asked. "I think that would be smarter than bringing them to one of the gates. My guess is there's probably an army of media waiting in the terminal."

"I agree," Leo said. "We can send Henry a message."

Donovan thought for a moment. "Just tell him to bring that airplane home and we'll have transportation ready to get him and Matt to the hospital."

"Done." Leo authorized the message with a simple nod. Moments later Glen sent it via ACARS, a glorified airborne fax machine. The words would be printed out in Henry's cockpit in a matter of seconds.

"How can I get to the hangar? I'd like to be there when they land." Donovan looked around for Emmett, but couldn't find him. "I also need to retrieve Dr. McKenna's purse. I think she left it here?"

"I'll drive you there myself," Preston said as he signaled one of his men to get the purse Cyrus had given him earlier. "I need to be there when they disembark."

"Let's go then," Donovan said. He turned and put his hand out to Leo. "It was a distinct pleasure to meet you."

"Thank you for everything you did today." Leo shook Donovan's hand. "I'll be in touch."

Preston pointed at one of his men to let him and Donovan through the door. Once free of Operations he radioed that he wanted a vehicle standing by. When he was confident his orders had been received, he turned to Donovan. "I have one question for you, though."

"What's that?" Donovan said as they stepped out into the blizzard. He searched for Emmett's truck—but it was nowhere to be seen.

Preston yelled above the howling wind. "Just who in the hell are you?"

CHAPTER THIRTY-NINE

"Do you see them yet?" Preston asked as he strained to find the Boeing out of the window of the truck.

"Not yet." Donovan looked at his watch. "It's only been two minutes since Henry and company had reported over the final approach fix. Give them another minute or so and they should be down."

Donovan and Preston had left Operations and were now making their way to the Wayfarer hanger across the field. Donovan had been listening to the transmissions between Henry's jet and the control tower. The weather had improved slightly. Donovan had every confidence that Henry and Michael would have the 737 on the ground shortly.

"I think I hear something." Preston cracked his window.

Donovan turned his head slightly and began to pick up a familiar sound—the noise a jet engine makes as it goes into reverse thrust. Donovan scanned the darkness until out of the gloom the distinct shape of a Boeing 737 appeared. Henry had the jet in maximum reverse; the billowing snow thrown up by the engines obscured the entire back half of the plane. The airplane was ablaze with lights as it raced past them on the nearby runway.

"Wow!" Preston said as the Boeing disappeared in a cloud of snow.

"O'Hare Tower, this is Boeing 31 Whiskey Alpha," Michael transmitted from the 737. "We're down and clearing onto taxiway Tango Four."

"Roger 31 Whiskey Alpha," Kate replied. "You're cleared to taxi north along the parallel to your hangar. Welcome home."

"Roger," Michael said.

"How much further?" Donovan asked.

"We should get there about the same time they do." Preston said. "We'll take taxiway Juliet to Yankee, come in the back way."

"How do you expect this to go down?"

"How many people are on this jet?" Preston asked. "Do you know all of them?"

"I think there are only four people," Donovan said. "I know two of the four very well. One is my fiancée, Dr. Lauren McKenna, plus Michael Ross, who is a man I've worked with for years. The other two are Henry Parrish and his son Matt."

"How old is the son?"

"He's a teenager."

"It could take a while. I'll need to interview each person myself and get a statement. If I think we're all in the clear as far as the law is concerned, they could be free to go by late tonight—possibly tomorrow."

"We don't have that kind of time," Donovan said. "Especially Henry and Matt. Matt's mother was one of those injured on 880. She's in critical condition. Is there any way you can do this later?"

"Afraid not." Preston shook his head. "I've got the top brass of Homeland Security breathing down my neck on this one. Anything I do here must be cleared at the highest level."

"Really?" Donovan cocked his head to one side and looked at the TSA agent. He knew Leo Singer had promised to get on the phone to straighten out a few things. "How long has it been since you've spoken with Washington?"

"If there was something going on they'd find me," Preston said. "Trust me on that one—my boss isn't particularly shy about things like that."

Donovan held on as Preston stepped heavily on the brakes and made a wide left turn. Down the row of hangars, through the heavy snow, he could just make out the bright glow of powerful lights. "That must be them."

"Has to be," Preston said as he straightened out the truck. He stepped on the gas and went as fast as he dared. "We're almost there. The lights you see on the right are coming from the hangar."

Donovan could see that the huge doors to the hangar stood open, and the 737 was being guided directly into the building. Official vehicles, red lights flashing, lined both sides of the airplane. The 737 taxied slowly into the hangar and came to a gentle stop. Immediately, the doors began to close. Preston brought the truck to a halt alongside a group of armed men.

"This section is off limits!" a plainclothes official with a gun said as Preston rolled down his window.

"It's okay," Preston called out.

The man shined his light inside the truck and inspected the occupants. Then, turning to his partner, said, "Let them pass."

They continued, and covered the short distance to the hangar. Donovan was able to leap from the truck and run through the snow just before the large doors fully closed. He stopped as his eyes adjusted to the harsh lights inside the cavernous building. Preston also slipped through the doors before they closed with a resounding thud that echoed through the space.

Donovan hurried toward the front of the plane. The big engines ticked as they cooled down. A small group of people started to roll a portable stairway into position near the nose as the heavy door on the 737 swung outward. It took Donovan a moment to recognize the man standing in the entryway. It had been nearly eighteen years since he'd seen him. But his features were unmistakable—Henry Parrish.

As Donovan drew closer, he found Henry was staring at him. Donovan knew his appearance had changed far more than the simple effects of time could account for. He gave Henry a casual salute; a small gesture of respect he used to give the man years ago. It might help his old friend make sense out what he was seeing—which was essentially a ghost.

Henry moved aside as another figure joined him at the door. It was Lauren. Despite her drawn face and unkempt hair, to him, she was still the most beautiful woman in the world. As their eyes locked, a smile washed across her face. She stepped onto the portable stairs the instant they were in place and rushed down to the floor. Donovan met her there, took her into his arms, and held her close.

"I was so afraid I'd never see you again," Lauren whispered in his ear.

"I'm here," Donovan said. "We have a date next weekend, remember?"

"I love you so much." Lauren kissed Donovan hard and deep, her hands gently touching his face as if for the first time.

Donovan closed his eyes and was enveloped by the feel of her. Moments later someone behind Lauren cleared his throat. He looked over her shoulder to find Henry and Michael standing there. Slightly behind them stood a young man who'd sheepishly turned away from their display of affection.

"They get like this all the time." Michael said. "I'm through apologizing for them. Oh, and Donovan—love the purse."

Donovan ignored Michael's barb and handed Lauren her purse. "You left this in Operations."

"Thanks." Lauren took her purse then locked her free arm around Donovan's neck as she turned to look at the others. "Donovan, I'd like to introduce Henry Parrish, and his son Matt."

Donovan pulled himself away from Lauren's embrace, and searched Henry's eyes for any hint of what his old friend might be thinking.

Henry shook Donovan's outstretched hand. "That was an impressive display of flying out there today."

Michael put his arm around Matt and nudged him forward. "Donovan. This is Matt. One of the most remarkable young men I've ever come across. Matt, this is Donovan Nash."

"Hi," Matt said, as Donovan vigorously shook his hand.

"What you did today was nothing short of a miracle," Donovan said to the young man. "I don't know if I would've been able to stay with you guys without the laser."

Matt shrugged.

"You and I will have to sit down sometime and compare notes," Donovan said, and winked. Later, he'd pull Matt aside and they'd talk.

"Cool," Matt replied, then shot a worried look at all of the security people waiting for the little reunion to end. "What's going to happen to us now?"

"I'm not sure. That's for the TSA to decide." Donovan searched for Preston, "Where'd Preston go?"

"Please wait here," a security man said. "Mr. Preston said he'd be back in a moment."

"Have you heard anything about Audrey yet?" Henry said quietly to Donovan.

Donovan shook his head. "Leo said he'd call us the second he knew anything."

"We'll talk later," Henry whispered, the words more of a threat than a suggestion.

"Yes, we will," Donovan moved closer to Lauren and pulled her out of earshot from the others.

"That sounded a little ominous." she said.

"I think Henry's still a little mad about a few things." Donovan put his arm around her. "He and I are going to talk later. Hopefully I can get Henry and Matt out of here and off to the hospital. Then, you and I need to sit down in private and see where we stand on things. Depending on what happens, our future could get a little tricky."

"Did Calvin come through?"

"In a big way." Donovan squeezed her hand. "He sent me the recording and it made all the difference. You were brilliant."

"No, I wasn't. If I were smart, none of this would have happened." Lauren shook her head. "I didn't want to tell Henry, but it was the only way."

Donovan kissed her. "You did what needed to be done. Don't worry, we'll figure it out."

"Nash!" Preston yelled out across the hangar floor. "Get in here!"

Donovan gave Lauren and the others a quizzical look. They all started to walk toward the office where Preston stood.

"Just Nash!" Preston called out. "The rest of you stay where you are!"

Donovan jogged over to where Preston was holding the door open for him. The agent gestured to a desk phone with a nod of his head. A flashing red light indicated there was someone on hold. "Is that for me?"

"Yeah." Preston closed the door behind them.

Donovan picked up the receiver and pushed the button. "Donovan Nash here."

"Mr. Nash. This is Richard Holcomb, Secretary of Homeland Security."

Donovan instantly pictured the heavyset Texan. Holcomb was a fireplug of a man; both his temper and intelligence were legendary in Washington. He was a high-powered career politician who was used to getting what he wanted. If it was the hot-headed Holcomb calling, this had the potential to be very painful. "Secretary Holcomb. What can I do for you?"

"You know what, Mr. Nash? Until a little while ago, I'd never heard of you," Holcomb began angrily. "Now, to tell you the truth—you're a goddamned burr under my saddle and it's pissing me off!"

"Sorry to hear that, sir," Donovan said politely. There was no reason to further agitate the man.

"First, I hear we've got terrorists stealing airplanes in Chicago. Now I'm to understand that's not the case? As if this sudden reversal isn't enough, I just got off the phone with the President. He and the Secretary of State are sitting in the Situation Room at the White House—and do you know what they told me?"

"No sir."

"They told me to let all of you go!" Holcomb bellowed loudly. "That's the biggest crock of shit I've heard all day! Then, as if all of this isn't enough, I'm supposed to spin today's events into some kind of success story for all concerned. What do you make of that?"

"I've always liked the President," Donovan said innocently. He wondered how much of this was Leo Singer's doing.

"No shit!" Holcomb shot back, then let out a long breath as he thought. "I like the President too, but he's left me in the ticklish position of trying to spin this episode a certain way. I can do that, but I need you and your little entourage to play along. Is that something you're prepared to do for me?"

"Of course."

"Okay. Listen up Mr. Nash, because I'm only going to say this once. Here's the way this whole damn mess is going to go down. You were never on flight 880. Donovan Nash will never be mentioned in the same breath as flight 880. The pilot who landed the plane is the Wayfarer pilot who took off from Dulles. I'm told he's hurt, but all the better story, don't you think?"

"Sounds good so far." Donovan had no reason to explain that being out of the limelight was exactly what he wanted.

"As far as the rescue plane is concerned, it too was piloted by Wayfarer pilots. This was a group effort on the part of Leo Singer and the airline. I think you'll agree we can't just have a bunch of gung-ho civilians out flying airliners around, now can we? It's just plain bad for business."

"I think your plan is admirable, but I have a request." Donovan knew this was the time to make sure they all walked away from this unscathed.

"What is it? I can warn you in advance, I'm not in a great mood, so don't push it."

"Understood. But since none of us were here, and this was a fully sanctioned event, then of course there's no way any of us are in trouble with the TSA, or the FAA, or anyone else for that matter. All involved are free to go on like nothing happened?"

"I've already taken care of that. Yes, you're free to go, and I'd prefer you left sooner than later," Holcomb said. "The President and I are counting on all of this working. Don't screw it up!"

"You have my word." Donovan sat back in the chair and put his feet up on the desk. Preston stood motionless, an uneasy smile frozen on his face.

"Then get the hell out of there!" Holcomb barked. "I don't want some goddamned exposé to show up in the *Washington Post*. I can promise you I'm the wrong man to make angry."

"I understand. Do you want to talk to Agent Preston?" Donovan eyed the nervous TSA agent.

"I've already spoken to him," Holcomb said. "He knows what to do."

"Thank you, sir." Donovan sat up straight in the chair. "I owe you one."

"You're damn right you do," Holcomb said dryly as he hung up.

"Okay." Donovan set the phone down and rubbed his hands together. "I guess that takes care of that. What's the best way for us to get to the hospital where they took the others?"

"The Chicago Fire Department has a helicopter on its way," Preston said, fatigue evident in his voice. "They've been instructed to take you there."

"That might be them now." The unmistakable sound of a helicopter's rotor beat in the distance.

"You never answered my question." Preston stood in front of the door. "Who are you?"

"I'm sworn to secrecy. Besides, as you know, I'm not even here." Donovan slipped past the confused agent and hurried toward Lauren and the others.

"What's up?" Michael called out as Donovan approached. "Who was that?"

"A friend," Donovan could hear the helicopter as it approached the hangar. "I'll explain everything on the way to the hospital. Our ride's here."

"We can leave?" Henry asked. "Just like that—they're going to let us walk out of here?"

"Yep." Donovan put his hand on Lauren's back and began to guide her toward the door, hoping everyone else would follow. "It's a little complicated, but like I said. I'll explain it to you in the helicopter."

The five of them exited out a small door into the teeth of the blizzard. Fifty yards away sat a Bell 412, its rotors still turning. A figure was making his way through the snow toward them.

"Is one of you Henry Parrish?" the crewman called out. "Are you the people we're taking to the hospital?"

"I'm Henry Parrish."

"Right this way, sir. Here, take my coat. You'll freeze out here."

Henry accepted the heavy coat and slipped it on. "Thanks."

"The weather came up enough for us to fly about half an hour ago," the crewman explained above the whine of the helicopter's engines. "Or we would have been here sooner. Sorry about your airplane, sir."

"Can we fly over it on our way out?"

"Yes, sir. You'll be able to see it. It's kind of hard to miss."

Several minutes later, all of them were seated and the Bell helicopter's blades became a blur as the engines spooled up. The skids pulled free of the snow and they rose straight into the sky. Once above the hangars, the pilot pivoted the helicopter smartly and turned southeast. Moments later, Donovan saw the eerie glow in front of them and pointed it out to the others. They all watched in silence as the wreckage from 880 came into view.

Donovan grimaced at the sight and Lauren took his hand. Banks of temporary lights had already been erected, bathing what was left of the 737 in brilliant white light. The flashing lights from a legion of emergency vehicles added to the horrific scene. Donovan could see from Henry's expression that he wasn't prepared for the image of Audrey's plane and how forlorn it looked sitting in the snow. From this vantage point, Donovan realized just how close he'd come to going over the edge of the thirty-foot embankment. The tail was cocked at an odd angle. He winced as he remembered how hard they hit. He also knew it was a miracle that another wrecked 737 wasn't burning nearby, one with Henry, Michael, Lauren and Matt inside. A sick feeling crept through him as he wondered what Henry and Matt must be thinking. They sped away, and Henry turned to take a final look at the wreckage.

"That's so weird, Dad," Matt said. "We were so close to it when it was still flying. But it's still pretty much intact. Maybe Mom's all right?"

Henry nodded and put his arm around Matt. "I hope so, son."

CHAPTER
FORTY

Donovan had just finished describing his conversation with Holcomb when the forward momentum of the helicopter slowed. Ahead was the brightly lit hospital. It only took Donovan a moment to locate the landing pad. The helicopter made a circling approach and set up into the wind. Moments later, the skids touched down firmly. The door was pulled open and the crewman helped them down to the ground.

"Good luck, Captain Parrish," the fireman called out, as the five of them steeled themselves against the cold and ran down the narrow walkway toward double glass doors.

Donovan kept Lauren's hand firmly in his own as they neared the entrance. The doors opened and a group of people stood waiting inside for them.

"I'm looking for my wife, Audrey Parrish!" Henry said to the first person he saw.

"Henry." A woman hurried in their direction. "Oh thank God you're here. Leo called and said you were on your way."

"Nancy." Henry reached out and gave the woman a gentle hug.

"I heard what you did." Her tears flowed as she held on to the man who had saved her husband. "I am so thankful." She looked at Matt and reached out to grasp his hand "You must be Matt. I haven't seen you since you were a little boy. I understand I have you to thank as well."

"Nancy, this is Donovan Nash." Henry pulled away and introduced the two. "Donovan, this is John's wife, Nancy."

"I'm so grateful for what you did up there. John couldn't tell me much, but he said he wouldn't be here if it weren't for you."

"I helped him a little bit here and there." Donovan said, though Henry would need to explain to her later, how important it was to keep his involvement a secret. "How is he?"

Nancy exhaled deeply and dabbed her tears with a tissue. "He has second and third degree burns and he suffered a concussion. But the doctor assured me he would recover. I can only sit with him for a few minutes at a time, so I thought I'd come meet you."

"What have you heard about Audrey?" Henry asked, but Nancy shook her head to indicate that she knew nothing. Henry looked around and found the female staff member he'd first spoken with. "Where can I go to find my wife?"

"If you'll follow me," she said, "I'll take you to a waiting area. Someone will be in to speak with you shortly."

Donovan felt a hand on his arm and turned to see it was Michael. "I've got to find a phone and call home. Susan still thinks I'm coming home tonight. I'm so glad none of this happened, I'd hate to have to explain my day to her. I'll catch up with you in a little while. Can I bring you some coffee or anything when I come back?"

"No thanks."

Lauren shook her head too, to show that she was fine for the moment. "Tell Susan hello from us."

"I will." Michael nodded and hurried away.

"Are you immediate family?" The nurse said to Donovan and Lauren as they caught up.

"Yes," Henry said without hesitation. "They're with us."

"Very well." The woman pointed down the spotless hallway to a bank of elevators. "The waiting room is up one floor and then to your left. There is a refreshment area to your right as you step off the elevator. I'll let someone know you're waiting."

"Thank you." Henry hurried off in the direction of the elevator.

Moments later, the small group entered the empty waiting room. There were rows of chairs, a few pictures on the wall, and a magazine rack. The room, though it tried to create a feeling of warmth, fell far short.

Donovan was still far too wired to sit and wait in the confining space.

"I've changed my mind. I think coffee sounds good. Who all would like some?"

"I'm fine." Lauren gave him a puzzled look. She knew Donovan rarely drank coffee after his second cup in the morning.

"I'll go with you," Henry said as Donovan started to leave the room.

Donovan walked to where he'd seen the machines when they got off the elevator. He dug in his pocket for some change, only to discover that he had none.

Henry pulled some singles out of his front pocket. "Maybe it'll take these."

The two men stood in the small alcove. Donovan's tension rose as Henry went about the process of feeding his dollar bills to the machine. He bought Donovan a cup, then himself.

"Let's you and I have a little talk," Henry said.

Donovan didn't really want to have this talk now, not here in the hospital while they were waiting to hear about Audrey. In his mind, this was something to be done later.

"Just who in the hell do you think you are?" Henry's words poured out with venom. "I can't believe you faked your death and deserted all of us. Was it so bad, you had to run off and hide—and leave us to clean up your mess?"

"I didn't leave much of a mess," Donovan said softly. "In fact, everyone who was hurt by my departure was well taken care of."

Henry stared Donovan down. "Let me fill you in on a few little details. After your plane crashed, first the FAA, then the insurance people, then finally the media, everyone was all over me."

"I did everything I could to calculate the fallout." Donovan recalled the painstaking planning that went into his final days as Robert Huntington. "The only aspect I didn't plan on was your insisting on trying to recover the airplane from the bottom of the ocean. It would have been a monumental task, but the investigators would have discovered enough clues to cast doubt on certain elements of the accident. I couldn't afford that kind of scrutiny."

"Is that when I was terminated?" Henry said. "When I wanted to raise the airplane."

Donovan nodded. "I was in Europe by then. I'm sorry Henry, I really am, but I can assure you no one paid a higher price for my actions than I did."

"Don't be so sure."

"Did it make you want to escape? When it felt like the entire world had you in their sights, did you ever feel like making it all go away?"

Henry seemed unfazed by Donovan's words.

"Now imagine what was going on in my life. I'd lost Meredith and the world was blaming me for her death. Imagine trying to get through each day with that kind of grief, while also trying to deal with death threats against friends, boycotts of the company. I would never try to minimize what you went through, Henry. But I will ask you to search inside, and see if there is even the smallest bit of empathy for what I was dealing with."

Henry looked up at Donovan "If you'd have asked, I would have probably helped you do what you needed to do."

"That's not the way it worked. I didn't tell anyone. I wouldn't put that burden on anyone else." Donovan paused to see if his words were having any effect. "Which brings us to the real issue at hand."

Henry stood rigid, his face flush with resentment.

"You and Audrey both know the truth about me." Donovan sought out Henry's eyes and held them with his own. "Henry—is my secret safe with you?"

Henry said nothing, his jaw clenched and his expression unyielding.

"You knew me for a long time," Donovan said, his tone softening. "You also knew Meredith. It's taken me almost twenty years to feel that way again. Lauren and my daughter mean everything to me. But if the world discovers I'm still alive, the backlash will be considerable. It's up to you."

"Dad?" Matt's voice carried down the quiet hallway. "Dad!"

"I'm in here," Henry called out to his son.

"Dad. They're showing the crash on the television. I think you'd better come see this."

"I better go see what's going on," Henry said, eyeing Donovan as if to say they'd talk later. Matt joined the two men and stood next to his father.

"Go," Donovan urged Henry, while putting out his hand and resting it on Matt's shoulder to get him to stay. Henry returned to the waiting room. "Hello Matt. I was hoping we'd have some time to talk." Donovan could clearly see both Audrey's and Henry's features in Matt's face. "I still can't get over how brave and resourceful you were today. Your mom was so proud of you."

"She was?"

"Yes." Donovan carefully measured his words. "She loved that you and your father were working together to help us. It was what she wanted most of all—."

"Did she really say that?"

"She also wanted me to tell you that she loved you. Some pretty amazing things happened today, but the most amazing person by far was your mother. She held things together, in the end; it was her that saved us from going into the lake. I owe her my life."

"Really?" Matt looked up. "She saved you?"

"She saved all of us," Donovan said.

"Excuse me? Are you by chance Henry Parrish?"

Donovan turned in the direction of the voice. A doctor stopped where he and Matt stood. He was wearing green surgical scrubs. An identically clad nurse was at his side. "Are you Mr. Parrish?"

"No." Donovan shook his head. "He's in the waiting room though. Do you have news about Audrey?"

"I really need to speak with her husband." The doctor said before continuing down the hall. Donovan, with Matt on his heels, followed the doctor into where the others waited. When they entered the room, Donovan saw that only Lauren and Henry remained; Nancy had left.

"Mr. Parrish?" the doctor repeated.

"I'm Henry Parrish." They shook hands briefly and Matt joined his father. "This is my son, Matt. Do you have news about my wife?"

"Hello, I'm Dr. Mueller." He hesitated for a moment. "I'm sorry—but we lost her. We did everything we could—but her injuries were just too severe. I'm deeply sorry."

EPILOGUE

It was a picture-perfect south Florida evening. A gentle breeze swayed the tall palm trees and the ocean waves lapped up onto the white sand. Donovan and Lauren, hand in hand, had quietly slipped away from the wedding reception. The ceremony had been beautiful. Michael had been the best man and Calvin Reynolds had given the bride away. They'd been man and wife now for nearly four hours. They walked across the patio, away from their reception at the Breakers Hotel.

"The air feels wonderful," Lauren said, as she leaned close, putting her head on Donovan's shoulder. "I hope they won't miss us."

"They'll be fine." Donovan kissed her cheek and slipped his arm around her waist. "It was down there on this very beach where we had our first kiss."

"I remember." Lauren smiled at the memory, then pointed out over the waves. "And somewhere out there you proposed."

Donovan nodded as they stopped at the ornate railing that looked out over the water. It had been a perfect day. Their friends and loved ones had made the trip to West Palm Beach for their wedding. Everyone was spending the weekend at the Breakers. The next day, he and Lauren were getting on a chartered jet and flying south to a private island. They'd marveled at the pictures of the luxurious house, pristine grounds and protected beach. It was going to be a memorable honeymoon.

"What do you think will happen from here?" Lauren said wistfully, asking the question that had been on both of their minds.

Each day they'd both devoured the newspapers and followed the media coverage of the dramatic events in Chicago. The aftershock had been wide and varied. As promised, neither Donovan, Lauren, or Eco-Watch had ever been mentioned. Leo Singer and Wayfarer Airlines had been the focal point of the after-crash media barrage. Henry's daring exploits had served to draw the attention away from the twenty-nine passengers who had been permanently damaged from lack of oxygen. The loss of his wife had served to make Henry an even bigger hero. Wayfarer had acted swiftly and decisively to spin the aftermath into a celebration of those who had lived and those who had helped facilitate the rescue. As far as Donovan knew, John and Christy were still in the hospital; both Captain Tucker and Keith were fine and had been released. Keith was back home in Aspen. Rafael was in Chicago getting ready to start school. In their statements to the press, everyone involved had carefully kept to the story orchestrated by Leo and Henry. Norman Wetzler had eagerly agreed to stay silent in return for a dismissal of the federal charges leveled against him. All of the personnel at O'Hare were quietly commended by the head of the FAA, as well as by the mayor of Chicago. The inadvertent shutdown of the Indianapolis Air Route Traffic Control Center was branded a freak accident, and additional steps were already underway to ensure that a repeat of the tragic events would never occur.

"I wish I knew," Donovan replied honestly. "But whatever happens we'll deal with it together. Maybe we could buy this island we're going to, and live there happily ever after."

"I like that idea. Run around naked for the next thirty or forty years."

Donovan smiled, but the shadow of the events in Chicago loomed heavily over their future. Lauren had bravely reassured him that whatever the future brought would be fine with her. But only he fully understood how dramatically their lives would shift if the secrets of his past were made public. His fortune could buy them a certain amount of privacy, but the price on their security and mobility would be high. Abigail would probably suffer the most. As the only child of billionaire Robert Huntington, she would grow up with the media focused on her every move. Any hope for a normal childhood would instantly vanish under the onslaught. It was that thought that made Donovan the saddest.

"Any regrets?" Lauren looked up into his eyes.

"Only that I didn't find you years ago."

"Good answer." Lauren smiled.

"Excuse me, am I interrupting?" a man's voice called out from behind them.

Donovan turned, not sure who had spoken. In the waning light someone was approaching. Several moments passed before he recognized Leo Singer.

"Well I'll be damned." Donovan faced Lauren. "Did you know about this?"

Lauren shook her head.

Donovan stood and waited for him to draw closer. He wasn't sure what to expect; he hadn't talked to Henry since the hospital. Leo Singer had been kind enough to call earlier in the week to give Donovan updates on everyone's condition. But after that he'd heard nothing.

"Hello," Lauren said.

"Congratulations. May I kiss the bride?" Leo put one arm around Lauren's waist and kissed her gently on the cheek. Then he put his hand out to Donovan.

Donovan shook Leo's hand, knowing that this wasn't a social call—something had happened. Donovan braced himself for the worst.

"I hope you don't mind that I crashed your wedding," Leo began, then hesitated as he searched for exactly what to say next. "There have been some developments."

"Uh oh." Donovan reached out and found Lauren's hand.

"Yesterday," Leo said, "A body was discovered in the Wayfarer employee parking lot. It was found buried under fifteen feet of snow. Apparently it took almost a week for the snow to melt enough to reveal the body. It has been identified as Cyrus Richtman."

"What?" Donovan shook his head at the news. "What happened?"

"The preliminary autopsy indicated that he suffocated," Leo said. "The authorities speculate that he must have inadvertently wandered into the path of a snow plow on the way to his car. They've ruled his death accidental."

Donovan squeezed Lauren's hand. With Cyrus dead, and by all appearances it looked as if he'd died shortly after he'd left the airport, there was almost no chance he'd told anyone what he knew about Donovan's past. A brief image of Emmett flashed through Donovan's mind. Had the grief stricken man taken justice into his own hands?

"There's more," Leo continued. "Henry and I have discussed much of what needs to be done before we can put this ordeal behind us—both professionally and personally. When Cyrus' demise was made public, I used that opportunity to announce that after an appropriate interval, Henry Parrish would be named as the new Chief Executive Officer of Wayfarer Airlines. It has to be voted on by the board, but I've been assured that it's merely a formality. I have you to thank for planting that seed."

"How are he and Matt doing?" Lauren asked. "We so wanted to come to Audrey's funeral, but under the circumstances, we knew we couldn't afford to be seen."

"Henry knows, and he understood. He and Matt are doing as well as can be expected. Thankfully, they have each other; otherwise I'm not sure they'd be doing very well at all. It'll just take time, I guess."

Donovan nodded in solemn agreement. "What else is going on? I'm just guessing, but there's more to you being here than that?"

"As I flew down here," Leo said, "I spent most of the flight thinking about your father, and the young Robert Huntington I knew all those years ago. It's still a shock to discover you're alive after all this time. It made me realize how much I owe you for everything that you've done in the past, as well as the present. I wanted to share that with you in person. You have my eternal thanks and know that I will carry your secret to my grave."

"You're welcome." Donovan tried to smile. "But what about Henry? How does he feel about everything?"

"It's the final reason I came down here." Leo reached inside his suit coat and pulled out an envelope. "Henry wanted me to hand deliver this, and under the circumstances I felt that I should."

"What is it?" Lauren asked as Donovan took the envelope from Leo and carefully slid his finger beneath the seal.

Dear Donovan:

Under regrettable circumstances, I'm sure you understand why I wasn't able to deliver this letter in person. You and Lauren have truly made an impact on my family, and if I could change anything, it would be for Audrey, Matt and myself to be there with you. But, as you know, that's not possible. I have learned a great deal in the past week, and as you can imagine, some of it is truly overwhelming. Through the most unusual of circumstances I discovered you were still alive. To be honest, I'm still trying to grasp the fact that the last twenty years weren't what I thought they were. But now, with the death of Audrey, I find myself in the unenviable position you once found yourself in after Meredith was killed. I can now see why you chose the path you did. I too, have had my moments where I'd love to shut everything down and vanish, but I don't have that luxury.

As you can imagine, a number of people involved with the events last Friday have come forward, they were kind enough to explain the chain of events as they saw them. I now know much of what happened after the midair collision. I understand how Audrey was hurt; how you did everything you could to save her. I want to thank you for that. I also learned from Leo what you did after you were on the ground as it pertained to Cyrus and the authorities. You averted what would have been a total disaster for all involved. More importantly, I guess I need to thank you for what you did nearly twenty years ago. I was so full of anger and resentment that it never occurred to me to question why I was contacted, and then hired by Wayfarer Airlines. I had no way to grasp the fact that it was you behind the scenes. All of that said, I guess I should get to the matter at hand. With everything that has happened, I need to finally tell you that I have no ill will toward you or Lauren. Your secret is safe, and I believe Leo will echo the same sentiment. There is nothing to be gained by your past becoming public once again. Call it a wedding present. It's difficult to pick a wedding gift for a billionaire, but I'm hopeful that you're both pleased. One day, in the not so distant future, I hope we can all get together under more pleasant circumstances. I know Matt would enjoy seeing you. He and I have grown immeasurably closer in the last week. I know it was Audrey's final wish and I thank you for helping make it happen. Good luck to you both.

Best Wishes,
Henry

"Did you read this?" Donovan asked Leo he handed the letter to Lauren.

"Yes." Leo nodded. "Henry wanted me to look at it. I think it was a difficult letter for him to compose."

"It's beautiful." Lauren finished the letter and passed it back to Donovan. "I think they'll both be just fine."

"I agree." Leo pulled a lighter out of his pocket as he took the letter out of Donovan's hand. He held one corner and lit the bottom edge. Moments later, nothing remained but a few black ashes that swirled and disintegrated in the evening breeze.

"In light of everything we've just heard—I think it's finally safe to give you this," Donovan said to Lauren as he removed something from his pocket.

"What is it?" Lauren had no idea what to think as Donovan placed a small, carefully wrapped box in her hands.

"Just a little wedding present." Donovan smiled, as he waited patiently for her to open the gift.

Lauren tugged on the ribbon and opened the box. Inside she found a key, with a small gold tag attached. As she studied the delicate engraving, it took her a moment to understand that it was an address. The address of the house she'd fallen in love with. She looked up at him, wide-eyed and speechless.

"I didn't want to give it to you until we were certain we weren't going to have to make a mad dash out of here. But I think we're okay."

"I can't believe—this is—amazing!" Lauren threw her arms around her husband, and after kissing and hugging him, whispered in his ear. "You had this all week didn't you? This is why you left me in Chicago and flew home. I knew it! I can't believe you would keep a secret like this from me."

Donovan could only smile as he shrugged off Lauren's accusations.

"I don't know what you gave her, but I know a happy woman when I see one. Well done." Leo rubbed his hands together. "I think we need to find some champagne—and toast our combined good fortune."

Donovan put one arm around Lauren, the other he placed on Leo's back. Together, the three of them walked back toward the party. "I think we can arrange that," Donovan said. "In fact, I'm buying."

Leo looked at Donovan, then at Lauren, and smiled broadly. "You bet you are."

PHILIP DONLAY

Philip S. Donlay is a professional pilot who has spanned the globe in jets for nearly three decades. A native of Kansas, he divides his time between Minneapolis and Northern Virginia. For more information go to
www.philipdonlay.com

For sales, editorial information, subsidiary rights information
or a catalog, please write or phone or e-mail

ibooks
1230 Park Avenue
New York, New York 10128, US
Sales: 1-800-68-BRICK
Tel: 212-427-7139 Fax: 212-860-8852
www.BrickTowerPress.com
email: bricktower@aol.com.

For sales in the United States, please contact
National Book Network
nbnbooks.com
Orders: 800-462-6420
Fax: 800-338-4550
custserv@nbnbooks.com

For sales in the UK and Europe please contact our distributor,
Gazelle Book Services
Falcon House, Queens Square
Lancaster, LA1 1RN, UK
Tel: (01524) 68765 Fax: (01524) 63232
email: gazelle4go@aol.com.

For Australian and New Zealand sales please contact
Bookwise International
174 Cormack Road
Wingfield, 5013, South Australia
Tel: 61(0) 419 340056 Fax: 61(0) 8268 1010
email:karen.emmerson@bookwise.com.au